MICHAL

THE WIVES of KING DAVID, BOOK 1

MICHAL

A NOVEL

Jill Eileen Smith

Revell

a division of Baker Publishing Group
Grand Rapids, Michigan

© 2009 by Jill Eileen Smith

Published by Revell
a division of Baker Publishing Group
P.O. Box 6287, Grand Rapids, MI 49516-6287
www.revellbooks.com

Printed in the United States of America

Library of Congress Cataloging-in-Publication Data
Smith, Jill Eileen, 1958–
    Michal : a novel / Jill Eileen Smith.
       p.   cm. — (The wives of King David ; 1)
    ISBN 978-0-8007-3320-9 (pbk.)
    1. Michal (Biblical figure)—Fiction. 2. David, King of Israel—Fiction. 3. Bible.
O.T.—History of Biblical events—Fiction. 4. Women in the Bible—Fiction. 5.
Queens—Fiction. I. Title.
PS3619.M58838M53 2009
813'.6—dc22   2008041193

11   12   13   14   15   9   8   7   6   5

And so it was, whenever the spirit from God was upon Saul, that David would take a harp and play it with his hand. Then Saul would become refreshed and well, and the distressing spirit would depart from him.

1 Samuel 16:23

Now Michal, Saul's daughter, loved David. And they told Saul, and the thing pleased him.

1 Samuel 18:20

1

Gibeah, 1023 BC

Michal ducked as a shard of pottery soared past her head. She took a step backward into the shadowed hall, gripping the stone wall for support.

"No! Please! Not my alabaster vase!"

Michal stiffened at her mother's shrill voice. She crept forward and looked around the heavy wooden door into the battlefield of her mother's spacious bedchamber.

Her father, the king of Israel, held the priceless Egyptian treasure above his head, his gaze taunting.

"Please, Saul!" Her mother rushed at him, her sheer robe drooping from one shoulder. She gripped the vase, trying to wrestle it from his grasp.

Michal's breath caught. Had her mother lost her mind?

She had to create a diversion. Get her father out of this room. Or pull her mother away before she died trying to protect that silly pottery collection.

"Give—me—my—vase!"

Her father's eerie laughter followed. Fabric ripped as he yanked her mother forward by her tunic. She gripped the vase hard. Snatched it from his grasp. A guttural sound came from his throat. He heaved her across the blue tile, and the vase shattered beneath her.

Her mother's screams faded.

Silence settled over the room.

Michal cowered, fingernails digging at the mortar between the stones.

Her father sank to his knees, face cupped between both hands. Soft weeping came from the corner where her mother lay. A moment passed.

Darting a quick look at her father, Michal hurried to her mother's side. "Are you all right, Mother?" She noted a jagged cut on her mother's arm. "You're bleeding."

"My vase . . ."

Was that all she could think about? "We'll get a new vase, Mother." Never mind that the urn had been in her mother's family since the exodus, dating back several centuries.

"Guards!" Michal called out, hoping one of the cowards was within hearing distance.

Her father's piercing wail startled her, followed by deep, throaty groans as he pushed his purple-draped body up from the floor. Dark, smoldering rage burned in the abyss of his gray eyes.

Michal tugged on her mother's arm, bending to whisper in her ear. "Come, Mother. Let's go!"

Her mother clutched a pottery shard to her chest. "I cannot."

Michal gritted her teeth, wishing she could fly away like a bird. To somewhere far from Gibeah and her father's unpredictable wrath.

"I'll get Jonathan," she said. Her brother was the only person who could control the king when he got like this. More importantly, her brother could issue the command to send for the singer.

David. The thought of him fluttered her stomach.

"Come here, Daughter."

She stared at her father in silence, his glare pinning her feet to the floor.

"I won't hurt you."

She'd heard the words before, their promise disappearing like water through shifting sand. Michal held her tongue, surprised at how calm she felt. After six months of putting up with her father's changing moods, maybe she was finally figuring out how to manage him. Though staying out of his way seemed like the wisest option.

She took one step, then whirled about and dashed to the door. On the third step, she felt her father's grip on her forearm. "Let me go!"

He yanked her to his chest. "Do you think you can outrun a warrior, Daughter?" His fingers dug into her flesh.

"You said you wouldn't hurt me!" With tears in her eyes, she writhed to get free. "Why, Father? Why do you do this?" She winced at the bruise he was giving her, hating him.

Her mother's weeping grew to loud wails.

Michal felt her father's fingers slowly release her arm.

"I shouldn't have . . ." With a wounded look on his face, he glanced about the room. One hand lifted to his temple as he sank to the floor again. Moaning, he dug both hands into his shoulder-length hair.

Michal resisted the urge to kick him and beat him with her fists. Instead, she drew in a calming breath and rested a hand on top of her father's head, brushing the golden crown.

"Don't worry, Father. The harpist will come soon, and you will be well."

When he didn't respond, she slipped from the room, disgust and despair mingling in her heart.

❦

Michal rushed along the cobbled stones, then stopped abruptly in front of a guard. "Joash, get Marta to help my mother. She's hurt." The guard hurried away, and Michal ran to the courtyard, where Jonathan sat with her brothers Abinadab and Malchishua, rubbing oil into their leather breastplates. "You must come at once, Jonathan." She bent forward, dragging in a breath of air. "The demons are after Father again."

Jonathan dropped the oilcloth and shield onto the stone bench and stood. "Tell me quickly, what has he done?"

Michal blurted out the scene in her mother's chambers, her words tumbling on top of one another. Her brother's left brow hiked up a notch, and his dark brown beard moved with the clenched muscle in his jaw.

"He's getting worse," she said, falling into step at Jonathan's side. His long legs carried him faster than she could keep up. "What are we going to do?" She hated the whiny quality her voice took on when she panicked, but she was grateful that Jonathan never seemed to notice.

"Send for the singer," Abinadab said, coming up behind them. "At least the house has some peace from the madness when he plucks those strings of his."

"I sent for him yesterday." Jonathan stopped at the entrance to their father's harem. "How badly was she hurt?" he asked Michal.

"She had a cut on her arm, maybe a few bruises. I sent for Marta."

"With that temper of his, it's a wonder he didn't kill her." Abinadab scowled.

"Keep your tone respectful, Brother. He's still our father and king."

"He doesn't act like a king." Michal tensed, wishing she could retract the words.

"Maybe not, but we must still keep in mind that he is the Lord's anointed."

Michal sighed, feeling far older than her fifteen years. A guard emerged from her mother's chambers, the king leaning on his arm. They stepped to the side, allowing the king to pass. His eyes held a dazed expression, as though he looked through them instead of at them.

"He's not a good king," Michal whispered, when their father had turned down the hall leading to his own chambers.

Jonathan's hand on her arm made her look up at him again. "We have to trust the Lord in this, Michal."

He walked on toward their mother's room. His earnest expression brought a sliver of hope into her heart, but in the same moment the old doubts rose to haunt her.

"Then why has the Lord forsaken our father?" she asked, hurrying to keep up. The question had burned within her since the day their father had returned from a battle with the Amalekites, shaken to the core. He'd never spoken of it, and she was desperate to understand. "Please, Jonathan, do you know why the Most High seems to torment Father rather than help him?"

Jonathan crossed the threshold to their mother's chambers, where Michal could see the woman resting on her couch, Marta at her side.

"The singer will ease Father's worries," he said. "Don't trouble yourself with the rest." He touched her arm. "I'll handle things here."

Michal nodded, relieved to be free of the whole ordeal. Grabbing up her skirts, she raced to the outside of the palace kitchens where stone steps led to the lookout area on the flat roof. *David*. If Jonathan had already sent for him, he could be coming up the hill from Bethlehem. She might be able to spot him from the rooftop.

She rounded a corner closest to the clay ovens, where scents of garlic and leeks mingled with the yeasty smells of baking bread. One sniff made her stomach growl, but she pressed a hand to her waist and grasped the rail. She raised her foot to climb the first step when the echoing sounds of her father's screams sent her hopes plummeting.

Her sister, Merab, came up behind her, dark hair flowing beneath a blue veil, arms crossed in her arrogant older sister pose. Sometimes Michal saw glimpses of her father in her sister's cold eyes and tight smile. She shuddered at the thought.

"There you are. Mother needs you," Merab said.

Michal let out a sigh. "Jonathan is with her. She doesn't need me." She had to get away from her mother's demands.

Merab lifted her chin. "Of course she does. It's always you she wants." She shifted from one foot to the other. "You best hurry—you know how she gets."

Yes. She knew only too well.

A feeling of rebellion made her pause. Of late her mother had grown almost as unreasonable as her father, even going so far as to bring teraphim into the palace. The household gods made her shiver every time she looked at them.

Michal glanced up at the roof, then back at her sister. "I'll be there soon." Before Merab could protest, Michal scurried up the stone steps to the lookout place between the dual towers.

A brisk breeze whipped her head cloth behind her while she gripped the stone parapet. She bent forward, straining to see against the glare of the fading sun.

David.

She swayed to the music of his name echoing in her heart. Leaning her weary limbs against the stone tower, she released an unsteady breath. Below her, ricocheting against the granite walls of the palace, the sounds of her father's raving madness carried through the open windows.

Any moment now the harpist, straddling his father's gray donkey, would trot through the imposing gates of Gibeah, straight to her father's side.

Oh, please hurry!

The incessant pounding of her heart increased at the sound of a sudden, earsplitting scream. She clamped her hands over her ears and rocked back on her heels.

Why, God? Why does my father act this way?

Michal bit back a sob and stretched farther over the rail's edge, begging her eyes to find the object of her desire, of her desperation. Truth be told, she needed the magic of the singer's music almost as much as her father did. Maybe then her fears would subside, her anxious thoughts cease.

She rushed to the other end of the roof. Her fingers trembling, she flipped her braided hair behind her back and peered around the towers toward the hills. For a moment the beauty of the sunset calmed her tattered nerves.

Please come. Don't make us wait another day.

Her father's guttural wail coming from below reduced

her fragile peace to ashes. She raised her fists in the air and screamed.

⁊ᵟ⳺

Cushioned couches lined the south wall of the king's court where Michal reclined beside her mother and sister, her gaze fixed on the singer. Though it was long after dark, David had finally come. His sweet music wooed her, and the strings of his harp mimicked the melodic trill of a nightingale. She closed her eyes, picturing the cascading blue-green waters of En Gedi.

Tension slipped from her shoulders, and her restless fears vanished. *David.* Had she spoken his name aloud? But David's gaze was focused on her father. King Saul was no longer the crazed madman of a few hours ago. His eyes were clear, and his lips curved in a smile.

Michal's heart stirred with something akin to compassion. She could almost love the king when he was like this.

The music drifted into stillness. David's head lifted, and he glanced in her direction. Michal's breath caught when their eyes connected. His casual, dimpled smile nearly made her heart stop. Could he read her thoughts? Could he tell how her heart yearned for him? His gaze moved past her and lingered on her sister. Michal shifted in her seat, catching the blush on Merab's cheeks.

In a suspended moment, Michal glanced from Merab to David, who had turned away to face Jonathan and the king. But not soon enough to hide the look that had passed between them. A look that told her more than words could begin to say.

David—the man who had captured her heart—was in love with her sister.

2

David's right hand clutched the sling circling in a wide arc, his grip tightening on the leather strings. Eyes fixed on the target—a chipped vase sitting at a distance on a natural rock projection—he twirled faster with easy, practiced determination, until finally he let loose the stone.

The air rang with a high-pitched *whoosh*, and the vase exploded with a handful of clinking pops.

"That was dead-on!"

"Glad that wasn't my head."

"Good thing he's on our side."

David heard the shouts of admiration amid the friendly backslapping as he stepped aside to allow the next of Saul's twenty-four armor bearers to take aim at another target. He turned at the touch of a hand on his shoulder. Prince Jonathan stood at his side.

David dipped his head. "My lord. I did not hear your footsteps."

"Never admit such a thing to your superiors, David. A warrior never lets his guard down." Jonathan's brown eyes danced.

David dropped a stone in the flat leather pad of his sling and glanced quickly in all directions. "Is that better, my lord?" He smiled, palmed the stone, and slipped it into the pouch at his belt. "I had assumed I was among friends."

Jonathan shifted the quiver of arrows at his shoulder, his angular face taking on a somber expression. "These days it's hard to tell friend from foe."

David followed Jonathan's gaze to the fifty men broken into smaller groups spaced about the field and practicing with bow and sling. His attention stopped at the pillarlike stone structure where the targets were placed by one of the young men at the edge of the field. They'd dubbed the stone *Ezel*, or "departure," due to its proximity to the road heading south of Gibeah—toward home in Bethlehem.

"So are you cleared to stay a month this time?" Jonathan asked.

"My father is pleased to allow me to serve the king as long as my lord wishes."

Jonathan nodded, turning east toward the stone palace fortress. "Let's walk."

David tucked the sling into his belt and followed the prince in the opposite direction of the practicing captains and armor bearers. A quiet camaraderie fell between them as the warm breeze blew puffs of white pollen into the air and rustled the dry grass beneath their sandals.

"I see your nephews followed you here again."

David nodded. "Joab and Abishai. I can't seem to lose them."

Jonathan laughed, his somber expression replaced by a wide smile. "We have another thing in common then. I have at least one family member I wouldn't mind losing for a while."

David glanced at Jonathan. "Things have not improved while I was away."

Near the edge of the palace grounds, Jonathan turned west toward a plateau where a large terebinth tree shaded the ground. They sat in the dirt among the gnarled roots, the wind playing with the leaves above them.

"Things will never improve until my father repents of his sin," Jonathan said, setting the quiver and bow between them. "You have heard the rumors, have you not?"

David looked up, meeting Jonathan's gaze. "Rumors, my lord?"

"About my father and the Amalekites and Samuel's prediction. You are aware of this?"

He knew, of course. But the prophet Samuel had warned him not to reveal his knowledge. Only a handful of people had heard Samuel's prediction to King Saul, and as long as Saul was in power, the less David should tell. So how much should he reveal to the future king of Israel—his rival?

"I know Samuel was unhappy when your father refused to kill all of the Amalekites." He picked a twig from the dirt and stole a glance at Jonathan.

The prince removed his leather helmet and ran a hand through his shoulder-length brown hair. "Not even my brothers know this. But I was there that day. I heard Samuel's prediction." He faced David then. "Tell me, David. Have you met the prophet?"

David's heart skipped a beat. He forced his gaze to hold steady, to keep from revealing the turmoil coursing through him. "Yes."

"When?"

David's stomach knotted. "A couple of months ago . . .

before I was summoned to play for your father." He paused. The chirping and echoing response of two birds broke the silence. "Why?"

Jonathan stroked his beard. "Samuel told my father that the Lord had torn the kingdom from him and would give it to another, his neighbor—someone better than him." He looked beyond David as though deep in thought. "I do not wish to pry into your affairs, David. But there is one thing I must know."

The hairs rose on David's arms. "What is that, my prince?"

Jonathan's hands stilled, resting on his knees. He looked into David's eyes, unwavering. "Did Samuel anoint you?"

❦

Michal raced down the stone corridors of the dank fortress—a sorry excuse for a palace. Where could he have gone? It was not like she cared overmuch for the carved wooden doll he'd stolen from her room, but Ishbosheth had a way of irritating her, and she was tired of his games. Besides, the doll was the first toy Jonathan had carved for her, and she intended to keep it.

She spotted her older brother hunched in a corner of the hall outside his sleeping quarters. With a shake of her head, Michal smoothed her robe and walked toward him. The action made the young man jump to his feet.

"Give it back, Ishby."

He held the doll above his head and laughed.

Michal moved closer. He tried to turn away but hit the wall. There was no place else to go.

"This is an idol." Ishbosheth pointed to the doll, then ran

his free hand through his scraggly brown hair, the way Jonathan always did.

Michal stumbled back a pace as though he'd slapped her. "No, it's not. Jonathan wouldn't make an idol."

"Yes, it is. I've seen bigger ones like it in Mama's room. She has them guarding the door."

The teraphim. Michal tried to peer through Ishbosheth's closed fingers at the carved, faceless doll, Jonathan's youthful attempt at carving. There was little resemblance to her mother's teraphim.

"Mama prays to the idols," Ishbosheth said.

She did?

"How do you know that?" Adonai would not be pleased about that. If there was one commandment Jonathan had taught her, it was "You shall have no other gods before me."

"I've seen her." He clutched Michal's doll. "Now I can pray to one too."

"No, Ishby, you mustn't ever pray to an idol." She patted his arm. If only he could understand. "Adonai doesn't like us to pray to anyone but Him."

Indecision flitted over his chunky face, and tears threatened, making the pale brown hues of his eyes glisten. "If I disobey Adonai, I could end up like Abba, couldn't I?" He thrust his hand forward, palm open. "Take it, Michal. Hurry, before the demons come for me."

Michal stared at the piece of wood, then at her brother. Maybe he was more aware than they gave him credit for. She took the doll from him and stuffed it into a pocket of her robe. "A wise choice, Ishby."

Ishbosheth grabbed Michal and gave her a fierce hug, startling her with his sudden affection. "Throw it away, Michal. Hurry."

"Good idea." She ran off, feet flying back the way she'd come. She would hide the doll in a better place this time, to protect Ishby.

❦

"Did you hear me, David? Or would you prefer not to answer?" Jonathan's clear eyes never wavered, his shoulders straight as an arrow. "Did Samuel anoint you?"

The truth. There was no getting around it now. David's gut clenched, his emotions spiraling downward. He dropped his gaze and studied the earth, assuring himself he still sat on solid ground.

Please, Lord, tell me what to do.

He lifted his head and gave the prince a slight nod.

Jonathan's shoulders lost their military pose. He stared into the distance. "I thought so."

Moments passed in tense silence until at last the prince stood, picked up his bow and quiver of arrows, and placed them at David's feet. Then before David could stop him, Jonathan knelt, head lowered.

"Please, do not bow to me, my prince," David said. "It is I who must bend the knee to you."

Jonathan looked intently into his eyes. "Time will tell us that, now won't it?" He stood, then gripped David's right hand, pulling him to his feet. "Now, how about I teach you to use these things? After all, a king must be a warrior first." He paused. "And if we consider Moses' teaching, I suppose the Most High would want him to possess a shepherd's heart as well."

❦

An hour passed. The wooden doll still lay tucked into the pocket of Michal's robe, the weight of it growing with every passing moment. She'd been cornered by her mother as she passed the kitchens, keeping her from fulfilling her promise to Ishby. Even there, centered on a wall above the ovens, Michal noticed a carved image—another teraph. Were they everywhere? When had her mother decorated the house with them?

A troubled feeling settled in her stomach as she stumbled down the dark halls. The doll pressing against her thigh seemed to burn her flesh at the slightest touch.

She rounded a corner, her mind whirling. Where to put it? Maybe she should have thrown it into one of the ovens' fuel supplies and let it turn to ash. But a part of her couldn't destroy what Jonathan's hands had made.

She had to hide it one way or the other.

She sprinted to the outer court. Passing through the door, she tripped, righted herself, and nearly banged into David.

"My lady! Are you hurt?"

She looked into David's vivid dark eyes and thought she might faint.

"Where are you going in such a hurry?"

His smile sent her heart into a wild gallop. She released a long, slow breath. "I was taking care of something."

"I see. It must be urgent."

"Yes—no—not exactly . . ." Warmth crept into her cheeks. She should love the chance to talk with him. So why did she suddenly feel like a lost little girl, tongue-tied and nervous? "I . . . it's a family matter."

"It's not your father again, is it?" A muscle worked along

his jaw, and he shifted as though ready to move—to hurry to the king's side.

"No, no, it's not that." She glanced at the leather sandals strapped to his dusty feet. Had no one offered to wash them when he entered the palace? Lazy servants! If she were in charge . . .

"I'm glad." His words brought her wandering thoughts back to him, and she found herself gazing into those fathomless eyes.

"What? Oh yes, so am I. Glad, I mean, about my father." She stopped short, cheeks flaming. Placing a hand over her fluttering heart, Michal drew a deep breath. "I'm sorry. I must sound like I've lost my mind." She summoned her courage and offered him a warm smile.

"Not at all, Princess. Just distracted." He smiled in return, clasped his hands behind him, and took a step backward. "If you'll excuse me, I have business to attend to."

"Yes, of course."

He turned, heading down the hall away from her.

"David?" There was so much more she wanted to say in such a rare moment alone.

He swiveled around, keeping his distance.

"Despite what everyone thinks, I'm not a child."

David looked at her, head tilted, brow lifted in question. Was that pity in his eyes? "Indeed."

"I mean . . . in case Jonathan or Father treats me like one . . . I'm not."

"That's quite obvious. And I understand. You are the youngest—as am I."

She let her eyes meet his and linger for a moment. "You are?"

22

He nodded, his ever-charming smile making her heart skip another beat. "Considered the runt of the litter, left out of important decisions, stuck with the sheep."

Michal's eyes widened. "Truly? So am I. I mean, my family is always calling me 'little sister,' as though I'm never going to grow up."

"Maybe you run too much. Don't most grown women walk with dignity—you know, head held high, chin tipped up?"

Michal giggled at his imitation, wishing the laugh had come out sounding more sophisticated. "Perhaps I do. I guess I'll have to become dull and elegant if they're ever going to see me as a woman."

David's look made Michal's palms moisten. "You'll never be dull, Michal." He moved farther away from her. "I will let you get back to wherever it is you were off to."

The field scent of him remained when he slipped from sight. Michal drank it in, wishing for all the world that he could stay and talk with her forever. She felt the wooden doll press against her thigh and pulled it from the folds of her robe. David's devotion to the God of Israel would never allow him to keep an idol.

She watched his retreating back, listening to the fading sounds of his footsteps. Then she walked with grace to the garden—head held high, chin tipped up. Once there, she got down on her knees and used a sharp stone to carve a hole in the dirt. With a vow never to go near an idol again, Michal dropped the image into the space and buried it.

3

Twelve uniformed jugglers, each wearing the embroidered insignia of an Israelite tribe, lifted a round, red pomegranate in their right hand high over their heads. Miniature, red-plumed helmets representing Philistine soldiers rested in each juggler's left hand.

A hush settled over the packed banquet hall. With rhythmic motions, one performer after another placed the tiny helmet on the fruit and tossed the overripe pomegranates into the air, then caught them and smashed them into the center of Saul's banquet hall. Each splat and spillage of the seeded fruit brought a cheer from the crowd and outright laughter from the king.

"And we'll slaughter you again, you Philistine dogs," Saul shouted when the last leathery skin split like an enemy head crushed in battle. "You think you can summon us to Elah and win? You dare come against the armies of Saul? We'll grind you to dust." Saul's voice rose with each syllable, his hardened face growing crimson with rage.

David sat in one corner of the room, his lyre resting on his knees, his eyes on the king. Saul's expression darkened, and his fingers rose to his temples.

"My harpist. Where is my harpist?"

David stood and strode toward the center of the room. The jugglers sloshed and slid in the smashed fruit, symbolically tramping in the blood of the enemy.

"Stop!"

The room fell silent.

David studied the king's lined face, assessing which mood to soothe. Was this another demon attack or merely a headache brought on by too much wine?

"Where is my harpist?" The demand grew to a wail, and Saul slumped forward. He raked both hands through his salty black hair, pushing the golden crown askew.

David strummed a harmonic chord on his lyre, stepping around the squashed pomegranates to take a seat near the king.

"Hear my cry, O God; attend to my prayer. From the end of the earth I will cry to You when my heart is overwhelmed. Lead me to the rock that is higher than I." David closed his eyes, praying as he sang. "For You have been a shelter for me, a strong tower from the enemy. I will abide in Your tabernacle forever, I will trust in the shelter of Your wings."

The creaking of a heavy wooden door pulled David's attention to the opposite side of the room. A royal guard marched with staccato steps across the hall, leading Saul's wife, Ahinoam, his concubine, Rizpah, and his two daughters, Merab and Michal. They stopped midstride.

David picked a light, melodic tune to mask the intrusion. Saul's women made a practice of a ritual farewell at these prewar events. But their timing couldn't have been worse.

He continued to play, singing words he'd crafted on long

nights alone with the sheep, ever aware of the riveted attention of the crowded room. There was power in music, as though the Lord had given humanity an inner pulse that beat only with the rhythmic cadence of song—a force that flowed through him to the people.

It was a heady feeling.

David looked over the room, catching glimpses of appreciation scattered among men and women alike. He stole a glance at Merab, whose elegant beauty made his heart race. Shiny, long brown hair shimmered beneath a striped red and blue veil. Her eyes were almost as dark, like polished onyx stones, and her olive skin was as smooth as the soft garment she wore. Her moist red lips drew him.

Heart hammering, he looked away. A discordant note came from his lyre as his fingers slipped on the strings. He corrected it, willing his thoughts into submission.

No woman should have such power over a man.

He turned his attention to the king and to Jonathan sitting at his right hand. Saul's eyes were closed, his head tipped back against the wooden throne. David moved to another melodic transition, plucking a tune suggesting spring rain and rustling leaves.

When the music ended, Saul's eyes were clear. David smiled. Power belonged to God Most High.

David breathed a deep sigh as Saul's women stepped forward to greet the king. He watched Merab's elegant, graceful steps across the tiled floor. When she stopped, she met his gaze with a beguiling one of her own. His hands tightened around the wood, his mouth dry. Swallowing hard, he shifted his attention behind her.

She held far too much sway over his emotions. Power

belonged to Adonai, he reminded himself, not Merab. Yet the thudding of his heart betrayed him.

"Come forward." At Saul's command his wife, Ahinoam, walked with royal grace to kneel at Saul's feet. She kissed his outstretched hand.

"My lord," she said in a thin, strained voice.

"Take your seat, woman," Saul said. His gaze drifted to his concubine, Rizpah.

"May my lord, King Saul, live forever." Rizpah's lilting voice carried across the room as she slowly bent forward, cradling her unborn child, and kissed the hem of Saul's outstretched sleeve. Saul dismissed her with a wave, relegating her to the seat farthest from him. Merab stepped forward and kissed the back of Saul's hand. David watched the exchange, unable to pull away.

"Have you come to wish your father victory, Daughter?"

David noted Saul's softening expression. Did she carry some mystic control over him as well?

"Yes, Father. May you bring the head of the Philistine king back on a silver platter."

Saul leaned his head against the chair and laughed. "I've trained you well. And if I am successful, what do you wish?"

David's interest piqued. This girl knew how to appease the king. So why didn't she try to do so more often when his moods rose and fell?

"I wish you to bring me your greatest warrior as a husband, Father. Someone who makes you proud."

The words came out in a honeyed tone. A typical female trick to get a man to do her bidding. He'd seen it often enough between his brothers and their wives.

"When we return victorious, you will have your pick of fine young men," Saul promised.

Merab turned and took a seat behind her mother, and Michal stepped forward and kissed Saul's signet ring.

"Come back to me safely, Abba," she said, leaning closer to kiss Saul's cheek. Saul's face relaxed, his eyes alight with affection.

David sat up straighter, intrigued. No syrupy tone, no haughty lift of the chin. No tempting power over a man.

"I'll always come back to you, Michal." Saul cupped both hands around her face. "Ten thousand Philistines couldn't keep me away."

Michal tilted her head against the palm of Saul's large hand and smiled. The image reminded David of when he'd held one of his smallest lambs close to his heart. When Saul released her, Michal started to walk away, then turned back to look into the king's eyes.

"I'm counting on you, Abba."

Saul's delighted expression made David pause. He looked at Michal, now sitting beside her sister. A pale blue head cloth covered rich, ebony hair, and her skin, even from a distance, held a rosy glow. She was younger than her sister by at least two years, but the curves of a woman truly did show beneath her striped robe. There was a quiet beauty about her—not elegant and beguiling like her sister, but innocent and fresh.

Easier to manage that kind of woman, if his brothers could be trusted.

He glanced at the king again.

Then again, maybe not.

David caught Jonathan's attention and the prince's slight nod. The prebattle feast would last through the night, then

Saul would gather his army of thousands and travel to the Valley of Elah. David stood and tucked his lyre under his arm, heading for the barracks.

Time to pack his bags and go home.

❦

"David, wait!" Michal stepped from the shadows of a row of trees that lined the walk from the palace to the barracks.

"Michal?" David tightened the leather strap around his lyre, securing it to his father's donkey. His gaze met hers, and Michal thought her heart would stop.

She drew closer, emotions clashing within her like rival swords. "They're still feasting. I came as soon as I could." She drew a breath, willing her pulse to slow. "I wanted to say good-bye."

His charismatic smile fluttered her stomach. "It appears that you already have."

Heat burned her cheeks, and she looked down. How was it possible that he always tied her tongue in knots? She heard the swish of his sandals moving toward her.

"Take care of yourself, Princess."

She pushed her raging emotions into a corner of her soul and met his gaze. "I will. I—we'll miss you."

He smiled again, making her heart skip a beat. "Perhaps we'll meet again someday."

Someday?

"You know my father will still need you. He shouldn't send you off so soon. What if the demons come back tonight?"

David's smile softened to a thoughtful expression. "Your father has a war to fight, Michal. He'll be too busy to allow the thoughts that torment him to gain control."

He took a step back yet was near enough for the earthy scent of him to reach her. *Oh, don't go! Stay!* The words sprang to her lips, but she silenced them.

"Why does the Lord let the demons trouble my father?"

He stroked his sparse, dark brown beard, compassion evident in his tender gaze. "I don't know, Princess."

"It's because he didn't kill all of the Amalekites, isn't it?" Michal averted her eyes. She chided herself for bringing up her father when David was leaving. She wanted to speak of love and marriage and her interest in him.

"That's a possibility, I suppose." He turned back to secure the donkey's sacks. "I really couldn't say for sure."

"What will you do when you get home?"

David glanced at the sky and patted the donkey's side, then looked into her eyes. Was she embarrassing him? "I'm a shepherd, Michal. I spend my days in the fields tending smelly sheep."

"Sheep aren't so smelly." She toyed with the sash of her multicolored robe. Was there a shepherdess he longed to return to?

David chuckled. "You haven't been around them much. It's a life far less glamorous than a palace."

Michal's lip curled. "I'd rather live with sheep."

She felt David's eyes on her, and her cheeks grew warm again. "You live a privileged life, Michal. Be grateful."

"I'd hardly call living in a dismal stone fortress with an unpredictable, hot-tempered father privileged." The words came out harsher than she intended. "Are you betrothed, David?"

His donkey snorted, and David turned his attention to the beast. He checked the donkey's bridle. Silence lengthened between them. Oh, to draw the words back and stuff them into her heart where they belonged. Not out in the open for him to see. She shifted from one foot to the other, wringing her folded hands. It was a foolish question and none of her business.

"Nevertheless, God has set your family above all others," David said at last, ignoring her question. His serious tone matched the concern in his brilliant, dark brown eyes. "Which makes you fortunate."

Michal's stomach quivered as she held his gaze.

"If you say so."

She watched his face take on the affection of an older brother. "I say so." He grabbed the donkey's reins, urging it forward. "And no, I'm not betrothed."

Michal fixed her gaze on David's back. In a heartbeat he turned, his eyes meeting hers. The momentary contact felt like a familiar touch, making Michal's heart skip again. He left her staring after him, a deep ache settling in her soul. She didn't want him to treat her like a sister. Couldn't he see that?

"Have a safe journey, David," she managed, fighting sudden tears. Before he rounded the bend leading through the arched gates of her father's fortress, Michal turned and ran back to the palace.

4

Jonathan stood on the hill overlooking the Valley of Elah, bow at his side, shield in his hand. On the opposite rise, the red-feathered helmets of the Philistine army were visible among row after row of enemy tents. Even from this distance, Jonathan could see the relaxed stance and hear the boisterous laughter and taunting jibes. Israel's old enemy was at it again, flexing their military might. In the last battle, with God's help, Jonathan had nearly single-handedly sent them running. Where was God now?

The sun hung low on the horizon, and Jonathan braced himself as the Philistine hoard came to attention, flanking the ridge. A distant rumble, like coming thunder, shook the earth. Giant feet holding up a mammoth of a man marched with deliberate strides to the edge of the ridge.

"Why have you come out to line up for battle? Am I not a Philistine, and you the servants of Saul?" The giant's shout caught the swift attention of his father's army, who'd been crouched near their tents for nearly forty days. "Choose a man for yourselves, and let him come down to me. If he is able to fight with me and kill me, then we will be your servants."

The oaf paused, letting a deep laugh erupt into a sneer. "But if I prevail against him and kill him, then you shall be our servants and serve us!"

Jonathan watched his father's men, comrades in peace and war, shrink from the hilltop back to their tents. They'd heard the same request, day after day. Why couldn't someone step up and fight the man? Why couldn't he?

With fingers stiff from clenching, Jonathan stuffed straight locks of hair back under his turban, out of his eyes. Courage. What had happened to his once dauntless courage? He bent to pick up a small rock and heaved it toward the valley, too far from the giant for him to notice, then turned with dogged steps toward his tent.

"Master Jonathan." A young armor bearer ran up beside him. "The king requests you come at once."

Now what? He turned a corner and meandered through the row of black goat-hair tents. Muted whispers drifted to his ears, but Jonathan shut them out. Never mind that his men looked at him with questioning eyes, wondering what to do. He didn't know what they should do. If the Philistine was a normal man, he'd gear up and attack at first light. But he stood almost twice as high as most of the men of Israel. Only a fool would attempt such a thing. Or a man of great faith.

So where is your faith, Jonathan?

The question hung in the air, as though someone had spoken in his ear. Where indeed?

Lifting the flap of his father's tent, Jonathan ducked through the opening and entered the dim interior. "You called for me, Father?"

Saul leaned against the tent post, sitting among an assortment of brown and yellow cushions. Abner, Israel's army commander and Saul's cousin, stood at attention. The only sign of his agitation was his right foot tapping an intermittent rhythm.

"Oh . . . we must do something, Jonathan. Do you hear what the men are saying? The whispers, the confusion. They're talking about deserting me."

"We need someone to take up the challenge." Abner touched one hand to his pate, smoothing the sparse brown hair.

"I could go, Father." Jonathan spoke the words with resignation. If he died in the process, so be it.

Silence. Then a guttural wail. "No!" Saul jumped to his feet, banging his head on the tent's ceiling post. "I will not allow my son, heir to my throne, to be butchered by that—that—heathen pig."

Jonathan did not care to be butchered by that heathen pig either. But he hid his thoughts. "What makes you think he'd win?" he asked.

Abner's left brow hiked up a notch. "Don't be ridiculous, Jonathan."

Saul put a hand to his head and groaned. "I've sent for your sister."

Jonathan stared at his father. "You're going to feed my sister to the giant?"

Saul shook his head. "No, no, of course not! She's our incentive."

Jonathan rubbed the back of his neck. "What are you talking about, Father?"

Saul fell back in a crumpled heap among the cushions and rocked back and forth. Abner walked over and placed one hand on Jonathan's shoulder. "Your father is offering tax exemption, riches, and Merab's hand in marriage to the slayer of Goliath. He's sent for her. Maybe if the men see her beauty, someone will step forth."

Jonathan shook off Abner's hand. "You cannot bring my sister into a war camp. This is no place for a woman!" He sent a penetrating look to Abner, strode to the tent's door, and summoned two soldiers. "Go after the men sent to bring my sister and tell them to return without her."

"But the king said—"

"The king has changed his mind."

The guards appeared doubtful and tried to peer beyond Jonathan into the tent.

"Now go." Jonathan dismissed the men with a wave of his hand before turning back to his father.

"I had no choice, Jonathan," Saul whined, still rocking back and forth, hands clasped around his knees.

"There is always a choice, Father."

The king's lips curved in a pout. "Well, I'm still offering her hand. Something must be done. Don't you see?"

Yes, he did see—all too clearly. Disgusted, he turned and stepped into the gathering dusk. He was a coward, along with all of the rest of the men in the camp. And all of the money, riches, or women in the world would not change that fact.

꿰꿴

Stacks of gray clouds shadowed the western foothills of Judah, blocking David's view of the approaching ridge. A far-off rumble grew with every step, and David urged the donkey into a faster trot up the mountain's winding path. The trail led through a grove of sycamore trees, and when he rounded a wide bend, the black goat-hair tents of the Israelite camp came into view. One quick glance told him the place was deserted except for a handful of sentries standing guard.

In the distance, excited shouts and stomping feet preceded a collective battle cry. David's heart thumped, spurring him forward. He spotted a lone tent off to the right surrounded by leather packs and saddlebags. A middle-aged man stood tying a goatskin sack to the low branch of a tall oak tree. David rushed toward him.

"Are you the baggage keeper?" he asked, hopping off the donkey.

"Yes, yes. That would be me, yes." The man turned to give David a toothless grin. "Come to watch the battle, boy?"

"Actually, I've come to find how the battle goes and to bring word to my father of how my brothers fare." David handed the donkey's reins to the man. "Are they up on the ridge?"

The man nodded. "Won't be there long, though. Should be comin' back to camp soon enough, if it goes like it's been goin'."

David gave the man a quizzical look. "What do you mean?" He fidgeted at the sound of another earthshaking battle cry. If he didn't hurry, the army would rush forward, and a bloodbath would begin before he had a chance to see his brothers.

The keeper stroked the donkey's nose and shrugged. "Run along and see for yourself."

David stepped over a sack of grain and raced around a row of tents, then sprinted the rest of the way up the hill. Row upon row of Israelite soldiers filled his vision, bordering the edge of the hill overlooking the Valley of Elah. Across the wide, green valley, columns of red-feathered helmets moved forward. Moments later they began to bob in time with the stomping feet and hoarse cries of the Philistine army. They stopped abruptly at the summit of the opposite hill.

Another returning, deafening shout erupted from the Israelites while David scanned the rows for Judah's tribal banner and some sign of his brothers. There, four rows down, he spotted them and ran behind the battle lines to greet them.

"There you are, Shammah."

"David!" Shammah clapped his thick arm around David's shoulder and nearly squeezed the air from David's lungs. "Did Father send you? Oh, tell me he sent some decent food."

David smiled. "Some of Mother's best bread." He turned at a tap on his shoulder to face his second-oldest brother. "Abinadab, I've missed you."

Abinadab wrapped large arms around David in a brotherly hug. "Hey, little brother! What brings you here?" He bent closer to David's ear. "Did the king send for you again?"

David shook his head. "Father was worried. There's been no word for over a month. What's going on?"

Abinadab opened his mouth to speak when a collective hush fell in waves over the multiple rows of men. Across the valley a lone Philistine stepped out from the sea of heathens with red-feathered helmets and stood at the highest tip of the ridge.

"Servants of Saul." Was that booming roar a human voice?

"Servants of Saul." The words came clearer now, prodding David to push closer to the front lines, while the men around him took several unobtrusive steps backward.

"Why have you come out to line up for battle? Am I not a Philistine, and you the servants of Saul? Choose a man for yourselves and let him come down to me. If he is able to fight

37

with me and kill me, then we will be your servants, but if I prevail against him and kill him, then you will be our servants and serve us." He paused, lifted a huge spear, and shook it at the heavens. "I defy the armies of Israel this day! Give me a man, that we may fight together."

David stared at the huge man, the Philistine's words registering in his heart. This was no ordinary Philistine. He had to be close to six cubits and a span, covered from head to foot in plated armor. And his shield bearer was as sturdy as a brawny tree.

Yet God was bigger. Did this Philistine think his size alone could defeat the men whose God fought for them? David's fists flexed open and closed, and he whirled about to return to his brothers, but he found the ridge suddenly deserted. He glimpsed the backs of the retreating Israelites. Where were they going? He turned back at the sound of the giant's bellowing laugh.

"Still afraid of me, are you?" The man beat on his chest and shook his fist at the sky. "Some God you serve, Israelites! He cannot even save you from the likes of me!"

Indignation burned in David's chest like a living, breathing fire. He spun around again and ran after the withdrawing men. Pockets of soldiers grouped by tribes huddled near their tents. David slowed his pace and approached one of them.

"What will be done for the man who kills this Philistine and takes away the reproach from Israel? For who is this uncircumcised Philistine, that he should defy the armies of the living God?"

A hardened soldier wearing the colors of the tribe of Asher folded his arms, eyeing David up and down. "I heard the king has offered his daughter's hand in marriage."

David faced another soldier, but the man averted his gaze as though he were ashamed. Well, he should be. David turned to a third. "Is that all he said?"

"I don't know about a marriage proposal, but I heard there is a promise of no taxes," the third said. "Not that it will do us any good dead."

David jogged to another group sitting under the banner of Ephraim. "What will the king do for the man who slays this Philistine?"

"He's promised great riches, and he'll make him his son-in-law," one said, scowling, then he walked off.

"If you don't believe us, ask Prince Jonathan," another man said. "They say he had to stop the king from bringing her to camp." The man's tone held disgust, matching David's own. This was no place for a woman, least of all the beautiful, beguiling Merab. He could only imagine what would happen to her should she be taken among the spoils of war. A shudder passed through him.

The sound of shuffling feet met David's ear. "What are you doing here, little brother?" Eliab, David's oldest brother, grabbed the back of David's tunic and spun him around, pulling him close and nearly spitting in his face. "And with whom have you left those few sheep in the wilderness? I know your pride and your wicked heart. You came to see the battle."

Irritation spread through David, and he shoved both hands against Eliab's chest, breaking free of his grip. "What have I done now? Is there not a cause?" His gaze met the burning coals of Eliab's hardened eyes.

"Your questions aren't helping anything." He straightened his shoulders and tossed David a final, haughty glare. "Do not make a nuisance of yourself, little brother." He stomped off.

David lifted his chin and stared after Eliab. His brother would never change. If anything, he'd only become more antagonistic since David's anointing by the prophet Samuel. Must he always meet with such opposition?

He walked on to the next tribe and came upon a group of Benjamites about a stone's throw from the ornate tent of the king. Armed guards stood watch outside, and servants scurried about, carrying skins of wine and trays of roasted meat into the tent. Something was seriously wrong here. Saul should be walking among his men, encouraging them, seeking the Lord's guidance in what to do about this Philistine.

"Has the king consulted with the priests to determine the will of the Lord?" David asked a man who sat in front of his tent hugging his knees to his chest. He knew the prophet Samuel wouldn't be coming. Samuel had told him months ago that he would no longer appear in Saul's court or anywhere else in the vicinity of the king.

The man lifted troubled eyes to David, and his shoulders slumped in a deep sigh. "The king has offered riches, tax exemption, and his daughter's hand in marriage to the slayer of Goliath."

"Goliath?" So that was his name.

"Goliath of Gath. They say he's one of the sons of Anak." He studied his feet. "He's too strong for us, you know. There isn't a man in Israel who comes close to his height. Not even the king."

King Saul was well known for his stature in Israel, towering head and shoulders above most men. Yet David bristled, the hairs on his arms prickling his flesh. What difference did a man's height make? "The Lord is on our side," he said, straightening. "We have nothing to fear."

The man looked at David as though he had lost his mind. David was about to turn away when he felt a hand touch his shoulder. He looked into the face of Saul's general, Abner.

"Are you the young man who asked about the Philistine?"

"Yes, my lord."

Abner motioned with his hand. "Come with me."

The commander, with a stiff-backed march, led David to the king's tent. As Abner lifted the black flap, flickering light spilled over the entrance. David removed his sandals and ducked his head to enter the plush oriental interior. He took in the room and found King Saul seated upon a raised dais of embroidered pillows, Jonathan to his right. Abner approached and knelt at Saul's feet.

"This is the one who's been asking the questions, my king." Abner extended his arm in David's direction.

"The harpist."

"Yes, my lord," David said. Abner rose to stand at Saul's side, and David took his place, kneeling before the king.

"What is this I hear about you? They say you want to know what the king will do for the man who will slay the giant. Do you know such a man, my son?"

David swallowed, forcing down his rising anger at their lack of faith. He met the king's steady gaze. Peace settled over him, and the same sense of expectancy he'd felt the morning of his anointing filled him from head to toe. God would defend His honor. No uncircumcised barbarian was going to defame the Name and live!

Resolve tightened his gut and clenched the muscles in his arms. He took a steadying breath. "Let no man's heart fail because of this Philistine, my lord. Your servant will fight with him."

Saul's cold, gray eyes narrowed, contempt flickering in their depths. "You are not able to fight this Philistine. You are only a boy. He's been a warrior from his youth."

David rose slightly, his elbow resting on one knee. Passion burned in his soul. "My king, your servant used to keep his father's sheep, and when a lion or a bear came and took a lamb out of the flock, I went out after it and struck it and delivered the lamb from its mouth. When it rose against me, I caught it by its beard and struck and killed it. Your servant has killed both lion and bear, and this uncircumcised Philistine will be like one of them, seeing he has defied the armies of the living God. The Lord who delivered me from the paw of the lion and the paw of the bear will deliver me from the hand of this Philistine."

A telltale twitch began above Saul's left eye. He directed a skeptical glance at Abner and Jonathan, who both tipped their heads forward in reluctant nods.

Saul cleared his throat and gripped the edges of the pillows at his side. "He's but a boy."

"The Lord is with David, Father." Jonathan's low voice rang in the ensuing silence.

Saul nodded in mute ascent, his gaze troubled.

"No one else has come forward, my lord," Abner interjected, eyeing David.

Saul stared at his counselors one at a time, then studied David again. At last he heaved a deep sigh and leaned back against the cushions, resignation lining his grizzled face. "Go, and the Lord be with you."

❦

Michal's jeweled sandals struck the smooth round stones of the family court, taking one slow step after another. No sense hurrying. There was nothing to do with the men away at war unless she wanted to sit and listen to Merab complain about the food, the servants' attitudes, or the lack of male attention. Maybe if Father's strategy worked, Merab would soon marry, leaving Michal free run of the palace without a haughty sibling guardian to interfere with her plans. And if Merab married the giant slayer, she would no longer be Michal's rival for David's attention. That is, if someone in Israel actually had that much courage.

"Why the sullen look today, Michal? You look like you've swallowed sour grapes." Ahinoam's arched nose tilted, and her eyes squinted as Michal met her in the large palace kitchens.

"There's nothing to do, Mother." How long did it take to win a war anyway?

Ahinoam turned toward one of the open windows, her gaze pensive. "There are still a household of servants to feed and manage, Michal. You will never be queen, but you must still know how to manage a home. Your husband will need you to be a disciplined, industrious woman."

Who says I will never be queen? The thought slipped unbidden to her mind. It was something she had long pondered, but of course, the whole thing was impossible. If Jonathan succeeded Father, his wife, Sarah, would be queen. But what if he didn't? If the rumors were true . . . But her mother would not understand the direction of her traitorous thoughts.

"So what should I do?"

The braying of a donkey and the creaking of an oxcart came through the open window.

"He's late." Merab entered the room with regal grace, passing five serving girls bent over wooden kneading troughs.

"Who's late, Mother?" Michal picked up her skirts and hurried after Ahinoam, annoyance nipping at her. She was frustrated that Merab should know something she didn't.

"Adriel, the merchant," Merab answered before Ahinoam could. "Really, Michal, you should pay more attention to overseeing the servants, otherwise things will get out of hand. In this case, the vegetables should have been here at dawn."

"Why? Did they have an appointment with someone?" Michal studied the turbaned merchant leading an uncooperative donkey up the stone walk.

"Don't be impertinent, Michal." Ahinoam brushed past her daughter to meet Adriel at the door. Merab followed two paces behind.

The burly guard Benaiah, who was left to protect the king's household, had allowed Adriel access to the palace kitchens. There was nothing unusual about the sight before her. Benaiah and a handful of other guards were fixtures she encountered at every turn. And she'd seen Adriel bring food to her father's table almost daily for over a year. With the men gone, getting here at dawn didn't seem to make much difference.

Michal lifted one hand to inspect the dark orange henna on her fingernails, then turned to where Adriel and her mother stood looking over a clay tablet checklist. Every now and then the man's gaze drifted to Merab. Was that admiration in his eyes? Michal studied the quiet merchant a moment longer, gauging Merab's demure reaction to him. Adriel was older, probably in his late twenties. Chances are he had a wife and a quiver of sons already. Still, some men took more than one wife.

The stiff staccato of sandaled feet made Michal turn. Benaiah marched across the tiled floor to make his circle of the grounds. He was a dark, average-looking man, but larger than most, his size dwarfing Michal by comparison. He paused at the arch of the door and turned to scan the room. For a long moment he looked at her, then courted a hesitant smile and turned away. Michal studied his back, for the briefest instant warming to the power of her own physical appeal. She shook her head. He couldn't possibly be interested in her. He was just a guard. Then again, he'd paused when he saw Merab too. Maybe Benaiah and Adriel were both attracted to her sister. Like David.

A sick feeling settled over her. Would her sister's beauty always outshine hers? Michal looked again at the merchant, and her thoughts pondered her father's decree sent the day before. Merab would marry the slayer of the giant.

If someone did kill the giant, Father would likely promote him, and he could end up someday as Jonathan's right-hand man, like Abner was for Father. If Merab married him, she could be the second most powerful woman in the land next to Sarah. Suddenly irritated and cross, Michal slipped away from the kitchen and walked slowly out of the room toward her rooftop retreat. She clenched her hands into tight fists. She couldn't let that happen.

❧☙

The air felt thick and still in the wide Valley of Elah, which separated the Philistine camp from the Israelites. Overhead a lone black hawk circled the sky. David stood, watching the carrion bird swoop low toward the Philistine ranks, then fly westward in the direction of Gath, then swing back toward the enemy army again. If God intended to send him a sign of his coming victory, the bird surely made it clear. Not that it mattered. Without a doubt, David knew the Most High had called him to this moment, and nothing anyone could do or say would shake his confidence in the Almighty.

David rested his left hand on the pouch of stones at his side. His sling draped from his right hand. He walked to the top of the ridge, ever aware of the silent army of Israel at his back.

On the opposite rise, Goliath stepped from the battle lines and followed his armor bearer to the point where he usually barked his challenge. David began his descent to the valley floor before Goliath's mouth opened. No sense giving the man what he expected. When the giant saw that someone had come forward to accept his challenge, he lumbered down the hill, each footfall shaking the ground. David's heart beat double time with every approaching step.

With his left hand, David slipped one of his five smooth stones into the pocket of his sling, eyes scanning the armor-plated giant for some kind of chink, a space unprotected. He squinted against the rays of morning sun bouncing off the giant's bronze helmet and coat of brass-scaled armor. Even his legs were cloaked in shining brass greaves. The man looked impenetrable—until a shaft of sunlight moved like an arrow to the center of Goliath's forehead, as though God's finger had pointed to the exact spot David needed to aim his weapon.

David's feet touched the valley floor and began the trek up the other side of the hill. The giant stopped, took two steps forward, and lifted one hand to shade his eyes. David drew closer, but not near enough for the man's javelin to reach him. He stopped within aiming distance.

Sneering laughter bellowed from Goliath's throat. "Am I a dog that you come to me with sticks?" A string of curses spilled like vomit from his mouth. "Come to me, and I will give your flesh to the birds of the air and the beasts of the field."

David extended his arm and began to twirl the sling. "You come to me with sword and spear and javelin, but I come to you in the name of the Lord of Hosts, the God of the armies of Israel, whom you have defied. This day the Lord will deliver you into my hand, and I will strike you down and take your head from you. And this day I will give the carcasses of the camp of the Philistines to the birds of the air and the beasts of the earth, that all the earth may know there is a God in Israel."

"May Dagon grant me victory. I'll have your head first, boy!" The giant lifted his heavily plated leg. *Thud. Clop.* Dust rose from the earth with every step. The Philistine armor bearer ran closer to David.

The black hawk screeched, then a collective hush blanketed the valley. The giant's huge hand straightened the plated coat of mail, then moved to the shaft of his spear. David whirled the sling in one fluid motion at his side. Goliath raised his spear to shoulder height as David flung the stone. He reached for a second stone, his gaze never leaving the path of the first. Time stretched into eternity.

The stone jolted the giant's head back, hitting its mark. Goliath tilted, his expression clouding. His arm pulled back the spear. A dazed look crossed his huge face. David held his breath, clutching the sling.

Out of the corner of his eye, David saw a flock of black hawks join the lone sentinel and fly in circles above the heads of the Philistine army, as though waiting to feast on their flesh. The giant's armor bearer glanced up, his face riddled with terror. He dropped the heavy shield meant to protect Goliath and ran for the top of the hill. David heard the birds' incessant screeching, but his gaze was focused on Goliath.

A moment passed. The giant teetered, both hands pressed to his feathered helmet. Like a tree falling in a forest, Goliath toppled face forward into the dust.

David ran toward him with cautious strides. The spear clattered to the dirt behind the giant, but when David reached it, he knew he'd never be able to lift the thing. He stepped closer and found Goliath's sword still in its scabbard. He tugged it loose and squinted as the sun glinted off the shiny metal. The giant didn't move, but there was no sense taking any chances. He swung the blade high over his head and brought it down on the Philistine's thick neck. Blood spurted over his sandals and onto his tunic.

David tugged the feathered helmet from the severed head, wrapped his fingers around the locks of dark hair, and raised the bloody trophy like a banner high into the air.

"For the Lord and for Israel," he shouted at the Israelite army watching on the ridge.

"For the Lord and for Israel." The thunderous roar shook the ground. Pounding feet pummeled the dirt as battle cries echoed to the opposite hill. As men surged into the valley and climbed up the other side, David grabbed Goliath's sword again and led them to pursue their fleeing enemies.

🦅

"Here is the head of the king's enemy. May all your enemies become as this one, my lord." David stood outside Saul's tent, bowing low before the king, the bloody head of Goliath at his feet. The stench of sweat and blood filled David's nostrils, while the buzz of excited male voices carried to him on the evening's cool breeze.

"Whose son are you, young man?"

David's head lifted at Abner's question. The commander's brawny arms were crossed, his gaze looking David up and down.

"I am the son of your servant Jesse the Bethlehemite."

"The harpist." Saul's dark gray eyes flickered in recognition, his thin lips lifting his beard in a half smile.

"Yes, my lord."

"You've done a good thing in Israel today, my son." Saul's brows dipped ever so slightly. David straightened, his weary senses alert to Saul's mood. Would the demons attack him after such a victory?

"Thank you, my lord."

David's peripheral vision caught Jonathan's lithe form striding across the compound toward them. "God be praised for you, David!" The prince clapped David's back. "You have performed a great feat. May all who hear of it bless the Lord God, for there is indeed a God in Israel!"

David fell to one knee and bowed his head. "Thank you, my prince."

Jonathan grabbed David's arm and lifted him to his feet. "David has done a great service for you, Father. I assume you plan to reward him."

Saul's pinched expression moved from the bloody trophy to David. He interlaced his long fingers and began twirling his thumbs around each other. "Of course, my son. This is why we asked his lineage." He glanced briefly at Abner. "His family will receive tax-exempt status and wealth beyond compare."

"And Merab's hand in marriage," Jonathan stated.

"Of course . . . Merab's hand in marriage. My daughter will get her wish, and the harpist will become my son-in-law. We'll make the arrangements when we return to Gibeah." Saul ducked into his tent, Abner at his heels, as the last words trailed behind him. Was the king regretting his promise?

Jonathan spoke to a standing guard and pointed to Goliath's bloody head. "Take this trophy and impale it on the top of the ridge overlooking the Valley of Elah—in case our enemies should ever care to come this way again." He looked at David and smiled. "Come to my tent, David. I have something for you."

David followed in silence. Fires dotted the starlit camp, and the voices of the men reached his ears.

"Did you see the way David walked with such confidence toward Goliath?"

"And the look on Goliath's face when the stone hit its mark."

"They're singing your praises, David." Jonathan lifted the flap of his tent and ushered David inside.

"Yes, my lord. But it was God who gave the victory."

Jonathan lit a clay lamp and hung it from the center tent post. "Sit down a moment."

David sat on a woolen mat, noting the simple furnishings—a few cushions, a change of clothes, a water jug, a sword and shield, a bow leaning against one wall, and a closed food basket hanging from the ceiling. In wartime, the prince of Israel did not live in luxury like his father.

Jonathan stood silent, head bowed. Was he praying? When he lifted his head, his eyes were clear, and a serious smile turned the corners of his mouth. "Would you stand now, David?"

"Of course, my lord." He jumped to his feet, ignoring the ache in his strained muscles—the evidence of his first battle.

Jonathan walked toward him, released his leather belt, and slipped his blue and purple robe from his back. He draped the robe over David's shoulders and tied the belt around his waist. He walked to the side of the tent, grabbed his shield, sword, and bow, and set them at David's feet. Finally Jonathan fell to his knees and touched his head to the floor three times.

David's chest muscles tightened with emotion, and a lump formed in his throat. Jonathan's robe covered his own legs and formed a pool of folded cloth at his feet, attesting to the prince's stature. David fingered the soft fabric and touched the fine, jeweled leather belt. It was a taste of the future, a small glimpse of the finery that would surround him when he was king.

"I know you will sit on my father's throne in my place, David," Jonathan was saying. "I knew it the moment I met you, as surely as I've felt my own breath. Samuel's anointing confirms what my heart has told me all along." He drew in a long, slow breath. "But today . . . today you had a courage I have lost." He looked beyond David to some point on the tent wall and let the silence hang between them. After a moment, he lifted clear eyes to David's and gave a wistful sigh.

"Once, when the Lord was with my father, I had great faith, planning from my earliest youth to follow in his footsteps. But ever since that day when he willfully disobeyed the Lord's command to destroy the people of Amalek, I knew I would never be king. And now I know the Lord has chosen you to take my place."

David clasped Jonathan's shoulder. "Do not bow to me, my lord. I would much prefer we be friends." He studied Jonathan's sober expression. Brotherly love was mirrored there, and the fire of friendship warmed David's heart.

"Promise me, David, when you come to power, not to kill me or wipe out my family."

David's heart skipped a beat. Kings had absolute power. And the kings of the east showed little mercy to a dethroned monarch or defeated foe.

"When the time comes, you have my solemn promise," David said. "But should the tables turn, promise me—will you do the same for me?"

"I stake my life on it, my friend."

ᔧ5ᔧ

Michal stood at the flat wooden table in the palace kitchen, her hands pressed into the soft wheat dough, kneading and stretching it into a thin layer. Across the spacious room, Marta, the cook, stirred a sticky, honey-raisin mixture over the open flame on the stove, and other maidservants mixed dates with butter and cinnamon to be spread and rolled in leavened dough.

Michal rarely helped with domestic chores, but today the task was more than distraction, it was necessity. The honey cakes and raisin pastries would be among the succulent dishes laid out at the victory feast and subsequent betrothal ceremony. A betrothal she couldn't bear to see come to pass.

How could this disaster have happened? Three days ago word had come from the battle. The war was finally over, and the giant slayer would be honored in a huge victory celebration. How was it possible that the giant slayer was David? He wasn't even in the regular army.

With a violent jerk Michal ripped off a small section from the ball of dough and shoved the heel of her right hand into the grainy mass, making it slide to the center of the table and causing Michal to nearly lose her balance. The action made the elastic dough too thin, producing a gaping hole where a dollop of dates should go.

"Oh bother!" Michal snatched the dough from the table and punched it into a ball again. Merab couldn't marry David. Not ever!

"Having trouble, little sister?" Merab's haughty tone grated against Michal's ears like fingernails on limestone.

"Nothing I can't handle." Michal avoided eye contact, her gaze riveted to the ball of dough as she began pushing and stretching again.

Merab sauntered about the wide kitchen with an air of authority, then settled into a chair opposite Michal.

"Isn't it exciting?"

Michal could feel Merab's scrutinizing look and wished with all her might that the earth would suddenly swallow her sister whole.

"Isn't what exciting?" Michal shoved the heel of her hand into the dough again, glanced up for a moment, then looked back to her work.

"The wedding, of course! What else would I be talking about?"

Michal smoothed the dough into a square and shrugged her shoulders, ignoring the annoyance in Merab's tone.

"I told you they said David was valiant as well as talented. Can you imagine living with such a man? And he's soooo handsome! I can't believe he killed a giant of all things! Father promised me his best warrior. I just never expected to end up with one I like so well."

Yes, but do you love him? The thought made Michal's jaw tighten as she studied the shape of the dough. Merab didn't

54

deserve a man like David. She couldn't possibly know how to love a man of his caliber.

"Yes, well, the wedding hasn't happened yet." Michal reached for the date mixture to drop into the center of the dough.

"What is that supposed to mean?"

Michal felt the searing heat of Merab's gaze and lifted her head to look at her sister. "Exactly what it sounded like. How many times in the past year has Father promised to find you a husband, only to put it off again? I say don't count on it happening until you've been to the marriage tent with David."

The look of surprise on Merab's face sent a shiver of satisfaction through Michal's soul. If only her words were true. This time Father had a man picked out. It wasn't likely he would go back on his public word.

Michal dragged the wooden spoon along the insides of the clay bowl and dropped the last of the date mixture onto the pastry dough.

"Are you jealous, Michal?" Merab leaned toward the table and narrowed her eyes at Michal. "You are jealous, aren't you? You'd like nothing better than to see Father change his mind. You think you can marry before I do, is that it? Or is it David you want?" Her eyes widened to dark, round orbs. "Ah, I've touched a nerve. My, how red your cheeks grow when you're found out, little sister."

"I'm not jealous." Michal glared at Merab. "And if you want David so much, you can have him! I just think you should worry that Father might not keep his word, that's all."

Merab sat back and tapped her forefingers together. "I think you're lying, Michal. I think the person I should worry about is you."

Michal forced herself not to look away. "I don't know what

you're talking about. I'm too young to marry—at least by Father's definition. Besides, I've got my eye on someone else."

Merab studied one hennaed nail, then looked at her sister again. "Truly?"

"Truly."

"Who?"

"None of your business."

Michal hated to lie, but she couldn't, wouldn't, give Merab the satisfaction of being right. God forgive her, but she must find a way to stop Merab's betrothal to David.

Merab rose in one graceful motion and smoothed her red and yellow linen robe. She gave Michal one last penetrating look and turned to go, then apparently thought better of it and looked at her again.

"If I find out you're lying or you do anything to stop this wedding, Michal, I'll make sure Father gives you to your worst enemy as a wife. Don't you forget it!"

An involuntary shudder swept up Michal's spine as the steady slap of Merab's sandals on the stone floor faded away. If she was going to stop the wedding, she'd better do it in such a way that Merab never discovered the part she played.

❦

Michal sprinted up the steps to the roof and positioned herself between the twin towers, eyes on the winding road beyond Gibeah's gates. Clouds of dust billowed beneath the feet of the returning army. Women and children craned their necks in the grasses lining the path. Ahead of the shouting men, young virgins, veils drawn over their faces, shook tambourines and danced, while others accompanied by flutes and lyres sang the victory song.

56

"Saul has slain his thousands, and David his ten thousands."

The words, usually a tribute to her father, stung Michal's ears. The women repeated the phrase in varying tunes over and over until it resounded like an incessant drumroll in her head. Michal looked to and fro in the crowd. Her father rode a brownish black donkey at the head of the throng, and his brooding expression confirmed her worst fears.

The virgins' song would become a threat to David.

She dragged her gaze from her father to David and Jonathan, who rode their donkeys side by side behind him. The sight of David made her heart twist with desire. She leaned forward, straining for a closer view. Sudden, swift longing rose in Michal, followed by a painful shot of despair. David's beard had filled in, and he sat taller than the last time she'd seen him. And there was no denying his handsome features or the piercing honesty of his dark brown eyes. With candid humility, confidence, and dignity, he nodded to the women and children, offering them an enchanting smile. He seemed oblivious to the stinging effect of the virgins' song.

"Saul has slain his thousands, and David his ten thousands."

The consistent song cut through the fabric of Michal's thoughts. Her fists clenched, and she forced her eyes from David back to her father. The grim set to his jaw, the smoldering gray of his gaze, and the nervous twitch of his worn hands grasping the donkey's saddle told Michal his true feelings. She must warn David. If she didn't, there would be no end of trouble.

❦

David's eyes adjusted to the dim light casting shadows over the gray stone walls of the king's banquet hall. Tables laden with roast lamb, dates, raisins, lentil stew, leeks, and sweet cakes sent tempting, succulent aromas drifting across the room. David's stomach rumbled as his gaze moved in an arc over this hall of contrasts. Bright embroidered tapestries hung along one wall, and bronze and leather foreign shields—trophies in battle—graced the other, as though Saul were trying to mix war and peace. David stood, tucking the picture of the place in his memory for future use. His palace would have its own trophy room, separate from the banquet hall entirely. When the time came.

He smiled at a table of fellow soldiers as he passed. The drone of men's voices joined the clanking of tableware about him. Hurried footsteps of a handful of servants added to the din.

"David, my son." Saul's voice echoed across the noisy hall. "Come, take the seat next to Jonathan. That's it. Don't be shy." Saul's narrowed gaze moved down the long table toward his commanders. "Our hero certainly wasn't shy when he faced the giant, now was he?" Saul's sardonic laughter was met with a trickle of agreement, but the captains looked embarrassed.

David sensed their pride and compassion with each step he took toward Saul. They seemed to admire his victory over the giant, despite Saul's mixed approval. Before taking the seat offered him, David stopped in front of Saul and bent forward, touching his head to one knee. "Thank you, my lord. May the Lord be praised for the victory He gave us today."

"The Lord be praised!" Jonathan said, raising his goblet of wine.

"The Lord be praised!" all the men echoed, doing the same.

The meal dragged. Hours passed until David grew weary of Saul's repeated stories of long-ago glory days. He uttered a soft sigh when the king rose at last and let his guards escort him to his chambers. Jonathan leaned toward David.

"I've heard those stories my entire life." He gave David a rueful smile. "I could repeat them backward in my sleep . . . and probably do." He chuckled.

David rested against the couch and stretched. "They do get tiresome after a while."

Jonathan took another sip of wine. "Well, my friend. I have a wife I must go home to."

David stood. "Good night, my lord."

Jonathan strode from the banquet hall while David moved in the opposite direction. He shivered, his warm blood cooled by the high granite walls of the passageways, which led through the palace toward the soldiers' quarters. He tugged on the folds of his robe.

"David. Psst . . . David."

David's hands stilled, and his head twisted from side to side. "Who's there?"

A mirage with luxurious raven hair, doelike dark brown eyes, and lips the shade of wild poppies slipped from the shadows. She wore a pure white tunic and a royal blue robe tied with a golden sash, covering a shapely, slender frame. David's heart kicked into a hard gallop, and he struggled to swallow. The scent of sweet perfume wafted from her skin.

"Michal?"

"Yes, David, it's me," she whispered.

She moved closer to him, making his pulse thunder in his ears. Could this be the child of Saul—the one who two months ago would not have turned his knees to mush?

"What are you doing here?"

"I need to speak with you. You must listen to me." Her gaze darted in all directions, and she stepped within a handbreadth of his chest. When she rested her delicate hand on his arm, he thought his heart would stop. "My father. You must be careful around him."

David groped to understand her meaning. Every nerve ending screamed for him to dig his fingers through her hair and bury his face against her neck. He took in a deep, steadying mouthful of air. "What are you talking about?"

Michal's breath touched his neck as she leaned against his ear. His blood raced through his veins, and he had to force his mind to focus on her words. "I heard the virgins' song. The 'Saul has slain his thousands, and David his ten thousands.'" She looked at him then, her heart in her eyes.

"What about it?" David managed.

"My father hated it." She held his gaze.

Raging temptation tugged at him. She was doing strange things to his senses. "How do you know this?" He stepped back a pace, fighting for inner control.

"I know my father." She stepped closer and placed one hand on his chest. "He will try to harm you, David. He is jealous beyond reason. I could see it in his eyes."

The steady hammering of his heart throbbed in his throat, and her touch made heat flood his face. On impulse he closed his fingers over her hand and lifted it from his chest. "What do you suggest I do?"

The shock of his touch registered across her flawless face, and David watched her bronze skin blush crimson and her eyes lower. Was she attracted to him, as he was to her? But he was promised to her sister.

"I don't know. Just be careful, please."

He felt her cool fingers against his skin, and he squeezed them once before releasing his hold. "Thank you. I will."

She gave him a bright smile, then turned abruptly and hurried around a corner and out of sight.

❦

David settled on a woolen mat on the hard ground, trying to sleep. Images of Michal floated through his thoughts. The girl was gorgeous—and tonight seemed even prettier than her sister. And the things she did to his senses still made his blood race like hot oil through his veins. The soft scent of myrrh clung to his tunic where her hand had rested, and he clenched his fingers open and closed, imagining the soft tendrils of her raven hair flowing between them. He had to stop thinking like this.

He flopped onto his back, tucked his arms beneath his head, and stared at the wooden beams running along the ceiling. The barracks door creaked open, and David's eyes darted to the moonlight spilling into the room. Footsteps tiptoed closer.

"David?"

He rose up on one elbow. "Yes?"

"Come with me." David recognized one of the king's personal guards motioning him forward.

Without question, David stood.

"And bring your lyre."

David pulled on his robe, quickly tying the belt, then grabbed the goatskin bag holding his lyre and followed the guard back to the palace.

"The king can't sleep." Abner met David at Saul's door. David peered beyond the man to Saul, who was propped up on his wide bed, fingering his spear.

He will try to harm you, David. Michal's words suddenly made sense.

David pulled a chair close to the open door.

His fingers plucked the soothing tunes, eyes riveted on the king. His body poised for action, David played by rote feel, nerves as taut as the strings on his lyre.

"The heavens declare the glory of God, and the firmament shows His handiwork. Day unto day utters speech, and night unto night reveals knowledge."

He forced the song past parched lips, grateful for the years he'd spent in the hills with the sheep, committing the words to memory. If he'd had to come up with something new now . . .

He jerked as Saul shifted on the bed and tightened his grip on the spear, lifting the tip off the ground. David held the lyre closer to his chest, his right hand missing a note, then another. Saul's head snapped up, and he looked directly at him. David quickly finished the song, and Saul lowered the spear to the floor.

"Your music is lacking tonight, harpist. Play something else."

David drew in a slow breath. His hands trembled on the strings. What was wrong with him? He'd just killed a giant twice the king's size. But here his only weapon was a lyre, and in his exhaustion, his skill was failing him.

But he plucked a new tune just the same.

"O Adonai, our Lord, how excellent is Your name in all the earth, who have set Your glory above the heavens!" He kept a wary eye on the king, whose movement suddenly stilled. "When I consider Your heavens, the work of Your fingers, the moon and the stars, which You have ordained, what is man that You are mindful of him, and the son of man that You visit him?"

"Stop singing about Adonai!" Saul's eyes resembled glittering ice. The spear twisted in his hand. David closed his mouth, silent prayers for wisdom aimed heavenward. He let his fingers move over the strings again, playing songs without words, begging for relief for the king and for himself.

Moments ticked by, but Saul's gaze did not soften. The strength of his anger heated the room.

David flexed his shoulders. Saul straightened, tensing. Another chord spread from David's fingers, and he searched his mind for words that didn't ultimately focus on Adonai. Finding none, he moved from melodic to harmonic transitions, switching from one key to another. He blew out a soft breath as Saul relaxed against the cushions. At last!

But a moment later, Saul sat up again, his face lined with tension. David swallowed, his throat in desperate need of water. The music was doing nothing to soothe the king's soul. What was wrong with the man? He usually drifted to sleep by now.

David stretched his brows wide, fighting the need to yawn. Exhaustion warred with duty, compassion with suspicion.

Leather sandals slapped against the stone floor, and David's gaze darted to the door to see who was coming. In the space of the moment his gaze left the king, Saul hurled the spear straight for David's heart.

David leaped from his seat toward the open door. A guard blocked his way, but David pushed past him, lyre in hand. Heart pounding with the rhythm of his feet, David ran breathless back to the barracks.

6

The feasting and celebrating over the Philistine victory lasted a week. On the final day Michal slipped into the shadows to watch the dancers and the plethora of musicians playing for her father's entertainment. At the end of the performance, David picked up his lyre and strode to the center of the room. His clear voice carried to the farthest corner, sending a shiver of delight up Michal's spine.

Hidden behind a large crowd of men, she leaned against the wall just inside the entrance of the banquet hall, her heart stirring, her hands clammy. In the next breath, she silently begged him to sing a song of love—for her.

"Listening to David's singing again I see, eh, little sister?"

Michal jumped at her sister's whispered words, released an irritated growl, and whirled to look at Merab. "Looks like you're no different," she hissed, keeping her voice low.

Merab's chin raised a notch, and her eyes held disdain. "I have a reason to be here. Father summoned me."

Michal bit back a curt retort and looked her sister up and down. She wore an elegant gown and jeweled sandals, and a sheer veil covered her face. Her long hair was piled high with shell-shaped combs, and a golden sash held her scarlet-and-blue-striped robe together.

"Why are you wearing your best robe?"

Merab rolled her eyes. "Really, Michal, I can't go into Father's banquet hall and meet my betrothed in my normal attire, now can I?"

Michal swallowed, her jaw clenched. "You're not betrothed yet."

"If Father has his way, I will be before the day is done. He's going to surprise David by offering me to him now."

A swell of nausea turned Michal's stomach. Merab couldn't marry David. Not now. She'd had no time to do anything to stop it. And stop it she must.

"Once the betrothal ceremony takes place, I won't have you to worry about anymore, now will I, Michal?"

Before Michal could answer, Merab, followed by her maids, swept past her into the center of the banquet hall.

Michal trailed her sister at a distance. The crowd of men parted to let her pass, and she straightened her back, holding her head high as though she was fully aware of what was happening and had a perfect right to be there.

A hush settled over the room as Merab approached Father's throne, her bearing regal, her maids two paces behind. She knelt before the king, then stood. Father rose as well and came to stand in front of Merab.

"Men of Israel—my oldest daughter, Merab." Father put a hand on Merab's shoulder and turned her to face the company of gawking men. Though Merab stood rigid and appeared serene, Michal sensed her discomfort. Or maybe it was her own discomfort she was feeling, closed in as she was by too many interested men. She took a step forward, moving farther from the crowd to slide against the wall near the antechamber, where she could see the throne from a safer distance.

She scanned the room, spotting David as he stood and handed his lyre to a servant. Had Father told him? By the look on his face, he had to know. Oh, why did it have to come to this?

"David, son of Jesse, come." Her father's command held the full weight of his kingly authority, making Michal's heart sink. Her father was in his right mind, which did not bode well for her.

David walked across the hall and bowed three times at the king's feet. When he stood, her father stepped forward and grasped his hand, placing it in Merab's.

"Behold my older daughter, Merab." The king looked at David. "I will give her to you for a wife, only be valiant for me and fight the Lord's battles."

But David had already proven he was the most valiant man in Israel. How could her father think to suggest that he needed to do more?

Silence settled over the room, pressing in on her. Michal's heart skipped a beat, then another, her stomach twisting in dread. She searched David's face, trying to read his expression, but he had masked his emotions well. He looked from her father to her sister, the silence lengthening. She should do something to distract him, to keep him from making a commitment she would never be able to accept, but her mind would not formulate a single plan, and she couldn't pull her gaze from him.

"Who am I, and what is my life or my father's family, that I should be son-in-law to the king?" David's words made her breath catch, matching the sharp intake of breath coming from Merab.

An unreadable expression crossed her father's face. His jeweled, age-scarred fingers pulled Merab's hand from David's, and he dismissed Merab with a nod. Relief flooded Michal so quickly she nearly fainted.

As Merab walked from the room without a backward glance, head held high, Michal slipped away from the banquet hall through another door and hurried to her room. She flopped facedown on her sleeping couch, then rolled onto her back and clutched a pillow to her chest. There was no question she would be miserable if Merab married David. But David's words made no sense. He was supposed to marry her sister because he killed the giant. Why turn down such an opportunity? If anything, marriage to the king's daughter would help his future.

Michal dug her fingers into the embroidered pillow, curling it into a tight ball. David's actions today had brought a reprieve, and Michal's heart sang with tentative hope. Now all she had to do was convince her father to give Merab to another, then persuade him to let her marry David in her sister's place.

❦

Saul paced the length of the banquet hall moments after the last commander had left for the evening. His royal robes flowed about his feet, girded at the waist with a golden sash, and he clutched his bronze, iron-tipped spear in his left hand. He'd sent the young upstart David to the guardhouse with a new title—captain over a thousand. It was his only recourse. After the young fool had refused to marry his daughter, he had to reward his act of bravery in battle somehow. His men would never trust him again if he didn't offer their young hero some compensation.

His long legs carried him to the opposite wall, where bronze shields taken in battle from the Ammonites and Philistines stood on display. Saul stared at a shield emblazoned with the Ammonites' colors and symbols, then turned his attention to a similar Philistine one. The giant, Goliath, had possessed such a shield and carried an even more ornate sword. David owned that sword now.

Brash, arrogant, youthful, popular David. Saul cursed under his breath. The boy was a blight, a pestilence to be rid of.

Without warning, the melancholy thoughts slid under his skin again. He whirled around and stomped across the tiled floor.

"Ahh!" He flailed his spear at the air as he walked. Let David be captain of his thousand. "Take that!" Let him fight battles and skirmishes and full-scale wars. "And that!" Let the Philistines come against him. "Argghh!" Then he, Saul, would be free of shedding the boy's blood.

Saul leaned against the wall, spent from his imaginary battle. The scraping of wooden hinges made his pulse jump. He looked up.

"Forgive me, my lord, for intruding," David said, taking one step into the room, "but Commander Abner suggested I play the lyre for you this evening."

Saul stared at him as though he were seeing a ghost. He twisted the blade around, slapping the shaft in the palm of one hand. He glanced down at the spear, then lifted his head, his vision blurred.

Pin him to the wall. Be done with him, the voices screamed at him. *You can kill him with one thrust. Then the kingdom will be yours, and your son's after you, and your son's son forever and ever, and you won't be tormented anymore.*

Saul grimaced. He didn't want to hear the thoughts. Trying to thrust David through last time hadn't worked. He was too quick.

No, he's not. He doesn't suspect you now. Not after you offered your daughter to him.

But the boy had refused her. Why did he act like he didn't deserve to marry her? Perhaps he was trying to act humble to gain the favor of the people.

"My king? Are you all right?"

David's words mingled with the other voices in his head. He glanced up at the boy. A handsome lad. Too handsome. The people might love him more.

Saul has slain his thousands, and David his ten thousands.

They already did.

Saul's eyes bored into David's.

Do it! You have nothing to lose!

The voices grew louder, shouting, blaring their demands, until at last—*whoosh!* The spear flew from his experienced hands, aiming straight for David's heart.

The spear imbedded into the wooden frame. Saul stared in disbelief and let out his breath. The boy had evaded the weapon and slipped back through the door into the night.

Saul's body began to tremble, and he rubbed his arms and hugged them to his chest, trying to still the shaking. Sinking to the floor in a heap, he buried his face in his hands. He hunkered down, succumbed to his body's violent shudders, and wept.

7

Despite the usually cool predawn hour, the breezes wafting across the palace roof promised oppressive heat later in the day. Dressed in her finest multicolored robe and white tunic, her braided hair hanging beneath a soft veil, Michal found her favorite viewing spot.

A thousand soldiers lined up in regiments of one hundred each outside the barracks, stretching almost to the gates of Gibeah. Michal lifted one hand to shade her eyes and squinted, searching for David. If only Father hadn't gotten so insanely jealous of the man. Sending him away was no solution. She wanted him here, with her.

But she'd heard the shouts and bitter curses, the pottery shattering and the wood splintering. No one was safe when her father got like this. He acted as though a demon were nipping at his heels.

Michal sighed and looked closer at the barracks. There he stood, the wind whipping his tunic, revealing muscular arms and a tall, strong body. His dark, nearly shoulder-length brown hair skipped across his ruddy complexion and poked out from under his tan turban. Jonathan's belt girded his waist, and his sword hung from his side. What a specimen of manhood! Michal's breath caught, imagining what it would be like to be held in his arms.

Her mind drifted to the moment in the palace hall when she'd warned him to be careful. She would never forget the scent of him or the startled way he'd stepped back, as though her presence had unnerved him.

"Watching our young hero head out to battle the Philistines?" Merab's voice came from behind her.

Michal jumped, a storm of anger suddenly bursting in her chest.

"I thought I'd find you here hiding from the madness." Merab strode to the parapet and stood an arm's length from Michal. "Isn't it sweet of David to go so soon to battle to prove himself? Once he wins this one, Father will surely seal our betrothal."

Michal focused again on finding David, who had walked away from where he'd been standing. Leave it to Merab to ruin her favorite sanctuary. Maybe if she ignored her sister, she would go away.

She found David moving swiftly through each regiment, conferring with each captain, until at last he took his place at the head of the troop.

"He'll make a great commander," Merab said, squeezing between Michal and one of the twin towers. "I just hope he lives to prove it."

"He'll live." Michal spoke the words with a certainty she did not feel. David had to live. *Please, God, let him live.* She couldn't bear to lose him after just discovering she loved him.

She stole a glance at her sister. What if Merab loved him too?

"Well, let's hope so. If he dies, Father will have to start all over again finding a husband for me." Merab's slender fingers lifted long, smooth brown braids to cascade past her shoulders almost to her waist. She looked beyond Michal to the men below.

"Is there someone else you'd recommend?" Michal kept her eyes trained on David, not wanting to see Merab's reaction.

Merab stepped away from the parapet. "If there was, little sister, I certainly wouldn't tell you."

Of course you wouldn't, you arrogant little . . . The desire to turn and scratch Merab's perfectly sculpted makeup off her face nearly choked Michal.

"Why not, *older* sister? Afraid you'll never find a man willing to take you? Or are you worried I'll try to steal him too?"

"Why, you little beast!" Merab stepped forward and yanked a handful of Michal's hair.

"Ow!" Michal jerked away and snatched one of Merab's dark braids, snapping her head backward.

"Oooo!" Merab lost her balance and fell to the roof's dusty floor amid the sound of ripping fabric.

"Move out!" Michal heard David shout. She turned back toward the soldiers. A thousand men fell into line, some on donkeys and horses, others on foot. She watched David mount a sleek black stallion, lean toward its mane to rub its neck, and then sit back in a comfortable stance. Even the horse listened to him.

"I'm going to kill you, Michal!" Merab squealed after scrambling to her feet and examining her torn robe.

Michal pulled her attention from David to Merab. "Do not fight with me, Merab. I'm tired of you treating me like a troublesome, pesky child. I'm as much a woman as you are. And don't you forget it!"

⁂

A number of fires dotted the open field where David's men made camp for the night. In another day or two they would advance on the enemy stronghold, but for tonight they huddled together, going over battle strategies.

The buzz of voices floated to David on the evening's cool breeze. He stood on a low ridge overlooking the group, his gaze traversing the blackened sky.

Teach me, Lord. Train my hands for this war. Show me what You want me to learn from Saul's treachery, and let me come out stronger for it.

As if in answer, a plethora of dazzling stars burst like sparks across the expanse of heaven. Peace settled over him, replacing the confusion Saul's hatred caused. God had not abandoned him.

I praise You, O Lord, for You will not forget Your servant.

⁂

Michal slipped into the antechamber connected to her father's audience hall and settled on a gilded couch to watch the proceedings. When the last delegate delivered the final message of the day, Michal's breath came harder, a bead of perspiration trickling down her spine. It was the best place for her meeting with the king, especially since Merab avoided the audience chamber unless David was there playing his lyre.

She waited until the scribes rolled up their scrolls and Abner and her brothers rose to leave before opening the side door and walking with a casual air toward the king.

"Did you want something, Michal?" Jonathan asked as she drew closer to her father.

"I want to see Abba." She glanced at her father, gauging his mood. Timing was everything. "Alone," she added, giving her brothers a childish pout. Let them treat her like a little girl who simply needed her father this one last time. The sacrifice to her adulthood was worth it if she got her wish.

"Come here, my dove." Her father's use of her childhood nickname took her back a pace. Maybe the sacrifice was in fact too great. But the thought of David spurred her forward.

She reached the throne and knelt at her father's feet, taking his right hand between both of hers.

"What can I do for you, Daughter?" Saul asked, looking down at her with the exact benevolent expression she was hoping for.

"Send them away first." She turned her head to indicate everyone left in the room.

"You heard the girl." Her father's light laugh lifted her spirits. She had picked a good day.

When the room emptied of everyone but the guards near the door, Michal stood and leaned close to her father's ear. "I know a secret." It was the way they used to begin their private games in the earlier days of her childhood, during her father's first years as king—before the demons came.

Saul laughed outright. "Tell me your secret, little dove," he said, playing along.

"Merab has a suitor. A wealthy merchant."

"Does she now?" He cupped her cheek.

Michal nodded against his open palm. "His name is Adriel of Meholath."

"Indeed?"

74

She kissed his weathered cheek. "I thought you'd like to know." She stepped back, holding her breath. Would he take the bait?

"Thank you, Daughter." He smiled, signaling the end to their game.

Michal exited from the room the way she'd come. When she stepped from the antechamber into the hall, she rushed toward the roof, hoping for some sign of the returning army.

Suddenly Merab moved into her path, arms crossed and eyes flashing. "What are you doing, Michal?"

⚜

"Tell me, Uncle, why did you turn down the king's offer to become his son-in-law?" Joab sat on a large rock before the campfire, sharpening his dagger with a stone. Despite his stocky build, he could keep up with the better soldiers in the fiercest battle. What he lacked in stature, he made up for in cunning.

"I didn't refuse his offer." David plucked and tuned the strings on his lyre. He trusted Joab—to a point—but a wrong response on his part could bring him into greater disfavor with the king. "I was simply taken aback by the way she was presented to me. I had nothing to offer as a dowry and didn't know what to say."

"Killing Goliath was dowry enough." Joab held the blade toward the fire, turning it over in his hand. Apparently satisfied that it was sharp enough, he tucked it into the leather pouch at his side. "He defrauded you, David. You should have agreed to marry the girl right then and there."

David plucked a string, tightened it more, then plucked it again. "Well, I didn't, now did I?" He would marry when he was good and ready, when he had earned the right and paid the bride price.

❦

"What do you mean, what am I doing? I'm going to the roof." Michal's pulse sounded in her ears. Had Merab somehow heard her conversation with her father?

Merab's dark eyes narrowed. "If you think watching the road is going to bring him back any sooner, think again, Michal. David is at war, and the last thing he is thinking about is you!"

"And who said anything about David?" Though his name made her heart beat faster, Michal's breathing slowed to a more normal rhythm. Merab didn't seem to know anything. "I like feeling the evening breeze as it moves across the fields. It's cooler on the roof than in these confined walls."

Merab tilted her chin, looking down her nose at Michal. "See that it's all you do." She walked off in a huff, her anger obviously still smoldering.

Michal shook her uneasiness aside. Something had put Merab in a foul mood, but that was not her concern. She raced to the roof, to her quiet sanctuary, to think about David instead of her sister.

8

Saul's fortresslike palace came into David's line of sight, and his men quickly dispersed toward the barracks or their homes, leaving him blissfully alone.

He glanced toward the roof. Would Michal be there? A glimpse of Saul's youngest had caught his attention the day he left for war three months before. Had she been standing there on account of him?

He didn't see her today. But maybe that was a good thing. He couldn't think about Michal when he had so recently refused Merab. Like Laban of old, Saul wouldn't allow the younger daughter to marry before the older one. And he was less likely to offer David the chance to become his son-in-law a second time, so to dwell on Michal was useless. Still, David couldn't deny the rapid twittering of his heart or the quiver in his stomach at every thought of her. A feeling he fought to suppress.

The horse trotted beneath him, drawing nearer to the palace fortress. No welcoming crowd greeted him on this return, only the standing guards who nodded as he passed through the gate. His weary limbs begged to do nothing more than rest, and perhaps fill his belly with a hot meal. But on closer inspection, David realized the palace was whitewashed and draped with palm fronds. Torches stood on poles that were set in large clay pots filled with sand, and vases of flowers were everywhere.

Was a wedding planned? Three months ago no one in Saul's household was yet betrothed. So who would marry so soon?

He drew up beside the barracks and reined in his mount, an uneasy feeling settling in his gut. A groomsman approached, took the stallion, and led it back toward the stables. Guards and servants hurried to and fro in the yard, seemingly oblivious to David's return. Voices drifted to him as he moved toward the guardhouse.

"The princess wants the red poppies lining the path to the chuppah, not the purple anemones."

"That's not what I heard . . ."

Which princess? He should stop someone, ask what was going on, and put an end to his uneasiness. But he ducked into the guardhouse instead, moved toward his small corner of the open room, and reminded himself that he had no right to know or care. If Merab was the princess of which they spoke, he should be relieved. He had come to realize that she was too beguiling and manipulative for his taste. And if it were Michal, well, then he could stop thinking about her and get on with the important matter of preparing to one day be king. Either way, it was no concern of his.

But he donned a fresh tunic and scrubbed the dried blood from his hands and arms just the same. He deserved an answer, if only for his own peace of mind.

"Welcome back, Captain," one of the guards said as he

approached the outer court and stood before the palace doors. "We've heard glowing reports of your success."

"Have you now? Then I can presume the king is pleased." He thrust both hands behind his back and assumed a relaxed pose. He nodded toward the yard beyond him, where the heady cones of incense burned and the multicolored wedding tent stood like a proud sentinel for all to see. "Tell me, Soldier, what is all this about?"

The man blanched. "You mean you don't know?" He averted his gaze as though he were suddenly uncomfortable, and he cursed under his breath. "The king should have sent word to you. Leave it to crazy old King Saul to do something like this behind your back."

The knot in his stomach cinched tighter. "What has the king done?"

The man looked at him then. Was that pity in his eyes? An undeniable sense of anger and foreboding pressed in on him.

"The king's daughter Merab is being wed to Adriel of Meholath this evening."

David curled his hands into fists. "Barely three months ago, Saul promised her to me." Yet the soldier's words brought a surprising sense of relief. The bride wasn't Michal.

"The king felt you had refused his offer. Word came to him of Adriel's interest in his daughter, so he sought him out, and they sealed the betrothal."

"I didn't refuse the girl," David said with clenched teeth, though a deeper part of him knew he had. "I merely pointed out that I didn't deserve the position." Perhaps he didn't. Was this God's way of showing him He had other plans?

David forced his clamped muscles to relax and drew in a

slow, easy breath. "May God bless their union." He turned, needing to be alone, then glanced back at the man. "Thank you, Soldier."

"You're welcome, Captain."

❦

The relentless wedding drum reverberated in Michal's ears, like the barking of wild dogs circling their prey. She had seen the wary look in Merab's eyes, and for a brief moment Michal's heart tripped with guilt. Maybe she'd done the wrong thing.

She's just suffering bridal jitters.

Of course, that's what it was. Mother had said every new bride came to her husband in fear. And Merab barely knew Adriel. Perhaps she didn't even like him.

At least she wasn't marrying David. And Adriel had grown wealthy over the years. But the fact that his first wife had died in childbirth, something Michal discovered after the betrothal was secure, hadn't helped the situation. She didn't really wish Merab ill fortune. She just didn't want her to have David.

When the fanfare of the groom's entrance drew the crowd's attention, Michal caught the resigned sadness that flickered across her sister's face, which intensified Michal's guilt. She twisted the belt at her waist and slipped away from her maid and the other women of her father's court, past the virgin dancers and the appreciative young men watching them dance, on through the garden gate. A grove of olive trees rested beyond the walled garden but within the more extensive fortress, which included the servants' quarters and housing for the on-duty soldiers.

With quiet steps, Michal maneuvered through the crowd,

80

glancing over her shoulder to be sure she wasn't being followed. Perhaps she had overstepped her bounds this time. If she had not spoken to Father about Adriel's interest in Merab—an assumed interest at best—Merab might at this moment be resting in David's arms. Michal shivered, and her stomach twisted until she felt physically sick.

Her jeweled sandals trampled the soft earth toward the olive grove. Moonlight cast eerie shadows over the place, and Michal considered turning back. Maybe she shouldn't have come here alone at night like this.

She cocked her head to listen. The steady drum continued to beat, pushing the newlyweds toward the bridal tent with unseen hands. Michal didn't want to be there when Adriel returned to the merrymakers. She didn't want to be reminded of her part in it all.

"Isn't it a bit late for a princess to be out by herself so far from the safety of the palace?"

Michal jumped back at the familiar voice. She tripped on a protruding tree root but caught a branch and righted herself. David stepped from the shadows and touched her arm, steadying her. He turned her to face him. "What are you doing here, Michal? Shouldn't you be at the wedding?"

He sounded stern, but his eyes twinkled in the moon's glow, and he courted a smile. Michal's heart stopped and then soared at his touch, and when she looked into his handsome face, she couldn't speak.

David's gaze penetrated Michal's soul, and amid her racing heart she imagined lifting one hand to brush the wavy strands of dark hair from his forehead. Instead she lowered her lashes and studied his feet.

"Aren't you going to answer me?"

She lifted her head and met his steady gaze. "I needed to get away—to think."

He took one step back and clasped his hands behind him. "I see. It seems we have the same idea. I too came here to think . . . and pray."

Michal reached out to a low olive branch, gripping it for support. His nearness was making her head spin. "What did you need to think about?"

David shifted positions, and Michal watched his gaze travel the length of her. He looked beyond her, then back to her face. His feet moved closer. "I've been wondering why your father gave my intended bride to another."

Michal's heart hammered, and she clutched the branch harder, all too aware of the intensity of David's gaze.

"Do you know why, Michal?"

She looked away, thankful for the dark of night to hide the warmth she could feel filling her cheeks. If she told him the truth, he might reject her forever. But if she lied and he found out about it, all hope of gaining his favor would be lost.

"Father thought you had refused her, and when he learned of Adriel's interest in Merab, he contacted him. Adriel is older than Merab by almost eleven years and had acquired enough wealth to supply a healthy bride price. So my father betrothed her to him. Honestly, David, my father thought you would die fighting the Philistines, and he didn't want to marry Merab to someone whose life stood in such a precarious position."

She stole a glance at him then. He lifted one hand to his chin and stroked his dark brown beard, a thoughtful look on his face.

"Considering your father has twice sought to take my life, I can understand his thinking."

Michal nodded, then slowly stepped away from the tree until she stood within a pace of him. Her pulse thudded as she took in his masculine scent and watched the breeze play with a tendril of his hair. "That's not the whole truth."

David gave her a curious look. "No?"

She shook her head and looked at the dirt beneath her feet. "I told Father about Adriel's interest in Merab. The problem is . . . I think she might have preferred to marry you."

"What are you trying to say, Michal?"

The wild galloping of a thousand horses couldn't match the thumping of Michal's heart against her chest. Her palms grew sweaty, and she struggled to control her trembling.

I love you, David. I want you to marry me.

She squeezed her eyes shut and shook herself. *Don't be ridiculous.* And yet he stood there, so close she could feel the strength of him, asking her for the truth. She attempted to swallow in her suddenly dry throat.

"Merab wasn't right for you," Michal choked out. "Even though she thought she cared for you, she wouldn't have been good for you when God gives you the kingdom."

She looked up at David's sharp intake of breath. "Who told you I would be king? Your father is king, and Jonathan is his heir."

"Jonathan believes you will be king." She dropped her gaze again, her cheeks flaming. Surely it was the truth, and though Jonathan had not confided in her, she could tell it in the way her brother looked at David, as though this man who stood before her now deserved special honor. "And so do I." Saying it made the prospect believable, a certainty even, despite the doubt flitting through her mind.

She drew in a breath, fearing she had just destroyed any

trust he had once placed in her or her brother. Had she betrayed them both? The familiar guilt assailed her, nearly drowning out the heady feeling of his nearness. She should turn around and run back to her rooms. She took a step away from him instead.

But in the next instant, David took two steps closer. He touched the tips of his fingers to her cheek, then slipped them under her chin, gently lifting it to force her to look at him. "And what makes you think Merab isn't right for me?"

Michal released the breath she'd been holding. No mention of the kingdom. Good. She held his steady gaze, her heart picking up its erratic rhythm, all sense of guilt gone. "My sister is too arrogant and self-seeking. She has little compassion for others. A king needs a wife who will support him, help him achieve his goals, and love him." She shifted uncomfortably under David's perusal.

"I see. Do you know someone who fits that description, Michal?"

The question hung in the air between them, and Michal thought she would drown in the depths of his liquid gaze. "Yes."

Silence.

"Who?"

Michal cleared the dryness in her throat and averted her eyes.

"Who, Michal?"

She swallowed again, feeling faint. "Me, my lord."

There, she'd said it. She looked into his face, noting his tender expression. He leaned closer, studying her, his lips parted. A muscle flexed along his jaw, and his right hand cupped her hot cheek. Michal held her breath, silently begging him to kiss her. But in the next instant, he dropped his hand from her face and backed away.

"You shouldn't be here, Michal. Let me walk you back to the palace. It isn't safe."

Disappointment stung her, and Michal stiffened. "Considering I'm with the man who has slain a giant, I should think I am perfectly safe."

David stepped beside her and placed one hand on the small of her back, urging her forward. His touch sent pinpricks of delight through her soul. "Some giants are easier to slay than others," he said softly, leading her toward the garden gate. "You are far too tempting a foe, and I am too weak a man."

She turned to him then and searched his face. His bright eyes bespoke the fire of longing, and Michal's heart leaped for joy. Perhaps in time he could love her too. Maybe she hadn't done the wrong thing where Merab was concerned after all.

Bolstered by this sudden thought, Michal leaned forward and kissed his bearded cheek. "I love you, David," she whispered, then spun around and fled back to the palace.

9

The morning sun glinted off the metal blade David held in one hand. With the other hand, he took a rough stone and rubbed it back and forth over the sword. Almost a month had passed since their last battle—and that fateful night of Merab's wedding and Michal's declaration of love. If he closed his eyes, he could still feel the warmth of her smile and see the blush on her cheeks. His chest lifted in a deep sigh.

It was just as well that nothing had come of it. He could not afford to give his heart, his sensibility, to a woman. She was simply a testament to his own weakness.

Still, she was an interesting creature, if nothing else.

He bent over the sword again, scraping the metal, the noise grating on his ears. The thought of marrying her had crossed his mind more than once, but the obvious impossibility of it all squelched the idea. The Most High would find a way to give him the throne—with or without marriage to Saul's daughter.

A noise behind jolted him. In one swift motion he dropped the stone and turned the blade on the intruder. Seeing his nephew, he lowered his arm.

"Joab, don't come up behind me like that. I could have killed you!"

"Sorry, Uncle. But we aren't at war. Why are you so jumpy?"

David gave Joab a cursory glance. "What do you want?" David picked up the stone he had dropped and readied the sword to begin sharpening it again.

"I've heard talk."

David lifted his head. "What kind of talk?"

"I believe Saul wants to offer you the position of son-in-law again."

The steady beat of David's heart increased. He rested the sword across his lap. "How do you know this?"

"Saul has sent a delegation of his men to speak with you. I just wanted to warn you ahead of time."

And take the credit for the news, David thought. He stroked his beard, then picked up the sword again and bent over the stone. "I'm still a poor man with no dowry to offer him, Joab."

"You underestimate your worth, Uncle."

Out of the corner of his eye, he saw Joab walk away.

An hour later, a handful of palace servants found him oiling his shield in the guardhouse.

"Greetings, Captain."

"Brothers." David nodded to the men, setting his shield on a low table. "What can I do for you?"

"We have a message for you," said one servant whom David recognized as a personal attendant to the king.

"I'm listening."

"The king delights in you, and all his servants love you, therefore the king desires you to become his son-in-law."

David studied the group. Thanks to Joab, he'd had time to

consider the matter. But every way he looked at the situation, the problems of his lineage and lack of wealth remained. He was no rich merchant who could drop gold coins into Saul's purse like Merab's new husband did. "Do you think it is a small matter to become son-in-law to the king? I am a poor man and lightly esteemed."

"Nevertheless, the king delights in you. He's giving you a second chance to become his son-in-law."

This had to be Michal's doing. But he still could not accept. "I'm sorry, brothers. I cannot go to the king empty-handed."

David watched the men walk away dejected. Their expressions matched the feelings in his heart. But there was nothing else he could do.

❦

David bent over the curved shield, rubbing until his fingers ached. At the creaking of the wooden door, he looked up. The delegation of Saul's servants strode toward him, smiling.

"You're back," David said. He wiped the last of the oil from his hands, then carried the shield to his corner of the room.

"The king has set a dowry."

David studied Saul's personal attendant. "Indeed?"

"The king said to tell you that he desires no other dowry than one hundred Philistine foreskins, to take vengeance on his enemies."

No doubt the king hoped he would die in the process. David surveyed the roomful of men, then the light outside the open window. The sun had moved halfway to the middle of the sky. If they went now, they could be back by first light, God willing.

"Tell the king the terms are acceptable."

David turned to his men, noting their eager expressions. "Listening to my conversations, are we?" he asked. A few nodded sheepishly. "Volunteers willing to help me secure the bride price—let's go."

❦

"Send the servants to gather palm fronds and wildflowers for the baskets, Mother. If we don't start to decorate soon, David will be back, and nothing will be ready for our wedding." Michal stood in the arch of the door to her mother's bedchamber, hands on her hips.

Ahinoam sat at an ornate dressing table, her maid pulling a shell-shaped comb through her long, graying hair. "A bit anxious, aren't we, Daughter? And confident too." She swiveled in her seat to look at Michal, her expression tender. "At lunch, your father couldn't stop gloating over his cleverness. He seems to think your young hero will die trying to secure the dowry."

"Which is exactly what he wants, Mother. But God is with David. He'll be back, and I want to be ready." Michal stepped into the room and knelt at her mother's side. "Please, Mother, couldn't we have the kitchen staff begin preparations? Father doesn't need to know. Then, if David should succeed, there will be nothing to stop our wedding."

"And if he fails, Michal? Whatever will we do with so much food?" Ahinoam placed one hand on Michal's shoulder, then reached to stroke her cheek. "I know you love the boy, but you must be realistic. This caper is not an easy feat, not to mention gruesome. If just one man is not completely dead when David goes to snatch his—" She looked away, but not before Michal caught the disgusted scowl on her face. "Can you imagine? What was your father thinking?"

Michal chewed one nail, then thought better of it. She'd gotten Father to pursue her marriage this far. She couldn't stop now. "He was thinking he'd finally found a way to rid himself of his worst enemy, Mother. But just in case I'm right, and God is truly with David, couldn't we start preparations? If David dies, Father can throw a feast with the extra food to celebrate."

She shivered at the thought, knowing full well her father would pretend to mourn rather than make merry. But the people of Israel would grieve for months. And the king would do anything, even grieve for his enemy, to please the people.

"Your father wouldn't celebrate, Michal. At least not publicly. But I suppose a few plans are in order." She turned back to the table to allow her maid to finish pinning up her hair. "Go and tell Marta to secure extra food and help. Send a runner to contact Adriel for more food. Oh, and send for your sister. She should be part of this, regardless of your father's broken promises."

Michal stood and bent to kiss her mother's cheek. "Thank you, Mother. I'll get started right away." She fairly skipped out of the room, down the long, shadowed halls, to see Marta.

❧❧

"You've got your hundred foreskins, David." Joab slapped the last piece of bloody flesh on the pile at David's feet and sighed. "Let's go home."

David looked across the Philistine camp at the bodies lined up in rows for easy counting purposes. The raiding party they'd come across held two hundred men, and after a swift but bloody battle, the soldiers under his command destroyed them all. Now the mutilated foreskins of one hundred men sat below him in a heap. But what if they lost one on the way back? What if they'd miscounted?

"Double it." David unsheathed his flint knife. "I don't want to take any chances." He strode to the line of blood-soaked Philistines, whose tunics still covered their legs.

"You heard the captain," Joab shouted to the exhausted soldiers. "Double the dowry."

Before long, the sun edged closer to the western horizon. The mission had been accomplished sooner than David expected. He dropped the last slimy foreskin into a goatskin pouch and tied the bag to his horse's saddle. He cast a long look at the Philistine camp. Overhead, carrion birds flew in circles, creating wide arcs in the cloudless sky, and then swooped low, waiting to devour the dead.

"Let's go."

❧❧

"David, son of Jesse, respectfully requests to see King Saul." David spoke to the guard blocking the audience chamber door a few hours later. "I have brought the dowry he requested."

The guard opened the heavy door, walking ahead of David to announce his presence. David followed, set the pouch on the stone floor, and knelt.

"I have done as you have requested, my lord. Behold two hundred Philistine foreskins to take vengeance on my lord's enemies and provide the dowry for your daughter Michal to become my wife."

Saul's expression moved from disinterest to suspicion. *Please, Lord, after giving us such quick success, don't let him defraud me again.*

Footsteps sounded behind David. He waited until the source came into view, not daring to look away from Saul.

"It looks like we're about to have a wedding, Father." Jonathan's voice sent peace straight to David's heart.

"Mother and Michal have been planning all day, decorating and preparing food. Now that David has supplied an appropriate dowry, there is no reason to wait. Are you ready to become son-in-law to the king, David?"

"Yes, my lord." David could not suppress an appreciative smile.

"Count them!" The king's demand echoed off the stone walls like crashing thunder. "I want to see every last one."

Jonathan's eyes flashed as he drew himself up to his full height and took two steps forward. "You can trust David, Father."

David began to untie the bag. The putrid scent of blood and decaying flesh sickened him, but he held his breath and dumped the contents onto the floor. With painstaking accuracy, David picked up and counted each one—"One, two, three . . ."—through all two hundred pieces of flesh.

"Are you satisfied now, Father?"

"You doubled the amount." The king's jaw slackened in disbelief, then closed again. A look of resignation was evident in his slumped shoulders and dipped head.

"Yes, my lord. In case some were lost—I wanted to be sure."

Saul gave David a thoughtful look. "My daughter loves you."

"Yes, my lord. And I am offering to spread my garment over her, to care for her."

"He's met your requirement, Father," Jonathan said.

Saul nodded. "He doubled it."

"Yes, he did."

Silence descended over the room until not even a scribe's reed pen could be heard scratching against parchment. All eyes were riveted on the king, and servants and advisors held their collective breath.

"You'd better clean up for your wedding, Son." Saul's strong, sure voice put David at ease. "Tonight you will become my son-in-law."

❦

Michal sat on the dais in the colorful banquet hall, her heart keeping time with the steady beat of the drum. Her trembling fingers picked at her muted gold and blue robe, and she cinched it closer to her neck. She felt a rush of gratitude for the blue-fringed, striped veil closing her in her own private canopy. The filmy material allowed her a blurred view of her ten virgin maids and the servants milling about—some fanning the area around her with large palm fronds, others carrying trays of food and drink to the excited guests. Across the room the voice of her beloved carried to her above the din of male laughter.

He would come for her soon. Perspiration beaded her upper lip despite the circulating air, and she dabbed it with a square of white linen. Every thought of David's arms holding her, of his lips tasting hers, sent her pulse racing and her emotions soaring with anticipation. And dread.

Mother had warned her that the marriage bed was not a pleasant place for a woman. At least not at first. But when Michal had pressed her for details, her mother had changed the subject. The women who had accompanied her to the ritual mikvah a few hours earlier were no better, though they seemed to enjoy teasing her enough.

The rapid increase of the drum's steady beat jolted her. Michal's stomach fluttered. Boisterous voices settled into silence, and in the next moment, Michal heard David's sandals slap against the stone floor. They stopped in front of her.

"It's time, my love." His strong, callused fingers grasped her cold hand and pulled her to her feet.

"Yes, my lord," she whispered past a suddenly dry throat. Would David love her—truly love her?

Her anxious feet followed his lead across the banquet hall, his strength seeping through his fingers to her hand, warming her. The crowd fell in behind, trailing them to the multicolored wedding tent shining in the palace garden like jasper. At the tent's entrance, David turned to the noisy crowd and smiled, then lifted the flap. He pulled Michal in with him.

The heady scent of spikenard wafted from David's muscular body, and Michal glimpsed a few well-placed lamps perched throughout the tent. A raised bed dominated the room. It was the reason they were here, and the people outside, particularly her father, would not leave until David emerged with proof of his bride's virginity.

Michal felt David's nearness, but she stood frozen to the spot just inside the door. The beat of the drum continued, matching the racing thump of her heart. She trembled at the touch of David's fingers lifting the veil away from her face and dropping it onto the carpeted tent floor. His nimble fingers pulled the golden combs from her hair, sending tingling waves down her back. He gently sifted her smooth strands over his palms. His dark eyes assessed her, as though trying to read her thoughts.

She averted her gaze to his wavy locks of dark hair. A ring of gold encircled his head. A groom's crown. She lowered her eyes to meet his, shaken by the intensity aflame in their depths. His look absorbed the very core of her soul in a suspended moment of time. He slipped from his shoulders the multicolored mantle he had placed over her to pledge his protection. Tanned muscles showed beneath a white tunic.

His fingers traced a line along her cheek. "Do you have any idea how beautiful you are, my love?"

Michal's throat tightened in response, and when he loosened the golden sash from her waist and pulled her against his chest, a hundred butterflies took flight in her stomach.

"I'm not very beautiful." She shivered.

His captivating smile faded, and his warm, sweetened breath touched her neck. A trail of kisses fell from his lips, traveling from her neck to her ear. "You are ravishingly beautiful, Michal."

Pinpricks of delight spread over her skin, and Michal's breath nearly stopped as his lips parted, first touching and then consuming hers. The fire of passion, which she'd often seen igniting his gaze when he sang a song of worship or discussed war with her brother, now turned on her, all wrapped up in his ever-deepening kiss.

Michal's head swam, and her heart galloped like a runaway horse. With trembling fingers, she reached blindly to lift the crown of gold from his dark locks. The action made him pull away to look into her eyes. His entrancing smile returned, and when he pulled her down beside him on the bed, she felt like she was floating, carried on angels' wings.

The incessant drum and anxious crowd slipped from Michal's thoughts, blocked by the rush of blood pumping through her veins. What was her mother so worried about?

Her hands came up around David's neck, and she felt him respond when she returned his kiss. His strong arms tightened around her, and Michal's dread slipped away, sharing the joy and exquisite bliss of her husband's love.

PART II

Thus Saul saw and knew that the LORD was with David, and that Michal, Saul's daughter, loved him; and Saul was still more afraid of David. So Saul became David's enemy continually.

1 Samuel 18:28–29

Saul also sent messengers to David's house to watch him and to kill him in the morning. And Michal, David's wife, told him, saying, "If you do not save your life tonight, tomorrow you will be killed." So Michal let David down through a window. And he went and fled and escaped.

1 Samuel 19:11–12

II

≈10≈

"Please, David, don't go." Michal sat on the foot of their bed, hands outstretched in supplication. "We've only been married seven months, and you've gone to war three times." She let a tear slip down her cheek. "I can't bear it when you leave. I'm so afraid."

David straightened his tunic and tightened his belt before coming to kneel at her side. He took both of her hands in his. "I won't let anything happen to you. What are you afraid of, beloved?"

Hot tears wet Michal's cheeks, and she felt his scarred fingers brush them away. "How can you protect me when you're not here? You know how my father acts when the demons attack him. What if he tries to hurt me?"

David bent to kiss her moist face, then pulled her against his chest, stroking her plaited hair. A deep sigh escaped his lips, and Michal felt his shoulders slump as though in defeat. "If I stay, your father will find more reasons to become annoyed with me, Michal. While I hate leaving you, it is better for all of us the less I'm around your father."

"We could move away, David. Just the two of us. Then

we'd never have to see my father again." Though they lived apart from the palace in a home of their own, the house still belonged to her father on palace grounds. Too close to breathe easily or to feel like their home was truly their own.

David held her at arm's length. "And do what, beloved? Tend sheep? Live in caves? Your father is king. He could find us if he wanted to. Israel isn't that big." He kissed her nose. "Besides, God doesn't want me to live my life in seclusion. You knew that when we married."

A shiver ran through her. Every time David left her alone, nagging doubts filled her. What if he didn't come back? He would never sit on the throne of Israel with her at his side if he died in battle.

She felt his hands slip from her shoulders as he released her and stood. He pulled his striped brown robe over his tan tunic and attached the leather girdle holding his sling and sword.

"I have to go, Michal." He turned to face her again, his expression grim. "Please don't make this harder than it is."

A lump formed in Michal's throat, and she blinked back tears. She stood and walked with him to the front entrance. Two household, man-sized teraphim guarded either side of the wooden door. David looked at them, then turned to her, his brows furrowed. "I don't know why we keep these statues, Michal. They certainly can't be pleasing to Yahweh."

Heat rushed to Michal's cheeks. Hadn't she felt the same the moment her mother dropped them at their door? A wedding gift, she'd said. Michal closed her eyes at the memory. Ishbosheth had stood behind their mother, shaking his head, his penetrating gaze accusing her.

"They're idols, Michal," David said. "We shouldn't keep them."

"Would you turn my mother against us too?" Her lower lip trembled despite her attempt at defiance.

David's expression softened, and his arms came around her again. "Of course not. If it pleases you, keep them—for now. We can decide what to do with them later."

"If there is a later."

His kiss silenced her skepticism, and for one brief moment she felt protected and loved. In the distance a trumpet sounded, and David released her and opened the door.

"There will be," he said, his tone cheerful. "When I return, things will change. You'll see." He stepped onto the landing and walked slowly down the steps to the street below. Michal leaned against the railing and watched him wave to her and smile. His confidence did nothing to quell the sinking feeling in her heart.

❦

Two months later, Saul paced the small chamber inside the city gate, waiting for some sign of the triumphant returning army. Word had reached him that morning of the throngs lining the city streets from Gibeah to the Philistine border. His choice soldiers under the command of Abner, Jonathan, and David had made a significant dent in the enemy's strongholds in Israel.

Saul's fists clenched so tight that his nails dug into his palms and his arms began to ache. He should have gone with them. By allowing them to go without him, that upstart, no-good son-in-law of his had grown more famous as he'd led the men to yet another victory. A victory that should have been his.

He folded his arms across his chest and gripped his biceps, willing his body to become still, to stop the trembling. He must get hold of himself. What kind of a king worried about an insignificant army commander? With shaking hands, he smoothed the wrinkles from his purple robe. He must speak to the servants. A king's robe should never be wrinkled.

He left the chamber and climbed the steps into the tower. From this vantage point, he could see the crowds four and five people deep on either side of the dirt path through the gates and along the winding road that led to Gibeah. Dust rose in great clouds in the distance, indicating the coming of a large company. The jingling sound of a tambourine joined the melodic trill of a flute. Moments later a loud chorus of women began singing.

"Saul has slain his thousands, and David his ten thousands. Saul has slain his thousands, and David his ten thousands."

The dust settled behind the feet of three thousand soldiers as they marched toward Gibeah. At their head, Saul's three commanders rode black horses. They pranced toward the gates as Saul hurried down the steps. He would meet them in a special chamber in the gate, where complaints were often brought and judgments were passed. A raised dais of ivory inlaid with gold stood along the center of the back wall. Guards flanked either side of the throne, and Saul took his place between them. He was king, he reminded himself as he tried to block out the sound of the infamous victory song. The people were only praising David because he'd killed the giant. They'd forget about him soon enough.

The noise grew louder as the crowd drew closer to the gate. A horse whinnied and another snorted.

What's taking them so long?

"David . . . David . . . David . . . David . . ."

A chant began outside, and Saul walked to the window to

look out. David waved his arms and waited for the crowd to quiet. "Thank you. The Lord is good."

The people cheered, and David held up his hand for silence. "The Lord gave the armies of Israel a great victory. Let us remember that it is not by the strength of man but by the Lord's might that we are successful."

Women took up the flute and tambourine again, but David stopped them with a disapproving shake of his head. "Sing your praises to the Lord Most High, not to me." He hopped off his horse and followed Abner and Jonathan into the judgment chamber.

Saul slipped back to his throne, seething. How dare the people praise David over Abner and Jonathan. His son-in-law's status was rising above his own son, heir to his throne. He clenched and unclenched his fists. David would continue to snatch the glory away from Jonathan. There would be no end of it. Every time Saul had sent him to war in the last nine months, he had returned victorious. Only this time the crowds were larger, the praises louder.

"Saul has slain his thousands, and David his ten thousands."

The song came through the walls of the tower, growing and swelling like a living thing as his three commanders filed through the door and knelt at his feet.

He drummed the arm of the chair with tense fingers while Abner began to speak. What was he saying? Something about routing the Philistines. The voices in his head kept pace with the song, blocking out Abner's words. Who were the Philistines? Oh, that's right. The enemy. The defeated enemy.

Saul lifted both hands to his ears. *Stop screaming at me!*

"Are you all right, Father?"

Who said that? His gaze drifted from Jonathan to David. He lifted his arm and pointed at his son-in-law.

"Send him home."

The room began spinning, and a sharp pain shot against his left ear. Saul leaned his head back against the coolness of the stone and closed his eyes briefly. Blinking them open again, he tried to move but could only focus on blurred objects in front of him. Time seemed to stand still until he drifted into merciful blackness.

❦

The moment Michal caught sight of David trudging a slow path toward their house, she flew down the mud-brick steps from the roof to meet him.

"David! Oh, David. You're back."

Her heart melted at his tender look, and he dropped the weapons he carried and whisked her into his arms. "I've missed you," he whispered. His fingers sifted through her undone hair, and he buried his face against her ear. "Just hold me, Michal."

Her arms slid around his neck, and she kissed his sun-drenched cheek. He smelled of fields and fresh air, and her heart sighed with relief at the scent of him, then soared with delight at his gentle touch.

"Let's go inside." He spoke against her ear, one arm around her waist, the other scooping his gear in one hand.

Michal leaned into him and smiled. "I've made your favorite pastries, David, and fresh wine is cooling in a tub of water." He released her to close the door, and Michal hurried toward the kitchen. "If you sit on the couch, Keziah can wash your feet."

She turned to pick up a tray of pastries and hurried back toward the sitting room, nearly bumping into David, who still stood where she had left him.

"My lord, I thought you would sit and rest your feet—" His look halted her words, and her heart jumped to her throat. She swallowed and lowered the tray to a table. "What's wrong?"

David cupped his sturdy hands over hers. "We defeated the Philistines."

"You're distressed over a victory?"

"No, of course not. It's what happened at the gate afterward, as we returned home."

Michal watched the discouragement flicker in his eyes. She pulled one hand from his grip to brush the hair from his wrinkled brow. "Tell me."

He studied her with searching intensity. "Your father collapsed."

Stunned, Michal felt her knees grow weak. "What do you mean? Is he dead?"

"No, no, he's fine . . . physically."

Michal's heartbeat slowed, and she wrapped her fingers around David's and squeezed. "The demons?"

David nodded. "The women were singing your father's favorite tune as we entered the city."

Michal groaned. "Not again."

David gave her a rueful smile. "Yes, again. Only this time they started chanting my name when they finished the song, then sang it all over again, though I tried to stop them." He draped one arm over her shoulder and pulled her close, kissing the top of her head. "I'm weary of your father, Michal."

"Then don't think about him." She leaned into his chest, the fatigue in his body pervading hers. "Come," she said softly, leading him to the couch. "For tonight we will not speak of him again. We will pretend my father is dead and you are king, beloved."

"I can't pretend such things."

She urged him to sit and pulled his sandals from his dusty feet. "Yes, you can. And if not, I will pretend enough for both of us."

❦

The twittering of the birds the next morning woke Jonathan from a sporadic night's rest on a mat in a corner of his father's room. He should have been home greeting his wife, but duty called before pleasure, and Jonathan's obligation was with his father.

The yellow glow of the rising sun filtered through a slit in the heavy red curtains, which were drawn to allow the king more time to sleep. After collapsing, then wakening in a rage, then passing out again, he needed all the rest he could get.

Jonathan sighed. A longing to see Sarah again struck with such ferocity that he felt ill. Then again, maybe the nausea was due to sleeping in tents and riding rough terrain, then coming home and sleeping on a hard floor next to a restless, unpredictable monarch.

Standing and stretching to his full height, Jonathan strode to the window and peered through the crack to watch the explosion of warm color accompany the dawn. The beauty of the Most High's creation sifted through him. How he longed for tranquility. To walk the highlands and listen to the whispers of nature would do wonders to erase the frustration in his soul.

O Lord, how long? The prayer echoed from deep within

him. How long must he live with his father's madness? How long until he could help David lead the people back to true worship of Adonai? *When, Lord? When?*

Yesterday, when they had returned from the battle, David had refused the praises his father reveled in. David had turned the people's focus back to the Lord. As it should be. If only Israel could have a leader who would always point them in that direction.

Not until Father is dead.

The thought disturbed him. He didn't wish his father harm. But he longed for peace—a blissful entity that seemed a long time in coming.

"Jonathan?" The voice of his father startled him.

"Yes, Father, I'm here." Jonathan strode to the king's large bed and sat beside him. "Are you feeling better?"

Saul shook his head as though to clear it. He looked around the room, a dazed expression on his face. His gaze settled on Jonathan, and his eyes became cloudy and then hardened, the lines around his mouth stretching taut. Sitting straight up in bed, his father gripped the edges of the wooden frame, every muscle in his arms and neck strained. With a fierce growl, he leaned forward and grabbed Jonathan's tunic.

"David must die!"

Jonathan bit back a retort and pried himself loose from his father's grip. He gently patted his arm. "You're distraught, Father. You need rest." *Please, God, give him more rest.*

"No! As long as the son of Jesse lives on the earth, you will never be king. He must die!"

"If killing David is the only way to make me king, I would rather die myself. Please, Father, think of all David has done for you. We would be captives of the Philistines by now if it weren't for him."

Saul jumped from his bed and marched out of his bedroom and down the hall. "David must die!"

Jonathan sat in stunned silence, exhaustion slowing his reactions. What had just happened here?

"David must die!" Saul's words grew dimmer as he strode farther from the bedchamber.

Adrenaline rushed like a raging river through Jonathan's veins. He jumped to his feet and ran from the room, down the long corridors, and across the field at the back of the palace grounds.

To warn David.

❧❦

"I'll leave right away." David bent to fasten his sandals. "Thank you for telling me." Jonathan's strong arms pulled David into a fierce embrace.

"Be careful, David. I will take my father to the practice field and meet you at the stone Ezel after I try to talk some sense into him."

David swallowed the bitter lump in his throat, his shoulders sagging. This constant running was getting tiresome. Hardly a day went by when he didn't fear for his life. Had God changed His mind? Maybe Samuel had made a mistake.

David snatched his leather belt from a peg on the wall and girded himself with his sword and sling. Michal's quiet weeping cut deep into his heart. Oh, that he could take her away, as she had requested, and hide her from her father's insanity. He walked to her side and pulled her close.

"Don't worry, beloved. God will protect me." He had to

believe it. He lifted her chin with his fingers and kissed her. "I must go."

He released his grip on her arms and watched her collapse into a chair. Her emotional state was not helping him. With an about-face, he turned to Jonathan and followed him into the courtyard.

"Fear not, my friend," Jonathan said, clutching David's shoulders. "You know how unstable my father can be. He changes with the wind, and I'm certain this time will be no different."

David gave him a cheerless smile. "I hope you're right."

ᗯ11ᗯ

The mournful cry of a dove woke Michal from her cramped position on the couch. A stiff layer of dried tears coated her cheeks, and she struggled to open her swollen eyes. Her stomach twisted into a hard knot with each waking breath, and worry blanketed her thoughts.

Through blurred vision she glanced at the opposite wall, where a ceramic dish lay on the floor in a shattered heap. The rush of memory made her tremble from head to toe. She'd thrown the vase in an angry fit last night.

Just like Father.

A sudden headache made her temples throb, and she rolled her neck, fighting tears. Thinking like this would only add to her problems. A kink in her back forced her to stand and stretch, and she followed the sound of the dove's tuneless melody to the open window. One hand shoved the curtain aside, and her gaze riveted on the large field where David lay hidden, waiting for her father's wrath to subside. *David, oh, David.*

A knock on the solid wooden door startled her, and she turned in time to see her half-Nubian, half-Hebrew maid,

Keziah, slip from the servants' quarters to answer the call. Michal hurried into her bedroom. She lifted the polished bronze mirror from the oak table and peered at her reflection. Smudges of black kohl still rimmed her eyes, and her black hair hung down her back in a tangled heap. With shaking fingers she tugged the golden comb through her tresses, wincing.

"Is my sister home?" Merab's voice drifted through the sitting room to grate on Michal's ears. "I haven't seen her in days, Keziah. Is David here too?"

"Your sister has just arisen, and Master David is not here, my lady."

Michal let out her breath, praying Keziah would say no more. She didn't need Merab's prying, and David's struggles with Father were none of Merab's business.

Michal heard footsteps coming in her direction. She quickly poured water from a ceramic jar into a silver bowl, snatched a white linen cloth, and rubbed the remnants of makeup from her face.

"Did I wake you?" Merab pushed the bedroom door open and sat on Michal's raised bed.

"The birds woke me a few moments ago." She continued washing, her back to her sister. "You're up early."

"Adriel is always up before the birds, and he likes me to join him for the morning meal," Merab said in a lilting tone.

Michal dried her face with the towel and sat in front of the dressing table before turning to glance at Merab. "So what are you doing here?"

"I came to see you, of course. It's been almost a week."

"I suppose it has." Michal picked up the mirror and examined her face.

Merab shifted positions on the bed. "Where's David?"

"He had business to attend to. He'll be back later." Michal set the mirror down as Keziah entered the room, picked up a clay pot, and began stirring cosmetic mixtures. She grasped a long-handled, narrow brush and leaned toward Michal to reapply kohl to her eyes.

Merab rose and walked over to hold the mirror steady so that Michal could see what Keziah was doing. "Your lids are all puffy. Have you been crying?"

"They were swollen when I awoke." Michal averted her gaze. It was the truth, as much as she cared to tell of it.

"Has this happened before?"

Michal turned at the concern in Merab's tone, certain her sister had an ulterior motive.

"On occasion." She studied Merab's uncharacteristically humble, almost embarrassed gaze. Something had happened.

"Why did you come?"

"What do you mean?" Merab wore a look of surprise and set the mirror facedown on the linen table covering.

"You have something to tell me. What is it?"

Merab smiled evenly, her straight white teeth gleaming in her tanned face. "You always were good at reading my mind, weren't you?"

The muscles in Michal's shoulders ached, stiff from worry and a restless night's sleep. "I suppose. But don't keep me waiting. Tell me."

Merab lowered her long, dark lashes in another shy gesture, then held Michal's gaze. "I am with child."

Michal masked the stab of jealousy with a smile. "I'm happy for you."

Merab strode to the window and lifted the curtain, her back to Michal. "Are you?"

"Of course. Every woman longs for such a thing."

An uncomfortable silence followed, with Merab staring out the window and Michal's heart warring with bitterness. David was the one who deserved sons.

"Too bad David isn't home long enough to give you a child. Adriel is so attentive. He treats me like a queen." Merab turned, giving Michal a scrutinizing look.

"David is needed in more important matters right now." Michal lifted her chin, her eyes narrowing. "Besides, David loves me."

Merab's eyes flashed, and her chin tipped up. "I better go. I promised Mother I'd visit today, and I haven't told her the news. I don't want to keep her waiting."

Michal watched her sister walk to the door. "Greet Mother for me."

Merab looked down her nose with a proud, disdainful air. "One of these days you'll have to join us, little sister." She walked off while Michal looked on, emotions raging.

"Can I get you anything, my lady?" Keziah stood beside her, watching Merab go. "Some breakfast, perhaps?"

"I'm not hungry, Keziah." Sick was closer to reality. David had to return. Now more than ever she needed to give him an heir. Surely Jonathan would persuade Father to cancel the death threat. Unless God was punishing her for her part in Merab failing to marry David. The pain in her head intensified, and she stumbled over to the couch and sat down.

"Are you sure I can't get you anything?" Keziah bent her tall, dark frame beside Michal and touched her arm.

"A cold cloth." Michal leaned against the cushions and

113

closed her eyes. Merab could be so irritating. Of course this pregnancy was bound to happen sooner or later. But the timing couldn't have been worse. If Father couldn't be appeased and David didn't come home again, she would never have a son, and she'd never be queen. There was no way she was going to let that happen if it was within her power to stop it.

❦

"I'm going shooting, Father. I'd like you to come with me." Jonathan stood in the dining hall, bow slung over his shoulder, watching his father swallow the last bite of goat cheese and drink from his silver water goblet.

Saul stood, eyeing his son. "I'm coming."

The two strode through cool palace halls, along the cobbled path of the courtyard, and past the gardens to an adjoining field. Jonathan fitted an arrow in his bow, took aim, and shot toward a stack of flax, left there for that purpose.

"Good shot, Son. Too bad the target wasn't your brother-in-law." Saul's voice erupted into gales of laughter. "Maybe that's what I should do. Tie him to a tree and then cast my spear at him. He's too quick otherwise."

Jonathan held his tongue, praying for wisdom. "Father, why would you harm an innocent man? David has done nothing to deserve death." He watched his father's lips curl in a childish pout. "Remember when he killed the Philistine? He took his life in his hands then, and you rejoiced to see such a victory. And every battle since then, David has handled himself with wisdom and skill to the benefit of your kingdom, Father. You are seeking his life without cause."

Saul folded his arms over his muscular chest, and his lower

lip quivered. "But he wants my kingdom. You are my heir, Jonathan. David will take your place if we let him live."

"If God is the one who wants David to rule, who are we to fight against Him, Father? I would rather obey God than men."

Jonathan held his breath, gauging his father's stiffened back and the proud tilt to his head.

"You would choose David over me?" Saul's dark gaze glittered like embers.

"I would choose to obey the Lord. Wouldn't you, Father?"

Jonathan studied the indecision moving in waves over Saul's features. The prophet Samuel had once accused the king of rebellion, and Jonathan knew his father's heart held no real desire to obey Adonai.

"You're right, of course." Saul's shoulders slumped beneath his royal robe, and his head drooped forward in defeat. "I've played the fool, Jonathan." Tears formed small pools in his eyes, and his voice cracked. "As the Lord lives, David will not die. I will cancel the order right now." He whirled about and set out at a brisk pace for the palace.

Jonathan jogged to his father's side. "Thank you, Father. Do you want me to come with you?"

Saul shook his head. "No, no. I need to be alone." He paused, his expression uncharacteristically humble. "Sometimes, when a man does a foolish thing, he doesn't want an audience."

Jonathan watched until his father's feet passed through the gardens and out of sight before walking over to a large stone where he knew David was hiding. "Did you hear what he said, my friend?"

David brushed the dirt from his tunic and rolled his

shoulders, stretching his arms behind his back. "Not clearly. What did he tell you?"

"He swore by the Lord you would not die. I told you he'd change his mind." Jonathan hugged David, then held him at arm's length. "I'll take you to him myself as soon as I collect my arrows."

"Are you sure it's safe?"

Jonathan looked into David's worried face. "As sure as one can ever be of my father." There was no sense trying to deceive the man. "I'd like to tell you this will never happen again, David. But only God knows."

❦

The sun had reached its zenith in a cloudless blue sky when David finally trudged the path from the palace to his mud-brick home just outside the king's fortress. The meeting with Saul had gone well enough. The king had fallen on his neck and kissed him, apologizing for the misunderstanding and praising him for his military conquests. Then David had played his harp for old time's sake and left the palace with Saul in high spirits. But David's own spirit sagged with defeat. He needed time to rest, to enjoy his wife, to sleep without fear.

As he reached the stones of the courtyard, the door swung open, and Michal raced toward him, arms outstretched. He caught her and swung her around.

"I told you I'd be back," he said after lifting his lips from her inviting mouth. She smelled like sweet apricot blossoms, and her full lips tasted like mint.

"Is everything all right now, David? Did my father put away his threats?"

David nodded, then swooped her into his arms and carried

her inside. He buried his face in her long, soft hair and sniffed. "You smell good enough to eat."

She giggled as his beard tickled her neck. "Not that good."

His pulse quickened at the twinkle in her dark eyes. He set her among the cushions of the couch and bent to kiss her again. "Yes, that good," he whispered.

"Oh, David . . ."

He sensed she had more to say, but his kiss silenced her.

~12~

Michal awoke to the sound of David's footsteps tiptoeing across the wooden floor beside their bed. Summer's unbearable heat filtered through the open window, and Michal rolled over, her hand to her stomach. She pressed her lips together, trying to suppress the urge to vomit, then bounced out of bed and made it to the chamber pot with no time to spare. The contents of last night's supper—what little was left—emptied into the bowl, and Michal sat back on her heels, shaking.

"Sick again?" David asked, coming up behind her and helping her off the floor. "This is every morning for the past week, isn't it?"

Michal wiped her trembling mouth on the towel he handed her and nodded. "You've been counting?"

"I get concerned when my best girl is sick all the time. You've barely eaten, Michal, and your eyes have dark circles under them."

Michal looked at him. "Best girl?"

"Only girl," he corrected.

He walked over to the dressing table and picked up the comb. Two months had passed since her father's death threat had been lifted, and Michal relished these rare moments together. Usually Michal's maid helped her freshen up and dress. Today David drew the comb through her long tresses. His gentle fingers lifted a strand and slowly worked the teeth through her tangles. Tears dampened Michal's cheeks.

"You're too good to me."

"I'm worried about you."

"Thank you." She leaned her weary head against him. She was so tired. And this constant queasiness was taking its toll. Was God punishing her? Was she dying?

"I've called for your mother." David's tender voice cut through her thoughts, and he swabbed her perspiring forehead with a soft cloth.

"All right." Her heavy eyelids closed of their own accord.

❦

David paced the small courtyard of his home, his head cocked, listening for some sign of movement within. Muffled voices and the sound of shuffling feet met his ear, but the door remained closed. He released an impatient breath. This was taking too long. He whirled about and strode to the front of the house. Two man-sized teraphim made of carved wood stared at him from either side of his front door. He restrained the urge to curse, sighing instead. Michal's mother had taken charge the moment she stepped under his roof. She'd summoned the palace physician, sent servants rushing to and fro, and proclaimed his presence a nuisance.

His hands clenched one at a time, and he flexed his muscles in a rhythmic pattern. Future king indeed! He couldn't even control his own mother-in-law. How was he supposed to rule a kingdom?

The sound of hurried footsteps made him turn toward the door leading to the sitting room. He caught Keziah's sturdy arm.

"What's going on, Keziah? How is your mistress?"

Michal's maid lifted large, fear-filled eyes to David before dropping her gaze to her feet. He released his grip on her arm.

"My lord, I'm afraid I do not know. Her color is pallid, and the doctor doesn't say anything except to send me for cool water and fresh rags." She lowered her voice. "The queen just sits at her side, holding her hand and moaning, 'My baby.' I'm afraid we're losing her, my lord."

Losing her? Ahinoam had the audacity to send him away when Michal might be dying? Angry now, David marched to his bedchamber and burst through the closed door.

"What's wrong with her?" David looked down at the bed, where his wife lay shaking among a pile of blankets. He faced the physician.

The wiry man bent over Michal, touching her forehead. "She has a fever, my lord, and she is delirious. Keeps mumbling your name and—" His words slid to a halt.

"And what? Tell me." David heaved a sigh, reining in his temper.

A nervous laugh stumbled from the doctor's lips. "Of all things, she has been"—he looked around the room and leaned toward David—"cursing the king."

David hid a smile. Maybe not so delirious. He pushed past the worried little man and stood in front of Ahinoam.

"Excuse me, Mother, but I'd like to be alone with my wife, please."

Ahinoam straightened, her hands still clutching Michal's

frail arm. She assumed her typical aristocratic pose. "I see no reason to leave."

"I do."

Ahinoam tossed him a look of utter disdain. "My daughter needs me."

"She's asking for me." David met Ahinoam's stiff glare.

"She's delirious. She doesn't know what she's saying."

"Nevertheless, she's my wife." David's eyes traveled to Michal's sunken ones. His stomach did an uncomfortable flip. If he was losing her, he needed to hold her again, to tell her how much he loved her. And he couldn't do that with an audience.

"Please give me some time with her, Mother." He turned to Ahinoam and smiled. "Afterward, I'll sing for her, and you can come back and listen."

The anxious creases on Ahinoam's forehead smoothed, and she returned his smile. "Very well."

When the door closed behind the small entourage, David sat on the bed and let his fingers stroke Michal's warm cheek. Her eyes fluttered open at his touch.

"David?"

"I'm here, my love."

Her eyes closed again. Silence followed. David laid his ear against her chest, listening to Michal's breathing. *Please, Lord, let her be well. I don't know how to help her. But You are* Adonai Roph'ekha, *and I know You can heal. Please heal her.*

Her dark, somber eyes opened again. "I lost your baby, David." The words were lifeless, like fallen leaves in winter.

David's breath caught. Baby? He hadn't even known she was expecting his baby.

"I didn't want to tell you until I was sure, but when I got

121

sicker and sicker, I couldn't hide it anymore." She lowered her lashes, perspiration beading her brow.

David smoothed the wet tendrils of hair from her face. "Don't talk, beloved."

Michal shook her head. "I have to, David. If I die . . ."

"You're not going to die."

Her lips quivered, and tears filled her luminous eyes. "I wanted to have your son, my lord."

"And you still will someday." He gripped her hand in his, intertwining their fingers. "You just need to rest and get well, Michal."

"You're not angry with me?"

"For what?"

The tears spilled over and fell from the corners of her eyes to the matted pillow beneath her head. "For losing the baby."

"You couldn't have stopped it, Michal. It wasn't your fault." He'd seen enough miscarriages among the sheep to understand the spontaneity of such an action.

Silent tears met his words. He kissed her wet cheek. "I love you, Michal. Nothing you could ever do will change the way I feel."

He released his grip on her hand and snatched his lyre from one corner of the room. Perhaps his music would lift her from the depths of her pain. And in the process perhaps the Lord would grant him comfort as well.

❧❧

"It seems like the normal frontline battle attack isn't the best strategy," Joab said, changing the direction of the advisors' meeting at David's home two weeks later.

David studied Joab's expression, then glanced around the

courtyard at Abner, Jonathan, and Abishai, Joab's brother. "You have a better suggestion?"

Abner straightened, his proud chin lifting. He folded his arms over his burly chest. "We've employed sneak attacks and come-from-behind strategies before, Joab, when we've come upon small groups of the enemy. But you know as well as I do that meeting the Philistines at the edge of their territory, especially in a valley, is going to make any kind of sneak attack difficult—to say the least."

"Any attempt to enter the valley and opposite mountain would be seen by their sentries," Jonathan said, accepting a cold drink from Keziah, who moved about the courtyard offering refreshments.

"Unless we strike after dark." David crossed his legs at the ankles and leaned against the cushions. Keziah stepped beside him and refilled his goblet with watered wine. He straightened and touched Keziah's arm. She bent close to his ear.

"Yes, my lord?"

"How is your mistress?" David whispered. Michal's condition had improved beyond the danger point, but the knowledge that he was leaving at the end of the week for yet another battle with the Philistines had sent her spirits sinking.

"She is sleeping, my lord."

David nodded, dismissing her. Maybe Michal's mood would improve when she awoke. He looked at Jonathan. "If we wait until dark, we could send scouts into their camp, even hiding near enough to strike before dawn."

"We would need torches—they'd see us," Abishai said.

"We would wait for the light of a full moon." David sipped his wine, his thoughts turning. "Besides, the Lord can save by many or few. A better strategy would be to ask Him what we should do."

"Indeed." Jonathan smiled. He rose and stretched, glancing at the sundial. "I need to give a report to the king. We can talk more tomorrow."

Abner followed Jonathan through the gate, but Joab and Abishai hung back.

"Do you trust them, Uncle?" Joab stood at David's side, his voice low.

David's wide eyes met Joab's beady ones. "Why wouldn't I?"

"They are loyal to Saul. Saul hates you."

"Jonathan is my friend. And this mission is for Israel. What are you worried about, Joab?" David studied his nephew, noting the way his thick brows drew together in a straight line whenever he was deep in thought.

Joab shifted his weight from one foot to the other, still staring after Abner and Jonathan. "I don't trust Abner."

"For what reason?"

"I don't know. I just don't trust him."

David looked beyond them into the gathering dusk. "When you come up with a reason, I'll think about taking you seriously. Time to go, my brothers."

Joab grunted, and Abishai followed him out. Abishai looked back when they reached the front gate. "Be careful, David," he called. "Joab is usually right."

~13~

The roof of her father's fortresslike palace afforded a better view of the returning army than did Michal's home. She stood in her old youthful hideaway between the twin guard towers facing the road, the wind tugging at her robe and plastering it against her too-thin frame. The scent of heavy dew hung in the air and still clung to her jeweled sandals from the short walk to the king's estate. Paltiel, one of her father's guards, had become her personal shadow since David's departure. He'd been summoned by David to protect her until his return. The young man, barely past puberty but probably close to her age, had run to her shortly after sunup with the news of the army's imminent return.

How was it that three months could feel like years? She would never get used to David's military life. A shiver worked down her spine, making her wish she'd brought an extra cloak, but she was too stubborn to summon a servant to fetch one.

Fog hung in the misty air, and Michal strained to see. Already the loyal citizens of Gibeah had left their homes and walked through the gates to line the path to the city. Men carrying large banners emblazoned with the symbol of each tribe were spaced symmetrically on either side of the road.

Despite the early hour, the festive spirit of celebration filled the air. Musicians began tuning their instruments, and children danced in the middle of the road, their voices beginning the fateful song her father despised. In the distance, Michal spotted the swirling dust, and within moments the earth began to shake with the thundering of horses' hooves. The crowd grew quiet, almost trancelike, as they watched the victorious men approach. Then without warning, like a joyous sentry a young boy cried out, "Saul has slain his thousands . . ."

A group of little girls responded, "And David his ten thousands."

More boys joined the first, the pitch higher and louder. "Saul has slain his thousands . . ."

The women joined the children. "And David his ten thousands."

Michal stood transfixed, enthralled by the wild cheering for her husband. If any man in Israel deserved to be king besides her brother, it was David. The people loved him, and as he came into view, riding with royal grace atop his black stallion, her heart leaped. How she loved him! What she wouldn't give to sit beside him now, leading the nation.

Her gaze traveled from her husband to her father standing atop the palace steps that led to his audience chamber. She leaned over the parapet to get a better look. He wasn't smiling. He stood decked out in royal garb, arms folded across his chest, eyes trained on David.

The women and children continued the famous chant, thrusting darts of fear straight to Michal's heart. She turned away from the scene, one hand pressed against her stomach, and staggered toward the roof stairs. Her breath came in short gasps, and she teetered, nearly stumbling in her hurry to descend. She grabbed the rail for support, heart thumping.

David would never be safe from the king. As long as breath remained in his body, her father would never be rid of his hatred, and the demons would never give him rest. In all her life she had never dreamed her marriage would be so fraught with danger, so riddled with fear. She was supposed to help her husband rise to power in Israel, to sit beside him as he ruled the nation in her father's place.

What a fool she'd been. Her father would never give up the throne of Israel to an outsider. He would fight to the death for Jonathan to be king—and David's life was forfeit. All her well-laid plans were crumbling about her, the last vestiges of control slipping from her grasp. She was a snare to her husband's safety, keeping him near the man who hated him most.

❧

David felt the king's frigid gaze fixed on him throughout the celebration feast. When the last guest parted for the night, David stayed in the dining hall, per Saul's request, to play his lyre.

Saul sat back against one wall, his spear in his hand. David chose the opposite wall, a safe distance away, ever aware of a path for a quick escape.

"The Lord is my light and my salvation; whom shall I fear?" The words were said more as his own desperate prayer than for Saul's comfort. "The Lord is the strength of my life—"

The words hung in midair, cut off by Saul's flying spear. As

David dove to the mosaic-tiled floor, the spear just missed his left ear and imbedded in the wall behind him. David scooped up his lyre and sprinted to the door. Like a deer fleeing the lion's jaws, he did not slow until he reached the relative safety of his own courtyard.

His feet stumbled over each other as he staggered into the house and bolted the door.

Michal jumped from the gilded couch and rushed to his side. "What is it?"

"Your father . . ." David bent forward, hands on his thighs, forcing air back into his lungs.

"He tried to kill you again." The simple statement sounded uncharacteristically calm.

He looked into her troubled eyes. "Missed me by less than a handbreadth. I ran all the way home." David panted, still gasping for breath.

Michal led him to the couch, where he collapsed in relief. She retrieved a jug of water and poured him a cup. He took the chalice, giving her a grateful smile. When at last his breathing slowed to normal, she reached for his hands, cradling them between her palms. "You must leave, David. If you do not save your life this night, my father will send men to kill you by morning."

David studied every detail of her flawless face. Her eyes were luminous and sad, but she was no longer the weeping woman he expected. "You cannot be sure of this."

Her resigned smile made his hopes plummet. "I know my father, David. I watched his expression when you rode into town. I have never seen such a frigid glare, even from him. If the demons start whispering, he will commission your death."

She cupped his bearded cheek in her hand, a heavy sigh slipping from her lips. "I've been sitting here thinking about this all afternoon, David. My father will never stop hating you. So I think we should go away—leave Israel, like your ancestors Elimelech and Naomi did. It would only be for a time, until my father is dead."

Pain twisted like a barbed dagger in his gut. "You want to run away with me this night?"

"Why not? If we wait, my father will kill you."

"I would be guilty of kidnapping you, Michal. Despite what the people say, and even though you are my wife, I am considered a guest in your father's house. Just as Laban once thought Rachel and Leah belonged to him even though they were Jacob's wives, your father still thinks you are his to protect, not mine. Since he is king, he would have no trouble getting every man in Israel to take his side."

"Rachel and Leah followed Jacob."

"And Laban caught up to them—only Laban had more mercy."

Michal studied her hands as she clasped them around David's. "Then you must go." She lifted tear-filled eyes to his. "I will help you."

He pulled her close, and his pulse kicked up a notch. Her lips tasted like fresh mint, and David prolonged the kiss, hating to ruin the brief moment of peace.

"I'll come back for you," he said at last. "After I am settled somewhere, I will send for you, and we will be together again." Someday when he could be sure she would be safe. When her father was no longer a threat.

David felt her fingers dig into the flesh of his arms, clinging to him. He kissed her again, his whole body aching to rest beside her rather than slip through the window and run back out into the night.

"We must hurry," she whispered. "My father's men could come at any moment."

Together they entered the bedroom. David tied one end of a wide woolen blanket to the bedpost and tossed the other end out the window. He tugged on it, testing the knot. Michal handed him a satchel with date cakes and figs, which he attached to his girdle. One foot on the window ledge, one on the floor, David pulled Michal to him one last time.

"I'm sorry, beloved." He kissed her cheek.

"Just come back for me."

He kissed her again, then abruptly released her and stepped through the window, hanging onto the makeshift rope.

"I will," he promised, then dropped to the ground and ran off into the night.

❦

Michal's gaze lingered on David's retreating form, her heart deluged in a sudden rush of pain. Would she ever see him again? Despite his parting promise, was it in his power to do as he said? Moments after he slipped from view, sudden movement from the direction of the palace caught her eye.

She rubbed her wet lashes and blinked to clear her focus. Someone was coming. How many? Two? Four?

Michal pulled the window shut and closed the curtains, trying not to attract attention. She tiptoed past the servants' quarters where Keziah was sleeping, then to the front door to retrieve one of the tall teraphim. Half dragging, half lifting it, she pulled the wooden image onto the bed and covered it with one of David's tunics and the blanket she had removed from the window. Draped over a wooden chair in the corner of the room lay a coarser blanket made of goats' hair, which David used in the fields on military raids. It would do. She snatched the fabric in trembling hands, tucked it around the head of the household idol, and stepped back to survey her work. The ruse would buy David some time, at least.

Please, God, let it work.

A knock at the door sent her pulse into a wild gallop. Should she answer it or ignore it and feign sleep? Michal stalled. She yanked her best robe from her shoulders and slipped into her night tunic. She mussed her hair and smudged her makeup, hoping she looked sleepy. The knock came again, and she tucked a blanket around her and stumbled to the door.

"Who is it?" she asked.

"The king's messengers. Open the door."

"What do you want?"

"The king wishes to see David."

Michal stood silent, debating with herself whether to obey. She hesitated. David needed more time. But if she waited too long, they might suspect the lie. Praying that her decision weighed on the side of good judgment, Michal undid the bolt and cracked the door. The young guard Paltiel, who had quickly endeared himself to her father in David's place, stood at the head of six guards, Joash and Benaiah included.

"Yes?" She tried to sound sleepy and unconcerned despite the rapid pounding of her heart. "Is there a problem?"

Paltiel looked her over. His dark eyes filled with appreciation, sending an uneasy blush to her cheeks. "Your father sent us to bring David to him."

"Tell my father that David is ill and must respectfully decline the invitation."

"David is ill." She didn't miss the sarcasm in his tone. "He seemed fine an hour ago."

"Well, he must have eaten something at the banquet that disagreed with him, because he's been sick ever since he got home." She placed one hand on Paltiel's arm and looked past him to Joash and Benaiah. "I can't disturb him now. He just fell asleep."

Paltiel peered past her as if trying to see into the bedroom, then turned his gaze to her. Michal abruptly dropped her grip, uncomfortable with his perusal.

"Please, give my apologies to my father." She pushed on the door, trying to narrow the gap and give the guards the hint to leave.

To Michal's surprise, Paltiel stepped back and bowed to her. "I will tell him, Princess."

"Tell the captain we hope he feels better soon," Benaiah added, his low voice carrying to her. She looked into his large, concerned face, amazed at the gentleness of the huge young man. Warmth crept under her skin. She used to think Benaiah cared for her, but she'd never shown him even a hint of interest. He was just a guard, after all. And yet now, having a soldier on her side might not be such a bad idea.

Michal shrugged the thought aside, bolted the door behind the guards, and leaned against it, sighing deeply. A tremble rushed through her body, and she pulled the blanket close to her neck to ward off the chill. Paltiel had no right to look at her like that. Benaiah had at least shown some sympathy.

Oh, but what would she do if they returned, if her father would not be appeased by her words? Her shaking gave way to uncontrollable fear, and Michal slumped to the floor and wept.

The scuttle of tromping feet caught David's attention, and he slipped into the shadows along the wall, making his way to a copse of trees behind the house. He couldn't stay here. Despite the warm reception he'd received earlier today, the citizens of Gibeah would side with the king against him.

In the distance, the shouted orders of Saul's men sounded like wild dogs barking and prowling, hunting their prey.

Protect me from their hatred. They seek my life to destroy it, Lord.

Brief indecision caused his feet to slow before he lost sight of the house. His pulse could have outrun the fastest horse, and he nearly choked on his breath. The guards were circling his house now. *Please, God, don't let them hurt Michal.* Saul wasn't so desperate he would harm his own daughter.

Bolstered by the certainty, David turned, pacing himself at a steady jog to the city gates. Somehow he had to get past the guards. He slowed to a walk and straightened his tunic, head held high. With a slow, steadying breath, he willed his pounding heart to calm down and approached one of the sentries.

"Good evening, Soldier."

"Evening, Captain. Going somewhere?"

"The king has sent me on an urgent errand." David smiled at the man and stepped forward through the gate, not waiting for permission to leave. He exuded a confidence he did not feel.

"Should you be going off alone, Captain?"

David halted, stung by the skeptical tone of the guard.

133

"It isn't safe outside the city at night," the guard continued.

David touched the leather sling at his side. "The Lord will protect me. And I am well armed."

The guard's silent nod was his only response, and David continued walking between the wide stone pillars. The guards up ahead opened the gate for him on a signal from their superior. Once through, David continued an even gait until the doors closed behind him and he passed from view of the guards on the towers. After one last backward glance, he broke into a solid run, widening the distance from everything he held dear.

✎✎

With her last ounce of energy, Michal pushed up from the tiled floor and staggered to the cushioned couch. She swiped at the trail of tears still trickling down her face and gulped the remnants of her heart-wrenching sobs.

David. Oh, David!

Despite his protests and logical advice, she knew without a doubt she should have gone with him. A wild, tingling sensation slid down her arms, and her head felt light.

Oh, God, what will I do if the guards return? How on earth can I face my father?

Jonathan. She could run to her brother. Surely he would protect her.

New courage rushed through her, and she sprang to her feet and ran to the bedroom. She snatched a spare tunic and robe from the peg and stuffed them into the bottom of a wicker basket sitting next to the wooden dressing table. In one glance she surveyed the room, her anxious eyes searching for anything she might need on the run with David. She carefully wrapped her makeup jars in a linen towel and laid her comb and mirror in the folds of her tunic. The rest of her belongings would have to stay.

Michal thrust both arms into her day robe, cinched it closed over her night tunic, and bent to tie one sandal on her foot. Should she try to maneuver through the window or go out the door? Would guards be watching the house? She slipped on the other shoe and walked to the window, peering into the inky darkness. Nothing moved other than the slight breeze dancing with the branches of the distant trees.

She turned, picked up the basket, and tiptoed to the door, fearful of waking Keziah. She grasped the bar and was about to lift it from the door when she heard voices and the sound of tramping feet enter her courtyard. Michal's heart tripped, her fingers frozen to the wood.

"Open up in the name of the king!" Fists slammed against the oak door, causing Michal to drop the basket and lurch back in terror. She recognized Paltiel's voice and couldn't believe he would shout at her. Her throat closed, and she uttered a strangled cry. What was she going to do?

On tiptoe she raced to the bedroom window and peeked through the curtain. The incessant pounding carried through the house. Could she slide to the ground without attracting their attention? She rested a shaky hand on the latch and winced at the noticeable squeak when it turned.

Did they hear?

She cast a furtive glance behind her and pushed on the window. She grabbed the blanket from the bed, exposing the wooden idol, and tied one end to the post as David had done.

The other end dropped through the opening, and Michal lifted one leg, stepping onto the ledge.

"Open up, I say!" The slamming of fists continued, and she heard Keziah in the hall outside her room, probably headed to open the door. She had to hurry.

Quickly now. One foot on the sill, one over the edge.

Her hands slipped on the woolen fabric. Heart racing, she dug her fingers into the folds of the cloth. *You can do this.*

She bit her bottom lip against the urge to cry out and trusted her weight to the blanket. But she hadn't made the knot tight enough. The material grew slack as she crept down the mud-brick wall.

No!

The loosened fabric gave way, and she skidded to the ground. She landed in the dirt with a loud thud and couldn't stop a choked groan.

"Going somewhere, Michal?" Michal flinched at Paltiel's hand on her shoulder. She jerked free and scrambled to her feet.

With an agility that surprised her, Michal sprinted toward the grove of trees, ignoring Paltiel's startled look. But she had twisted her ankle in the fall and now stumbled to her knees a few paces from the guard. She shoved both hands into the dirt, overlooked the pain, and ran past him. His chuckle incensed her, and she turned toward the field. Jonathan's house was at the other end.

If she could only make it there before the guard caught her.

She threw a quick glance over her shoulder. Paltiel had started jogging toward her with Joash right behind. Either one of them would close the gap in moments. But they couldn't catch her. She wouldn't let them. Her feet flew faster, every step making her ankle scream in anguish.

"Where are you running to, Michal?" Paltiel shouted, his breath coming hard.

If she dared speak, her pace would slow. Oh, why didn't she insist that David take her with him? By now the other guards would have discovered her ruse.

Jonathan's house seemed no closer, no matter how fast she ran. It was too dark to see where she was running. But she must press on.

Hurry, Michal. You can make it.

Her foot twisted on the uneven ground, and she heard a popping sound, which accompanied a shooting pain in her ankle. An animal-like cry escaped her lips, and she fell forward, crumpling in the dirt.

"Michal?" The guard's voice held a surprisingly tender quality. He knelt beside her, out of breath. "Are you all right?"

"My leg. I think I broke something." She doubled over, clutched her stomach, and fought off a sudden, overpowering wave of nausea.

"Let me see," Paltiel commanded. His gentle hand touched her leg and probed from her knee to her foot.

"Ow!"

He squinted in the moonlight, bending closer to inspect the wound. "Can you walk?"

She shook her head. At that moment Joash reached them.

"Then I'll carry you," Paltiel said.

"No! Don't touch me." She looked to Joash. "You can help me."

"Don't be ridiculous, Michal." Paltiel's tone was insistent. "Joash isn't strong enough to lift you."

Tears slid down both cheeks. She didn't trust this man, and she didn't like the way he looked at her. "Then you can both let me lean on your shoulders."

Paltiel shook his head. "It could be broken. I'll carry you."

Michal choked on a sob. No telling what this man would do to her. "Then take me to Jonathan. Please, Paltiel, don't take me to my father." She grabbed his tunic with one hand, but her strength quickly ebbed, and she released him. "Please . . ."

She felt his hands slip beneath her and lift her to his chest. The shifting movement on her leg made pain slice through her afresh. Michal closed her eyes, sinking below the surface of deep darkness.

~14~

Moonlight cast variegated shadows across the stony path David walked from Gibeah to Ramah, to the prophet Samuel's home. Pain shot through his bruised feet, and his legs felt like they were on fire. He stopped only long enough to drag more air into his lungs before plunging forward, running, fleeing the pursuit of a mad king.

Ramah came into view as the pinkish gray light of dawn crept into the eastern sky. A handful of women dressed in colorful, flowing robes and headdresses already stood at the large well in Sechu. David approached them, half stumbling, and sat on a large rock. One of them, a girl with dark almond eyes and hair the color of ripened wheat, approached.

"May I get you a drink, my lord?"

Lungs silently gasping for air, David held up a hand and nodded. The girl walked with measured steps to the stone well, lowered a rope-bound clay jar, and then pulled its contents to the top of the well. She lifted the container with ease and strode toward David, handing him a dipper.

David anxiously scanned his surroundings. The area seemed safe enough. His racing heart still collided with his chest, but his breathing slowed, reminding him again of the ache in his throat. He took the dipper from the girl's slender fingers, noting the tanned smoothness of the skin on her bare forearm. Leaning forward, he filled the scoop and lifted it to his parched lips. He drained it dry and filled it again.

"Do not drink so fast, my lord. You'll be sick."

David drew a deep breath and sat back on the rock, taking in the girl's distinct beauty.

"Where can I find the prophet Samuel?" he asked, forcing himself to look away from the oriental splendor of her eyes.

"His home is within the town of Ramah, but he often spends time with his students at Naioth. If you walk down the street of the potters, turn away from the sun and walk six more paces. His home is facing east."

David nodded and lifted both hands around the clay cup, accepting one more drink.

"Is everything all right, my lord?"

She certainly was the talkative type. He glanced into her curious eyes and smiled. "I've been traveling all night. Nothing is wrong that rest and a good meal won't fix." He willed his aching muscles to stand. "Thank you for the drink."

Blisters on the balls of his feet made him wince, and he stumbled despite his attempt at bravado. He felt the girl's hand on his arm. "Let me help you, my lord. My cousins will wait for me. I will take you to Samuel."

With more strength than David would have expected, the girl supported him with her arm and began to walk with him. The scent of cinnamon wafted from either her hair or her skin—he couldn't tell—filling him with emotions he did not want to feel. He stopped abruptly and released her arm.

"I'm fine. Truly." He glanced at her. "Thank you."

She stepped away from him and lowered her head, but not before he caught the blush coloring her face. Sudden pity filled him. "Whose daughter are you?"

Shy eyes met his. "I am Ahinoam, daughter of Lemuel of Jezreel. I am living in Ramah with my uncle since my father died."

He dropped his hand to his side. "I am sorry about your father."

She nodded, taking another step away from him. "Thank you, my lord."

Her look gave him the distinct feeling he'd somehow hurt her. But he couldn't accept her help. He couldn't risk Saul's men finding out she'd assisted him. "You're welcome." He offered her a warm smile and trudged forward alone.

A servant met him at Samuel's door and led him into the cool entryway. At least the girl's directions were accurate. David lowered his aching body to the wooden bench and released a deep sigh. Moments later, shuffling footsteps sounded along the tiled hall and stopped in front of him.

"David, my son." Samuel spoke slowly, but concern laced his tone. "To what do I owe the honor of this visit?"

David met the prophet's steady gaze, sudden tears threatening. "Saul is seeking my life," he said, his voice coming out in a hoarse whisper.

In two strides the old prophet's strong arms pulled David to his feet and embraced him. David fell on his neck and wept.

꧁꧂

"Why did you help my enemy escape?" Saul's words rumbled in a low growl, his gaze menacing.

Michal used her arms to push to a sitting position, but the slight movement made the pain in her foot intensify, forcing her to lean back against her mother's cushions. "I had no choice, Father."

"No choice?" He whirled around, his hands thrust in the air. "What do you mean you had no choice? You always have a choice, Daughter." Saul lurched forward, dug his fingers into Michal's forearms, and shoved her farther into the couch. "Now tell me the truth. Why did you help my enemy escape?"

"I told you, I had no choice."

His hand raised, then she felt the harsh slap of his palm against her cheek.

"The truth, Michal, or I'll do worse to you than that!"

She choked back the uncontrollable urge to weep. "I already told—"

The second slap caught her off guard. "Abba, please!"

She raised both arms to protect her stinging cheeks, feeling more humiliated than when he'd taken her over his knee in front of her sister when she was small. Did he hate her as he hated David?

"Then tell me the truth!" His angry voice echoed in the chamber, and one glance into his heated face told her now was not the time for truth. His eyes flamed like embers from the pit of Sheol. He stopped in front of her, grabbed her wrist, and dragged her half off the couch.

"Please, Saul, you can see she's hurt." Her mother's words seemed to bounce off him, not registering. His nails dug into her skin until she cried out in pain.

"He said he would kill me if I didn't help him. What else could I do?" She choked on the words, sobbing.

He released his grip and staggered backward.

"That no-good son of a nobody threatened my daughter?" Saul shrieked. In one swift motion, he unsheathed his sword and held it in the air. "I make you this promise, Michal. As I live, we will find this traitorous husband of yours and feed his body to the beasts of the field."

No! her heart screamed in protest, but she couldn't retract her words.

"Send out a search party." Her father's barked order made her sob all the more. "Find David and bring him to me—so that I may kill him."

❧❧

"I'm sorry to awaken you so soon, my son, but I thought it wise to move you to safer quarters." Samuel's sorrowful, rheumy gaze rested on David.

David squeezed his blurry eyes, trying to focus on the old prophet in the dim light of an oil lamp. "Has Saul found me?" David pushed into a sitting position, heart racing, his gaze resting on the shuttered window.

"I haven't heard anything unusual. But dusk has fallen. It will soon be dark enough to travel about unnoticed."

David nodded. He sat up and tested his weight on his blistered feet. The healing balm Samuel's servant had wrapped around them had helped, reducing the pain immensely. "Where are we going?"

"To Naioth. I have several students housed on the outskirts of Ramah. The buildings are old, added on to over the years, with many secret rooms and places of refuge. You will be safe there."

❧❧

A delegation of Edomite shepherds who tended Saul's sheep in the hills surrounding Gibeah stood in the king's audience chamber.

"David has been seen in Ramah at Naioth," their leader, Doeg, said.

Paltiel stood at attention to the right of the throne, acting as one of the king's bodyguards. He expected such news to come, but not quite so soon. In the two days since David escaped, Saul had rarely slept as he paced the palace halls, breathing venomous accusations against his former captain and son-in-law.

"Guards!" Saul shouted to the men standing at the door to the audience chamber. Two men rushed forward and knelt.

"Go at once to Samuel at Naioth and bring David to me. Take ten men with you."

"Yes, my lord," one of them said. "May my lord, King Saul, live forever."

Paltiel watched the two do an about-face and march out the door. What would Michal do when she saw her husband executed? With Saul's propensity toward madness, David's chances of a quick death were slim. Any number of gruesome thoughts of torture made Paltiel's stomach turn. Even he wouldn't wish such evil against David. While death was inevitable, swift was best. No sense putting Michal through the trauma of watching her husband suffer.

A sudden, acute protectiveness rose in his chest. He had to shelter her from the gruesome ordeal. He couldn't bear to see anguish in those dark eyes. A shiver worked down his spine, and he wiped damp palms down the front of his tunic. Should he speak to the king? One glance at his monarch's menacing features stopped the words in his throat. After David was dead, maybe he would make his wishes known.

⚘15⚘

"It's no longer safe for me to stay with you, Samuel." David spoke with deep regret, wondering if he would ever see the old prophet again.

Samuel placed two gnarled hands on David's shoulders and gazed into his eyes. "I know Saul's guards keep coming, but never forget, my son, God has chosen you to be the next king. Despite his efforts, Saul will not succeed."

David bowed his head, accepting Samuel's kiss on each cheek. "Thank you, my lord, but thirty soldiers have come in the month I've been here. Now your servants have spotted Saul's own retinue headed this way. It is time for me to leave."

Samuel dropped his hands and nodded. "Understood." He handed a satchel of food to David. "Where will you go?"

David ran his callused fingers through his scraggly beard. He needed to see the palace barber. But he had more important needs to attend to first. "I'm going to see Jonathan. He succeeded once before in talking some sense into his father. Saul has never taken his pursuit this far. Maybe Jonathan can tell me what's going on."

Samuel touched David's arm as he turned to leave. "Be careful, my son. And God go with you."

❦

"David!" Jonathan greeted his brother-in-law with a fierce embrace and kissed each cheek. "Come in, my friend." He clapped one arm around David's shoulder and drew him into the secluded sitting room.

"What are you doing here?" In the dim light of the clay lamps, he studied David's disheveled, haggard appearance. The pain in David's expression made Jonathan's throat go dry. "You look terrible. What happened?"

"I've come to beg you for my life, Jonathan."

Jonathan swallowed hard, uneasiness creeping up his spine. "What are you talking about?"

"A month ago your father tried to kill me. I escaped to my home, where Michal helped me slip through a window. I've spent these past weeks with Samuel in Ramah, but your father has sent guards continually and is on his way there now to capture me and kill me." He paused, ran a hand over his beard. "What have I done? What is my sin before your father, that he seeks my life?"

"Impossible! You shall not die!" Jonathan said, but a sick feeling twisted his gut just the same. He walked to the window, raked one hand through his hair, and walked back to where David stood.

"My father will do nothing great or small without first telling me. And why should my father hide this thing from me? It is not so!"

"Your father knows that I've found favor in your eyes, and he has said, 'Do not let Jonathan know this, lest he be grieved.'

146

But truly, as Adonai lives and as your soul lives, there is but a step between me and death." David lifted both hands in a defenseless gesture. "If there is iniquity in me, kill me yourself. But do not take me to your father."

Jonathan raised his hands in the air. "God forbid! If there is evil planned against you, wouldn't I tell you?"

"I hope so." David spoke so softly that Jonathan almost missed his words. His friend looked ten years older, worry lines etched on his brow.

Jonathan embraced David again. "I will talk to my father. If I find out he plans to harm you, surely I will tell you and send you away safely."

"How will I know what he says?"

Jonathan's mind whirled with a thousand thoughts, but a plan emerged as though given to him by an unseen hand. He bent closer and whispered in David's ear. "This is what we'll do."

❦

"The Lord is my light and my salvation . . . whom shall I fear . . . fear . . . fear . . . Your father is trying to kill me, Michal . . . Michal . . . Michal . . . I will be back . . ."

"I love you, David . . . David . . . David . . ."

Michal woke with a start, her nightshirt drenched in sweat, her pulse racing. What began as a pleasant dream with David's sweet voice and God-honoring words to allay her fears ended in stark terror, all the awful memories weighing down on her again. For more than a month she had been back in her old bedchamber in the palace recuperating. Though it felt more like prison. While her mother insisted she stay where the servants could look after her and Marta could tend her leg, Michal knew without a doubt that she was not free to go home.

Deep grief filled her, and she placed one hand over her heart as though the action could bring relief. She had to get out of here. How would she know if David tried to contact her? Even Jonathan had been kept away from her and unaware of their father's plot against David. Try as she might, she had no one to trust who could take him word.

Agitated, Michal swung her legs over the edge of the bed and tested the pain level by pressing down on the wounded foot. So far, so good. She gripped the wooden post protruding from her bed and forced herself to stand. A dull ache still accompanied the effort to walk, but if she took it slow, she might be able to finally leave her old bedchamber and get a bit of fresh air. The gray walls of the palace always gave Michal a closed-in feeling, and she longed to be free of the place. More than anything, she wanted to go home—to David.

Using a wooden walking stick Paltiel had fashioned for her, Michal managed to dress and maneuver the halls to the family's courtyard. When she passed the kitchen, her stomach growled as if on cue, reminding her how hungry she was. Keziah glanced up from some wheat she was grinding and hurried to her side.

"My lady, I didn't know you were up. I would have come to help you if I had."

Michal gave in to a half smile. "Never mind that now. I needed to do something for myself anyway. I am hungry, though."

"Of course you are. I will bring food to your room right away."

"Bring it to the courtyard, Keziah. I don't want to see that room again for a long time."

Keziah gave her a quizzical look.

"I want to go home," she whispered, bending toward the girl's ear. "Is there any chance you can figure out a way to take me there?"

Keziah glanced over her shoulder at the other women busily working, then back at Michal. "I do not know, my lady. Your father is back from Ramah and is planning the new moon feast for tonight. There is much to be done, and your mother bid me help."

"My mother is not your mistress. My father gave you to me as a wedding gift."

The girl's tightly wound black braid flipped forward as she sent another wary look over her shoulder. She straightened and took Michal's arm. "I will help you to the courtyard, my lady. Then I will bring your food." She spoke loud enough for the others to hear. When the two were out of earshot, Keziah leaned closer. "You might want to sit down."

Her tone set Michal's teeth on edge, but she obediently lowered her body onto a stone bench. "What is it, Keziah? Tell me quickly." She couldn't bear suspense. It only added to her overwhelming fear and the guilt of her lies to her father—the lies that had made her prisoner here.

"Your father is talking of annulling your marriage to David and giving you to another man."

A thick lump in her throat made it impossible to swallow, and Michal nearly choked on her saliva.

Keziah settled her lithe body on the stone bench at Michal's side and placed one hand on Michal's knee, her look earnest. "I heard it myself, my lady. I was in the hall outside your mother's room when your father came in, black with rage. I hid from view until he stepped into the room, then I peeked through a crack in the door.

"After three tries sending servants to fetch David, your father went after your husband himself. But the same mysterious malady that came over the guards hit your father the moment he entered Naioth." She paused and glanced around, then clasped her hands and lowered her voice further.

"He was stomping back and forth, cursing, and was about to throw one of your mother's priceless vases when he fell in a heap at her feet and wept like a child. It was hard to hear his exact words at first, even though I pressed my ear as close to the door as I dared. But then he grew louder and wailed that he was humiliated by the whole affair. He had actually removed his royal robes and lay down like a commoner on the floor of the prophet's house, muttering praises to the Most High. The moment he became aware of what he was doing, he grabbed his clothes and ran off. Of course, by then David was gone."

"But what does that have to do with my marriage to David?" Michal whispered, at last able to speak.

Keziah glanced about the court, eyes wary. "When your mother tried to soothe your father, he started to calm. She changed the subject and mentioned that your foot was healing nicely. The mention of your name must have made him think of David, because he started cursing again and stood up, fists clenched, pacing the room. This time he smashed your mother's vase against the wall, and she started to cry."

The girl straightened, flipped her braid behind her back, and rubbed her hands together. The recollection of that night obviously caused her agitation, but Michal felt her own impatience rising.

"Tell me the rest, Keziah. Hurry now, before someone comes."

Keziah's nervous gaze rested on Michal, but she nodded her obedience. "I don't remember the rest very well, mistress. I was afraid the king would come stomping out of the room and catch me listening. So I took a step back and slid around the corner. Good thing too, because I was right. He left your mother's room like a horse rearing its legs, ready to strike."

"But when did you hear him threaten my marriage?" She was getting weary of this conversation. So what if her father missed out on catching her husband? All the better for David. Perhaps this whole thing was a result of Keziah's overactive imagination.

"When he stormed down the hall, I was hiding around the corner, and I heard him shout for Joash. He told him to summon the scribes." Keziah twisted her hands together. "Joash said, 'The scribes, my lord?' And your father said, 'Yes, the scribes. If I cannot put an end to David's life, at least I can put him out of my house. His contract with my daughter is at an end. He is no longer fit to be called son-in-law to the king.'" Keziah's breath came fast, her dark face flushed with the telling of such news. "I'm sorry, my lady. May I bring food for you now, that you may break your fast?"

Michal shook her head, too numb to speak. Her appetite had fled.

She had been David's wife for over a year. No scribe could write words across parchment and annul their marriage just because her father no longer cared for her husband.

Michal chewed on one of her knuckles, fighting tears.

Keziah had to be wrong. But she had never known the girl to lie. She closed her eyes against gritty tears and stifled a sob.

David . . . Oh, David . . . why didn't I run away with you when I had the chance? How will you ever come to me now?

A multitude of questions stormed her thoughts. What would happen to her if she were no longer David's wife? Who would her father give her to? Maybe she could still run after David.

She pushed her foot onto the stone floor of the court, giving her ankle more weight than she had before. The dull ache intensified to a sharper pain, bringing instant tears. She could never run away in her condition. But she could not sit back waiting to see what her father would do.

She must act.

With a desperate shove, Michal pushed herself halfway up from the bench but fell back in defeat and despair, the pain in her foot matching the pain in her heart.

Oh, David, what should I do?

≈16≈

Jonathan spread nervous fingers through his thick, shoulder-length hair, looking up in silence at the mammoth oak door leading to the banquet hall. His father would already be seated, his back to the wall, eyes wary and ever watchful. Yesterday, the first day of the new moon feast, David had stayed away. Father had said nothing of David's absence.

Jonathan lowered his hands to his sides and clenched them. No telling what would happen when David didn't show up this time, though after Father's actions of late, no one else would expect him to. He blew a shaky breath and pulled the door open, sending a silent prayer heavenward.

"You're late, my son." Saul tapped the shaft of his spear with one finger. "We almost decided to start without you."

Jonathan glanced around the table. Abner sat to the king's left, and his brothers, Malchishua, Abinadab, and Ishbosheth, were on his right. His place opposite his father remained open, waiting for him, and as planned, David's seat next to Abner was empty.

"I'm sorry, Father. Something came up." He slipped into

his seat at the end of the table, watching his father for a reaction.

Saul's pitiless eyes flashed, and his silver brows arched as he leaned toward his son. "I suppose David has a similar excuse? Where is he, Jonathan? Why has the son of Jesse not come to eat, either yesterday or today?"

Jonathan's stomach dipped, then knotted. This was it. Saul's response would give him the answer he and David were looking to find.

Please, God, let David be able to come home.

"David begged me to allow him to go to Bethlehem, my lord. His family is having a sacrifice in the city, and his brother commanded him to be there. I said he could go. This is why David has not been present at the king's table."

The stillness grew thick enough to choke a man, and Jonathan forced saliva down his throat to keep breathing normally. Saul's weathered hand clutched his spear, his knuckles white. His round pupils glowed like smoldering coals in a dying fire.

"You son of a perverse, rebellious woman! Don't you think I know you've sided with the son of Jesse to your own shame and to the shame of the mother who bore you? As long as the son of Jesse lives on the earth, neither you nor your kingdom will be established. Now bring him to me, for he must die."

The air grew thick with collective dread. Jonathan felt all eyes trained on him. He met his father's bitter gaze.

"Why, Father? Why should he be killed? What has he done?"

Murder simmered in the king's eyes. Saul's fingers took aim with his spear as Jonathan had seen him do a hundred times in battle. Jonathan placed both hands on the table.

Saul lifted his spear as Jonathan shoved the bench aside and backed away from the table. His heart pounded. Which way would he throw the spear?

Saul pulled his arm back, and the weapon flew from his hand. Jonathan ducked and sprinted toward the door. The spear whizzed past and clattered across the tile floor.

Heat flooded Jonathan's cheeks. He glanced back at the shocked faces of his brothers and the king's advisors. What madness was this? Did his father actually think he could fight against God and win?

When he reached the ornate door, Jonathan looked one last time at his father, pulse racing, bile rising in his throat. So this was how it was going to be. The king's blackened gaze still burned, and his face contorted in a disgusted scowl. Jonathan's eyes settled on him long enough to make his father turn away, then he whirled about and strode with dogged steps out of the palace.

When he reached the cool night air, fresh anguish assaulted him. *David.* A heavy, boulderlike lump lay where his heart should be. What would become of his friend now? He couldn't stay here. Father would never stop seeking his life.

A large stone caught the lip of his sandal, and he kicked it aside mercilessly. Such a fool he'd been! To think he, heir apparent to the throne of Israel, would somehow be able to just hand the kingdom over to David with his father's blessing sounded ludicrous to him now. His father had shown little sense since the second year of his reign, when he'd impatiently offered a sacrifice in Samuel's place. Then there were those two rash oaths Saul had taken during a war with the Philistines.

Jonathan's shoulders lifted in a heavy, defeated sigh. One

of those oaths had nearly gotten him killed. If it weren't for the people of Israel taking his side in the matter, his father would have executed him to save his own pride.

He ran a shaky hand through his hair and glanced at the winking, starlit sky. His father didn't deserve to be king. David deserved to wear the crown in his father's place.

If David lived that long.

His shoulders slumped, and his feet grew leaden with every weary step. He desperately needed to pray before he took the bad news to David.

❦

David stretched his stiff body from its cramped position in a huge rock crevice. Three nights of sleeping in the fields was nothing new. He'd spent countless weeks and months tending sheep and enacting military campaigns in similar spots. But few had left such a resigned ache in his gut.

He tilted his head and stood, rolling his shoulders to ease the kinks in his neck. Beyond the outcropping of rocks, tufts of grass began to glisten with the morning dew.

David crouched, grabbed a stick, and poked the last few embers of the dying fire. His stomach groaned. Only a handful of dates and almonds remained in the sack Jonathan had given him, and the bread was long gone.

A soft, cool breeze tickled the hair on his bare legs. He cinched his striped robe at the neck, closing the gap, and glanced at the lightening sky. Jonathan would come soon. At least then he would know.

The stick exposed a few glowing ashes, and David tossed a handful of dirt on them, killing the fire. One knee touched the dusty earth, and in the next instant David dropped face forward, hands spread in front of him.

"O Lord, my enemies surround me, and my life hangs by a breath."

Raw emotion scraped his throat. Words he ached to say died on his lips. What good could possibly come from all of this?

The sound of muffled voices in the distance reached him. He pushed up from the ground and stood, brushing the layer of dust from his robe. A man and a boy were walking toward him. Jonathan was early.

The voices grew louder until they were within shooting distance of a bow.

"Now run, find the arrows that I shoot," David heard Jonathan say.

A zinging dart whizzed past the reddish clay boulder that hid David from easy view. Quick, young feet pounded the earth a stone's throw from David.

"Is not the arrow beyond you? Make haste, hurry, do not delay."

The words wounded, their meaning clear.

"Go, carry them to the city."

Jonathan must have given the lad his weapons. David peeked around the edge of the rock, watching the boy's back through blurred vision. When he disappeared from sight, David rubbed rough fingers over his eyes, then smoothed his rumpled robe. With hesitant feet, he stepped from behind the outcropping of rocks and walked to the middle of the field where Jonathan stood.

He stopped in front of his friend and fell to his knees. He bowed to the ground three times, then remained prostrate, his face to the dirt. His head lifted at Jonathan's touch. In an instant, the prince pulled him to his feet and kissed each cheek.

David swallowed the heavy lump wedged in his throat. "I take it your father missed me?" He attempted a wry smile, his nervous fingers raking one hand through his unkempt hair.

"You could say that." Jonathan's royal robe flapped behind him, and the wind tugged at his silver-crowned hair. His gaze held no trace of mirth—only sadness.

A rush of emotion again blurred David's vision. "This is good-bye, then." What was he supposed to do now? Where could he go where Saul could not find him?

"Go in peace, since we have both sworn in Adonai's name, saying, 'May Adonai be between you and me, and between your descendants and my descendants, forever.'" Jonathan's usually steady voice faltered, and his right hand gripped David's shoulder. "Surely we will meet again someday."

David searched the prince's teary gaze. Would that it were true! His throat closed with an ache as sharp as a sword. Thick, stinging tears coated his beard. Jonathan's muscular arms wrapped David in a fierce hug.

"You must hurry, my friend, before the sun rises much higher in the sky. My father already has his guards on alert, and if you're not careful, he may have men combing the area soon."

He held David at arm's length. "God go with you, David." He kissed each tear-soaked cheek again.

David bowed low one last time. "And with you, my prince."

The sun had fully crested the horizon now, and David turned south—away from Gibeah, away from Michal and

Jonathan, away from all he held dear. His weary feet picked up the pace as a sudden noise fueled gut-twisting fear. *What was that?*

One swift glance over his shoulder attempted to put his mind at ease. Must have been an animal or bird. But just the same he clung to the shadows and ran through forests and tall grasses of neighboring fields.

His prayers came in desperate spurts, and his blood thudded through his veins like a horse's pounding hooves.

Help. Please, God, let someone give me food and shelter, at least until I can figure out where to go and what to do.

❦

The *clop*, hobble, *clop* of Michal using her walking stick on the stone floor reminded her of the crippled old man that begged near the city gate. She'd seen the toothless beggar when she'd ridden her donkey behind her father in a royal parade. Now, bent over and limping, she imagined herself gnarled and old like him. She would be grateful when her foot healed and she could cast the stick to the dogs.

The palace walls gave off an oppressive air today, smothering her. Something had changed. The guards were tense, the servants nervous. Merab had stayed home, and Mother was off somewhere. She'd passed her father's concubine, Rizpah, when she left the dining hall. The seductive woman had entered the west door with her infant son while Michal had struggled to walk through the opposite way. Otherwise the place held a stony silence.

The family courtyard stretched before her, and Michal tried to walk unaided the last few steps to a wooden bench. If she could just get her foot used to her weight again, she could leave the palace and go home. Home to David. Had he come for her? Would he know where to find her?

She used the strength in her arms to lower her body to the bench. A walk through the connecting gardens would be so refreshing. The garden where she and David had met before their wedding—the night Merab married Adriel and David indicated his interest in her. She allowed the tension in her back to slowly release and flipped the long strands of her braided hair over the bench.

She had to get away from the captivity of her father's house. Surely David would come for her soon. If only she could get a message to him. She squeezed her eyes shut, trying to ward off the oppression, to dispel the ever-present fear.

"Michal," a voice whispered from the direction of the gardens.

Michal's eyes flew open, and she sat up straight, peering across the wide courtyard. She leaned forward and grabbed the stick, forcing herself to stand again.

"Who's there?" The *clop*, hobble, *clop* on the courtyard stones almost drowned out the sound of her voice as she walked toward the gardens. Fear raised the hair on her arms, and Michal stopped when she reached the gardens' gate. "Who's there?"

"Don't raise your voice." Jonathan stepped from the shadows and gripped Michal's arm. His eyes were ringed in dark circles, and ashes coated his hair and beard. In one swift glance Michal noted his torn robe and bare feet. Had someone died?

Her stomach leaped to her racing heart, and her knees wanted to crumple beneath her weight. "What happened, Jonathan? Is it David?" Her voice came out in a high-pitched squeak.

She felt Jonathan's strong arms pull her against his chest, and his head bent to her ear. "Shhh . . . Be quiet, Michal." His older-brother sternness held a certain comfort. "What I'm about to tell you must remain our secret. Do you promise?"

"I promise." She would do anything for David.

"Father is committed to killing your husband." Jonathan paused. "I've sent him away, Michal. He'll never be safe in the king's court again."

Michal's stomach dropped and somersaulted, and she bit down hard on her lower lip, fighting tears. "I want to go with him, Jonathan. You must take me to him!"

Jonathan held her at arm's length and looked into her eyes, his own haggard with emotion. "You can't go with him, Michal. You can barely walk. David will need to run far and fast. You would only put him in more danger."

He was right, of course.

"When I'm well then. Promise me you'll take me to him then, Jonathan."

Jonathan studied her with resigned sadness. "I can't make a promise like that, Michal. You can see how I came to tell you this. If Father catches me here, there'll be no end of trouble. He threw his spear at me yesterday."

Michal's free hand clutched her stomach. Father tried to kill his own son? Heir to his throne?

Tears squeezed past her closed lids, and Michal sniffed back a sob. "What am I going to do, Jonathan?" she asked. "I can't stay here without David. I'm going out of my mind in this place." A slow shudder worked its way through her body, making her tremble uncontrollably. "What am I going to do?"

Jonathan pulled her close again and kissed the top of her

head. "We will do what we always do, Michal. We will live with our father's madness and pray for David's safety. The rest is out of our control." He released his grip, looked at her until she acknowledged his words with a nod, and left.

The moment Michal knew Jonathan was out of earshot, her legs gave way and she crumpled in a heap.

David!

She groaned like a wounded animal, wrapped both arms around her knees, and rocked back and forth on the dusty ground. There must be something she could do to help him. He needed her. More importantly, she needed him.

Her tears spent, she dried her eyes on the edge of her sleeve and used her walking stick to force her legs to stand. Tingly sensations ran from her knee to her sore foot, and Michal gently shook it, trying to wake it up and release the added pain. She needed to do something, however small. But whom could she trust?

Clop, hobble, *clop*. The familiar, annoying sound broke the silence of the courtyard as she made her way back to her prisonlike room. Halfway down the deserted hall, Michal stopped. What if she could get to the stable and find David's horse? She could ride after him and give him the horse, which would help him go farther faster. Then they could sleep in caves together, alone, away from all the distractions that had plagued their marriage from the beginning.

Hope sprang anew, quickening Michal's step. She hurried the rest of the way to her room and shoved open the door. She would need to gather a few things in a bundle to tie to the back of the horse. Maybe she could get some food from the kitchen and a cooking pot or a camp oven like the one David used to take into battle.

With the door closed behind her, Michal began to forage through her clothes. Only a few items could go—there wouldn't be room for much. She glanced at her mirror and pots of makeup. They would have to stay.

After perusing her collection of clothing, Michal settled on two pale blue tunics and the multicolored robe she was wearing, a few personal items, and combs for her hair. And her veil, of course. The dust alone would make it necessary to wear one.

Oh, but what if she couldn't find David? Israel was a big place, and she'd never gone far from Gibeah in all of her seventeen years. She stared at the items laid out on the bed in front of her. Could she do this? In her condition?

David! Her body swayed like one keening for the dead.

She had to do this—for David's sake, if not her own. The horse would help him, and if for some reason her father found them, she could plead for her husband's life. Father had always listened to her in the past.

Before she could change her mind, Michal wrapped everything in a wool blanket, tied it with a piece of leather, and put it under the foot of her bed. She would go to the kitchen and gather a few more things, then find Keziah. The girl had proved trustworthy in the past. She would have to trust her again if her plan was to succeed. Her feet nearly flew amid the clop of the stick over the stone floors. If all went well, she could be on her way by nightfall.

☙❧

"But how are you going to find David in the dark all by yourself, my lady? There are thieves and malcontents roaming the fields and living in caves. At least let me go with you."

Michal shook her head and met Keziah's concerned gaze as the gray light of dusk curtained the sky. "I'll be fine, Keziah," she promised with a confidence she did not feel. "Just help me get the horse out of the stable and mounted."

"But what if the king finds out? What will I tell him? He'll kill me!"

"No, he won't. Besides, I need you here to cover for me." She paused midhobble and placed one hand on the girl's arm. "Please, Keziah, don't worry."

Michal watched Keziah clamp her mouth shut, a telltale sign she would soon open it again.

"But it's not safe, my lady," she blurted moments later. They were within a few paces of the stables now, and Michal's heart tripped. Perhaps she should have left Keziah out of her plans.

Michal put a finger to her lips, motioning for Keziah to be quiet. The caretaker's house was built above the stable, a place once used as an inn. Her father had hired the man to care for his animals, leaving no room to house the donkeys and horses of travelers. Another inn had opened for that closer to the city gate.

When she reached the door, Michal glanced overhead for any sign of the caretaker's family. Voices could be heard, muffled by the thick walls. A good sign. Maybe she could actually get David's black stallion out of the stall undetected. Her hand grasped the rope handle and pulled. Relief slipped from her in an unbidden sigh. At least the door wasn't locked.

She tiptoe-hobbled over the hard-packed earth, Keziah at her heels. One of these horses had to be David's. Too bad she didn't have use of a torch. She squinted in the gray light, wishing the moon's glow were visible through the door. Thankfully dusk had not given way to blackest night yet. With soft steps, Michal crept along, hoping, praying for success.

"Is that the horse, my lady?" Keziah touched her shoulder and pointed to the end of the row.

"Maybe. It's too dark to see." Michal limped closer, ignoring the pain in her foot. She'd put too much weight on it walking around all day. If she could just get on the horse, she could let it rest.

When she came to the far wall at the back of the stable, she found a large black horse munching hay. One clear look at him through the dim moonlight turned her hope to despair. The animal was huge! How would she ever mount the beast, let alone ride him? She gripped the walking stick for support and stared at the sleek stallion. Maybe she should ride her donkey instead. Oh, but it would take so much longer to reach David!

Squaring her shoulders, Michal looked around for the bit and reins, realizing with a jolt that she had no idea how to prepare such an animal for riding. Servants and stable hands had always done such things for her. Strong men had even lifted her onto her donkey whenever she'd ridden in a royal march through Gibeah's crowded streets.

Whatever had possessed her to think she could mount David's horse alone, much less find him in the barren hills of Judah?

She turned and walked back to the front of the stable, defeat surging through her in a torrent. Keziah was right. She should go back to her father's palace and hope that someday he would change and welcome her husband's return, praying that peace would somehow find her in those dismal stone halls.

165

But as she reached the front of the stable, truth hit her full force. Her father would never change. And if Keziah had heard correctly, her marriage to David would soon be a distant memory. She could not let that happen!

"Did you hear that? I think someone is coming," Keziah said, making Michal's heart kick into a gallop. She rested one hand on a wooden rail and cocked her head. The only sound was her own labored breathing.

"I don't hear anything." She walked on, pausing at the narrow stall that held her personal donkey. Relief flooded her. This one she could manage. She dropped her packs over the animal's sides. "I'll take her instead, Keziah. Fix the bit in her mouth so I can mount."

Keziah did as she was told, though Michal could sense the girl's fear in her quick, jerky movements. It had been a mistake to bring her this far. But it was too late to go back now.

Keziah spread a multicolored blanket over the animal's back and helped Michal mount. Moments later Keziah led the animal through the door and into the night.

"Where will you go, my lady? It's so dark."

Where indeed? Probably to Bethlehem, but she wasn't going to tell Keziah everything. No telling what her father would drag out of the girl.

"Do not worry overmuch for me, Keziah." They were away from the stable now, headed toward the field. She would have to take the long way around to where the hill made a natural town border, past the stone Ezel, away from the guards at the city gate. "Just hurry home before I'm missed."

Keziah stared at her mistress, the whites of her eyes visible in the distant glow of the moon. "Will you not reconsider, my lady?"

Michal shook her head. "I cannot go back there, Keziah. David needs me. Now go!" She watched the dejected girl turn around and begin the long walk to the palace. Anxious to be off, she kicked the donkey's side. Truth be told, David might do well without her. But she was lost without him.

17

The glowing lights of the tabernacle winked at David through the falling dusk. Refuge. Surely the priests in the house of God would offer provisions, perhaps even give him helpful advice or inquire of the Lord for him. It was worth a try.

Please, Lord, let there be food and a weapon I can use.

He stood on a low ridge overlooking Nob, the city of priests, anxious for daybreak. He'd walked for hours since leaving Gibeah, grateful for the handful of men who'd caught up to him. Joab, Abishai, and six soldiers of David's tribe had run off to find David the moment Jonathan brought word of Saul's rage. No one from Bethlehem would be safe in Gibeah, especially those who shared David's blood.

"Why not go tonight, Uncle?" The sound of crunching stones accompanied Joab's approach.

"Because daylight looks less suspicious. I can't have Ahimelech reporting to Saul as soon as I leave. Nob is too close to Gibeah." Sabbath or not, he would speak to Ahimelech and get what he needed.

"But cover of night would give us an advantage over Saul's men."

David pulled the turban from its place and dug his fingers through his dusty hair. Joab had a point.

"We're hungry now, David. At least go and ask the man for bread," Abishai said.

Exhaustion warred against common sense. All he wanted to do was sleep, but his gnawing stomach demanded action. He looked at his men, too tired to argue, too hungry to care. "All right. I'll go."

❦

"Keziah! What are you doing out here in the dark?" Paltiel shifted the pack he was carrying to his left shoulder and studied the girl. Keziah's dark eyes widened, and her full lips trembled. He scanned her narrow frame. "What's wrong, Keziah? You can tell me. Maybe I can help."

Her slender fingers were fidgeting with the sash of her tan robe, and she looked like a cornered animal. He eased the sack off his shoulder and stooped slightly to meet her at eye level.

Keziah tucked her lower lip beneath her teeth and looked beyond him. Her obvious struggle to trust him sent pinpricks of dread up his spine. He wanted to shake the girl, to make her speak. If something had happened to Michal . . . Surely not. Michal was back at the palace in the safety of the fortress walls.

"My mistress . . ."

Paltiel's thoughts leaped to attention. "You mean Princess Michal?"

Keziah nodded. "She's . . ." The girl chewed her lip again, tears slipping down her cheeks.

"She's what, Keziah? I can't help you if you don't tell me."

169

He bit back his frustration and placed a comforting hand on her arm.

Keziah looked at him, hands clasped in supplication. "Please, sir, promise me you won't tell the king."

Paltiel bent his head in a slight nod but held his peace. "Just tell me, Keziah."

"My lady has gone off after her husband. I'm afraid for her, Paltiel. It's not safe for a woman alone."

Impossible! Michal couldn't even walk straight. How could she run off into the wilderness? She didn't even know where David was. Did she?

"How? When?" He studied the girl while a niggling fear worked through him. What if it were true? She could be hurt.

"We secured a donkey from the king's stable."

"Just now?" Paltiel glanced at the sky. Dots of glittering light began poking through the cloudless canopy.

"I left her a few moments ago."

"What direction was she headed?"

Keziah's dark brows knitted in confusion. "I'm not sure. She wouldn't tell me."

Paltiel let out a frustrated breath. He'd have to act now. But he still had this bundle to deliver, and he should help Keziah return to safety. Indecision made him curse under his breath. He knew the princess was stubborn, but this was just foolishness. His gaze roamed the sky again, then glanced back at the girl standing before him.

"Come, Keziah. Let me take you home. Then I'll saddle a horse and ride after your mistress. Hopefully she hasn't gone and gotten herself injured or killed in the meantime."

He snatched the sack from the ground and grabbed Keziah's

arm. If he hurried, he might catch up to Michal before she got out of the city.

☙❧

"Captain David, why are you here?" Ahimelech's pinched expression suggested worry more than surprise. Or was David imagining things?

"I'm here on the king's business," David said. Ahimelech's visible shaking rattled the clay lamp he carried and raised tingling flesh on David's arms. "I want you to inquire of the Lord for me."

"So late? Are you alone, my son?" Ahimelech shifted from foot to foot, his gaze shooting past David into the shadows.

David's quickened pulse throbbed in his neck, and his cheeks grew warm. Why was the priest so wary? Had he already heard Saul's decree? "My men are waiting for me, and the king's business is private and urgent. May I come in?" David produced his most charming smile and touched Ahimelech's shoulder.

The old man grew flustered and backed into the room, holding the door open. "Yes, yes. You simply startled me."

David glanced around the spacious room, home of the high priest. It was adjacent to the ancient tabernacle of meeting, which housed the holy articles—minus the ark of God. Israel had gone without access to the ark, the symbol of God's grace, for too long. Would they ever again worship before it in truth?

An inner sense of loss filled David's spirit. How glorious it must have looked. If only he could have been privileged to pray here, knowing the Lord's presence rested between the cherubim of the mercy seat. Maybe someday, when he was king . . .

Ahimelech cleared his gravelly throat. David shook himself and looked into the priest's light brown eyes. "Come, sit by the fire," the priest said.

Ahimelech glanced beyond David before closing the door. One gnarled hand adjusted the sash of his robe as he walked David to the courtyard. David followed, darting wary looks down shadowed halls, wondering how safe the priest's home really was. When they reached the family's inner courtyard, David spotted a shepherd warming himself near the fire pit. He stepped closer. The man looked familiar. When he glanced up from rubbing his hands, recognition hit David full force. Doeg the Edomite, Saul's chief shepherd, would waste no time telling Saul of David's whereabouts.

He should never have come.

"Let me get the ephod." Ahimelech hurried to an opposite door, and David followed close on his heels.

"What's the Edomite doing here?" he whispered.

The priest stopped at a closed door and met David's gaze, suspicion evident in his pale eyes. "He came to offer a sacrifice."

"Then why is he still here?"

"The Sabbath has started, David. Surely you aren't planning to travel, even on the king's business, on the Sabbath."

The accusing words stung, but fear for his life overruled the law of travel. "I am the king's servant, Ahimelech. I must obey orders."

"Yes, but surely the law of God—"

"Which I do my best to obey, but I need provisions. I ran off so quickly I forgot my weapon, and we've run out of food. I came here for help."

Ahimelech pulled on the rope latch and opened the door. "We don't have any food on hand except the holy bread and—"

"It will do."

Ahimelech entered the room where the priestly ephod hung on a prominent wall. Gold, blue, purple, and scarlet hues danced in a patterned rainbow in the glow of the clay lamp. The high priest's holy garment surpassed the king's in crafted beauty. As it should.

Ahimelech set the lamp on a low table near the wall and approached the ephod. He removed the two polished Urim and Thummim, stones engraved with the names of the twelve tribes of Israel. "What question shall I ask Him?" The priest gave David a calculated look.

"Shall I pursue this course of action?" *El De'ot*, the God of knowledge, knew what was on his mind.

The high priest wrapped one hand around each stone, lifted his head, and closed his eyes. David watched, heart galloping. A moment passed. Another. Would He answer?

Ahimelech's lids popped open, his gaze fixed on David.

"What did He say?" A tremor passed over David.

The priest broke eye contact and tucked the stones back into the ephod. "He said, 'Go.'"

David rubbed his arms in an attempt to stop the shivering. "Was that all? Did He say where?"

Ahimelech's curious look turned suspicious again. "I thought you were on the king's business, David. Don't you know where you're going?"

"Of course." David drew a slow breath. "I meant after I finished the task."

"I see." The priest's silence was deafening.

"Would you retrieve the bread now?" He had to get out of here.

"You realize this isn't just any bread. Have the young men kept themselves from women?"

Michal's alluring young figure flitted through David's thoughts. How long had it been? Three weeks? A month? Too long. He glanced at the priest. "The men's bodies are pure."

Ahimelech looked doubtful, but he hurried to the adjoining room to gather the bread, food the priests normally ate. He stuffed it in a straw basket and handed it to David.

"Thank you, Ahimelech. Is there a weapon here?"

Ahimelech clutched one hand to his chest and vigorously shook his head. "Oh my, no. We are priests, David. We don't keep weapons here." A sudden frown creased his brow. "Wait. There is the sword of Goliath, whom you killed in the Valley of Elah. It's wrapped in a cloth behind the ephod there. Take it if you want it."

Elah seemed a lifetime ago.

"There is none like it. Give it to me."

༄

Crickets sang their mating songs as the night breeze played a whimsical tune among the leaves in the sycamore trees. Michal's heart flipped over in fear with every step of the donkey's plodding feet. What was she doing out here? She would never find David in the dark. She didn't even know where she was going.

Oh, David, why didn't you just take me with you? Why didn't I insist on it? I need you.

She followed the path the moon splashed across the field, silently begging the donkey not to lose its footing the way she had done trying to run to Jonathan's house. What would she do if something happened to the beast?

A screech like the cry of a wounded animal sounded. Her heart stopped in her throat, and she cupped her mouth, stifling a scream. Overhead the rhythmic flapping of wings caught her attention. She glanced in the direction of the sound in time to see a bird swoop upward, prey clenched between its talons.

An owl. Probably snatched a field mouse or some other unfortunate creature. A shudder passed over her while perspiration beaded her forehead. Good thing she wasn't small enough to be food for an owl. A lion or bear or jackal might not think so ill of her, though.

She pulled the donkey's reins, bringing the animal to a halt. The ebony stillness of the starry night, once a beautiful sight from the safety of her home, now made her shiver with dread. Home. She should just turn around and go home before she was missed.

No. She must go on. Too much was at stake. David's life was in danger. If anyone could help him, surely she could. She held more sway over her father than most.

Panic wedged a sharp pain in her heart. Indecision made her throat constrict with tears. *David, David, what should I do?*

Michal's chest rose and fell as she released a huge sigh. She kicked the donkey's sides again and pointed the beast south. Perhaps she would find shelter in a cave along the way. In any case, she wasn't about to give up.

❧❧

"We can't stay here." David dropped to his knees, out of breath from running uphill at top speed. "Doeg the Edomite is spending the night in the priest's house. He saw me and will surely tell Saul."

"Where should we go?" Abishai pulled a loaf of bread from the basket, broke off the end, and stuffed it into his mouth.

"Anywhere is better than here," Joab said, handing a similar loaf to each man.

"Saul will find us anywhere in Israel," another man said.

"Israel has plenty of caves and vast deserts. Saul would be hard-pressed to find us there," Joab countered.

David ripped off an end of his loaf, his thoughts spinning. "Gath is closer than the desert. Saul would never enter Philistine territory in pursuit. Perhaps King Achish can be persuaded to take us in as mercenaries."

"Have you lost your mind, David? Goliath was from Gath. You killed the man—their champion—remember?" Joab's round eyes hardened under heavy black brows. "Isn't that his sword?"

"Joab's right, David. Not a wise move." Abishai wiped grainy crumbs from his dark brown beard, his normally smiling face somber.

David chewed in silence, glaring at his impertinent nephews. Suddenly he didn't care what they thought. He would go himself then.

"Consider me a fool, but I'm going to Gath. If Saul hears of it, maybe he will give up hunting me."

"Don't be ridiculous, Uncle. You can't do this," Joab said.

"I can and I will. Who will go with me?" David scanned the group. "No one?" He hid his disappointment and stood. "Fine. I'll go myself."

Abishai stood as well. "I'll go with you to the border, David."

David nodded and began a brisk pace to the west.

"They'll kill you, David," Joab called from behind.

"If I stay, Saul will kill me, and if I flee, I face the same fate. What choice do I have?"

⁊⥾

Weariness caused Michal's heavy lids to droop, and she fought to stay focused on the road. She couldn't let the donkey walk without staying aware of the direction she was headed. All she needed was for the dumb beast to turn around and head for home without her realizing it. Ahead of her, an outcropping of rocks indicated a set of limestone caves. Relief flooded her, draining what little strength she possessed. She could rest here until dawn. Perhaps God was smiling on her.

She shifted, trying to get comfortable, and steered the donkey toward the crevice. *Please, don't let anyone else be there.* What would she do if she came upon a group of men?

A sudden noise made her head snap around. Fully awake now, she twisted from side to side, squinting into the darkness. Her heart hammered. Palms sweaty, she clutched the reins. Someone was coming.

The distinct sound of horses' hooves beat the distant earth. Michal leaned close to the donkey's ear, the way she'd seen David do. "Come on, girl, just a little farther," she whispered. "We have to get behind those rocks."

The beast dropped its neck and began to nibble a patch of grass, oblivious to Michal's urging. "Please, donkey." Michal forced her sweetest high-pitched tone past her tight lips and stroked the animal's mane. The beast didn't budge.

Michal blew out a frustrated breath, fighting tears. If only her foot were healed. She would jump down and push the

177

beast forward. Or better yet, she'd run across Israel and never look back.

The earth shook, announcing the approaching horses. Michal kicked the donkey with her good foot again and again. *Move, you stupid beast!* The rumbling grew closer. Michal kicked harder, tears choking her. *Come on! Move!* She wanted to scream and flail her arms and throw a tantrum like a little girl, but she forced the words down her throat and leaned forward in silence.

Waves of dry earth billowed with each pounding hoofbeat, filling the air with stale dust. The donkey finally complied with Michal's wishes and sauntered a couple of paces forward. Still within sight.

Michal sat helplessly, watching the horses advance. Within moments, she recognized her father's guards Paltiel, Joash, and Benaiah. Her heart sank even as her anger flared. Keziah must have told. How else would they have come so soon?

The horses came to an abrupt stop a short distance from her. Paltiel jumped down, still holding the reins.

"Michal?" He peered at her, closing the gap between them.

She held her tongue, too angry to speak, and watched his brows furrow and his lips thin.

"What are you doing out here alone, Michal?"

Michal lifted her chin a notch. "Shouldn't you be addressing me as 'Princess'?"

Paltiel's dark eyes narrowed. "Not when you don't act like one."

Michal met his gaze. How dare he! He was a guard, not an equal. "What do you want, Paltiel?"

"I'm taking you home."

"To David—fine. You can all accompany me, then leave when I find him."

"Not to David. To your father, the king."

Their eyes met. There was a stern set to his jaw and an authority in his tone she'd never heard before. He looked haggard and irritated, if she read him correctly. Well, she could be stubborn too. And he had no right to tell her what to do.

"I'm not going." She clutched the donkey's reins and tried to swing the beast around to trot away. Never mind that Benaiah was strong enough to lift her with one hand. By himself he could force her to comply. Then again, Benaiah had once shown an interest in her. She glanced past Paltiel to the burly soldier and gave him a pleading look. Maybe he could be convinced to help her now.

The animal took one plodding step, but Paltiel's hand grabbed the bridle, stopping it.

"You can't make me go with you, Paltiel. I'm going to join my husband."

"He's not your husband anymore."

He was lying. David belonged to her, and she to him. "Unless you can prove David is dead, you are mistaken."

The look Paltiel gave her sent a shudder down her spine.

"There are other ways to end a marriage."

"I have no certificate of divorce. David wouldn't do that. He loves me."

"David wouldn't, but your father would—in fact, did."

Michal stared at him. He was wrong. He had to be. "What are you talking about?"

She watched the guard study her with a familiarity that made her skin crawl. She didn't like this man. She glanced

179

again at Benaiah. The pained look in his eyes sent jagged throbs up the back of her neck and tied her stomach in knots.

"I'm telling you, Michal, that your father summoned one of the scribes to annul your marriage to David. He has decided that David is as good as dead and has promised you to another. That's why we're here. To take you home to your new husband."

Michal tried to swallow but couldn't get past the dryness, so she tried again, nearly choking. She wouldn't let them do this to her. She wanted David.

David!

"He's not lying to you, Michal." Benaiah's gentle tone startled her, but when she searched his face for some sign of an ally, she found nothing but resigned sadness. The realization hit with a force that nearly knocked her off the donkey. She leaned forward, clutching the animal's mane.

"Who?" she managed to squeak through clenched teeth. Her gaze still rested on Benaiah. He wasn't going to help her get to David. Could it be his past interest in her had never ceased?

"You mean who is your new husband?" Joash asked.

She nodded, her throat aching with unshed tears.

Paltiel reached a gentle hand to brush a loose strand of hair from her cheek and smiled at her. "The king, your father, had no idea whom he wanted to give you to. When he found out you'd run away, he promised I could have you if I could find you. I'm to be your new husband, Michal."

~18~

Ginger-hued brick towers rose above an open, arched gate—an imposing structure used to welcome visitors or bar enemies from entering the city of Gath. Two weeks had passed since his visit to Ahimelech—two weeks of him and his men wandering south through Judah, avoiding places where people could recognize him, hiding in caves, scrounging for food, and finally reaching the Philistine city. David stood on the outskirts of the town now, watching heavily laden merchant carts pass under the inspection of guards flanking the solid wooden and metal doors. How to join their ranks was the question. Could he get inside undetected? Or maybe he should just announce his intentions up front. How else did one find an audience with the king?

"So, do I look ragged enough?" David turned to Abishai and sported a look of desperation. "Do you think the king will believe me when I tell him I'm seeking refuge?"

Abishai's thick, dark brown mustache twitched in response. He sized David up and down, crossing his arms. Joab and the rest of his men had eventually agreed with Abishai and followed David to the border, but they had stayed behind when

David and Abishai had broken camp that morning. David was weary of their harassment and questioning of his decisions. Abishai was the only one he trusted with this mission.

"You look ragged, all right. But, David, this is a fool's mission. Please reconsider."

"Don't start sounding like your brother, Abishai. My mind is set."

Abishai uncrossed his arms and tucked both hands in the pockets of his robe. "So, how do you plan to get inside?"

David looked back at the gate. A line of merchant carts still awaited entrance.

"Guess I'll join a caravan." He took two steps forward, then turned and embraced Abishai in a fierce hug, kissing each of his cheeks.

"God go with you, Uncle."

David released him and unfastened Goliath's sword from his belt. He handed it to Abishai. "Keep it for me . . . until I return."

"I will."

David set out at a brisk pace for the gates of Gath. He should have talked with some of the merchants around their campfires the night before. It would have given him an advantage he didn't have now.

When he reached the end of the line, his stomach knotted. He wasn't sure what he was so worried about. He'd spent years in a king's court. How different could it be?

"You, Israelite! State your business."

David snapped to attention. How had they spotted him from this distance? He glanced up to the guards decked along the walls, then down at the two stationed at the gate. A third soldier he hadn't seen before strode purposefully toward him.

"You there." He pointed a bony finger at David. "State your business."

David swallowed hard and met the man's scrutiny. "I'm here to request an audience with King Achish." It was too late to do anything else.

The youthful guard adjusted his red-feathered helmet and studied David. "For what purpose?" His voice was stern, his gaze calculating.

"To seek refuge . . . and offer my services." David lifted his chin and straightened his shoulders.

The guard turned. "Follow me." He walked past the rest of the merchant carts, leading David through the gate to the King's Highway. Multicolored ornamental pillars and grotesque statues carved of white marble lined the street. Signs hanging from metal poles announced places of business—an apothecary here, a temple there, a theater at the corner of an intersecting street. Philistines of varying levels of economic status bustled about, children raced around produce carts, men and women haggled over prices, a donkey brayed in the distance. David took in the scene while his feet kept pace with the guard's hurried gait until they reached the limestone steps of the jeweled palace of Achish, king of Gath.

"This Israelite requests a meeting with the king," the man said when they stopped at the scribe's desk outside the closed audience chamber.

The scribe lifted his turbaned head and rested beady eyes on David. "State your name, please."

"David, son of Jesse, of Bethlehem."

The scribe dipped a thin brush in a clay pot and jotted strange letters on a sheet of beige papyrus. David watched the man with a wary gaze, then scanned the enclosed portico.

To his right, two servants huddled, whispering. Behind him a group of guards approached.

"Isn't that David, the king of the land?" one of the guards said, his tone a mix of curiosity and condemnation.

David crossed his arms, feeling the heavy thudding of his heart beneath his fingers. This was not good.

"Yeah, that's him." Another guard took three steps closer, inspecting David like a farmer would scrutinize a lamb for sacrifice. The man stepped back and turned to his companions. "What's he doing here?"

"Said he wants to see the king." This from the guard who'd led David to the palace. "This ought to be good."

"Maybe the king will take him prisoner."

Another guard approached. "Hey, Israelite! Aren't you the one they sing about in their dances—Saul has slain his thousands, and David his ten thousands?"

"Yeah, I'll bet he's seen plenty of Philistine blood on the end of his sword."

David's heartbeat slowed, every rhythmic thump sluggish, blood draining from his face. Coming here was a big mistake.

"The king will see you now." The scribe spoke, the words distant.

They knew who he was, and they would use the knowledge against him. Saul's threats were nothing compared to what he had walked into here. They would surely torture him before they finally allowed him the escape of death. The vision of himself impaled on a stake made his knees weak. This was no lion or bear or wolf going after a lamb. His sling was useless among so many Philistine swords.

The room tilted, and he closed his eyes, clutching the edge

of the scribe's table for support. Dread, relentless and deep, spiraled downward into the pit of his soul.

O El Yeshuati, God of my salvation, help me now.

"Did you hear me, Israelite?" The scribe spoke again, louder this time, but the words barely penetrated David's fear-induced stupor. "What's wrong with you, man?"

"Maybe he needs a little prodding." A soldier lifted his sandaled foot and kicked David from behind. "Move along, Israelite! Don't keep the king waiting."

David stumbled forward as his self-preservation instinct swiftly rose, putting every nerve ending on high alert. His natural impulse screamed at him to whirl around and kick the man in return. But wisdom told him to ignore the insult. His mind raced with the best way to handle the Philistine king.

In the space it took him to totter and waver his way through the ornate doors, flanked by guards who grabbed his arms and tugged him toward the king, he knew what he should do.

"Who is this you've brought to me?" King Achish wrapped nimble fingers one at a time over the head of his staff. His dark eyes were intelligent, penetrating.

The guards shoved David to his knees, and he fell forward, hands braced against the cool mosaic floor.

"An Israelite, my lord. I believe we've captured their king without even trying. Seems he seeks refuge among us."

David kept his gaze on the red and blue tiles, simultaneously berating his own foolishness and begging Adonai for wisdom and rescue.

"What is your name?" Achish's tone was stern, menacing.

To not answer could get him killed, but to speak would reveal his own clear thinking. On impulse, he slid his hands forward, then tilted his head to look behind him. His gaze grazed the king's as he let his eyes roll back. In slow motion he stood, grasping at air, spittle pooling in his mouth. He let his lips go slack, the fluid dripping onto his beard. He turned away from the king, stumbled to one of the marble pillars, and dug his fingernails along the smooth surface.

Forgive me, Adonai. I should never have come. If You could just see Your way clear to intervene . . .

Had he gone too far? Would God change His mind and reject him as king before he ever started to rule? The thought made him physically ill. He'd be better off a madman than to forfeit the privilege to lead Israel. He was a complete and utter fool.

"Look, you see the man is insane. Why have you brought him to me?" Achish said. "Have I need of madmen, that you have brought this fellow to play the madman in my presence? Shall this fellow come into my house? Take him away." Two staccato claps followed his words.

Guards moved in, encircling him. They stood for a moment as if uncertain how to approach him in his new irrational state. At last, when the king's impatience grew in a string of angry curses, two Philistine soldiers gripped David's arms and half dragged him out the palace doors, through the city streets, and to the guard towers framing the gate. His heartbeat quickened from a state of near dead to a normal rhythm when they shoved him through and stationed a guard to bar his reentry.

❦

"I won't marry him, Mother! You can't make me." Michal limped from her narrow bed to the curtained window, ignoring the pain in her foot. "I'm David's wife! Father can't just deny that fact." Her voice rose with every syllable, and a deep shudder swept through her. Michal leaned forward, elbows on the window ledge, her senses assaulted by the pungent odor of roasting meat. Armfuls of wildflowers were being arranged in earthen vases around the large courtyard. In the garden, in the exact location where she'd first shared David's love, the wedding tent stood like a lone sentry watching for signs of an approaching battle. If her father made her go through with this, there'd be a battle all right.

She whirled on her good heel and stared at her mother, who calmly brushed lint from Michal's wedding clothes, the ones she'd worn over a year ago—for David.

"I'm not wearing that, Mother." Michal's throat felt raw from the tears she'd shed the moment Paltiel, Benaiah, and Joash had deposited her back at the palace. "I'm not marrying that man!"

"Don't be ridiculous, Michal. You don't actually think you can go against your father, do you?" Her mother looked her up and down. "Now come. Wash your face so Keziah can reapply your makeup. You've got kohl streaked over your cheeks from your tears. Then I'll take you to the mikvah and you can wash yourself. No man wants a dirty, disheveled bride."

"Aren't you listening, Mother? I'm not going to marry Paltiel. I'm David's wife, and I'm going to wait for him." She limped over to the bed and flopped on her back, arms behind her head, staring stubbornly at the ceiling.

"Now listen to me, young lady."

Michal kept her gaze on the ceiling despite her mother's harsh tone.

"Your father has been good to you all these years, giving you everything you wanted, including David, when it went against his wishes. Now your husband has deserted you and is threatening your father's life. Do you honestly think he will let you return to the man?"

Michal turned on her side and rose up on one elbow. "Why not? Father is the true threat here. He has tried to kill David repeatedly. David has never once raised his hand against him."

"How do you know for sure, Michal? Do you really know David? Didn't you say he threatened to kill you, his own wife, if you didn't help him escape? How can your father trust the man to take care of you if he's threatened to hurt you?" Ahinoam shook her graying head, her long turquoise earrings swinging with the movement. "David will soon be dead anyway, if your father has his way." She stepped closer to the bed and placed one hand on Michal's arm. "Let the king take care of his baby girl, Michal. Cooperate with this marriage. It's for your own protection."

Michal's whole body gave in to a tingling sensation. She couldn't decide if she was going to pass out or be sick. Had her lie to protect herself from her father allowed him to think he should give her to another man? Had she forfeited her marriage because of fear?

She rolled onto her stomach and stuffed a pillow to her lips to muffle the sobs rising within her. *Oh, David!*

What had she done?

❦

"So how does it feel to be marrying a man you don't want, little sister? I'd say you're getting what you deserve." Merab walked up to where Michal was standing between the main hall and the center court.

The earlier sick feeling invaded Michal's stomach again.

She lifted one hand to her middle in an effort to quell the fear-induced nausea and met Merab's triumphant gaze.

"What are you talking about?"

Merab's lip curled in a smirk. "Oh, come on, Michal. You know I was supposed to marry David, and Father just happened to find out about Adriel's interest in me and betrothed me to him instead. Now who would have spoken that idea in his ear? Adriel says Father approached him. But who told Father?"

"Any one of the servants could have suggested the idea."

"You were the only one with a reason."

"As far as you know, you mean." Michal's limbs shook with nervous tension. She should just tell Merab the truth. It didn't matter now anyway. "I don't know what you're so upset about. Adriel loves you. If Paltiel loved me, he'd return me to David." Michal's gaze darted past her sister, and she lowered her voice. "Besides, you didn't love David the way I do."

"You have no idea how I felt about him." Merab's sharp tone slashed through Michal's heart.

A distant look passed through Merab's dark eyes, and she cradled her protruding abdomen in a protective gesture. The movement pierced an arrow of jealousy through Michal's soul.

"Just leave me alone, Merab." She knew her tone carried waves of hurt, and her throat closed as she fought tears.

Merab studied her sister for a long moment. "You won David deceitfully, Michal. And now Paltiel has done the same with you. I hope you're happy."

She stalked off, her bitter words meshing with the discordant notes of the tuning musicians. Michal pulled her multicolored robe tightly across her body, a sudden chill shaking her.

189

The musicians, their instruments now ready, began one of the wedding songs, and her father appeared in the courtyard dressed in full royal garb.

A touch on her shoulder made her jump. She turned to stare at Benaiah.

"What do you want, Benaiah? Haven't you done enough?"

She glanced into the young man's mammoth face, curious at the sorrow etching his brow.

"Forgive me, Princess." He motioned her closer to the shadows, his wary gaze darting about before resting on her. "If I can arrange it, I will try to take you to David."

Michal blinked burning eyes and gaped at him. "How?" He hadn't helped her when Paltiel came for her.

"During the feast, before Paltiel leads you to the bridal tent, I'll be standing guard over you. Watch for my signal."

"You'll never get me past my father's soldiers, Benaiah. They've been watching every entrance like a pack of jackals."

"I have it all worked out, Princess. Trust me."

The tapping sound of hurried footsteps sent Benaiah scurrying down the hall and out of sight.

"Are you ready, my dear?" Her mother appeared in the arch of the door, killing Michal's hope and bringing all of her fears back in a rush. "It's time to join your husband under the chuppah."

Michal pressed her glossed lips together and nodded, thankful no words were required of her. She couldn't believe she was letting them do this to her. Just the thought of Paltiel's touch sickened her. Maybe in time she could convince him to return her to David.

Unless Benaiah could be trusted.

Her leaden feet moved to the canopy where Paltiel stood

waiting, smiling down at her. She glanced about and spotted Benaiah a few paces from her father. He nodded in her direction before she looked back at Paltiel. When she stopped beside him, he draped one end of his robe across her shoulders and solemnly promised to love and protect her.

"To the marriage tent at once!" her father said.

Michal's heart leaped, and the hairs on her arms rose in little bumps. She turned and saw her father standing with a gleam in his crazed eyes. This wasn't the proper way to start a wedding. Benaiah would never be able to whisk her away if she had no time to sit on the dais and greet well-wishers.

"At once!" Her father's voice rose in intensity. He stalked over to the two of them, grasped their arms, and looked sternly at Paltiel. "You must fulfill your vows at once! She must become odious to David. Now!"

Michal frantically searched for Benaiah. Where had he gone? Through blurred vision, Michal looked at Paltiel's profile. His head dipped forward in acquiescence. "Yes, my lord."

"Good." Her father took a step back, allowing Paltiel to grasp Michal's hand and tug her toward the wedding tent. An occasional cough or an awkward laugh filtered from the stunned crowd. The drum began its steady cadence, reminiscent of a year ago when David had pulled her from the dais. She had felt his excitement seep through his fingers, which had been tightly clasped around hers. Paltiel's hands were clammy, and she wondered what thoughts raced through his mind. How would she convince him to wait with her father standing guard outside? And where was Benaiah?

Paltiel lifted the flap and motioned Michal to pass under his raised arm. She ducked into the candlelit tent, a thousand romantic memories assaulting her. When the flap dropped in place and Paltiel moved closer to her in the center of the room, she backed away from him, wishing somehow she could rush past him, past her father, to David. If she had a knife, she would slit the tent's linen fabric and crawl through, away from this awful night. Instead, she stood rigid, willing him to keep his distance.

"Are you afraid of me, Michal?" Paltiel's tender tone surprised her. He took a step toward her, then another, until he was within arm's length. His fingers touched a smooth strand of her hair and tickled the back of her ear. She turned away, embarrassed and confused. Why did his touch send pleasant feelings through her?

"Stay away from me, Paltiel."

Silence.

"Let her go, Paltiel. She belongs to David."

Benaiah! He must have slipped in through the back of the tent. Hope surged, and Michal took a step toward the sound of Benaiah's whispered voice.

"Don't be a fool, Benaiah. One word from me, and Saul's guards will cut you down. There is no escape for either of you. Do you honestly think I would be foolish enough to disobey the king?"

"You can't do this. She's another man's wife!"

The drumbeat masked their heated, whispered words until Paltiel raised his voice. "If you don't leave now, Benaiah, I will call the guard at once and have you put out of Gibeah. I suggest you disappear, before the king does worse things to you than Michal will ever experience from my hand."

Michal studied the young guard, her heart sinking. Despite his obvious strength and massive size, he was outnumbered. Like David, running from danger was his only option.

"You must go, Benaiah. And God be with you." She met his miserable gaze and forced a smile, her back to Paltiel. *David.* Her mouth formed the word, and she caught the guard's almost imperceptible nod. A moment later he slid under the back of the tent, leaving her alone again with Paltiel.

Paltiel's hand on her shoulder made her jump. She scooted toward the back of the tent. "Do not touch me, Paltiel."

She watched his dark eyes grow impatient, smoldering. He took a step forward.

"I can't do that, Michal. Your father is waiting."

Heat flamed her cheeks, and she set her gaze on him. "Let him wait," she whispered. "Please, Paltiel. If you love me, take me to David." She hated the emotion in her voice.

His sudden look of compassion and pity both comforted and irritated her.

He closed the gap farther between them and toyed with the fringe of her veil. "I don't want to take you to David, Michal. Besides, why would I want to give you back to a man who deserted you? One who will soon be dead anyway? Do you really want to wait until you are widowed to share my love?"

She lowered her lashes and studied the sand-colored hairs curling around the cuffs of his striped robe. Silent tears clung to her lashes. Paltiel's fingers cupped her warm cheek before reaching to remove the veil from her hair. She stood immovable as he pulled the combs from her long tresses, her tears spilling onto his arm.

Despite his tender ministrations, Michal's tears continued. And when he donned his robe and strode from the tent to the boisterous laughter of friends and the approving backslaps of her father, Michal wept.

19

"David . . . Uncle . . . there you are."

David stepped out from behind a rock monolith above the cave at Adullam. "What is it, Joab?"

"There is a man here to see you."

"I've noticed the multitudes of men joining us. I'll be down to meet with all of them shortly." He looked out over the terracotta landscape at the valley's winding dirt road.

Joab stood with arms crossed, his feet set in a commanding stance. "Nevertheless, I wouldn't have interrupted you if this weren't important, David. You need to meet this man right away."

"Is Saul coming up the road?"

"No."

"Then I'll be down shortly." He dismissed Joab with a wave of his hand and walked back to the edge of the cliff until he heard his nephew's footfalls drift into the distance. Joab forgot his place too often these days. Sometimes David wondered who was really in charge. Would his family follow the leading of their youngest without question? He glanced over his shoulder at his secret praying spot and sighed.

O Adonai, in You I put my trust. Let me never be ashamed.

He stood, arms raised, longing gaze toward the heavens.

Pull me out of the net that they have laid for me, for You are my strength. Into Your hand I commit my spirit.

Peace settled, raising his confidence.

You have redeemed me, O Lord, God of truth.

With sure-footed ease, David descended the hill and entered the mouth of the biggest cave. A fire blazed in the center near the front, where several men congregated. He spotted Joab, who sprang to his feet the moment their gazes connected and motioned David toward the darker recesses of the cave. David took a torch from beside the fire and touched it to the flame, then followed.

"This way." Joab pointed to a tunnel leading off to the right. "He traveled for two nights to get here with nothing but the clothes on his back. I didn't know how long you would be off by yourself praying, so I bid the baggage keeper to find him a blanket and told him to rest."

"How uncharacteristically kind of you, Nephew." He gave Joab a pointed look, ignoring the subtle reprimand in Joab's tone.

"It was the least I could do." Joab's sarcasm was not lost on David.

"So who is this man?"

"Saul's guard Benaiah." Joab stopped walking and nodded toward a man sprawled out on a blanket, his breathing shallow as though he were lightly dozing.

At David's approach the guard stirred, and at the sight of David he stood. "My lord." He knelt at David's feet. "I have come to pledge allegiance to you. King Saul has done something . . ." He paused, his thick shoulders lifting in a pronounced sigh, as though the next words pained him. "I cannot be loyal to a man who does not follow the laws of the God of Israel."

A throbbing began at the back of David's neck, and the man's expression filled him with uneasy tension. "Explain yourself, Soldier."

Benaiah straightened and lifted a meaty hand in an act of surrender. "I am your servant, my lord. King Saul cannot be trusted . . . not after what he's done."

David read a message in Benaiah's eyes he wasn't sure he wanted to see. He scraped one hand through his already rumpled hair.

"What has he done? Tell me quickly."

The guard's expression grew pensive. Was that pity in his eyes? Or anger?

"He has annulled your marriage to his daughter Michal."

"His action carries no weight. We are married in the sight of God."

"As I said, my lord, the king does not follow the laws of our God."

As was evidenced by the king's relentless pursuit to kill him, but that was nothing new.

"So we'll get her back. Take some men with you, Benaiah, and sneak into Gibeah and bring her to me. I paid a high price for her. She's mine." When Benaiah didn't move, David said, "Don't just stand there, Soldier. Do what I tell you."

"Yes, my lord. But there is something else you must know."

Something stirred inside him, a fear so deep he couldn't bear to know the truth—and couldn't bear not to. An all-over trembling spread through his limbs, and heat filled his face. "Tell me."

Benaiah dropped his gaze as he fidgeted with his hands. David wanted to wrench the words from him and at the same time command him never to speak again. He drew in a slow breath, forcing his impatience in check.

"My lord, the king has given your wife to another man. Two nights ago she married Paltiel, son of Laish of Gallim."

His words hung in the oppressive silence. David's lungs burned, nearly bursting with the need to take a deep breath. The torch flickered as if the air had been drained from the small space to suffocate them all. He whirled about, gasping, and rushed through the dark tunnel to the mouth of the cave.

Oh, Adonai, not Michal. Have You not taken everything else? His home, his position, his good name, his best friend . . . He couldn't take Michal too.

What do You want from me, Lord?

Like a drunken man, David staggered out of the cave, pushing past the hundreds of men flocking the area, men who had come to him for refuge. But he was nobody's refuge. He was not a shepherd of men as Jonathan had once thought. He couldn't even protect his own wife.

Michal.

He stumbled on, trudging blindly hand over hand up the side of the mountain again. Jagged rocks cut into his palms, and pebbles scraped his knees. Oblivious to the stinging pain, David scrambled higher until he reached his sanctuary, where he collapsed in a heap.

Michal. Oh, God, why?

He should never have left her behind in the first place. Even now, if he had even a hint of authority, he ought to be able to reclaim her. But truth be told, he had no authority, no power to command. He could not undo what the king had chosen to do. Not until he was king himself. Which could happen tomorrow . . . or ten years hence.

He laid his head in the dirt and tossed dust over his hair. It was too much. If this was the cost of gaining the kingdom, he didn't want it anymore.

Take it away, Lord. I am not worthy to be king.

Unable to sustain his emotion any longer, David crawled over to a secluded crevice and retched.

∼20∼

One Year Later

Michal paced from parapet to twin towers to descending stairs and back again. The roof still afforded a small semblance of refuge. At least here she could escape the dim halls and prisonlike structure of the palace as well as the house she once shared with David—which she was now forced to live in with Paltiel. Despite their year together, Michal could not accept the man as her true husband, barely tolerating his presence and his touch.

She strode to the edge of the roof overlooking the road to the city gate. A lifetime had passed since the days when she stood here waiting for the harpist to comfort her, to strum his gentle fingers over the chords of her heart. Would she ever see him again? Would he want her if she did?

Unwanted memories of her first night with Paltiel and her father's resultant glee vexed her overwrought nerves. If only she'd gone with David. Even now she could be with him, listening to the melodic strains of his sweet voice easing her worries.

"What are you doing here, Michal?" Paltiel's harsh voice startled her, and she whirled to face him.

"I think I can go where I want to in my father's house." Anger flared at his intrusion. How dare he interrupt her quiet place!

"Not anymore." He stepped closer and gripped her arm. "You're coming with me."

She wrenched free of his grasp and spit in his beard. "Leave me alone, Paltiel! You can't control me."

He wiped his beard with his sleeve, then looked at her, his stern gaze fixing her feet to the roof's floor. "You misunderstand the meaning of husband, Michal. Perhaps David was too weak to control his wife, but I'm not." His fingers closed over her wrist in a painful grip, and he pulled her close enough to feel his hot breath on her face. "You will go where I tell you and do what I tell you, Michal. And you will not come up to this roof again. Do you understand, Wife?"

How dare he! How dare he, a common guard, tell her, a princess in Israel, what she could and could not do!

"Why are you treating me like this, Paltiel? You got what you wanted." She allowed her voice a hint of emotion, and tears filled her eyes.

"I don't trust you, Michal. You've run away more than once."

"And gotten nowhere." Her voice raised a notch. "Please, you're hurting me."

He pulled her closer. "I'm not hurting you, Michal. Stop the pretending."

She twisted her wrist in an unsuccessful attempt to get him to release his grip. "You are too hurting me!" The fact that he hadn't slapped her for spitting in his face amazed her. She had treated him horribly much of the past year when most of the time, if she were honest with herself, he had done his best to be kind to her. Still, she shouldn't belong to him. And she didn't want to.

"I'll overlook your disrespect for the moment, Michal, though I should punish you for it. Don't think I haven't considered the thought." He bent next to her ear. "But if you don't change your attitude, I will be forced to resort to other measures."

Every fiber in her being longed to jerk free and run from him, but common sense told her that feigned submission was probably better. Someday, when David returned for her and she was queen, she'd repay Paltiel for his impertinence. In the meantime, if she wanted to gain control, she must give in once in a while.

"I'm sorry, my lord. Forgive your maidservant." She lowered her lashes in a humble stance. "I don't understand why you don't want me to come up here, though."

Paltiel's eyes assessed her. "Let's just say you don't need to be reminded of the past." He kissed her forehead. "Understand?" He released his grip and guided her toward the steps.

"Yes, my lord." She understood plenty. It didn't mean she had to obey.

༺༻

Cool mountain breezes lifted the turban from David's forehead as he stood with staff in hand watching the road, a mere threadlike line winding away from the cliffs westward toward the sea. A sea clearly visible from the hills of Gath, but in the desert stronghold, a mere memory against the cloudless blue sky. His gaze lingered on the far-off horizon just the same. Oh, to be like a bird and fly off to such places. He blew out a slow breath. At least the stronghold offered them safety. After months at Adullam and his trek into Moab to Mizpah to deliver his parents to safety, it felt good to rest without having to constantly watch his back. Even if Saul coaxed every man in Israel to attack him here, they'd never scale the cliff sidewalls of the mountaintop fortress undetected.

He pulled his eyes away from the comforting vista and looked down on the bustling city below. His contingent of six hundred men now burgeoned with women and children, creating a community rather than a military atmosphere.

If only Michal could have joined him here. That a year had passed since he'd lost her . . . The news Benaiah had brought still grieved him, and it irked him to realize that he had allowed her to have such a hold over him. It was time to put her aside and take a new bride. If Adonai still planned to make him king, a promise he intermittently doubted and clung to, then he needed a wife to give him sons.

The king has given your wife to another man.

His fists involuntarily flexed, jaw clenching. He stared at the view before him and sighed. Yes, he needed a wife. But who? On impulse, he turned and began the slow climb down from his lookout post. He passed a group of women sitting around a fire pit, grinding wheat kernels. A short distance from them, another handful of women sat pounding dried tree bark. The spicy scent lingered in the puffs of reddish-brown air, and David stood still, groping for a distant memory. Glancing up, he spotted Joab trotting toward him.

"Joab, smell that." He sniffed and pointed to the second group of women. "Where have I smelled that scent before?"

Joab quirked one eyebrow at David. "Cinnamon is familiar

fare, David. You've smelled the spice all your life." His quizzical look deepened into a scowl. "Are you all right, Uncle?"

David rubbed his scraggly beard. "I've smelled it some-place, though. It came from a woman, like her skin or hair was dipped in the scent."

Joab lifted both brows now and smiled. "Women often mix different spices to create appealing perfumes, my lord. You probably got a whiff of one of them."

David shook his head and stuffed his hands in the folds of his robe. His gaze traversed the compound, his mind whir-ring. A moment later he slapped his thigh.

"Samuel! I smelled it the last time I saw him."

"Well, of course, Samuel's anointing oil was scented with cinnamon," Joab said. His doubtful expression made David chuckle. "I hardly think your anointing was a laughing mat-ter, my lord."

David sobered but still courted an irrepressible smile. "No, no, Nephew, that's not what I mean. When I was running from Saul, I went to see Samuel, and I met a girl at the well. What was her name?" He scratched his turbaned head. "Ahinoam! Yes. I remember because it was the same name as Michal's mother." He looked at Joab. "She was from Jezreel, but she was living with an uncle in Ramah."

"So?" Joab tapped an impatient foot.

"So, I want you to get her for me. If I can't have Michal, I must take another wife." David's pulse picked up its pace, and for the first time in months, hope pierced his heart.

"What if she's already spoken for?" Joab asked.

David clasped his hands over the end of his staff. Joab had a point. The girl had been of marriageable age when he'd met her over a year ago. The chances of her being available were slim. "Obviously I will have to find someone else then." He took two steps away from Joab, then abruptly turned back. "You don't usually run to greet me—what did you want?"

Joab glanced behind him, then faced David. "A prophet has come to see you."

David looked beyond Joab. The prophet Gad, one of Samuel's students, walked with purpose toward him. David brushed past his nephew and embraced Gad, kissing each cheek. Joab came up behind David, greeting the prophet with a nod.

"Welcome." David stepped aside to look at the man. "What brings you to our humble dwelling?" He moved his arm in a wide, sweeping arc toward the surrounding homes that had become their village.

"The Lord sent me."

David studied the prophet for a moment, uneasiness tickling his neck.

"Has something happened to my parents? The king of Moab assured me of his protection when we took them there, but if he's hurt them—"

"Your parents are well," Gad interrupted, his glowing eyes steadily holding David's.

"Is it Jonathan then? Or Michal?" His heart raced.

"I honestly don't know how they fare, David. I've heard nothing."

David's chest rose and fell in a deep sigh. "What does the Lord want then?"

Trust Me, David.

The thought swept over him, bringing with it waves of peace.

"The Lord says to leave the stronghold. He wants you to return to Israel."

"Where Saul can easily find us," Joab said.

David looked at his nephew, then turned serious eyes on Gad. "We will leave at dawn. Whatever the Lord wants, we will do."

❧❦

The black goat-hair tents were easily camouflaged among the trees of the forest of Hereth, giving David a small amount of comfort. It wasn't the most inviting place to bring a new bride, but Ahinoam had seemed pleased with the prospect of marrying him, despite the circumstances.

He watched her now as he sat shaving the bark from a sturdy piece of olive wood to shape into a flute for one of the young men, a promising musician. She looked up from the mortar and pestle to sift the soft grains of wheat into a clay bowl. A soft blush covered her cheeks when he smiled at her. She smiled in return but quickly averted her gaze. She was more skittish than he remembered, as though in constant fear of offending him. The thought grated, but he brushed it aside, certain he was imagining things. She was simply adjusting to marriage and would soon grow accustomed to him. Still, their love did not hold the longing and passion he'd had with Michal.

The familiar feeling of betrayal filled him, and he bent his head over the olive wood once more. Adonai surely had a purpose in allowing things to continue as they did, just as surely as He had a reason to move him from the stronghold to the forest. He only wished he understood what that purpose was. What gain was there in his going to the ground? His death would not accomplish Adonai's purposes, not if his anointing meant what Samuel had insisted it did.

He took a breath and released it, running his thumb along the smooth wood. He'd already learned the hard way that obedience to Adonai was far better than taking matters into his own hands—as he'd seen all too clearly in Gath—even if he lost his life in the process. Though he wasn't exactly thrilled with the prospect of landing in Sheol just yet.

"David?" Joab's voice came to him before his nephew emerged from the trees.

"What is it?" He set the wood aside and stood, grateful for the interruption to his unsettling thoughts.

Joab walked forward, his expression clearly troubled. "We have a visitor."

A visitor was nothing unusual. Disgruntled men from every tribe, especially the tribe of Judah, continually joined him.

"Who is it?"

"Abiathar, the priest."

David's stomach tightened. "Take me to him." Ahinoam should not be witness to whatever had troubled Joab.

"I couldn't get a word out of him," Joab said. David followed him through the trees to a clearing near Joab's tent, where a man sat near the cold fire pit. "Perhaps you will have more success." Joab pointed to a small man whose arms were wrapped around his bent knees. David felt a punch in his gut when the man lifted his head to meet David's gaze.

"Abiathar?" He'd seen the priest's son helping his father with the sacrifices on his numerous visits to the tabernacle. But one look at him now told David something was terribly wrong. "What happened?"

The young man released his grip on his knees and scooped up handfuls of ash and dust over his head to mingle with his already ash-coated hair and beard. It was then David noticed the torn robe and the priestly ephod lain out at his feet. The man sat unmoving, then slowly rocked back and forth, a soft moaning coming from his lips.

David glanced at Joab, who shrugged his confusion, his dark scowl telling David more than words could say. Handling a crisis, dealing with people, or knowing the right thing to do or say in any given situation demanded wisdom—wisdom deeper and greater than any he'd learned in the sheepfolds, when God had taught him to shepherd helpless animals. Now more than ever, he needed Adonai to teach him to shepherd people.

O Adonai, give me strength.

He lowered his body to the dust, knelt beside Abiathar, and placed a hand on his shoulder. The man's moaning grew to loud keening, and David felt his own tears of sympathy dampen his beard. When at last the young man's tears were spent, he wiped them from his cheeks with his sleeve and looked into David's eyes.

"Saul has murdered all the priests of Nob, all the women, all the children, my father, my mother, my brothers, my sisters. I alone escaped to tell you."

He'd guessed it was bad, but hearing the truth . . . Waves of shock rolled over him, stealing his breath. "What happened? Please tell me," David finally said.

Abiathar worked his jaw, but no words came out. David waited, patting the man's shoulder. "It's all right. Later, when time has passed, you can tell me—"

"No, I want to tell you now."

David nodded and sat back, hands clasped beneath his chin, giving Abiathar his full attention.

"Saul called for my father . . ." He averted his gaze and

coughed to clear his throat. "He demanded to know why my father had helped you when you came to him a year ago. My father defended you, so Saul told his guards to kill him and all of my relatives who were with him—the other priests." His chest lifted in a shuddering sigh. "They wouldn't do it. They knew the old king was out of his mind. So Saul turned to the man who had betrayed you and my father."

"Doeg the Edomite." Hadn't he known? David's stomach twisted. "How did you escape?"

"I ran away. I saw what Doeg intended to do, and I fled. Not a single guard followed me. Father urged me to go. I would have stayed with him . . ."

"You did the right thing." David studied the trees behind Abiathar, then at last met the young man's troubled gaze. "I knew when I saw Doeg there that day that he would surely tell Saul. I've caused the death of everyone in your father's house." He spread his hands in front of him in a gesture of supplication. "I'm sorry, Abiathar." David released a slow breath at the man's nod. He deserved the man's blame, not his forgiveness. "Stay with me, Abiathar. Do not fear. For he who seeks my life seeks your life, but you will be safe with me."

David rested his hand again on Abiathar's slumped shoulder and stood. He strode from the area, Joab on his heels. "See that he has everything he needs," he told Joab, then moved beyond him back to his tent.

Shepherding lambs was far less draining.

~21~

Two Years Later

After mounting his donkey and kicking its sides, Jonathan beat a swift path across the field to his father's house. Arrow prayers darted heavenward. The rumors couldn't be true. He tugged the animal's reins until it came to a stop, hopped off, and stalked toward the king's audience chamber.

"Jonathan, what are you doing here at this hour?"

"I could ask you the same question, Paltiel." He eyed his brother-in-law with marked disdain. It wasn't like him to show outward antagonism, but this man had defrauded his best friend, and despite the ensuing three years of Paltiel's marriage to his sister, the fact remained that nothing he could ever do would improve Jonathan's opinion of him.

"Did the king summon you?" Paltiel asked, matching strides with Jonathan's long ones.

"I don't need an invitation to meet with my father. I am heir apparent to the throne, in case you've forgotten."

"I hadn't. But everyone else thinks you have."

Jonathan came to an abrupt stop. He whirled to face his

nemesis. "I haven't forgotten my father's intentions. I've simply chosen the will of the Lord instead."

Not waiting for a reply, Jonathan took off down the darkened hall again, Paltiel on his heels.

"How can you be sure of the Lord's will, Jonathan? What if His plan is for you to be king? You're throwing it all away."

Jonathan ignored the barb and flung open the door to the audience chamber. His father sat on a raised dais, observing a flutist and a scantily clad dancer perform. The music came to a halt and the dancer's movements stilled as Jonathan stormed across the stone floor.

"Tell me it isn't true, Father."

Saul reached for a cluster of red grapes and plucked one, popping it into his mouth. His eyes held a curious gleam, and his mouth curved in an amused smile.

"Tell you what isn't true, Jonathan?"

Jonathan waved away the fruit a servant offered. "I heard you've called the troops to prepare for war—not against a mortal enemy like the Philistines or the Moabites, but against your own son-in-law, your faithful captain, David. What are you expecting to do, Father? Chase him completely out of Israel? You can't keep doing this."

"I can't? I, the anointed king of Israel, can't? I can do whatever I like, Jonathan."

"Not when you're breaking the laws of Adonai."

"I haven't broken any laws."

Did the man possess no remorse? "Father, killing the priests was not commanded by the Lord—"

"*Don't!* . . . Don't even speak of them." Saul's countenance darkened, and a brooding expression clouded his glowering eyes.

"Why? Because of the constant guilt you feel? Because the pain in your head and the misery you feel is worse since you killed eighty innocent people?" Jonathan regretted the ruthless way he flung the words, but the momentum of his anger propelled him forward. "And now you're going to gather the armies of Israel and run after David to kill him, when you have no good reason for doing so. You know David will one day be king. He is the Lord's anointed too, Father. I will be second to him. Why does this make you hate him? It is not David you fight against, Father." He rubbed one hand down the back of his neck. "You fight against God."

"Stop!" Saul's scream pierced Jonathan's heart. He'd said too much. But he didn't care. He watched his father clutch his temples and begin to moan. David wouldn't be there to soothe his restless soul. The household would endure a night of bitter agony—something Jonathan had done more times than he could count.

"Ohhh . . . Jonathan. Why do you torment me? I'm only doing this for you."

Any hint of pity Jonathan started to feel fled. "For me?" He fairly shouted the words. "You would kill David for me?" With one last glare at the man who had given him life, he turned on his heel and strode toward the door. When he reached the entrance, he paused and glanced over his shoulder.

"If you loved me, Father, you would let David live and allow Adonai's plan to unfold for both of us."

Ignoring the rising moans coming from the king, Jonathan stormed out of the palace.

※

"How will you know where to find David, my lord?" one of Jonathan's men asked. "Rumor has it he is staying in the stronghold near the Salt Sea."

"No, no, he left there over a month ago. Just last week the king got word of him living in the walled city of Keilah," another of his men said.

"Are you sure? I thought he went back to the wilderness after he left Keilah." This from a third of the five men accompanying him.

Jonathan listened to the banter with interest. Such confusion could be just the edge David needed to keep one step ahead of his father. He glanced into the shadowed face of the servant on his right and said, "I've no doubt David has been in all three places, some more than once. But my sources told me David's men were spotted in the Wilderness of Ziph. He is hiding in the forests there."

"What happens if your father catches up to us? He might kill you too, my lord," the second servant said.

"My father will never find David. God is with him."

Jonathan fell silent and urged the donkey forward. They would rest when he was closer to David and farther from the armies of a mad king.

❧

The brush of soft flesh on David's arm coaxed him from slumber. His new young wife lay sleeping, her golden brown hair cascading like a waterfall over her bare arms. She stirred, turning toward him. When she bumped against his bare chest, her dark, almond eyes flew open, and she reached for the blanket, tucking it around her.

David chuckled, his voice low. "Ahinoam, I'm your husband.

You don't need to act like a frightened doe every time you share my bed." His laughter deepened at the look of indignation flashing across her face.

"You scared me, that's all." She looked away from him, bright spots of crimson dotting her cheeks.

"Well, get used to it, beloved. You're not going to get rid of me that easily."

He reached for her, unable to still his amusement. The pale light of dawn began to filter through cracks in the ceiling of the cave. The rest of the camp would awaken soon, including the men and women sharing their small abode. Nevertheless, he wanted to feel the warmth of this delightful girl's arms around his neck, to taste her moist lips once more.

She giggled when his beard tickled her neck. He lifted the smooth strands of her hair and sifted them through his fingers. Had they truly been married only a month?

"David?" She interrupted his attempted kiss. "Will you still want me when you're king—when you take other wives?"

"Who said I'm going to take other wives?"

Ahinoam shrugged her slender shoulders, and David pulled her against his chest, kissing her forehead. "Don't worry about the future, my love. Who knows what tomorrow may bring? I only know I have you now. And you can count on that."

He moved closer, his lips brushing hers, when a hushed voice called from the mouth of the cave. "David? Are you awake?"

David lifted his head and gave her an impish grin. "It's only Joab. Maybe I can ignore him a bit."

She giggled again, accepting his kiss.

"David!" The whisper became louder, more insistent. "You have company."

Reluctantly David released Ahinoam and set her at arm's length. He stood, draped his tunic over his head, and secured his robe with a leather belt. He walked to the cave's mouth without a backward glance.

The pink sky illuminated the fire pit, and David saw a man sitting in the shadows. When David approached, he stood.

"Jonathan!" Sudden, memory-laden emotion made his knees weak. How was it possible? And yet here he was.

"David! Brother." Jonathan gripped David's shoulders, and as he accepted Jonathan's kiss of greeting, he could feel the prince's tears mingling with his own.

"How did you find me?" David motioned for Jonathan to sit, noting the dark circles under his eyes and the deep lines furrowing his brow.

"Men are always sending reports to my father. I have loyal sources in the palace who keep me informed."

"Please, my friend, tell me how it fares with you."

"I am well, all things considered. My father does not trust me." Jonathan accepted a flask of water from one of the women. He looked into its depth before taking a long drink. "He spends every waking moment trying to find you, David. He thinks he won't rest until you're dead. But he's mistaken."

"Don't be so sure, my friend."

Jonathan touched David's arm. "I have every right to be sure. You will be king over Israel, and I will be second to you. Even my father knows this." He looked back at the goatskin flask in his hand. "Don't be afraid. My father will not lay a hand on you."

"I wish I had your faith." David leaned forward, elbows on his knees, and stared into the fire.

"Didn't Samuel pour anointing oil on your head? Hasn't God brought you safely out of every difficulty thus far? The throne may not be yours yet, but it will be."

David nodded, his thoughts a jumbled mess. If only he shared Jonathan's confidence.

"This could be His time of preparing you, though." Jonathan studied him, then looked beyond David into the distance. "We don't always know why God allows trials. We do know He wants us to trust Him."

David focused on the smoldering fire. He knew that. Only a few months ago, when the prophet Gad had come to him at the stronghold, he'd heard the Lord's quiet voice whisper those very words.

Trust Me, David.

"When you come into power," Jonathan was saying, "promise me you will show kindness to my family—to me."

David's head came up. Was that defeat in Jonathan's expression? "You know I would never hurt you, my prince. Should God allow me to reign as king, you will be second to me."

"But if I die—"

"You're not going to die." The thought pierced David's heart.

"Nevertheless, *if* I die . . . please . . . protect Sarah and any children born to us. Promise me you will deal kindly with us."

David swallowed the thick knot in his throat. "You have my word, my prince. May God deal with me, be it ever so severely, if I ever betray this trust."

☙22☙

Four Years Later

"Nothing will ever be right again, Keziah." Michal picked up the golden-handled comb and started to sift through her tangled hair. Her father's moods had become worse since he'd ordered the deaths of the priests, and when Paltiel had joined Father's military campaigns against David, Jonathan had refused to set foot in their home again. She had taken to meeting him now and then in the gardens, in secret, but even then the tension and the memory of better times with David made their encounters uncomfortable at best. Sometimes the memories and the stress of it all made her want to scream . . . or weep.

"Let me do that, mistress." Keziah gently took the comb from Michal's clenched hands. Michal sank onto a low stool and placed the mirror on the table. She didn't care what she looked like anymore.

"One of the servants just returned from the palace, my lady," Keziah said in an obvious attempt to interest her.

"Mm-hm."

"There is news of David."

Michal's stomach did a familiar flip, but she forced indifference into her expression. "What news? And please spare me the long explanations."

Keziah lowered her head, and Michal suspected she'd hurt the girl's feelings, but her own nerves were stretched like taut bowstrings, nearing the breaking point. She gritted her teeth, trying to still her impatience.

"David has been seen in the Wilderness of Maon—"

"We know that already, Keziah. He's been there for months, if Jonathan's sources are accurate."

"Yes, but while he was there he met one of the wealthy landowners. He and his men protected the man's sheep, and when sheepshearing time rolled around, he requested payment for his services—"

"A reasonable action." Michal's interest piqued, and she waved her hand, urging the girl to continue.

"Yes, well, the man refused to pay any compensation, so they say David got ready to kill the landowner and all in his household."

Michal's heart sank. If David took vengeance, despite his right to receive payment for services rendered, the people of Israel would change their opinion of him. If he reacted, shedding innocent blood, the men in Israel's army would turn against him, the way so many had deserted her father when he killed the priests. The face of Benaiah, one of the few guards she had trusted, flashed in her thoughts. Had he fled to David as she'd urged him to?

She placed one hand over her stomach to control the uneasiness. If David killed innocent Israelites, he could never be king. And if he never became king—as Jonathan was convinced he would someday—then he would never be able to get her back, and she would never be queen.

"Did he? Kill the man, I mean?" The words were stiff and choked, and Michal chided herself for caring so much. David had deserted her, after all, and had taken another wife, if the rumors were true. Still, she couldn't deny the curious tug to her heart that news of him brought.

Keziah shook her head. "The man's wife stopped him."

"What do you mean?"

"The man was a fool, to hear the servants tell it. His wife knew it, and when she heard David was coming in anger, she loaded up donkeys with the provisions David had requested, and more so, and met him with the gift."

Michal's shoulders slumped, relief washing over her. "Oh, good." A tiny flame of hope flickered in her heart. Maybe David could still come for her after all.

"There's more, my lady."

Michal's heart jumped at her tone. "More?"

Keziah nodded. "The landowner died ten days after his wife gave David the food. When he died . . ." Keziah paused. Michal hated the girl's drawn-out storytelling at times like this—especially when she asked her not to. She could have her flogged for it, but she didn't have the heart. She held the girl's gaze instead, apprehensive of what she read in her expression.

"David asked the woman to be his wife after her husband died. She accepted."

The depression she'd awakened with could not match the sinking despair now dragging her soul to the pit. Why did David need another wife? And why could he accept someone

218

he didn't know but leave her, his true wife, to languish in the home of another man?

Like a drunkard, Michal staggered to the open window and clutched the ledge. Hot tears scalded her throat. Perhaps David didn't want her anymore. Could it be true? But he loved her! He'd doubled her father's gruesome dowry just to marry her.

David asked the woman to be his wife.

How could he do that?

He doesn't love you. If he did, he would have found a way to get you back.

She stood rigid, emotion draining from her. Was it true? If David didn't love her, why was she pining for him year after year? Why not make a home with Paltiel? At least he cared for her, however misguided his care might be.

With trembling fingers, Michal pushed the curtain aside and studied the ground below her bedroom window where David's feet had landed and he'd promised to come back for her so long ago. Not a day had gone by since she'd returned home that she didn't stare at this spot and beg God to bring him back to her.

Well, no more. If David could so easily cast her aside and embrace another—two others, in fact—she would toss her love for him away as well. Let Paltiel come home from this pursuit of David—and from this war, however futile, that her father thought he could win—and she would welcome him. Even if David one day became king, she was through with him.

PART III

Now the Philistines fought against Israel; and the men of Israel fled from before the Philistines, and fell slain on Mount Gilboa. Then the Philistines followed hard after Saul and his sons. And the Philistines killed Jonathan, Abinadab, and Malchishua, Saul's sons.

1 Samuel 31:1–2

So Saul, his three sons, his armorbearer, and all his men died together that same day.

1 Samuel 31:6

≈23≈

Three Years Later

The blackness of night gave way to a diffused yellow glow, and Paltiel lifted the flap and stepped into the morning dew. His sandals did little to protect his feet from the moist ground, but he ignored the cool tingle and walked slowly through the sleeping camp to the edge of the ridge. Word had it that David was among the Philistine warriors. A tremor swept through Paltiel, and he rubbed both arms, trying to calm his anxious nerves. What he wouldn't give to be the one to shoot the arrow straight through David's heart. If the fool could walk away and leave his wife just to save his own skin, he deserved to die. Besides, if David were dead, he could never reclaim Michal.

The thumping of someone walking toward Paltiel made him turn. At the sight of Saul, he bowed low.

"My king."

Saul approached the cliff, flanked by two sentries. He nodded at Paltiel, who stood and stepped back to give the king a better view. Saul glanced at the brightening sky, blinked twice, then squinted hard, his head moving from side to side. He stood still a moment, then staggered backward. The guards stopped him from falling.

"Are you all right, my lord?" Paltiel rushed closer and fell to one knee.

"How many?" Saul's hoarse voice croaked, and his arms were shaking.

Paltiel studied the king a moment, trying to understand the question. "How many what, my lord?"

Saul's whole body began to tremble now, and he struggled to speak. "How . . . many . . . men?"

Insight dawned, and Paltiel turned to examine the Philistine army once again. How many soldiers were there? A hundred thousand?

"I'm not sure, my lord," he said, turning to face the king. "Many thousands at least."

Saul's body shook like a leaf carried on the desert khamsin. Paltiel had never seen his monarch so visibly shaken. The image unnerved him, sending a flutter of fear to his own heart. An army couldn't follow if Saul wasn't prepared to lead. He looked over the sea of Israelite tents. If Saul didn't lead them, Jonathan would have to take up the cause. Assuming Jonathan had the strength to do so.

"What will we do?" Saul's voice, usually so strong and deep, now rose to a thin whine on the still morning air. "They're too strong for us."

"Surely not, my king. The Lord is with us."

Saul sank to the dew-drenched earth and buried his head in his hands. "Is He?" He looked at Paltiel. "I need to ask Him. Send for the priests, Paltiel. I need to find out if the Lord is with us."

Paltiel swallowed hard. "The priests are dead, my lord."

Had Saul forgotten his own order to kill them? The Urim and Thummim had been missing ever since as well, probably carted off by Abiathar, the one survivor unaccounted for. Had he taken them to David?

A sinking despair began to work its way into his gut.

Saul rocked back and forth, covering his face. He stopped abruptly. "A prophet then? Surely there is a prophet in the land."

Paltiel shrugged and averted his gaze. "I don't know, my lord. Samuel is dead, and I don't know what happened to the prophets he trained."

At the sound of quiet sobs, Paltiel turned, bewildered to find the king weeping. "I have to find out somehow. If He would just speak to me, in a dream perhaps." His gray eyes blinked to focus on Paltiel. "I can't fight this battle alone. I need the Lord to tell me what to do."

Paltiel stared at the man, suddenly aware of his silver-streaked hair and lined face. Saul was afraid. Unlike the fear he'd shown toward David, this fear, this terror, stripped him of his dignity and reduced him to a common man. Paltiel lifted his head and scanned the camp. The men were stirring. Soon everyone would know of Saul's ineptness, his paralyzed inability to lead. Paltiel had to do something.

His mind skipped over a handful of scenarios. They could pull back, retreat until the king could get a grip on himself. Or they could pose a challenge like the one when David fought Goliath. Perhaps a select few could fight for the whole. He glanced at the king, who was still rocking back and forth like a scared child. No, they needed something more.

With tentative steps he backed away from Saul and looked once again at the imposing Philistine army flanking the opposite ridge. Red-feathered helmets now dotted the landscape. The camp was waking. Would they surge forward to fight today?

Paltiel impatiently tapped his foot. He had to figure out a plan. If God wouldn't answer the king's pleas, there must be some other way to guess the future, even if it wasn't true, to bring some sort of peace to the man.

"Find me a woman who is a medium, that I may go to her and inquire of her." Saul's whimpering voice carried to Paltiel's ears. He turned in disbelief to face the king. After David had left Israel a year and a half ago to live among the Philistines, Saul had banished all mediums and spiritists, when the demons taunting him could no longer be appeased. Michal had told him her father thought it would somehow bring him relief, grant him favor in God's eyes. Paltiel released a frustrated breath. Did Saul honestly think the Lord would somehow bless him and now speak to him through a medium?

"There is such a woman in En Dor, my lord," one of the servants said.

"Take me there." Saul's voice sounded surer now, and he stood, his shaking limbs growing steadier as he walked toward Paltiel. "You will accompany me." Paltiel squirmed under the scrutiny.

"But, my lord, En Dor is in Philistine territory. What if they see us?"

Saul's dark eyes sparked with sudden purpose. "We'll go at night and disguise ourselves."

"I could take you there, my lord," one of the guards said. A sinister feeling slithered down Paltiel's spine at the guard's empty, soulless look. Mediums practiced witchcraft, something Paltiel wanted nothing to do with.

"Good," Saul said, smiling now. "You can accompany me and my son-in-law."

"Perhaps someone else could go, my lord." Paltiel hated his cowardly tone, but the mission was foolish. How would he ever explain to Michal what he'd done?

The glowing embers of Saul's eyes grew cold, and he stared immovably at Paltiel. "Fine!" He barked the words and whirled about. "Find another servant," he said to the guard, "one more worthy to go with me. We'll leave at dusk for En Dor."

Paltiel's stomach twisted in a hard knot, while at the same time relief loosened his taut shoulders. At least he wouldn't be party to something so ridiculous. And yet the whole thing troubled him. Saul shouldn't be going at all. Perhaps if he could convince Jonathan to lead the army, none of this would be necessary. He released a slow sigh. Jonathan could barely tolerate him. Abner then? His mind whirled. No, Jonathan was the heir. Whether the man liked him or not, he must be told. There must be something they could do.

❦

Not a single star dotted the clouded heavens, though Jonathan searched for one, praying for some sign of God's light to dawn in his soul. But his yearnings went unheeded, and his heart ached. He paced slowly in front of his tent, intermittently stroking his beard, then paused to gaze north past the Philistine encampment at Shunem toward the town of En Dor. If his father made it there, going and coming past the thousands of Philistine warriors, he was still placing himself in the hands of an evil woman—a witch of all things!

They wouldn't be in this mess if his father had trusted Adonai and obeyed His word long ago. David wouldn't be fighting against them, and he, Jonathan, would be planning to succeed his father to Israel's throne.

Jonathan rubbed the back of his neck, trying to ward off a horrible headache. He didn't care, really. Being king had always been his father's ambition for him, not his. David's coming on the scene had almost been a relief.

His restless feet threaded their way through the camp to the place where Saul would likely come the moment he returned. He twisted the belt at his waist. How much longer? Why had he allowed his father to go through with this? His own aversion to Paltiel had caused him to nearly block his ears to the man's impassioned plea. Still, what would happen if Saul were captured and killed along the way to or from En Dor?

Once, long ago, Jonathan could have taken charge and led the armies to victory—in the days when he knew without a doubt the Lord was with him. But he couldn't be sure of that now.

The admission made the back of his neck throb, and Jonathan stretched and tipped his head from side to side, hoping for some relief. He looked north again and squinted. There, stumbling closer in the inky darkness, were three men. Jonathan drew a deep breath and took two steps toward them. Moments later, his father fell in a heap at his feet, weeping.

Jonathan looked at the ashen faces of the two sentries who had accompanied Saul, his heart sinking to his toes. "What happened?"

One of the guards just shook his head, the whites of his eyes visible in the light of the moon. The other spoke. "Samuel spoke with him." The words were blunt and quick as though he longed to be rid of them.

"Samuel's dead," Jonathan said. His headache intensified. How could a dead man speak?

"The woman got his spirit to come up, and he spoke to your father."

Saul's weeping quieted, and he lifted his hooded head to look into Jonathan's eyes. In that instant Jonathan saw straight through to his father's soul.

Saul was going to die.

That was it, wasn't it? Samuel had predicted his father's imminent death.

The fear in his father's gaze drifted to something akin to sadness during the silent exchange, and Jonathan's strength evaporated like mist before sunrise.

They were both going to die.

He swallowed a leaden lump in his throat. Hadn't he realized it all along? Hadn't he felt it in the hot wind and known it when he held Sarah and Mephibosheth the day they left for war?

He stumbled away from the small group of men, then groped his way to the edge of the rise overlooking the enemies who would be his undoing.

Are you out there, David? Will yours be the arrow that pierces my heart? Oh, God, may it never be!

He sank to his knees and buried his face in his hands. He didn't want to die. He wanted to live to hold his wife and son again, to watch Mephibosheth grow to manhood, to bless his grandchildren on his knees. Unshed tears threatened to choke him.

Should he run away to save his life?

Silent sobs racked his body, draining the last of his energy, even as he wrestled with his tormented thoughts. He slowly lifted his head to gaze once more at the heavens, tears blurring his vision. He blinked and brushed them away. His heart was warmed by the sight of a million stars, which were hidden from him moments ago, now winking like distant flames across the blackest sky he'd ever seen.

Are You trying to tell me something, Lord?

Peace settled over him, diffusing his last fragment of fear. God had a plan, and somehow, though it might mean the end of his earthly life, he was part of God's intended design. Pictures of Sarah and Mephibosheth flashed in his mind again, but the peace remained. And then he remembered his covenant with David.

David would soon be king. And David would take care of his family. Hadn't he promised as much? A half smile curved his mouth, his heart soaring with the stars. God would not abandon him to the grave. God still cared for his soul. He raised his arms heavenward and let the words of David play a melody through his thoughts.

My soul, wait silently for God alone, for my expectation is from Him. He only is my rock and my salvation. He is my defense; I will not be moved. In God is my salvation and my glory; the rock of my strength and my refuge is in God.

Jonathan bent his face to the dust and worshiped.

❦24❦

"The Philistines are coming! Hurry, grab what you can and come to the palace. We've got to get out of Gibeah." Joash barked the orders, stomping past Michal, where she sat embroidering a tunic. He shouted to the servants, then came back to face Michal.

"My lady, you must hurry. Gather what you need and come with me."

Michal's heart slammed against her chest, and her feet felt like millstones stuck to the wooden floor. She grabbed the front of Joash's robe. "What are you talking about? How can the Philistines be coming? We're supposed to be defeating them!"

Joash shook his head. "Not this time, mistress. If what I'm hearing is true, your father and brothers are dead, and the Philistine army is headed this way to capture as many cities as they can. Their target is Gibeah." He placed one hand over hers to uncurl her fingers from his robe and urge her along, but she tightened her grip.

"What about Paltiel? What's happened to my husband?"

Joash shrugged. "I haven't heard. Most of the casualties

will take a while to discover. The important thing is, Israel is without a king and without an heir."

The impact of Joash's words finally registered. Her father and brothers were dead? How was that possible? *Jonathan!* A swift, sharp pain filled her. Hadn't she sensed it in the look of resignation he'd given her at his departure for war? And Father. Was he finally at rest? Or did the demons torment him even in Sheol?

Joash managed to release her fingers from his robe and shook her arm. "We've got to go now, Michal."

Her clouded eyes cleared at the sound of her name, and she shoved her grief aside and dove into action. "Keziah, help me!" The young woman came running, and the two of them began stuffing clothing and essential items into baskets.

Joash moved to the door, then threw a parting word over his shoulder. "Be at the palace before the sundial moves to the next mark. Don't delay."

Michal ran from shelf to cupboard, filling the last basket with food. "Let's go."

A few paces from the closed door, Michal took a parting look at the home she had shared with two different men for the past eleven years of her life. What would become of this place that housed so many memories? So many unfulfilled dreams.

She felt Keziah's hand on her shoulder and whipped around to run with her maid toward the palace.

❧

Michal felt a measure of relief the moment she stepped under the gate of her father's fortress. Surely the strong stone walls could keep out the advancing Philistine army. Besides, a vast group of weary men carrying tents and supplies couldn't travel that quickly, could they? On the other hand, it stood to reason that killing Israel's king and his heirs had energized them—the way David's slaying of Goliath that long-ago day had turned her father's army from weak-kneed women into ardent warriors.

"Michal! Help me get the boys into the cart. Adriel's bringing Merab." Ahinoam's barked order brought Michal's wandering thoughts to the present. Michal stared at her mother, who carried two-year-old Jacob with one hand and held firmly to four-year-old Reuben with the other. She had aged twenty years since Michal had seen her two days ago. Michal rushed to her side, took Jacob from her arms, and grasped Reuben's hand.

"Where are the others?" Michal lugged Jacob and Reuben toward the cart, her mother at her side.

"Keziah, go get Merab's older boys. Merab's maid has baby Joel." Keziah hurried away. Michal lifted Jacob into the cart and looked into her mother's dull eyes.

"Why can't we stay here? The walls will protect us."

"Don't be ridiculous, Michal. Your father is dead. Do you want to join him?"

Michal turned her attention to Reuben and away from her mother's biting words. She hoisted the wide-eyed child into the cart next to his brother. In the distance, a piercing scream split the air. A mournful wail followed. What on earth . . . ?

Michal watched Joash drop a sack of grain into the cart and run toward the wailing sound. What other awful thing could possibly happen?

After settling Reuben into the straw-laden cart, Michal commanded the two children to scoot to the front and be still. Keziah came up behind them with Merab's two oldest sons, followed by Merab's maid carrying the infant.

"Malchi, Benni, climb in with your brothers." Ahinoam's tone was stern again, and Michal noted the rigid set to her jaw. The two boys scrambled over the side of the cart as if this were some grand adventure. "Michal, you get in with the children, and I'll hand you the baby. My old bones will not be able to take riding in a cart."

Michal started to protest but was interrupted by Rizpah, her father's concubine. "Can we ride with you, Michal?" The woman's sunken eyes bespoke a lengthy lack of sleep. She turned to Ahinoam. "Is that all right with you, my lady?"

Startled, Ahinoam averted her gaze. There was no love lost between the two rivals for her father's affections. Rizpah's humility took Michal completely by surprise. But her mother's nod of acquiescence stunned her more. "You have to ride somewhere."

Michal lifted one leg and began to climb into the cart when the mournful wail that had sent Joash running grew closer. She lowered her foot and whirled around. The sight sent her heart into her throat.

Mephibosheth!

She raced over to Joash, then noticed Sarah and her maid clinging to his sides. The guard carried Jonathan's limp son in his arms. The boy's legs were grotesquely misshapen, twisted in an unnatural way.

"What happened? Is he dead?" Michal's hand trembled as she reached to touch the boy's curly dark head.

Sarah stood silently weeping, one hand on her son's arm, and her maid's stricken, dejected look caught Michal's curiosity.

"What happened?" she asked again.

"I dropped him!" Sarah's maid wailed. "I was running . . . He'd just awakened from a nap . . . I didn't see the flowerpot . . ." She burst into tears. "I'm so sorry. I should have let him walk on his own. It's all my fault."

Joash carried the boy past Michal and laid him in the wagon, which was in front of the cart Michal would ride in with Merab's boys. Sarah climbed in and knelt at the boy's side, her tears dripping onto his brown tunic.

Michal stepped to the side of the cart and said, "Maybe someone can straighten his legs. Marta was always good at that. Surely someone can help." The memory of the family's cook brought a reminiscent ache to Michal's heart. Marta had ensured the healing of her own injured foot ten years before. If she were still alive, she would have done the same for Jonathan's small son.

Sarah lifted damp eyes to meet Michal's gaze. "He's all I have left." She turned back to her son without another word.

The command to move out came from Joash's lips. Michal ran back to the cart holding Merab's boys, settled herself among the matted straw, and took the baby from Merab's maid. Ahinoam sat on a separate donkey, and the bedraggled group made its way slowly through the gate.

"Where's Merab, Mother? We can't leave her here," Michal said.

"Adriel is with her at the back of the line. They must move more slowly because of her condition. If we get separated, she wanted the boys to be safe."

Michal's gaze swept the crowd of family and servants squeezed together, fighting panic in their hurry to escape an unknown fate. She spotted Adriel's head in the distance and could only imagine Merab lying in the cart he was driving. The sound of an infant sucking its thumb turned Michal's head to the baby in her arms. What was she supposed to do when the child wanted to eat? She'd never birthed or nursed a baby. It was a trial she bore with continual regret. Once in a while she could forget the yearning for a son, when she was in a state of dreamless sleep. But in her waking hours, not a day passed that her empty arms didn't long to be filled.

Was this God's punishment for marrying Paltiel? Would she remain forever barren because she'd scorned her vows as David's wife? She stroked the baby's downy cheek and fought tears. Where were these thoughts coming from? Bitter grief sliced through her as the wagon jostled her from side to side. She had grown to love Paltiel. But what if he too was dead along with her father?

Jonathan's face floated before her eyes, his gentle, reassuring voice whispering in her memory. *Trust in the Lord, Michal. Whatever happens, wait for Him.*

Wait for Him? Trust? How was she supposed to trust when everything she loved kept slipping through her fingers like sifted grain? She dug her nails into the folds of the baby's blanket and held Merab's infant son close to her wet cheek.

❧❦

"Do you think they got the message, Abner? Will our families be waiting at Bahurim when we get there?" Paltiel dragged one exhausted leg behind the other, trying to keep up with the brawny commander of Israel's defeated forces.

"They'll be moving slow with the women and children, but if the runner got to them, they'll go to Bahurim." Abner continued at a measured trot but finally slowed when Paltiel doubled over and sank to his knees in the dirt. He walked over to the man. "What's the matter with you, Soldier? You're younger than I am. Can't you keep up?"

Paltiel heaved a deep sigh, holding his stomach. "Guess not."

Abner placed one hand on his shoulder. "Catch your breath then. I'll wait." He walked to the side of the path and sat on a tree stump.

Paltiel's breathing slowed, and he sat back on his heels, placing both hands on his knees. When his wind returned, he rubbed one hand over his haggard, sweaty face. "What are we going to do with all of them gone?"

Abner wiped his palms along his bloodstained tunic. "We still have Ishbosheth. If we can get the people to rally around him, we can keep the kingdom together."

Paltiel's stomach twisted in a knot of fear, the realization of their plight rocking him. Ishbosheth might be of Saul's blood, but he was not capable of running a kingdom. Israel needed a strong king, one who could unite the disjointed twelve tribes. One who could defeat their enemies. One whom the people already hailed a hero.

David.

Hadn't God promised him the kingdom someday? Jonathan had repeatedly reminded his father of that fact every time one of their efforts to capture the man had failed. Every time David had turned an opportunity to kill the old king into a mission of compassion and forgiveness. Every time David had acted more like a king than Saul did.

"The people might prefer another." Paltiel looked into Abner's hard features. "What will you do if they turn to him?"

"You mean David."

"Yes."

"It's possible."

"So how will you keep him from taking over the kingdom? Especially if God is with him?" Paltiel sat back in the dirt, defeat and fear coursing through him.

Abner's unyielding gaze reminded him of Saul. "You of all people should know we can't let that happen. Unless you want to lose your wife the moment he takes the throne."

The words stung like a hand slapped across flesh. He knew better than anyone that he was living with another man's wife in an unlawful union. But he couldn't lose her. Not now. Not ever. He loved her. He would rather die first.

"We can't let him control Israel." Paltiel looked at Abner with an affirmative nod. "I'll do whatever it takes to help you keep David from becoming king."

≈25≈

"Paltiel! Oh, tell me it's really you." Tears of exhaustion covered Michal's face the moment the wagons came to a stop in Bahurim three days later. She squinted through a filmy haze at her battered husband, not certain whether to trust her vision.

"Michal?" The emotion-choked voice of the man she had grown to care for sounded distant, but in two strides he stood at her side, leaned over the cart, and pulled her to him.

His kiss awakened her deadened nerves, and when he released her, she sat back, out of breath. She looked around at the children clamoring for her attention, then back at Paltiel. Heat filled her cheeks at the bold look in his eyes.

"Get these children settled with their mother." He whispered the command as his fingers brushed the tears from her wet cheek. "I need you."

"I can't."

"What do you mean, you can't? Just do it, Michal."

Michal swallowed hard. Sometimes Paltiel demanded too much.

"Please, Paltiel, I have to take care of them. Merab isn't well, you know, and the journey has sent her into early labor. Mother is worried about her."

Paltiel squeezed her arm gently and bent to kiss her cheek. "Put them to bed then. I'll meet you on the roof."

❧❧

After tucking the children safely into bed some time later, Michal walked through the main part of the house. The small estate belonged to Shimei, a distant cousin of her father's—a man with no love for David. He'd welcomed them with open arms, giving them full use of the place, then discreetly kept his distance. She should be grateful that anyone would even take them in, but she didn't want to be here, didn't want to be faced with living as a fugitive.

She came to the end of the hall and stopped before entering the large, open courtyard. Twin palm trees graced the opening, and potted anemones in varying shades added a splash of color to the gray brick walkway and limestone benches of the court.

"How much damage do you think the Philistines will do?" Ishbosheth's timid voice caught Michal's attention, and she leaned against the wall, listening.

"Enough that it will take us a while to set them to flight again," Abner said, his tone weary.

Michal peered around the palm tree and studied the faces outlined in the torchlight. The three men looked unutterably weary, their fatigue matching her own. She stumbled toward the small group and settled next to Paltiel, resting her head on his shoulder.

"Just getting the army to come out for the fight could take

months," Paltiel said, drawing Michal closer in a comforting embrace. "The way they scattered after Saul fell . . . I never saw such chaos."

"Was David there?" Michal said without thinking.

"Does it matter?" Undeniable hurt laced Paltiel's words.

Somehow it did. "I suppose not," Michal said, measuring her words. "I was just curious."

"It's a good question, Michal," Abner said, shifting on the bench. "If David had been there fighting against Israel, we'd have enough ammunition against him to keep him from ever gaining the kingdom. As it is, he wasn't there at all. Not defending or opposing. Which makes our job all the more difficult."

"But not impossible," Paltiel insisted.

"Do you really think I'd make a good king?" Ishbosheth's uncertainty, reflected in his childlike tone, made Michal uncomfortable. Her brother was not capable of running a kingdom. Anyone giving him more than a cursory glance would know this.

"You'll do fine, Ishbosheth. Just do as I tell you and you'll be all right," Abner said, reaching over to pat the man on the arm.

"I'm not dumb, you know." He plucked a flower from one of the pots beside the bench and began to twist it between his fingers. "People think I'm dumb, but I'm not. I'll make a good king—better than Father, 'cause I don't worship idols." He mumbled the words to himself, and Michal lifted her head to glance from Paltiel to Abner. Ishby had been religious about not worshiping idols, but that didn't make him a qualified candidate for king. Were they really going to go

241

through with this? But of course they had to if they wanted to keep David from the throne.

She rose from her seat and left the courtyard, climbing to the small guest room on the roof to await Paltiel. Let them discuss their ridiculous plans. Maybe she could block out all of the nonsense and fall asleep before Paltiel joined her.

※※

The coarse goat-hair blanket brushed against David's cheek, its rough surface knocking some of the dust from his beard. The action woke him from a light sleep, and he tossed the black garment from him in a fit of annoyance. He hadn't intended to doze. But grief had forced sleep to overtake him. A man could only shed so many tears.

He rolled onto his back, clasped both hands behind his head, and stared at the tent ceiling. His dry eyes, swollen from crying on and off for seven days, ached to close. He squeezed them shut, trying to block the memory of that horrible day.

Storm clouds on the horizon should have warned him, did in fact send a shot of wariness through his soul. But whether he knew it then or the moment he saw the lone runner enter their burned-out village out of breath, David sensed the day would change his life forever.

He rolled onto his side and thrust one arm over his head, then flipped back over and stared at the opposite wall. Through the thin curtain separating his quarters from that of his wives, David could hear the women's steady breathing. Abigail had wanted to comfort him, but he needed time alone. Time to think.

Saul and Jonathan were dead.

Death. There was such finality to that word. His nemesis

would never again torment him. And his friend would never again bring him comfort. Why did he have to lose them both?

Certain that sleep would not return, David pushed up from the earthen floor and ducked under the tent flap into the starlit night. Ziklag, his Philistine home for the past year and a half, still carried the scent of ash, evidence of the Amalekite invasion that had nearly cost him the lives of his wives and the families of his entire retinue. Thank the Lord they didn't have to endure yet another loss.

He walked the length of the camp, past the rows of tents housing his men and their families. In the center of the makeshift town, guards sat before a dwindling fire. He recognized Benaiah, former guard of King Saul, now his own loyal officer.

"Couldn't sleep, Captain?" Benaiah asked. David sat back on his heels, poking the fire with a nearby stick.

"Too much to think about, Benaiah. So many questions slip through my thoughts." He scratched a sudden itch along the back of his neck and lifted his sooty hair away from his head. A dip in the river would refresh him. After seven days it was time.

"I suppose you've heard the talk of making you king."

David glanced at the burly bodyguard, who shifted his tall frame on a log placed before the fire. "Some. But I'm not sure it's the Lord's time."

"The camp is overflowing with men from Israel and Judah pledging allegiance to you. What more evidence do you need, my lord?"

David studied the resurging flames, fascinated by the orange and yellow tongues licking the charred logs. "I'll inquire of the Lord, Benaiah. Then I'll know."

Silence passed between them, and David's thoughts turned to Yahweh.

Show me Your will, O Lord. Guide my steps. He glanced up at the glittering sky and breathed deeply. *Let me know if Your time has come to grant me the kingdom.*

❦

Muted shadows of a pale pink dawn awakened David from his cramped position before the fire. Somehow the place where he'd heard the news of Jonathan's death brought him a measure of comfort. Peace settled over him, and he sensed this day would be different, despite his recent untold grief.

He rose before the women stirred to start the morning meal, slipped into his tent for a fresh tunic, and walked the short distance to the river. After a brisk scrub that rinsed the dust and ashes from his hair and beard, he stepped onto the shore and donned the clean tunic Abigail had fashioned for him. He glanced down at the intricate design of palm leaves etched in green and the line of purple and gold trimming the edges. The design made him pause. His fingers traced the delicate embroidery. This was no ordinary tunic. This pattern signified royalty and months of intricate work.

He remembered Abigail's words to him soon after he had taken her as his wife. "The Lord has chosen you to be king, David. You must have a wardrobe fitting your future position."

So this was what she had been up to. All those times when he'd seen her sitting with the women, stitching—forever stitching. She was making this kingly tunic for him. Was it possible

. . . could she have . . . ? He climbed the steep bank and trudged the short path to Ziklag, his heart picking up speed.

"Good morning, Captain!" Joab called from across the street.

"Yes, good morning, my lord," another man, one of the tribal leaders, called out.

David waved to both men and a group of other well-wishers, nodding and smiling before ducking into his tent.

"Abigail?"

Silence. He peeked into the women's quarters. Empty. They were probably off getting water or starting to prepare the morning meal. He stuck his head under the tent flap.

"Abigail!" If she were within earshot, she would surely hear him this time.

"Yes, my lord?" She came running from the fire pit.

"Come here." He lifted the flap for her and pulled her into his quarters.

Her thick chestnut-brown hair was pulled away from her face and tucked under a pale blue scarf, and her face and hands were streaked with flour. Her inky eyes held a fresh sparkle, and her full mouth dipped in concern, her breath coming fast from running.

"What is it? Is something wrong, my lord?"

"This." David touched one hand to the ornamented tunic. "This is what you were working on, isn't it?"

She nodded, eyes downcast. "You don't like it."

He looked at her. How could she think that? "Of course I like it. I just wondered if there was a robe to match."

She met his gaze, and her bright smile revealed evenly matched white teeth. "Oh yes, my lord. Let me get it." Before he could respond, she walked to the other side of the tent to

245

her sleeping mat and pulled a folded object from a wicker basket. He followed at her heels, and as she whirled to face him, she nearly bumped into him. He caught her elbow, and she gave him an awkward smile.

"I finished it two nights ago. I was going to give it to you sooner, but . . ."—she unfolded the purple fabric as she spoke— "the timing didn't seem appropriate."

David took the ornamented, kingly robe from her out-stretched hands and studied every line in the dim light. Some-where, deep within his soul, he knew. Abigail's work symbol-ized God's timing. And now that Saul was dead, the time was right.

He slipped his arms through the wide sleeves and allowed Abigail to wrap the golden sash around his waist. She hurried to another basket on the tent floor along the center divider and pulled a bronze mirror from its depths.

"It's hard to see in this light. Perhaps you'd rather step into the sunshine?" she asked, her shy gaze meeting his.

He studied his reflection for a long moment, then laid the mirror on the ground, pulling her into his arms. "Thank you," he whispered, his throat tight. "I don't know how you knew to make such fine garments, but . . . thank you." He kissed the sweet moistness of her parted lips.

The kiss lasted longer than he intended, but he couldn't pull away from the security of her arms. Somehow he knew that once he released her, his life course would take a turn, and his relationships with his men and his wives would be forever altered.

"But don't you think wearing this now is a bit presumptu-ous? No one has declared me king yet." He still held her close, letting her head rest against his chest.

She tilted her head to gaze at him. "You could wear the tunic and your captain's robe. I mended and washed the one you tore a week ago. A little royalty mixed with humility should be a good mix, my lord."

David released a slow breath, then kissed her again. "You are always so wise, my love." He brushed flour from her cheek with his thumb. "Thank you."

She helped him slip the royal robe from his arms and then folded it, setting it aside for a better day.

"You're welcome, my lord." She patted the garment lovingly and stood facing him.

His hands cupped her shoulders, emotion overwhelming him as he studied the depths of her gaze. What a blessing from the Lord this woman had been. First she had kept his hand from slaying innocent men. Then she somehow managed to keep the kidnapped women from panicking when he was not around to protect them. And now she was preparing for his future reign without being asked, humbly giving of herself to him.

Would Michal have done the same?

The thought troubled him. Guilt mixed with anger every time he thought of his first wife—his heart's first love. He should have gone back for her. And she should have waited for him.

David closed his eyes, hoping the action would block the tormenting guilt from his mind. He slipped one arm around Abigail's shoulders, walked her to the tent door, and placed another tender kiss on her cheek. "Wait for me tonight, my love."

"Yes, my lord." She gave him an appreciative smile and ducked under the flap, leaving David alone.

☙26❧

The earth shook. A stampede of horses grew closer. Dust billowed, filling the air, choking her.

Get away. Run, Michal, run!

Thunder split the sky. Fists pounded on the door. Violent screams.

Hurry, Michal!

They were coming for her.

Her breath came in short spurts, like the snap of a distant drum before an army marched off to war. She dragged for air. *Oh, help me!*

A hand on her arm. Gentle shaking.

"Michal, wake up! Do you hear me? Wake up, I say." Paltiel gripped her elbow, and Michal sat upright, eyes wary, fear constricting every muscle.

"Where am I?"

"In Bahurim, with me," Paltiel said softly against her cheek.

Michal blinked, trying to clear her vision. Below them she heard what sounded like muffled screams. "What was that?" Her heart refused to slow its destructive pace.

"Calm down, Michal. You had a bad dream. It's all right now." Paltiel's fingers stroked her bare arm. "Everything will be all right."

The muffled scream grew in intensity, doubling Michal's fear. "Then what is that?" she demanded. In one leap she jumped from the sleeping mat and strode to the door. If he wouldn't tell her, she would find out on her own.

"Michal, wait!" He dogged her heels, but she hurried down the steps ahead of him. The screams dwindled to an agonized groan.

Merab!

She darted across the courtyard to the room occupied by Merab and Adriel. Merab had spent the week since they'd come to Bahurim in bed, her labor pains stopping and starting, leaving her exhausted and weak. Had the baby finally come and not survived? The thought made Michal's stomach dip in dread. She slowed at her mother's approach.

"Michal. Oh, my dear, whatever will we do?" Ahinoam collapsed into Michal's arms. Unsteady from her jarred awakening, Michal nearly lost her balance, but Paltiel's hands supported her. She offered him a grateful look, then focused on her mother.

"What are you talking about, Mother? What's wrong with Merab?"

Ahinoam recovered a small sense of dignity and stepped back, resting one hand against her lined cheek. "You must come and help, Michal. I think we're losing her."

"What!" Michal burst through the closed door, startled to see Adriel at Merab's side, weeping. Had the screams and groans come from him? She studied Merab's pallid face in the lamplight. Her breathing was almost imperceptible, and all color had drained from her once rosy face. The bed where she lay was blood soaked.

Adriel lifted stricken eyes to meet her gaze, confirming in his look what her heart told her was true. Merab was dying.

Oh, God, not Merab. Not now.

Michal felt her body propelled forward almost against her will, and she knelt at Merab's side opposite Adriel. She wrapped both hands around Merab's cold, limp one and leaned forward to kiss her cheek.

"Oh, Merab. Don't leave me. Please . . . don't you know how much I need you?" Amazing how true the words had become over the years since David. She studied Merab's pale face.

The woman's eyelids fluttered, then opened a crack. She gave Michal a tired smile, and her words came slowly. "You always wanted children, Michal. Sometimes they . . . can be . . . the death of you."

Michal blinked hard against a rush of tears. "No! You can heal. You just need time." She squeezed Merab's hand.

"Take care . . . of my sons, Michal . . . for Adriel." Merab managed the last words through parched gray lips before sinking back against the mat, her forehead bathed in sweat. The effort to speak had weakened her further, and Michal held back the words she wanted to say, lest they exhaust her sister more.

She dipped a cloth in tepid water and placed it on Merab's forehead, her gaze catching Adriel's bent head buried against her sister's limp arm. Merab couldn't die.

Oh, God, please don't let her die.

Bitter tears coursed down Michal's damp cheeks, and she

stifled the urge to cry out, to raise her fist into the air and scream at God, if He was even listening.

A crackling rattle sounded in Merab's throat.

"Oh no! I told you we were losing her. Oh, baby!" Ahinoam rushed forward, throwing herself across Merab's still form.

"Oh, God . . . Merab, I love you!" Adriel's deep voice rose above her mother's clamoring, and he leaned over his wife, tears flowing, to kiss her cheek.

Michal stared at the two of them, unable to move or speak. She felt Paltiel's hand on her shoulder and glanced up at him.

She heard the death rattle once, then twice, until at last Merab's body jerked a final time, then stilled. Almost immediately her mother broke into a loud wail, and Adriel's moans carried through the household, waking any lingering sleepers. Michal looked on, longing to weep and cry out along with them, but no sound would escape her tightened throat. She turned away from Paltiel's concerned look and ran out of the room.

✺

"This is the place, my lord." Benaiah, head of David's personal guard, pulled his animal up beside David's and pointed to a spacious house, which was built atop a small rise surrounded by a lush olive grove on one side and terraced gardens on the other. "A fitting place for a king, don't you think?"

David took in the scene. He spotted a lone figure peek through one of the windows, then disappear behind a curtain, and a moment later burst through the front door. A short, balding, smiling man hurried down the cobbled steps as quickly as his portly legs would allow. He came to a stop at

David's side and bowed to the ground three times, touching his forehead to the earth.

"Welcome, my lord. My name is Hushai the Archite. I bid you welcome to Hebron."

David swung his leg over his donkey's side and hopped to the ground. He stepped forward and kissed Hushai on both cheeks. "Thank you, Hushai."

The man took a step back as though he felt he did not deserve such equal treatment. He recovered his dignity with a short laugh. "Yes, well, you are welcome, my lord. Please, won't you come in and rest yourself? See the place the elders of Judah have been preparing for you."

David nodded to Benaiah, and the two followed Hushai to the house.

"When you ran away from Saul and it became apparent that God would not allow the old king to harm you, your brethren from Judah decided to begin building a home for you. They believed, as many in Israel have, that you were chosen by the Most High to one day be king. So we all began giving what we could to provide the materials to build you a house to rule from, when the time came." They stepped over the threshold of the house into a spacious room.

Hushai motioned them forward and pushed open heavy oak doors, revealing a large audience chamber with a raised dais at one end. David glanced around at the cheery place with open windows spilling the midafternoon light across the wooden floor. A sense of humility and awe washed over him.

"This is more than I could have asked for or dreamed of, Hushai. But how could you all have known such a thing? How would you know I would want many windows and wooden floors, of all things?"

Hushai waddled up to David and smiled. "The men of Judah knew I was experienced in architecture. I had been to Saul's palace—was friends of the man who designed that dreary place. Saul had a history of dark moods, you know. He never really trusted anyone. I think he built a fortress to keep his enemies out. Too bad he never realized his worst enemy was coming from within." He looked at David. "I surmised that you would want your home to be the exact opposite of the man who tried to kill you."

David lifted his callused fingers to stroke the soft hairs of his beard, studying the remarkable man the Lord had placed before him. "You have much wisdom, Hushai." He placed one hand on the man's arm. "Thank you."

Hushai's face flushed a deep shade of crimson, and he lowered his head. "Oh, it is nothing, my lord. But I do appreciate the compliment." He glanced up, his countenance suddenly brightening. "Would you like to see the rest of the place?"

David stifled the urge to chuckle. He already liked this man. "Indeed," he said, patting Hushai on the back. "Lead the way."

❧❧

Michal's back ached as she pressed her palm into the mortar, pushing down on the rough stone pestle. Soft grains of wheat sat in a clay bowl beside her, and Michal glanced at the rising pile of flour and sighed. She should be sipping lemon tea or baking sweet cakes in her own kitchen rather than killing herself with labor usually relegated to servants.

"Do you want me to do some of that now, mistress?" Keziah asked from her seat beside Michal. She moved a clay sieve back and forth, letting the crushed hulls separate from the grain. "You look like you could use a break."

Michal leaned back against the stone bench, brushed stray hairs from her face, and smiled grimly. "Concentrating on this keeps my mind off other things. It's easier to face pain in my body than pain in my heart." She pushed the sleeves of her robe back up her arms and pressed both hands against her aching back, straightening. The week since they had laid Merab and her unborn child in the burial cave seemed like an eternity ago, and at the same time impossible to have happened. Maybe if she kept herself busy, she could continue to ignore the grief dogging her.

The distant rumble of a horse's hooves made her tense. She exchanged glances with Keziah.

"Who would be coming so fast?" Keziah asked.

Michal stood and walked through the courtyard to the front of the house. She glimpsed Paltiel, Abner, and Adriel walking out to the road to meet the lone horseman. Sudden wariness slipped under her skin, and her hand shook on the latch of the door. The words of the messenger were indiscernible, and she walked through the entrance, straining to hear.

"You are no longer safe here. David and his troops have moved into Hebron. The men of Judah have crowned him king over them," the messenger said, his animated arms pointing north and east. "You must escape before David sends men to capture all who are left of Saul's household."

Michal watched Abner pull a coin from a pouch at his side and place it in the man's hand. "We will leave at once," he said.

"Where will we go?" Paltiel asked after the man rode away.

Abner said something Michal couldn't hear. Nor did she care what he would say. So what if David captured the lot of them? He wouldn't kill them. She couldn't imagine him hurting her family. They'd already suffered enough. Her gaze flitted to her husband. Then again . . . he might not take kindly to Paltiel.

As though he could read her thoughts, Paltiel suddenly turned toward her and trotted across the front yard.

"You heard?" His dark eyes illuminated his fear.

She nodded. "Where will we go?"

Paltiel took her arm and ushered her into the house. "Abner has been checking our options, sending spies throughout Israel. He wants to get us as far from David as possible."

"Away from Judah, you mean." Impatience made her words terse.

"To the farthest border of Israel. To Mahanaim. Is there a problem with that?" She couldn't miss the hurt in his tone.

Defeat spread exhaustion through her. "I'm just tired of it all, Paltiel. I want to go home. I want to see Abba and Jonathan and Merab and Abinadab and Malchishua. I don't want to raise Merab's five boys. I want my own children. There is so much fighting and hatred, and nothing ever goes right." She looked at him, noting the softening of his gaze.

He cupped her cheek with one hand. "I know it's been hard for you, my love. I want to take you away from here, where nothing can ever hurt you again."

She attempted a smile but knew the effort only came out halfhearted. "That's impossible, Paltiel." Without a backward glance, Michal turned away from him and went to gather her things for the hurried journey out of Bahurim.

❦ 27 ❦

One Year Later

"What's the word on Abner and the house of Saul?" David lifted a silver chalice to his lips and sipped freshly fermented grape wine. He stretched both feet in front of him and rested them on a low stool. Evening shadows blanketed the informal sitting room of his home, and a servant carrying a narrow torch walked about lighting the lamps.

"Saul's family has firmly settled in the far north, in Mahanaim, and Abner is still working to gather all Israel to them there." Joab gulped a long drink from a matching goblet and wiped the droplets from his mouth with the back of his hand. "You know Abner will stop at nothing to make Ishbosheth king in Saul's place."

David studied the swirling red liquid in the shiny cup, wishing the answers to his current dilemma could be found in its depths. "Jonathan would have handed the kingdom to me without question." Why couldn't Saul's firstborn have lived? "Ishbosheth will do whatever Abner tells him to do."

"And Abner doesn't want to give up such a powerful position. I wouldn't be surprised to find that the desire to be king rests solely with him." Joab took another drink, then slammed the empty goblet on the table. He rose from the wooden chair to pace the length of the spacious room.

David's brows lifted, and he eyed his nephew with amusement. The man was impertinent and impatient. "Calm down, Joab. The kingdom will come under my control in God's time. Hasn't He brought me this far?"

Joab paused midstride to stare at David. "Nevertheless, you must not take Abner lightly, my lord. He is shrewd, and his cunning will make him a worse enemy to you than Saul ever was."

David set the silver cup on the table beside him and clasped his hands under his chin. "I'm well aware of Abner's ways, Nephew. You do remember that I married into the family. Not to mention serving under the commander for years."

Joab returned to sit on the edge of his seat. He leaned forward, elbows on his knees. "What if you thwarted Abner's efforts before he can gain any more of a foothold? Plant an enemy at his back door."

"Meaning?" David looked into Joab's beady gray eyes and pockmarked cheeks. His hardened look could scare a child, and his murderous stare, a grown man. Good thing this gruff underling was working for him, not against.

"Make an alliance."

The words caught David off guard, and he settled back against the cushions of the couch. "What kind of alliance?"

Joab's bushy black mustache twitched as he toyed with a mischievous smile. "The king of Geshur might like to keep peace."

Geshurite people had been among Israel's enemies. Some of their southern towns had been wiped out by David and his men when they had lived among the Philistines. It would do no good for the Geshurite king to know the details of those expeditions. Not if they expected to make him an ally. "Does he know of our past exploits?"

"Doubtful. He's afraid of you now that Judah has crowned you king."

"You think so?" David gave Joab a curious look. Joab may have a lot of information, but he wasn't about to take advice solely from him. "Perhaps we should call my counselors together, see if they agree."

Joab sat back and crossed both arms over his chest. "Your prerogative, of course."

David snapped his fingers, and a servant hurried to his side. "Call Hushai the Archite, Benaiah, Abiathar the priest, and Abishai to join us."

"Yes, my lord," the servant said, and rushed from the room.

A short time later David addressed the group. "Brothers, it has come to my attention that Talmai, king of Geshur, would like to be in our good graces. Furthermore, I am told that Abner's forces are gathering at Mahanaim, and as we suspected, he plans to make Ishbosheth king in Saul's place. An alliance has been suggested between my kingdom and the Geshurite kingdom—to have an ally north of Abner. Tell me, what do you think on the matter?"

"What kind of alliance?" Abiathar asked. "They are a heathen nation, after all."

"We would come to their aid, and they would join in our defense. No more raids on Geshurite villages," David said, toying with the fringe on the decorative pillow at his side.

"Talmai's afraid of us," Joab put in. "And I don't think he

ever cared for Saul. He's not happy to find Saul's son camped in his backyard, especially with the possibility of Israel uniting to make him king. If my guess is correct, Talmai would like to know that we would defend his small kingdom from Abner's forces."

"Abner has been gaining back territory lost to the Philistines," Abishai commented.

"It's been slow going, though," Joab said, rising to pace again. "In the year that David has ruled Judah, Abner has gathered less than half the forces he had before Saul was killed, and they've only gained back one town since then."

"I suspect that given enough time, he'll build momentum and recapture the other towns, particularly Gibeah." Benaiah accepted a raisin cake from a servant.

"You don't think he'll go back there, do you?" Abiathar asked.

"Not any time soon. Abner is no fool. He wouldn't want to be so close to Hebron. He knows David's power is increasing daily. God is with us, and Abner knows it." Joab paused midpace and grabbed another goblet of wine from a silver tray, downing a large gulp. "But I still think we need to make an alliance with Talmai. It would strengthen your kingdom, David." He turned to face his uncle. "In any case, it couldn't hurt."

David listened to the banter continue around him, momentarily lost in thought. If Abner hadn't slipped away so soon, he might have gotten Michal back. As it stood now, he would probably have a fight on his hands if he tried to claim what was rightfully his. And she was his. He'd paid for her in blood. Besides, bringing her home to him would strengthen his claim to the throne. Then again, how would he accomplish such a feat without harming more of Saul's family? He raked one hand through his shoulder-length hair and sighed. There must be a way.

"Uncle? Are you listening?" Joab's voice rose above the dissonance of his thoughts.

"I was thinking." He scanned the room, pausing to acknowledge each man. "I want to bring Michal home."

Silence followed his announcement.

"What does that have to do with making an alliance with Talmai, my lord?" Benaiah asked with obvious hesitance.

David stroked his beard, stalling. By the looks on their faces, they must think him completely mad. "Nothing, I suppose. But it will strengthen my claim to Israel's throne. The trick is getting her away from Abner without bloodshed."

Hushai slowly shook his head.

"You don't agree, Hushai?"

"The timing doesn't seem right, my lord. You could, as you say, find that it helps unite the kingdom. But with Abner obviously trying to thwart your efforts to become king in Saul's place, you could find the tribe of Benjamin, and perhaps others, rising up against you if you do such a thing too soon."

"Abner would undoubtedly see it as a declaration for war," Benaiah said. The broad-shouldered bodyguard leaned forward on the bench, his dark eyes on David. "I didn't think you wanted civil war on your hands, my lord."

"A war might be inevitable," Joab said, rubbing his hands together.

"So, what kind of alliance did you have in mind?" David asked, purposely changing the subject. No sense belaboring a lost cause.

"Word has it that Talmai has a daughter." Joab dropped

his agile body into a stiff-backed chair. "If you married her, you would make a more powerful treaty than one written on mere parchment."

"They say the girl is quite beautiful, my lord," Abishai added.

David reached for his silver chalice. "You want me to take another wife?"

"Not just any wife, my lord. A princess," Joab said.

"Like Michal?" David took a sip of the red wine, suddenly wishing he could drink enough to forget the woman. "You think I should start a harem, Joab? Three wives are enough trouble. Why should I concern myself with more?"

"David's right. And Adonai's law warns the king against taking many wives, lest they turn his heart away from Him," Abiathar said. The priest had read the law to David at his coronation as king over Judah, and the reminder only increased David's resistance.

"But as long as they don't turn his heart from Yahweh, what's the problem? Surely He knows that political alliances can avoid much bloodshed." Abishai's words cast doubt on David's own confused thoughts.

"Yes, and while my enemies avoid such turmoil, my household suffers from it." David frowned. "A houseful of women is not necessarily a blessing, Nephew."

"So you build them their own rooms, give them servants and children, and call for them when your heart desires. Some men would relish such an arrangement." Joab folded his arms across his brawny chest and gave David his no-nonsense smirk. "Personally, I don't see the problem here."

Chuckles passed among the men, and David courted a wry smile. He studied the last of the liquid in his cup. They didn't understand. He wasn't interested in marrying more women. He found Ahinoam charming and Abigail appealing in a physical and spiritual way, and when he could recapture Michal's love, his home would be complete. Another wife would just complicate his life.

He sighed, rubbing his knuckles along the pillow cushioning his arm. When he looked up, expectant eyes met his, and he knew that to refuse them would not get his kingdom off to a good start. Though being king might give some the illusion he could do as he pleased, he was finding he must also satisfy his advisors.

"Perhaps a meeting with Talmai is in order," he said, forcing a smile. "Send a delegation to Geshur and draw up the terms of the alliance. If he agrees . . ." He paused, wishing he could undo what he was about to say. "If he agrees, tell him I will consider the treaty sealed when I marry his daughter."

❦

Michal bent over the woolen mat where Joel lay sleeping, resisting the urge to stroke his soft brown hair. Her back ached from kneeling at his side over the past few days, dipping the cloth in cool water and begging God to reduce his fever. Exhaustion swept over her, and she suddenly felt like one of the limp rags she'd wrung out and pressed over Joel's body night and day.

She studied the shallow rising of the boy's chest, satisfied that he finally slept peacefully. At least his breathing was no longer labored, and the fever had broken that afternoon. Maybe sleep would come to her now as well.

She rose to her feet on shaking limbs and lifted damp tendrils of hair away from her perspiring face. The thought of losing yet another family member made her numb to the core. Thankfully, God appeared to have mercy this time. Joel would recover and go home to his father, and she could go back to being Paltiel's wife. Sometimes this intermittent motherhood took more energy than she possessed. Though she wasn't solely responsible for them, she wasn't sure she wanted to help Adriel raise his five boys. One at a time, born of her flesh, would have been better.

The child's steady breathing continued, and Michal slipped from the room. She walked to the larger sitting room and through the door into the courtyard. A balmy breeze brushed her hot cheeks like a soft caress. The last vestiges of orange and pink swept the distant horizon, wrapping the sky in ribbons of color. She loved this time of day. Somehow her world seemed smaller by comparison, her problems miniscule weighed against the vastness of space.

With a deep sigh, she turned and walked back into the house. She dipped a drinking gourd into a large clay urn of water and sipped the tepid liquid. The house held an eerie quiet with Keziah away visiting her family and Paltiel at war. What was David doing now? And why did thoughts of him always surface when she was alone? News had traveled fast that he'd added two more wives to his harem. It shouldn't matter, really. And yet her heart still turned over in silent pain every time she imagined him in another woman's arms.

She finished the cup of water and placed the gourd on the table beside a covered bowl of rising dough. Paltiel would fight for her to his dying day, but that thought did little to comfort her. Maybe she was just tired. Life was too hard. Pain was too real. And God didn't turn things in her favor anymore.

She moved to the bedroom, stretched out on the cot in

the corner, and closed her eyes as the lamp's flame flickered on a niche in the wall. If David managed to become king of all Israel, what would she say if she stood before him and saw him dressed in the finery her father once wore? If she went back to him, would he make her his queen?

In her mind's eye she glimpsed the young girl whose dream it was to be married to a man who would one day be king. That girl didn't exist anymore.

ᔕᖇ

Michal awoke from an uneasy sleep. Was it morning? One glance at the open window showed no sign of dawn. Middle-of-the-night stillness wrapped like a shroud around the house, making Michal's skin prickle with wariness.

She strained to listen. Was that rumbling the sound of trotting horses? She pushed up on one elbow. Someone was coming. Would Paltiel be traveling in the dark?

Fear plucked at her heart. She walked to the door and tested the bar that blocked the entrance. Maybe she should close the window.

On tiptoe she darted across the floor, hoping Joel didn't waken. She peeked through the inky darkness one more time. Even the moon offered little light to illuminate the intruders. She pulled the shutters closed over the window.

Heart pounding, Michal flattened herself against the wall and listened. The horses came to an abrupt stop outside her door, and running feet approached. She expected a violent banging on the wooden door, but a quiet tapping met her ears instead. Unsteady limbs carried her closer.

"Michal?" Paltiel's unmistakable voice filtered through the door.

Michal's trembling fingers fumbled with the bar until at last she lifted it, opening to Paltiel, Abner, and a few of their men. Paltiel's hungry arms dragged her to him, embracing her in a grip that feared to let go.

"What are you doing here at this hour? I thought you were a group of thieves." Michal willed her racing heart to regain a normal rhythm.

"We came from the battle," Paltiel said, pulling in a long, slow breath. "We walked back to where our horses were tethered and hurried home."

She studied the worry lines along his forehead, trying to read his expression in the dim light. "I take it things didn't go well."

"David's forces killed nineteen times more of our men than we did of his," Abner said, his face sullen.

"Worst of all, Abner was forced to kill Asahel, Joab's brother." Fear flickered in Paltiel's dark eyes. He looked at Michal and gripped her shoulders. "Lay out some extra mats for our guests, Michal. Abner and his men will sleep here until dawn."

His sudden commanding tone unnerved her. She was too tired to be ordered about. But it would do no good to argue. There were no servants to do the work for her, so she walked to a corner of the room to retrieve a stack of blankets. She spread them out across the wooden floor and slipped into the back room with Joel.

The muffled sound of voices kept her awake, and she crept closer to the door to hear what they were saying.

"You know your life is in danger now," Paltiel said. "David or Joab will surely retaliate for Asahel's death."

"Don't you think I know that?" Michal could hear the bitterness in Abner's voice.

"All the more reason to keep David from reigning through-out the land," Paltiel said with a yawn.

"Ishbosheth will never gain the following David has." The pitch in Abner's voice dropped so low that Michal edged closer to the door, struggling to hear.

"He must! David cannot rule here."

Silence followed her husband's outburst, and Michal held her breath, aching to know what Abner was thinking.

"Don't get yourself all in a lather, Paltiel. I'm working on a solution."

What solution? Michal wanted to barge into the room and demand answers. But the men's voices had drifted to silence, and before she knew it, the soft sound of their steady breathing pervaded the still night air.

It was obvious that Abner and Paltiel were more afraid of David now than they had been before they marched off to war. And Abner was right. Her brother would never be able to hold the kingdom against the charismatic personality of her former husband. Besides, hadn't God promised David the throne? But Abner and Paltiel could both die if David succeeded. The thought sent a shiver down her spine.

She crept back to the mat that hugged the wall in Joel's room. The boy rolled over in his sleep, and Michal laid her exhausted body across from him, closing her eyes. Dawn's pink shadows peeked over the horizon before Michal finally succumbed to slumber, her restless mind wondering how long they could keep fighting Adonai's plans.

∼28∼

Six Years Later

A clap of thunder signaled the coming storm, and Paltiel wondered if the sky could sense the raging of his own heart. If only he could do something to secure his future with Michal. Why did fear immobilize him?

He stood under the overhang of the flat roof of Ishbosheth's spacious home, debating with himself what to do next. Six long years had passed since the start of the civil war with David's kingdom, since that fateful day when Abner had killed David's nephew Asahel. They'd finally managed to rally enough support to crown Ishbosheth king of Israel four years after that battle. Not soon enough. And his kingdom had been standing on weak knees from the start.

Paltiel shivered. How many battles had he and Abner executed to little or no avail? How many men of Israel had died trying to keep David's men from advancing? Yet David's kingdom only grew stronger, and Abner's promised solutions had gotten them nowhere.

He stepped farther beneath the roof's protection, taking in the guards flanking each entry. Ishbosheth lived in fear for his life—when he wasn't distracted by food and drink and pleasures that had nothing to do with making the kingdom secure. The new king was late to rise—not an uncommon occurrence—and Paltiel wondered if Abner had the same problem this morning.

The clouds shifted and raced across the heavens as the wind picked up. Paltiel clutched the folds of his robe and cinched them tighter against his neck, scanning the short distance from Ishbosheth's home to Abner's. Between the two larger buildings, smaller buildings housing Saul's wife, his concubine, Rizpah, and Ishbosheth's wives stretched in an L-shape, creating a link from the king to his general. Abner's home continued the L-shape like a sprawling arm, as though the general's home was of equal importance to Israel's king. The setup was far different from Saul's fortress. But then Ishbosheth was not the warrior and leader his father had been.

And most of Israel knew it.

A sudden gust of cool wind slapped Paltiel across the face while rain dropped wide circles over the courtyard's stones. Through his peripheral vision he caught a flash of red and whipped his head toward the outcropping of buildings. Was that Abner leaving Rizpah's apartment? The general's new red-crested robe could point him out in any crowd, and Paltiel squinted to make sure it was truly him.

Sure enough. Despite the rain, Abner did not appear to be in a hurry. In fact, he lifted his chin and flung his shoulders back, strutting like a bridegroom emerging from his wedding tent. Could he have spent the night with Rizpah? Such an action was akin to laying claim to the kingdom! Was this Abner's ultimate solution—to take over as king?

Paltiel rested one hand against the mud-brick wall, his heart pounding. If Abner took over the throne, assuming Israel would follow him, they might stand a chance against David.

The *rat-a-tat-tat* of water on the roof drowned out all sound, and Paltiel took a step backward away from the spray dampening his clothes. He bumped into a solid body and whirled around, wondering who would have snuck up on him without his notice. Ishbosheth's fiery gaze, so like his father's, cornered him.

"Did my eyes deceive me, or was that Abner coming from the home of my concubine?"

Paltiel swallowed. He had never been afraid of Ishbosheth. The man didn't seem to possess the ability to invoke fear. But now the venom in his tone and his crossed arms bespoke fierce determination that could ruin everything.

"It could have been. One can never be sure from this distance," Paltiel lied.

Ishbosheth shook his gray head. "Yes, you can, Paltiel." He paused. "Abner wants my throne."

Flames exploded in Ishbosheth's pale brown eyes before he turned and walked down the hall to his audience chamber. Through the slowing rain Paltiel glanced back over his shoulder toward Abner's house. The general stood in the arch of the door, smiling.

⚬⚬

Changing shadows moved over the walls in Ishbosheth's audience chamber. Few lamps were lit despite the dark day, and Paltiel's skin shivered with impending dread.

"When we reach the throne, do as I do," Abner commanded in a hushed whisper.

"Don't I always?" The words tasted bitter on Paltiel's tongue.

Abner leveled him with a stern glance. Let him be angry. If this didn't go right, he'd have only himself to blame. Besides, it would be nice if the man would let him in on what was going on.

They came to a stop several paces from the raised dais where Ishbosheth sat, his expression a gloomy mask.

"Why have you gone in to my father's concubine?" Ishbosheth asked. "You're trying to take my throne." His flabby chest puffed out, and his double chin jutted forward.

Abner folded both arms across his brawny chest. "Am I a dog's head that belongs to Judah? Today I show loyalty to the house of Saul your father, to his brothers, and to his friends, and have not delivered you into the hand of David, and you charge me today with a fault concerning this woman?"

Ishbosheth gripped the sides of his chair, and the natural olive coloring of his skin paled. Fear showed in his expression, and he seemed incapable of giving Abner an answer.

The room grew silent, and Paltiel gritted his teeth, sensing Abner's anger. The stalwart general stood stock-still, the only sign of his indignation a twitch in his left eye.

Abner took a step toward Ishbosheth, causing the man to shrink from him. "May God do so to me, and more also," Abner said, his tone low and menacing, "if I don't do for David as the Lord has sworn to him—to transfer the kingdom from the house of Saul and set up the throne of David over Israel and Judah, from Dan to Beersheba."

Paltiel's breath came out in a sudden whoosh, and

Ishbosheth's face paled even further, if that were possible. What was this? Had Abner lost his mind?

Ishbosheth sat back in his chair and clasped his hands in his lap. The muscles in his face contorted in a visage of fear, and he began rocking back and forth. His lips were sealed together, and Paltiel could tell he would not give Abner a reply. Abner was the one who had placed Ishbosheth on the throne, and Abner could take it all away.

The sudden stomping of Abner's sandals across the tiles brought Paltiel out of his shocked stupor. If Abner went over to David's side, he could take Michal with him. Spurred by a greater fear than Ishbosheth had portrayed, Paltiel raced after Abner. He caught up with him in the outer court.

"Abner, wait!"

Abner halted his rapid stride and turned. Paltiel hurried to his side.

"You aren't serious. Are you?"

Abner's dark eyes held a determined glint. "I said so, didn't I?"

"But . . . I thought the purpose of taking Rizpah was to make a move to take over the throne. Don't you want to rule the land? Why give it over to David? We can't let him win." Paltiel fought back the temptation to break down and weep.

Abner's left eye twitched again, and Paltiel thought he noted a softening in his gaze. The general's strong hand grasped his shoulder.

"Initially that was my plan. Haven't I worked beside you to pull Israel together all these years?"

Paltiel nodded, hating the sting of unmanly tears.

"But as I stood there watching Ishbosheth . . . well, I realized the man was never meant to be king. And God did promise

David the land, you know. After losing so many men to him, I think it's time he sees God's promise fulfilled."

"And if you make it happen, you'll be second in command." Sudden clarity washed over him, replacing his tears and renewing his anger.

Abner removed his hand from Paltiel's shoulder and stiffened. "If that happens, so be it. But I will not have my cousin telling me what I can and cannot do. Ishbosheth's days as king are over." He turned his back to Paltiel then and stalked off.

Paltiel stood watching Abner head toward the guardhouse and stables. Before the sun reached its zenith in the sky, the general would be on his way to destroying Paltiel's life. Hopelessness filled him, followed by brewing indignation. Just because Abner was going over to David didn't mean everything had to change. Maybe now was the time to take Michal out of Israel—out of David's grasp.

With a surge of hope, he turned in the opposite direction and ran all the way home.

※

Continual scraping of stone on stone mixed with distant shouts and youthful laughter. Adriel's children raced in circles about the yard while Keziah sat working at the millstone. Michal knelt with a clay sieve in her hands and sifted the grain for the evening bread baking, watching the soft flour grow in a pile at her feet. She took comfort in the familiarity of such menial tasks. After seven years away from Gibeah and her father's fortress, the privileges of palace life held the vague fondness of a far-off memory.

"You come back here, Benni. I'm telling!" Jacob's shrill voice cut across the yard. "Aunt Michal!" His running feet came to an abrupt halt a few paces from the pot of freshly ground flour.

"What is it, Jacob?" Michal blew a loose strand of hair out of her eyes.

"Benni took my bow and won't give it back! I can't learn to shoot like Uncle Jonathan if I can't practice." The child's wail touched a chord of sympathy in Michal's heart. The second youngest of Merab's children reminded her the most of Jonathan.

"I'll talk to Benni, all right?" She glanced across the field to where Adriel's second oldest stood holding the bow aloft, taunting his little brother. She was about to raise her arm and motion for him to come when her gaze caught a man running toward the house.

He drew closer, and Michal recognized Paltiel's frantic gait. Something was wrong. She felt a soft tugging on the sleeve of her robe.

"He's running away, Aunt Michal."

Michal's gaze drifted to catch Benni streaking across the field toward his father's home, out of her immediate reach. A brief moment later she jerked her head in Paltiel's direction. Something in his expression sent Michal's heart into a wild gallop.

"I'll deal with him later, Jacob. Run along and be good for Aunt Michal." She barely glanced down at the child while patting his head. Midmorning sun warmed her already flushed cheeks as she stood and turned her attention to Paltiel who was now sprinting to her side. Michal still clutched the clay sieve in one hand.

"We have to leave right away," Paltiel blurted, bending forward and dragging in a long breath. "Pack your things. I'll bring the donkey and cart."

Michal stared at him. Was he out of his mind? She lifted her free hand to touch his sweaty arm. "Tell me what happened."

Paltiel gulped another breath, ripped the turban from his head, and raked his fingers through his sand-colored hair. "Abner has gone over to David. If he has his way, and you know he will, all Israel will be under David's rule. I have to get you out of here."

The sieve slipped from Michal's hand, shattering on the stones of the court. "I thought Abner was going to try to be king himself."

"So did I. But he had a run-in with Ishbosheth and apparently changed his mind. Besides, if he gets Israel to follow David without further bloodshed, he could end up second in command of the entire kingdom. Sounds like the general decided to set his sights higher than ruling a mere eleven tribes."

Michal didn't miss the sarcasm in Paltiel's tone, but at the same time, her thoughts turned to David and the possible consequences of his rule. Obviously Paltiel was convinced their marriage was in danger.

"Did you hear me, Michal? We have to leave Mahanaim. Once Abner meets with David, there's no telling what could happen to Saul's family. If David is in a foul mood, he might order our deaths. I have to protect you." He grabbed her arm and attempted to urge her into the house. "Keziah, start packing," he commanded with a backward glance.

Michal stood rigid, holding her ground. "David won't hurt my family, Paltiel. If he'd wanted to do that, he would have done so long ago."

Paltiel loosened his grip and looked into her eyes. "Yes, but he could take you away from me. If we leave Israel, he won't have any power over us." His expression held such deep pain that Michal's heart lurched, and she longed to comfort him. But another part of her held back. Whether it seemed like it or not, she was still a princess in Israel. She didn't want to live like an outcast in a foreign land.

"I'm not going, Paltiel. You can leave if you must, but I can't leave my homeland."

"But, Michal . . . I could lose you." His voice rose a notch, tinged with emotion.

"I'm a king's daughter, Paltiel. I would be no safer in another country than in my own. Besides, it's possible David has forgotten all about me. In that case, you'll have nothing to worry about. But in the meantime, I've got five boys to look out for, and I'm not leaving." She hadn't spoken so harshly since the early days of their marriage when she was still in love with David.

"Does our marriage mean nothing to you, Michal?"

She looked into his stricken face and fought the urge to hold him and promise him anything. Too many things hung in the balance. Too much was at stake.

"I don't know that our marriage is in any danger, my love. Let's just wait and see. Please." She touched his arm then and caught her breath when he hugged her in a sudden, firm embrace.

"I love you, Michal. I think you're wrong not to worry, and I should demand that you obey me." He paused, and she watched his Adam's apple rise and fall in his throat. "But for your sake . . . I will wait a few days. We will see what Abner will do." He held her at arm's length. "I only hope I don't live to regret it."

❧29❧

A cool breeze tickled the hairs on David's arms during his evening walk in the secluded courtyard set apart for his wives and children. A series of doors opened onto the court, designating the different apartments for the now six women in his harem. Strange how after acquiring Maacah, the Geshurite princess, he was able to take the rest without a second thought. Keeping the goodwill of the tribes and nations seemed a huge benefit for such a small price to pay.

And God had blessed him. Six sons and one lovely daughter had been born to him in Hebron. What better proof was there than this that the Lord was strengthening his house and at the same time weakening Saul's?

He sat down on a stone bench in the center of the court and gazed at the beauty of the surrounding garden. One of the doors squeaked open, and a dark-haired toddler poked his head out. At the sight of David, he burst through the door and came running full tilt.

"Abba!" he cried, flinging himself onto David's lap. He clasped his chubby arms around David's neck and hugged him tight.

David chuckled, returning the boy's exuberant embrace. "Absalom." He kissed the child's forehead and bounced the boy on one knee. "And how have you been today, my son?"

The boy's lip curled in a sudden pout. "Can I play in the field, Abba? Mama said no 'cause I'll get dirty!"

Unexpected indignation filled David, and for a moment he thought about marching into Maacah's apartment and demanding to know why she restricted his son from the simple pleasures of being a boy. He didn't want his sons growing up to be weak-kneed women. Getting dirty was part of the normal progression to manhood.

"Abba?" Absalom's chubby hand clutched his sleeve.

Before David could respond, other doors opened, and two more sons appeared at his side.

"I'll talk to your mother about it," he promised Absalom, rubbing the thick, dark curls back and forth across his head.

He continued to bounce the child as Amnon, his oldest, and Chileab, his second born, approached his side. "Good evening, Abba," Amnon said, eyes downcast. He stood shyly, almost afraid to speak—an action that annoyed David. He must speak to Ahinoam about the way she was raising him. Firstborn of his loins should be heir apparent to his throne, but Amnon did not strike him as the kind of child who possessed kingly qualities.

"How are you today, Amnon?" David asked, forcing himself to smile at the boy.

"I am well, thank you." He dropped his gaze again.

David turned to Chileab. "And how is Chileab this fine evening?"

The boy's eyes were bright, his smile genuine. He stepped

forward and crawled up on David's other knee, then leaned forward to kiss David's cheek. "I always feel best when you are here, Abba."

Chileab troubled David. His five-year-old frame was too thin, too weak. If not for the accident . . . He forced his mind not to focus on that now.

David hugged the two boys to him, then looked up to see Abigail and Maacah emerge from their apartments. Maacah carried his daughter, Tamar, on her hip. David was about to remove his two sons from his lap when rapid footsteps approached. He lifted his head and turned to see the intruder, his faithful guard Benaiah.

"My lord, I am sorry to interrupt, but you must come at once," Benaiah said, exhaling a swift breath.

Benaiah did not agitate easily, and David read his expression like a scroll. He felt Chileab kiss his cheek one more time and slip from his knee, but Absalom clung to his neck. "Can I come with you, Abba?" he whispered.

David looked into the boy's dark eyes so like his mother's. This child had a way of moving him. Maybe it was his engaging beauty. Maybe the boy just knew how to manipulate his heartstrings.

"Please, Abba!"

David usually gave in to his pleadings, but he heard Benaiah clear his throat, and one glance at the man made him change his mind.

"No, Absalom. Not this time. Abba will let you come to court some other day. Tonight we may be up well past your bedtime." He looked to Maacah for support, relieved when she stepped closer and extended her hand.

"Come along, Absalom. Abba has important business. He'll

come again later, when he can." She took the boy's hand when David set him on the ground, then cast David a beguiling smile. He knew she expected him to come back this night. He looked away, refusing to acknowledge the hidden message, then followed Benaiah back into the house.

❧❧

After donning his royal robe, David's brisk strides carried him to his paneled audience chamber, where he took his seat on a padded throne. Torches had been lit and placed in clay pots along the walls as dusk settled over the town. Benaiah stood watch at the entryway while David's recorder hurried over to his table, picked up a reed pen, and readied the scroll. Whatever transpired here this night would hold some significance, and David wanted a record of it.

Footsteps marching up the stone walk could be heard through the open windows. David's gaze followed the sound. Two men hurried to the door and knelt before Benaiah.

"We have a message for my lord, King David, from Abner, son of Ner."

Benaiah nodded and stepped away from the door. David sat straighter as the two men walked the length of the room, sandals echoing across the tiles, and fell prostrate at his feet.

"You may rise," David said after a lengthy pause. "What message do you bring?"

"Abner, son of Ner, has sent us. He says, 'Whose is the land? Make your covenant with me, and indeed my hand will be with you to bring all Israel to you.'"

David held the speaker's gaze, his mind whirling. Abner was obviously seeking a place of prominence in his kingdom, or he wouldn't make such a statement. After all these years, the uniting of his house with the house of Saul would finally come to fruition.

Which meant Michal could be returned to him at last.

What better way to show unity of the tribes? Michal represented his past and Israel's first kingdom. To bring her back would right the wrong done to him and give the nation greater cause to accept him without question.

His look shifted from one man to the other, and he leaned forward, clutching the arms of the chair.

"Tell Abner, 'Good. I will make a covenant with you. But one thing I require of you: you will not see my face unless you first bring Michal, Saul's daughter, when you come to see me.'"

He dismissed them then, and when they were gone, he clapped his hands, summoning Benaiah.

"Yes, my lord." Benaiah bent one knee and bowed his head.

"Send my own messengers to Ishbosheth. Since Abner is so quick to seek my favor, let the king of Israel do the same."

"What shall the messenger say, my lord?"

David stroked his beard, his thoughts dancing through a handful of memories. "Tell him . . ." He paused, struck by the enormity of what had just happened.

Michal was coming home.

"Tell him," he said after a lengthy silence, "'Give me my wife Michal, whom I betrothed to myself for a hundred foreskins of the Philistines.'"

Benaiah met David's gaze and nodded. "As you say, my lord. It will be done."

❦

Michal sat in a corner of her home, mending one of Jacob's torn tunics. The needle dipped into the fabric to the sound of the children's squabbling and laughter in the yard. Michal toyed with a smile as she tugged on the thread. A month had passed since Abner had gone over to David's side, yet nothing had changed. Perhaps her life would turn out all right after all.

Keziah stood at the table in the kitchen, rolling dough into square sections, filling them with a handful of dates, and drizzling them with honey. At the sound of men's voices in the courtyard, Keziah looked up from her work, and Michal's fingers stilled.

"What is it, Keziah?"

The young woman looked out the window, and at her worried expression, Michal set the tunic in a basket and stood, smoothing her robe with trembling hands. Her heart skipped a beat at the sudden pounding on her door.

Michal looked to Keziah, who shrank toward the corner. She would be no help. Michal released a slow breath and willed her timid feet forward. When she opened the door, the sight of Israelite guards startled her.

"Yes?" Her gaze swept the men before her, noting her brother's kingly insignia on their outer robes and tunics. These were no ordinary guards.

"King Ishbosheth has commanded that Michal, Saul's daughter, prepare to leave Mahanaim. She will accompany Abner, son of Ner, to Hebron to be reunited to her husband, King David." The guard said the words in a stiff monotone, as though he'd rehearsed them many times.

Michal stared at the man, barely noticing another figure running toward the house from across the field. "I'm to return to David? Now?" This couldn't be true. Besides, she couldn't leave. She had a life here, and Merab's children needed her.

"Yes, Princess. Abner sent messengers to David, whose first words were that Abner could not see his face unless he brought you with him. Then David sent messengers to Ishbosheth, bypassing Abner, to command your return. Your brother sent us to you moments after David's men reached Mahanaim."

David wanted her back? Before another thought could pass through her mind, Paltiel reached her side, out of breath.

"What's going on here?" He faced the guards, stepping in front of Michal and blocking her view of them.

"King Ishbosheth has sent us to take Michal to Abner. She is going with him to Hebron to be returned to King David."

Michal heard the words again, but they had yet to truly penetrate her conscious thought. But when she watched Paltiel turn toward her in fear, reality awakened her senses.

"Didn't I tell you?" His face contorted in misery, and Michal's heart lurched in pain. "I told you we should leave Israel. I knew David would do this. Didn't I tell you?" He pushed Michal into the house and swung the door shut in the guards' faces. Michal stumbled backward, barely catching her balance. She braced herself against the edge of the table, staring at Paltiel in a mute stupor. Paltiel stepped forward and fell to his knees, clutching her feet and weeping.

"You can't go, Michal. I'll bribe the guards. We can run away. Please, don't leave me."

How could she? How could David expect her to leave the man who had been her husband for nearly seventeen years? Her marriage to David had happened so long ago that it seemed like a passing dream. She had been just a girl then.

A girl with ambition and longings she thought David could fulfill. But her father had snatched her dreams away when he thrust her into Paltiel's arms. Too much time had elapsed for her to ever think she could capture them again.

A pounding at the door interrupted her troubled musings. The guards weren't leaving. Paltiel still clutched her feet and wept, and Michal stood immobile, her emotions a twisted mass.

"Shall I open the door, my lady?" Keziah whispered in Michal's ear. Michal hadn't heard her quiet approach. She looked at her, then glanced at Paltiel. The incessant pounding continued.

"If you don't come out, Princess, we'll take you by force," one of the guards shouted.

Michal nodded at Keziah, and she tiptoed around Paltiel and pulled the door open. The guards stepped through, and one plucked Paltiel's fingers away from Michal's ankles. Michal stepped back and turned toward the bedroom.

"Let me get my things," she said over her shoulder.

Spurred by sudden urgency, knowing now she had no choice, Michal grabbed her spare tunics from pegs on the wall and scooped her pots of makeup into a straw basket. The blankets and bedding, cooking utensils, and cleaning supplies would be unnecessary items for a princess in a palace. She glanced around the room again, then picked up her basket and satchel and walked into the sitting room. Her eyes scanned the small area and stopped when she spotted her sewing supplies next to the chair in the corner. With brisk steps, she walked over and picked up the sewing basket, pulled Jacob's unfinished tunic from it, and left the tunic in the chair.

She searched every section of the house as she hurried

through each room. Paltiel sat crumpled in one corner, his face a mask of misery. She allowed herself one last longing glance at him, then nodded to the guard.

"I'm ready," she said, forcing her eyes away from the silent sobbing of her husband. "No, wait." She turned to Keziah. "You're coming with me. Pack your things."

"Yes, my lady."

The guard started tapping his foot in an act of impatience. "Abner is waiting."

Michal pursed her lips in annoyance. "Let him wait. My maid is coming with me."

Keziah ran through the house and was back at Michal's side within moments. "We can go now, my lady."

Michal followed the guard past Paltiel and out of the house. Merab's two younger children were still running around playing bury and hunt in the neighboring field. She stopped. How could she leave them? How was it possible that what began as a burden dumped on her by her dying sister had turned into a duty she would miss? The sudden sting of tears made her throat ache. Jacob and Joel in particular had wrapped their little arms around her heart in love.

"Can I say good-bye?" she asked when the guard stopped to look at her.

He gave her a curt nod, then paused. Cupping both hands to his mouth, he shouted to the children to come.

"What's going on, Aunt Michal?" Joel asked.

"Yeah, why'd you stop our game?" Jacob looked at the guard, scowling.

Michal knelt to meet them at eye level, emotion nearly choking her. She set her baskets on the ground and tugged the children toward her.

"I'm leaving, and I don't know when I'll see you again." Tears threatened, but she quelled the urge to break down in front of the children. Instead she held them tight, then quickly released them.

"Why are you going, Aunt Michal?" Jacob asked, sniffing back his own tears. "You can't leave us. Who will fix my scrapes?"

"Or make us raisin pastries?" Joel cried unashamedly.

"Or fix my tunics?"

"Or nurse us when we're sick?"

Michal held up her hand to stop their protests. "I'm going back to my husband, David. You remember I told you how your grandfather, King Saul, took me away from him?"

They nodded in unison.

"Well, Grandfather Saul had no right to do that. You see, David paid a high price to marry me, and now that Abner is on David's side, David wants me back."

Jacob's scowl deepened. "I don't like David."

"King David," the guard corrected. "And you'd better like him because he's going to be in control of the whole kingdom. He won't like nasty little boys."

Michal winced at the hurt, angry look in Jacob's eyes and turned on the guard, heat rising in her face. "I doubt you have any idea who or what David will like. I suggest you keep your own nasty comments to yourself." She couldn't believe she was speaking like this, but the thought occurred to her that she just might wield some authority as David's wife. No reason why she couldn't assert a little now.

She whipped her head away from the guard's startled expression and looked at the two somber boys. She brushed the hair from Jacob's brow, then cupped Joel's cheek. "If I

285

can, I'll ask King David to let you come visit me sometime. Would that be all right?"

They nodded mutely.

"But if I can't, be good for your father. He'll need you to be more grown-up now, and your grandmother will probably come and stay with you. You'll like that, won't you?"

"Yes," Joel said softly. "But I'd rather have you." He threw his small body into Michal's arms, and this time she couldn't stop the tears. She held him in silence as Jacob looked on, his expression sour.

"Is that all right with you, Jacob?" she said at last, setting Joel away from her.

He shrugged, but when she beckoned, he clung to her neck until she thought he would choke her. "I still don't like David," he whispered. "When I grow up, he's going to be sorry he took you away."

She held the boy at arm's length, stunned. Before she could think of something to say, Jacob whirled around and raced across the field without looking back. Joel looked at her, indecision written on his fine features, but at last he turned and ran off after his brother.

Paltiel stumbled out of the house, eyes blotchy. "Don't go, Michal." The words came out choked, barely audible. The agony of leaving him sent a dagger through her heart. She cared deeply for Paltiel. After seventeen years, despite their beginnings, how could she simply forget all they'd shared?

"I'm sorry." She touched his cheek, feeling the dampness of his beard. Tears still lingered in his eyes. "There is nothing I can do."

His look told her he didn't believe her, and yet she could not have done as he had asked and leave Israel. Somewhere deep within her soul, she still loved David. The fact that he wanted her back had changed the way she'd come to feel about him. He hadn't forgotten her. Maybe he loved her too.

She picked up her baskets and followed the guard to the waiting donkeys, allowing the men to fasten her belongings to the sides. Paltiel's soft weeping continued behind her, and she glanced back. Their eyes met, but she looked swiftly away.

"Let's go," she ordered, mounting a donkey. Keziah sat on another one at her side. "Take me to David."

Therefore all the elders of Israel came to the king at Hebron, and King David made a covenant with them at Hebron before the LORD. And they anointed David king over Israel.

2 Samuel 5:3

Now as the ark of the LORD came into the City of David, Michal, Saul's daughter, looked through a window and saw King David leaping and whirling before the LORD; and she despised him in her heart.

2 Samuel 6:16

☙30❧

From the vantage point of his roof two months later, David caught a faint glimpse of Abner's caravan plodding toward Hebron's city gate. He lifted one hand to shade the half-risen sun from his eyes and counted the donkeys, searching. Abner's red-crested robe stood out among the rest. David allowed himself to study the man's stance as he approached the guard, almost afraid to focus on the object of his desire—the woman riding directly behind Abner.

Michal.

When he pondered her name, his eyes moved toward her with a will of their own, like a moth drawn to an alluring flame. She was too far away for him to see the details of her face clearly, and as the group passed through the wooden doors toward his palatial home, David stood back a pace, not wanting her to see him. Not yet. He would see her soon enough.

He watched the caravan until it reached the outer court of his home before he turned and walked down the steps toward the door of his audience chamber, Benaiah at his side.

"Would you like Princess Michal brought to your chambers

right away, my lord?" He looked at David, his face a stoic mask.

David paused at the door, where flag bearers and trumpeters awaited to announce his arrival. "Show her to the apartment I have prepared for her. I'll call for her when I'm ready." ·

"Yes, my lord."

David took his seat on the gilded throne while his scribes and servants took their places at tables or posts around the room. Moments later, Abner, followed by twenty leaders from Israel, crossed the tiled floor and fell prostrate at David's feet.

"May my lord, King David, live forever." Abner rose to one knee, head bowed.

David extended his royal scepter to the man. "Do you come in peace, Abner?"

"Yes, in peace, my lord. I have brought your wife Michal with me. And I will do more than that. I will arise and go, and gather all Israel to my lord the king, that they may make a covenant with you, and that you may reign over all that your heart desires." Abner's dark eyes held David's for a brief moment, then lowered again in respect.

David clapped his hands together. A servant scurried to his side.

"Yes, my lord?"

David glanced at Abner, then at the servant. "Prepare a feast for our guests. We will dine together for the midday meal."

"Yes, my lord." The servant hurried off.

"You will join me for a meal," David said, smiling. "Then I will allow you to do as you have requested."

Abner looked up again and stood. "Thank you, my lord. We gladly accept your hospitality."

"Princess Michal, you are to come with me," a guard said.

Michal nodded, too nervous to speak. The guard removed the satchel and baskets draped to her donkey's sides after helping her dismount. Keziah followed close behind, and the two walked in silence across the walled brick courtyard. Cultivated flowers graced the perimeter of the walkway, and they stopped at a narrow door in the wall. The guard knocked twice. A short, weathered older woman appeared, dressed in a simple olive green and reddish brown robe tied at the waist with a brown sash. Her matching striped veil covered most of her wispy gray hair, and her arms were folded across her chest in a no-nonsense stance. She scrutinized Michal from head to toe, then sighed.

"Another wife, Elias?" She shook her head. "Where are we going to put this one?"

The guard cleared his throat. "This is Princess Michal, Hannah. The king has been expecting her."

Hannah's head bobbed in understanding. "Yes, yes, of course." She dismissed Elias with a quick swish of her hand as though batting a fly and looked Michal up and down again. "You will want to bathe in the mikvah and change out of those dusty traveling clothes before your visit with the king. Come."

Michal followed the old woman across another courtyard, past a maze of connecting rooms.

"This is the family courtyard." Hannah's arm circled to include the enclosed court where a number of doors opened into the same spacious gardenlike area. "This is where the king comes to meet with his wives and children."

Wives and children. She knew that. All the way from Mahanaim, through Paltiel's loud weeping as he followed them to Bahurim, where Abner finally sent him home; over the hill country leading to the Jordan River; across the river; and past Jerusalem and David's childhood home of Bethlehem, to Hebron, Michal told herself she would not be David's only wife. But telling herself and seeing evidence of it firsthand were two different things. What would she do when she was forced to share their table and David's love?

"And this is your apartment." Hannah pushed open the door, then stepped back.

Michal entered with caution. Would David be waiting for her inside? But that was ridiculous. He was meeting with Abner. She looked around, noting with appreciation the gilded couches and cushioned chairs sitting beside ornate tables topped with decorative oil lamps. Soft lamb's wool cradled her sandaled feet, and light came from opposite windows, giving the room an open appearance.

She walked over to one of the windows and looked out at a small garden blooming with brilliant colors—a stone's throw from her back door.

"Is this for me?"

"Yes, my lady. The king built it for you soon after he was crowned king over Judah. It is for your own private use."

Michal's awe shifted to sudden emotion, making her throat ache to hold back the tears. "Do the other women have one?" She had to know.

Hannah shrugged. "They all have something the king has chosen specifically for them. I can't say what that is."

The answer didn't satisfy her, but Michal held her tongue, afraid her words would come out in a choked whisper.

"King David has said to make yourself comfortable," Hannah said, walking toward the door. Keziah stepped out of her way and walked to Michal's side. "He will call for you when he is ready." She turned and strode out of the house.

❦

"The food is excellent, my lord," Abner commented, lifting the silver chalice to his lips. "If you feed your enemies such exquisite fare, you will quickly turn them all into friends."

David chuckled. "So to avoid bloodshed I should either feed my enemies or marry their daughters? I suppose that would keep at least one of us happy. The question is, which one?"

He smiled as Abner let out a loud laugh and slapped his palm on the table. Snickers and laughter moved around the large room, though David wondered if any of them realized how much his attempt at humor bespoke truth. He held up his hand for silence.

"Nevertheless, let it be known today that we have no enemies here. I will make a covenant with Israel. Bring me the elders of the land, and I will rule them in peace." David tore a loaf of bread, pinched a handful of salt between his fingers, and sprinkled it on each half.

Abner sobered, reaching to take the torn piece of wheat bread David offered him. "I will go throughout the land from Dan to Beersheba to bring all Israel to you, fulfilling the Lord's promise to my lord to give you the kingdom."

David took the other half of the torn loaf and bit a piece from it. He chewed slowly, watching Abner do the same. He looked at the general, who nodded in understanding. Eating with the man signified acceptance. Bread and salt between them meant a covenant of loyalty, despite their past differences.

"Go in peace," David said when the meal ended. He embraced Abner, kissing each cheek. Abner returned the affection, then bowed his face to the ground.

"May God do so to me and more also if I do not keep my word." He turned, followed by his men, and left David's house.

❦

After a relaxing visit to the mikvah, Michal returned to her apartment, still amazed at the splendor surrounding her. The home of her youth could not compare to the beauty of the decorations in this spacious apartment. She glided over the plush carpets into the separate bedchamber. Her breath caught. The room looked exactly like the home she first shared with David in Gibeah.

Unsteady feet carried her to a wooden table where she felt the smooth, oiled surface. Pots of kohl and rouge were placed exactly where they used to sit in her old home. Every detail remained the same, down to the bronze mirror and the golden-handled comb.

Oh, David.

Her eyes roamed the room. A window with white linen curtains stood along the same wall as the one in their old bedchamber where David had slipped from her life so many years before. She stood and walked to the window to peer out. The sight was not the same. This time her gaze took in the beautiful walled garden created just for her.

"Do you like it?" The masculine voice startled her. But she would never forget its melodic timbre. "Is it what you expected, Michal?"

His footsteps were muffled on the soft carpet, but she

could feel his presence filling the room. She turned slowly, her heart beating with awareness. He stopped within arm's length.

"Much more," she said, taking in every facet of his royal garb. His hair was still dark beneath the golden, jeweled crown, his eyes fathomless and unsearchable. His purple-gilded and embroidered robe fit him perfectly, his muscular body exuding authority and strength. Far different from the young husband who once feared for his life. "So, you are a king now."

"Yes."

David stood unmoving, his gaze sweeping over her.

"With a harem."

"I have other wives and children, yes."

She looked away, trying to hide the stinging tears. Feelings conflicted in her spirit until she felt David's fingers brush a tendril of her undone hair over one shoulder. His hand moved to her chin, and he coaxed her to look at him again. Heart leaping like a wild gazelle at his touch, she met his gaze and couldn't turn away.

His thumb moved in circles over her heated cheek, and before she could think of what to say, he drew her against his chest and bent his lips to hers. His kiss was tentative, uncertain. He pulled back, searching her face.

"I've missed you," he said, his voice husky.

"I've often wondered about you." She felt like a girl of fifteen again, enamored with this handsome man she now had trouble thinking of as her husband. It had been so long. And she felt like an unfaithful traitor.

He stroked her cheek again and let his fingers filter through her hair. "You're as beautiful as the day we met."

Every touch sent shivers of delight racing through her. "You've grown more distinguished and handsome." She toyed with a soft smile.

He responded with a wide smile of his own, then grew serious and drew closer, his mouth claiming hers again. This time all timidity fled, their lost passion remembered. Michal's thoughts carried her away to their wedding week and the precious year she'd spent as David's wife. Surely they could recapture their banished love and live in harmony once again. Surely, in time, he would make her his queen.

With renewed purpose, Michal lifted the crown from David's head, an action reminiscent of their first night together. The action made David tighten his hold around her and laughter bubble from his lips. Hope sprang anew in Michal's heart, and she returned his kiss.

Boom! Boom! Boom!

Incessant pounding against the oak door made her jump and stopped David's fingers from sifting through her hair. He kissed her one more time as if unwilling to pull away, then disentangled himself from her embrace, scowling.

Boom! Boom! Boom!

"David!"

David looked toward the door and moved in that direction, then seemed to think better of it and clasped his hand in hers, pulling her with him. He released his hold in the sitting room near the door and gave her an impassioned smile. "A king's life is not his own."

His look suggested that she of all people should understand such a thing, and she didn't miss his increased annoyance with each brisk step to the clattering door. She crept behind him, her interest piqued. How would he handle such an intrusion?

His bearing exuded an authority she'd never seen in him before, thrilling her.

He grasped the handle and pulled back, ducking to the side of Joab's slamming fist. "You better have a good reason for interrupting my privacy, Joab. What are you doing back here so soon anyway? I thought you were on a raid."

"We finished early," Joab said. His turbaned head dipped from side to side in an obvious attempt to peer past David, who was blocking the view of the room and of her. She slipped farther behind David but close enough to hear. David stepped forward, pushing Joab back a pace, and pulled the door shut behind him. Michal pressed her ear to the door to hear their heated words.

"What have you done?" Joab's disrespectful tone surprised her. Didn't David have control of his nephew? "Why did you send Abner away already? Surely you realize that Abner the son of Ner came to deceive you, to know your going out and your coming in, and to know all that you are doing."

Michal strained to listen, her heart beating hard against her chest. "Abner came in peace, Joab, with proof of his sincerity."

"Just because the son of Ner brought the daughter of Saul back to you does not mean he proved his sincerity. It only shows the extent of his power and his clawing desire for more."

"Abner used his influence to obey my orders," David said, his tone low yet strained. "Something you would do well to learn, Nephew."

Good. Let David put his opinionated nephew in his place where he belonged.

Joab cursed loudly enough for her to hear before his

footsteps pounded on the stones of the court and faded into the distance. Silence met her ears, and she stepped away from the door. Would David return to her now?

"Do you want me to have him followed, my lord?" Benaiah's clear voice caught her attention, and she leaned against the closed door again. Benaiah's words held wisdom, but would David listen to him? David would do well to appoint Abner in Joab's place and send his nephew back to Bethlehem where he belonged.

"He just needs time to cool off," David said. The latch on the door turned, and she stepped back, stunned that David had not acted on Benaiah's obvious wisdom. "See that I am not disturbed again."

Before she could think of what to do or say, the door opened and David stepped into the room, closing the door behind him. He looked at her, clearly distracted, then shook his head as though to clear it and smiled.

"Your nephew has grown powerful," Michal said as he shortened the distance between them and took her hand in his. "I remember when he was a scrawny guard chasing your heels under my father's command."

David smoothed the folds of his robe with his free hand, then looked at her, his expression unreadable. "Joab is my army commander. He has proven a competent captain and has a good military mind."

"Not the most respectful servant though." Michal toyed with a smile, trying to lighten the mood. She was grateful for the vulnerable half smile he gave her in return, reminding her of the mere boy she had married. "Will you give Abner that chief position when the kingdom is united? You must admit, he is older and more experienced than Joab."

David tilted his head back and chuckled. He pulled her to him then and began running his forefinger over the sheer fabric of her pale blue robe. "Such matters should not concern you, my love. Leave the political affairs to me." He bent to kiss her again, but she stiffened and pulled away. She walked across the spacious room and looked toward the garden, where even the fresh colors could not bring joy to her sagging soul. Why did his attitude irritate her?

David stood in the spot she'd vacated. Silence fell like humid air between them. The oppression nearly suffocated her, and she strained to take a breath. How dare he treat her like some common woman! She was a king's daughter and a princess in Israel. Surely she should have some say in matters like this— especially if he was going to make her his queen.

The distant sound of children bickering floated on the oppressive air—an atmosphere she had created—reminding Michal of Merab's children and her home for the past seven years since Merab's death. Why had David asked for her? What did he want from her that one of his wives hadn't already given him?

A soft hand on her shoulder made her jump, and she lowered her head, fighting the emotions his gentle caress brought. When he turned her to face him, she swallowed hard.

"I haven't decided who will be my commander yet," David admitted. "But I didn't come here to discuss those things with you, Michal. I've been looking forward to this moment for too long to interrupt it with kingdom affairs." He searched her eyes, and she read in him the longing she recognized from years ago.

Heat crept into her face, and she lowered her lashes against his scrutiny. She felt his possessive arms wrap around her waist and his tender lips press against her cheek, then move down to her parted lips. All irritation with his political views melted with the remembered passion of their youth, and Michal allowed David to carry her away into the intimacy of his arms.

❦

Evening shadows fell outside the window in Michal's bedchamber, accompanied by the shrill laughter of children clamoring about the family courtyard. David stood across the room, expertly tying his purple sash about his waist and replacing the band of gold along his forehead. He smiled down at Michal still lying on the raised bed, the white sheet drawn under her chin.

"Must you go, my lord?" But she already knew the answer. Why should her marriage to David this time be any different than before? If anything, he would only be more distant, and their marriage would have less chance of the commitment she'd longed for.

David knelt beside her and stroked her face with his finger. "You know how busy palace life can be, my love. A king's time is rarely his own." He kissed her forehead. "I'm only grateful I could snatch this afternoon to get reacquainted. If you'll dress for dinner, I'll seat you nearest me at the women's table. Then afterward I'll give you a tour of the place. How's that?" His lips tasted hers again, and Michal allowed a shimmer of hope to replace her lapse into melancholy.

"I'll be there, my lord."

"Good," he said, then turned on his heel and walked out of the apartment.

~31~

The spacious banquet hall bore little resemblance to the stone structure where Michal's father often entertained dignitaries and heads of tribes. Limestone walls were whitewashed, and brightly colored oriental tapestries added a rich yet homey flavor to the decor. Windows gracing opposite ends of the hall allowed orange hues of the fading spring night to mingle with newly lit torches placed about the room.

Michal took in the beauty of the hall with growing appreciation for David's creative flare. He'd certainly changed from the homespun shepherd she'd loved in her youth. How long ago that had been. So much had changed.

At the head of the room an extended table spread with fruit and goblets of wine stood out as separate from the others. Covering the wood was a white cloth with an embroidered pattern of gold and purple fig leaves fanning away from the Judahite insignia of a fierce, golden lion. Obviously the king's table.

To the left and facing the king was a rectangular table with a few women and children already seated. Michal followed the guard Elias to the spot David had reserved for her, her heart thumping wildly. Where once she carried some semblance of leverage and control in her royal home, here she felt like an outcast, as one tossed about in a storm. Would the winds of change never cease?

With uncertain steps, she approached the table and lowered her shaking legs to the gilded couch Elias pointed to.

"Who's that, Mama?" A toddler with curly, dark hair and eyes lifted a chubby finger in Michal's direction. "Why is she sitting on Aunt Ahinoam's couch?"

Michal studied the bold child before looking at his mother, who was a foreigner. Though her dress followed the royal pattern of the other Hebrew wives of the king, the darker hues of her skin and her facial features spoke of Syrian or Aramean heritage. She met Michal's gaze with a bold one of her own until at last she turned her attention to the boy who had spoken.

Michal looked away, listening to the chattering voices of the other women drifting across the hall, as one by one they took their places at the table. A fairer-haired woman with a slender, shy boy tagging at her heels gave Michal a look of disdain before taking the seat beside her. Apparently Michal had been given the place of first wife, which rightfully belonged to her. She lifted her chin, ignoring the perusing gazes of David's six other wives.

A trumpet sounded, jolting her attention. All eyes traveled to the door of the banquet hall, where David followed the trumpeter, flag bearers, and armed guards to the place reserved for him.

Michal watched the fanfare with interest. Would he speak to her here? Would he single her out and place her at his side as queen? The thought sent tingling warmth through her.

After all, he had spent the afternoon with her despite other obvious demands on his time. And he'd prepared her apartment to match their first home together. Surely he loved her better than these other young beauties.

As David leaned back on the ornate couch, the servants began offering silver trays of roasted lamb, purple grapes, pistachios, almonds, dates, and figs first to the king, then to the men seated with him at his table. A short, thin servant in a white tunic lowered a wineskin toward Michal's carved chalice before moving down the line to fill each cup belonging to David's wives. The women began placing food on the plates of their children, chattering again among themselves. Michal's stomach turned over. How was she ever going to survive in a harem where she wasn't wanted—perhaps was even hated? At least with Paltiel her home had been her own.

She studied the delicacy-laden silver plate overflowing with some of her favorite foods. Had David ordered them prepared in her honor? She cast a discreet glance at him again, but he was preoccupied, talking with a man she didn't recognize seated at his side.

She slowly chewed on a grape. The children reminded her of Jacob and Joel. An ache lodged in her heart at every childish word spoken.

Oh, David, why did you bring me back?

The intense temptation to run from the hall all the way back to Mahanaim nearly choked her. The action would surely not endear her to David.

"We've just got to get David to take us back to En Gedi. Don't you think so, Abigail?"

Michal leaned forward on pretense of reaching for a raisin cake, listening.

"I would love to go back there, Ahinoam." The woman called Abigail cut a piece of meat for a frail-looking child. "The waters might do Chileab a world of good." She lifted dark lashes to glance at Ahinoam, and as she did, Michal caught her look of interest.

Michal averted her gaze. En Gedi was a beautiful garden atmosphere with thirst-quenching waterfalls and a pool as clear as polished stones. She'd gone there once as a child. Never with David, as these women obviously had done.

The sound of running feet across the tile floor pulled Michal's attention away from David's wives. A young man dressed in military garb flung himself at David's feet, panting.

"May my lord, King David, live forever!"

David sat straighter and nodded at the messenger. "Speak."

The boy leaned back on his heels. "My lord, I bring news. Bad news, I'm afraid."

David clasped his hands in front of him. "Go on."

"Joab, the king's nephew and commander, and his brother Abishai have killed Abner, son of Ner, general of Israel's army."

Michal's heart plummeted. Fear dried her throat, and her clammy hands began to shake. Abner was dead? Abner controlled most of Israel. Abner represented her father's last ruling power in the land. More than this, Abner was her cousin—one more loss in her family. Michal swallowed a remnant of grape skin still on her tongue, nearly choking on the ripe fruit. How many more members of her family would die in this constant vying for power?

"How did this happen?" She heard David's stricken voice and twisted in her seat for a better view of him.

"Joab sent word to Abner to return to Hebron. They met

at the gate, where Joab pulled him aside to speak with him privately. Only instead of talking, Joab stabbed him in the stomach to avenge the death of his brother Asahel." The boy's words came out in a rush, as though he couldn't say them fast enough.

Michal's gaze moved from the messenger to David. His complexion had paled, and he rose slowly to his feet. "Where is Joab now?"

"He is still at the gate, my lord, with his brother Abishai. His men are bringing Abner's body to your courtyard. What would you have us do, my lord?"

David's color returned in deeper hues, sparks flashing from his dark eyes. "Prepare Abner's body for burial. And send for Joab and Abishai." He glanced at the window. "We will summon the townspeople and go first thing in the morning to the burial cave." He dismissed the messenger with a wave of his hand, then summoned Benaiah with another.

"Yes, my lord." Benaiah bowed.

"Make sure Joab and Abishai are with us before dawn to join the procession of mourners."

"Yes, my lord."

Michal watched Benaiah march across the hall into the courtyard. The once luscious food now looked repulsive. She should follow the man and await Abner's body in the court, but she couldn't stomach the thought. Her gaze drifted to David, who was engaged in whispered conversation with the man on his right. His problems would be multiplied now. She stood, catching a glimpse of sympathy on the faces of some of David's wives. She straightened her shoulders. She didn't need their pity.

With purpose in her steps, Michal strode across the

banquet hall, head high, chin tipped up. Eyes fixed on the door, she walked back to her apartment where she might, if God were gracious, fall into a forgetful sleep.

⋙⋘

"Tear your clothes, gird yourselves with sackcloth, and mourn for Abner." David's steady voice carried across the court, spilling over the gathered crowd and into the surrounding fields. Michal stood near the bier, staring at the still form of her once vibrant cousin, her hands tucked into the folds of her already torn robe. A trail of ashes created smudge marks along her veil and floated from her hair to the ground.

Hundreds of townspeople lined the court, Joab and Abishai at their head. They should be executed for what they'd done. But Michal knew instinctively David could never order their deaths.

"My kingdom and I are guiltless before the Lord forever of the blood of Abner, son of Ner." Michal slowly turned at the sound of David's words. "Let it rest on the head of Joab and on his father's house, and let there never fail to be in the house of Joab one who has a discharge or is a leper, who leans on a staff or falls by the sword, or who lacks bread."

Michal caught David's expression and noted the fierce tone, recognizing his frustration. After a few curt commands from David, Joab and Abishai led the procession to the outskirts of town to a large burial cave. David stepped behind the bier, head bowed, but when the body passed in front of her, David extended his hand and pulled Michal to his side.

His warm fingers wrapped around her palm, making her eyes fill with fresh tears. She could feel his perusal, and as they walked, he whispered in her ear, "I'm so sorry, Michal. This was not my intent."

"A king can't always know what his subjects are up to, my lord." She glanced into his stricken face, stifling the longing to brush the ashes from his cheek.

"Would that he could," he said softly, squeezing her hand. "Abner deserved better."

David didn't know the many unkind things Abner had spoken of him in times past. If he did, he might welcome the loss. But Michal couldn't tell him. No sense sullying her family's name.

When they reached the burial cave, David released her hand and raised his arms toward heaven, weeping. Were his tears genuine? But Michal's own blurred vision kept her from studying her husband's expression.

"Should Abner die as a fool dies?" David's voice cut above the scattered wailing. "Your hands were not bound nor your feet put into fetters. As a man falls before wicked men, so you fell."

It would have been better if Abner had died in battle. At least that would have been honorable. Following David's example, Michal bent to scoop dirt from the ground and poured it over her veil of sackcloth, letting it mix with her tears. Abner's men rolled the heavy stone from the cave's entrance, picked up the bier, and carried Abner's lifeless body into the tomb. Michal's shoulders heaved, and she covered her face with her trembling hands. The touch of warm flesh on her arm made her jump, but in an instant she found herself wrapped in David's strong arms.

"Oh, David! I've lost everyone," she wailed against his sackcloth.

She felt his fingers rub circles along her back. "You've got me, beloved." He kissed her cheek and held her close for a long moment.

She didn't really have him. Not the way she used to. Not the way she wanted him. But she held her tongue. She allowed him to lead her back to his royal house, where a feast awaited the mourners. David personally seated her and sat beside her in the outer court of his home.

"My lord, the food is waiting. Can I get you something? Some wine perhaps?" a servant asked.

"Yes, my lord. You need your strength," another said.

A small group gathered around them, holding trays of food and urging David to eat.

David stood, his hands raised, quieting the crowd. "God do so to me, and more also, if I taste bread or anything else until the sun goes down!" He looked at his servants. Michal noticed Joab and Abishai at the edge of the crowd. "Don't you know that a prince and a great man has fallen this day in Israel? I am weak today, though anointed king, and these men, the sons of Zeruiah, are too harsh for me. The Lord will repay the evildoer according to his wickedness."

Michal watched admiration light the eyes of the men surrounding them. She glanced at her husband, her own pride swelling at his devotion to her family. If only they could have been together from the start of his reign. If only she had gone with him into exile and stayed forever at his side. She could have influenced David to give someone else control of the army—perhaps even Abner right from the beginning. So much could be different, so much loss avoided.

When he sat beside her again, awaiting the setting sun,

she slipped her hand through the crook of his arm. "You will make a good king," she whispered, leaning toward him.

The smile he gave her melted her heart.

❦

A cacophony of sounds filtered through the open window in David's private chambers, dragging Michal out of a deep, restful sleep. She stretched her arms overhead, stifling a yawn.

"Finally awake, sleepyhead?" David turned from looking down on his bustling household and walked toward her. "I was just about to dress for court." He sat beside her and began to trace the outline of her face with his forefinger before bending to kiss her cheek. "Did you sleep well, my love?"

"Better than I have in months." She pulled one hand from beneath the lamb's wool covers and touched the fine, curly dark hairs on his arm. "Are you going to announce a queen at your coronation, David? You really should give one of your wives priority over the others, you know. It keeps the bickering to a minimum."

She watched his eyes twinkle and a smile lift the edges of his wavy brown beard. One strong hand cupped her cheek, making her heart do a little flip.

"You're jumping ahead of yourself, Michal. I've still got to bring all the tribes together under my rule. Abner's death slowed things down, you know."

"Yes, but you will be king. You know you will. Surely you've begun preparations for your coronation day." She offered him a demure smile and let her fingers travel along his arm. "As your first wife and daughter of the previous king, I think I'm the most qualified for the job, don't you, my lord?"

He'd been so kind in the week since Abner's death, giving her the privileges of first wife and the exclusive right to his time, like she was a newly married bride. It gave her the courage to even pose the question.

His hand covered hers, and he lifted her fingers to his lips. "I'll give it some thought, my love. In the meantime—"

The sudden knock at the door stopped David's words. He rose to answer. Michal slid farther beneath the covers.

"My lord," Benaiah spoke loud enough for Michal to hear, "there are two men come from the court of Ishbosheth to see you. They are waiting in the audience chamber."

"Thank you, Benaiah, I'll be right there." He closed the door behind the retreating guard and retrieved his royal robe from a peg along the far wall.

Michal slipped from under the blanket and snatched her own robe from a chair beside the bed. She must get back to her apartment and change. Perhaps the messengers had come ahead of her brother to lead the tribal elders into an agreement with David. Surely even simple Ishby would see the wisdom in such a move now that Abner was dead. Unless Paltiel tried to convince him otherwise.

Her jaw clenched at the annoying thought. Paltiel had spent years keeping her from David. If he'd been any kind of decent man, he would have never taken her to be his wife. The thought surprised her. Had her love for Paltiel been mingled with this resentment all along? How quickly David had made her forget the man, reawakening the dreams and ambitions of her youth. If she could only convince David to do as she asked . . .

She heard David's feet march across the wooden floor and stop in front of her. "I'll see you tonight, my love." His promised warmed her, and she lifted her chin to accept his kiss before he strode from the room.

⊰⊱

Michal hurried along the corridors of the king's house, sandals slapping along the tiled floors to the door of her apartment. She yanked the latch, grateful she'd managed to avoid the perusing, glaring looks of the other women in the harem. If she had her way, she would never be forced to deal with them, at least without having some advantage to hold over them. Becoming David's favorite would certainly hold privileges for her.

"Help me dress quickly, Keziah." Michal caught the woman smoothing a freshly washed tunic. "I must look my best today. I think my brother is coming."

"Good thing we cleaned your best robe yesterday, my lady." Keziah took Michal's night robe from her outstretched hands.

"Yes, well, soon enough I will have sequined garments and priceless jeweled robes to replace these old things. A king's wife needs to look her best."

"Yes, my lady."

Silence settled between them as Michal allowed Keziah to comb her hair and lace it with jeweled combs. Michal took a pot of rouge from the wooden table and began to apply it to her already flushed cheeks, noting the thin lines at the edges of her eyes. It took more kohl to cover the flaws than it used to.

"Please, my lord, reconsider!" The shout came through the open window.

"We were only trying to help . . ."

313

Anguished cries split the stillness, and Michal's fingers froze in a clamped position around the clay pot.

"What is it, my lady?" Keziah whispered.

"I can't imagine." But a sick feeling settled in Michal's stomach. She forced her fingers loose, set the makeup on the table, and walked to the window.

"I can't see a thing from here. I'm going to the audience chamber." She raced back to the bedroom and lifted the bronze mirror to gaze at her reflection, then turned to Keziah. "Do I look all right?"

"You look beautiful, my lady."

Michal set the mirror down with a thump and slipped into her sandals, and Keziah bent to tie the laces. She lifted her skirts and hurried along the halls again.

The audience chamber was filled with men speaking in low tones. David sat on the raised dais, face ashen, head in his hands.

The sick feeling knotted her stomach. She moved like a sleepwalker across the long room, brushing past David's counselors and dignitaries, until she was within a handbreadth of a blood-spattered sheet spread on the floor in front of David. Her eyes followed the path of blood to discover the round, hairy head of a person, his eyes staring vacant. The soft gray curls still bore a silver crown.

Michal's head swam, and her knees buckled. She knew she would see that face in a thousand nightmares to come.

Ishby!

"No!" she cried, sinking to her knees. "No! No! No!" Her fists pounded the tile floor. "No!"

"Michal." David's voice reached her ears, and she felt herself being lifted from the floor and cradled in strong arms. "What are you doing here?"

"Ishby." The word pushed past her aching throat. "Why?"

"Two of his guards murdered him. Their bodies are now hanging by the pool in the center of Hebron. We will bury Ishbosheth today in the tomb of Abner. I'm so sorry."

She heard the words but fought the reality. She'd lost them all. Every sibling lay buried somewhere. A roaring in her ears began until the sounds around her floated above and below, just out of reach.

"Michal, can you hear me?" The urgency in David's tone faded, and she felt her body being lifted again. "Take her to her apartment and send for a physician. I'll check on her after we bury her brother."

"Yes, my lord." The words faded further still until Michal's world became utter blackness.

32

"My lord, Michal is awaiting an audience with you." Benaiah leaned close to David's ear as the two walked to the royal house from the pool of Hebron, where they would hold part of the coronation celebration. "She sent word. It sounds urgent."

David released a deep sigh and rubbed one hand along the back of his neck. Recent days since the death of Ishbosheth had proved fruitful. God seemed to be pouring blessing upon blessing down on him. The familiar sense of humility spread through him like warm oil spilling over his hair and trickling into his beard. He would feel that sensation literally in two days when all Israel anointed him king.

"Did she say what she wants?" David forced himself to focus on Benaiah's words.

"No, my lord. But I suspect you'll find out soon enough."

He hadn't spoken with Michal in days. Hadn't seen any of his wives or children, for that matter. There was only so much a man could give, and his multiple wives and children tended to drain the last remnants of his energy.

David looked up as he crossed into the royal courtyard.

Michal sat on one of the stone benches, her arms folded over her chest, her shiny dark hair tucked behind a sky blue veil.

"I guess I will." He slowed his pace and stopped within an arm's length of her.

"Hello, my love. Benaiah said you wished to speak with me." He lowered his exhilarated yet weary body onto the bench beside her, turning to look at her. "What can I do for you?"

Michal's dark lashes lowered, and she clasped her hands in her lap. She cleared her throat and looked at him. "Your coronation is almost here, my lord. Have you chosen who will stand at your side as queen?"

So that was it. Did she want political position more than love? Was that why she made no fuss about coming home to him, never mentioning the man who had claimed her to David's disgrace? He'd made sure Paltiel could never come close to her again, barring him from ever leaving Mahanaim on pain of death. The man was fortunate David hadn't had him executed. Did Michal still think of him?

David studied her dark eyes, searching for some motive behind her words. "Isn't my love enough for you, Michal?" He watched a surprised expression cross her beautiful face. What he wouldn't give to undo the past and start over again with only her. Couldn't she see that?

Michal fidgeted with the sash of her robe, all the while holding his gaze. "It would be enough if I were your only wife, my lord. But as it is, you have taken my position and given it to six others, then snatched me from a home where I had no competition. The least you can do is give me a place of prominence in your life."

So she did still think of him. "We have no heir, Michal."

There, he'd said it. The nagging thought had troubled him whenever he'd contemplated her request over the past two weeks. In the first year of their marriage, she had miscarried once. And in seventeen years with another man, she had remained childless. What if God never gave her a son?

He watched her tanned cheeks sport a rosy hue. "You have given every other wife a son, David. You could give me the same courtesy and devote yourself to me until we do." The heat in her face traveled to fire in her eyes.

"Do you think I am God, Michal? I cannot promise you this. A child is His gift, not mine." David wiped one hand over his mouth and beard. This was not the discussion he needed right now. "Nevertheless, until you have that son, I could hardly name you my queen. In fact, I've given this a lot of thought, Michal, and I do not plan to name anyone in that position for now. There is no rush, and I have too many things on my mind. Enjoy the privileges I've given you and leave it at that, all right?"

He watched the anger in her eyes turn into a smoldering ember. She released a disgruntled sigh.

"You won't name anyone then?"

He shook his head. "Not until the Lord gives me direction."

Her second sigh seemed more at peace. She lowered her lashes again. "Or until I bear a son?"

David's heart warmed with sudden compassion. How hard it must be for her to live among so many women with children. He must remember to make it up to her somehow. "Until then, my love."

❧❦

"How good and pleasant it is when brothers live together in unity. It is like precious oil poured on the head, running down on the beard."

David's fingers strummed the strings of his lyre, the song springing gratefully from his lips. Hours after the last tribal elder had returned to his tent, the spicy scent of cinnamon still clung to him from the oil permeating his hair and beard. It had been a good coronation day.

"They are still singing that song throughout the city," Benaiah said, taking a seat opposite the king in the cozy receiving chamber kept for David's private use. "You've won the hearts of the people with peace, my lord."

David placed the lyre in his lap and lifted his head. A handful of his counselors remained after the day's festivities, as if none of them wanted to see it end.

"There was a time when I never thought this day would come." David leaned back on his gilded couch and accepted a goblet of wine from a Cherethite servant, a defector from the Philistines.

"Even when you were among our people, we could tell you were called to greatness, my lord. Your God has surely brought this to pass." The speaker, Ittai the Gittite, had followed David seven years before when he left the protection of the king of Gath. His six hundred men now served David as mercenaries.

"Thank you, Ittai. This is the Lord's doing, and it is good." He sipped the chilled, tart liquid and sighed. "Peace at last."

"I'm not sure we can claim that for long, my lord." Hushai spoke up from a far corner of the room. He moved closer and perched on a low couch. "Despite the joy in Israel, there are rumors of discontent between the tribes. It seems that

Israel wants to argue with Judah over who has more claim to you."

"That's ridiculous," Benaiah said, crossing one ankle over the other. "Judah crowned him king first, and they share his blood. What claim do the other tribes have at all except that they come from Jacob's loins? They followed Saul's house all these years."

"Too true, but some don't see it that way. And truly, my lord," Hushai said, turning from Benaiah to David, "they have a point. Israel includes all twelve tribes, and if you are to be king, you must be king equally of them all."

David ran one finger around the rim of his silver cup. "I agree completely, Hushai. What do you suggest?" He glanced around the room at the handful of men. Joab and Abishai were conspicuously absent, since they had fallen out of his favor. A new counselor, Ahithophel the Gilonite, had offered his services when the elders came together to proclaim David king. "And what do you think, Ahithophel?"

Ahithophel nodded toward Hushai. "After you."

Hushai's thick face flushed, and he folded his hands in his lap. These counselors weren't likely to see eye to eye, but different viewpoints could be a good thing.

"I think you need a plan to unite them—perhaps pick members from each of the tribal leaders to serve on the king's court. Give them equal standing with the men from Judah who already serve you, my lord."

"That's a start," Ahithophel said, his silver hair gleaming in the light of twelve torches set around the room. "But I think the problem lies with the location of your headquarters, my lord. I think you need to leave Hebron and find a more neutral capital."

David set the goblet beside him and tented his fingers beneath his chin.

"Where are we going to find something neutral?" Benaiah asked, his thick brows furrowed. "Every other city in Israel belongs to one tribe or another. If we leave Hebron for, say, Ephraim or some other tribal lands, the people of Judah will resent it."

"Benaiah's right, my lord." Hushai leaned forward in the chair, placing both hands on his knees. "Unless you go outside of Israel—"

"That's exactly what we'll do." David stood and walked to the window, looking out at the settled dusk. He whirled around and faced his men. "We will take Jerusalem, and I will build my palace there."

Silence followed the announcement.

"Is there some problem, brothers?"

Hushai shook his head. "They say Jerusalem is impenetrable, my lord. How will you scale those walls?"

"I think it's a grand idea," Ahithophel said. "I'm sure our king will find a way."

"Our king needs men who can help him plan, not just give him untried assurances." Benaiah scowled, but David ignored the guard's concerns.

"Hasn't the Lord given us victory over all of our enemies?" David picked up the heavy pitcher of wine and walked about pouring the drink into each man's chalice. "Jerusalem is His to give, and if He wants us to have it for Israel, He'll show us a way to take it."

David filled his own cup last, then sat back on his couch and sipped, looking over his men. He was met by looks of embarrassment and astonishment.

"What? Do you think your king is above serving you? I am your servant as well as your king. Drink a covenant to the future. For Israel." David raised his cup, waiting until his men did the same, then took a long drink. "Tomorrow we will make plans to take Jerusalem."

❦

Two weeks after David's coronation, Michal strode through the public halls of his home and onto the large porch overlooking a walled outer courtyard. The king's attendants filled the court, and banners from each tribe fluttered in the morning breeze. David stood on an elevated platform, arms raised to quiet the crowd.

"Men of Israel, today we set out to take Jerusalem."

A cheer erupted from the thousands of soldiers spread out in the surrounding fields. David motioned for silence, and Michal stepped closer, curious. She'd heard the rumors, but who would lead such a charge? Joab had been barred from David's inner circle, and Abner was dead.

"Whoever climbs up by way of the water shaft and defeats the Jebusites will be chief and captain."

David's announcement startled Michal. By throwing it open to anyone, even Joab stood the chance of being reinstated to his former position. More commands followed David's stunning words, until at last the throng broke into groups and the divisions moved away from the king's home, David at their head.

Michal leaned against one of the pillars of the porch, her mind whirling. If Joab took over as captain of David's forces again, it would be a slap in the face to her family, to her tribe. How could he even suggest such a thing and possibly let that happen?

Furious, she stomped from the courtyard and returned to her rooms. Something must be done. But there was nothing she could do.

⋙⋘

"The men are returning, my lady." Keziah rushed into Michal's private gardens, out of breath. "They're coming up the path to the king's gates. King David is leading the way."

Michal set her embroidery in a wicker basket beside the wooden bench where she loved to sit and pass the time. Her heart fluttered at the news, and she hurried to follow Keziah to the outer courtyard.

"Do you know who the new commander is?" She hated relying so much on a servant for information, but even after months of living in the king's harem, she had no friends among her equals, David's other wives.

"I haven't heard, my lady."

Summer heat assaulted Michal as she stepped onto the covered porch and watched the fanfare of returning soldiers. Townspeople lined the street leading to the king's home, much like they did on the road to Gibeah during her father's reign. The only thing missing was that fateful song.

She watched the entourage enter the court. Men shouted, and David's children danced about. The other wives had joined them now, lined up for David's greeting. Michal hung back, not caring to be lumped together with the rest. Instead, she scanned the crowd of men, searching for the object of her hatred. If Joab had taken the city and resumed command, he would be decked out with the commander's insignia and following David's numerous attendants.

She spotted Benaiah faithfully guarding the king. She

stepped from the shade into the sunlit court and walked over to the guard. "Benaiah, may I have a word with you, please?"

The guard looked at her with a hint of surprise, then took a step closer, standing at attention. "What can I do for you, my lady?"

"Please tell me who is commander of the army." She held her breath, searching his large face.

"Joab took the city by way of the water shaft. The king has reinstated him as commander of the hosts of Israel."

Michal stared beyond Benaiah, at last sighting Joab among the crowd. Even from a distance she didn't miss the proud tilt to his chin or the haughty gleam in his eyes. She stumbled back a pace and felt a hand touch her arm.

"Michal, my love, come join the other women." David gripped her shoulders, turning her to face him. "We've taken Jerusalem! Come into the banquet hall and rejoice with us." He searched her face, his brow knit in puzzlement.

Shaken out of her momentary stupor, Michal looked into David's eyes, frustrated with the joy she saw written there. Joab's reinstatement did not bother him in the least. He was probably glad of it.

"Why did you make Joab commander again?" She spoke softly, not wanting to ruin the day for him despite the fact that he had destroyed it for her.

He gave her a curious look and released his grip on her arms. "He won the position fairly, Michal. There was nothing else I could do."

She turned to walk away from him, but he took hold of her hand and held her fast. "Don't worry yourself about political affairs, Michal. You are trying to control something that is beyond your grasp." He stepped closer and bent his head to hers. "Come, enjoy the feast, my love. This is a great day in Israel."

Michal nodded and sighed. "As you say, my lord." Let him think she approved of his choices. It would do no good to anger him now. But she would never forgive him.

33

Five Years Later

"There you are, my lord." Benaiah stepped from the shadows and crossed the roof of David's palace in Jerusalem, meeting David at the edge of the parapet. "Hushai and Ahithophel are here to see you."

David acknowledged the guard with a slight nod. "It's a beautiful city, isn't it, Benaiah?"

"Yes, my lord—with this palace being the crowning jewel. The Most High has blessed you indeed."

David glanced at the faithful guard, one of his chosen mighty men. "Yes, He has."

David fell silent again as he looked out over the surrounding homes of his neighbors. The afternoon chatter of women working over cooking fires and scolding children mingled with the clatter of merchant carts and braying donkeys. Men returned from the fields or from selling their wares, signaling the end of another summer day.

"So shall I send your counselors to the roof, my lord?"

Shaken from his preoccupied thoughts, David turned away from the sight below him. "Yes, of course."

The guard walked over to the stairs and motioned to the two men. David walked over to greet them. "Come, my friends, join me in the pavilion."

The two men followed David into a half-enclosed tent, visibly open on one side. He took his seat in the center, among a pile of cushions on a padded, gilded couch.

"What can I do for you?"

Hushai took a seat opposite David while Ahithophel sat to his right.

"There has been talk, my lord. It seems some of Saul's grandsons are stirring up trouble in the tribe of Benjamin. I think Michal is fueling their efforts," Ahithophel said, toying with the fringe of his robe.

David drummed his fingers on the cushion at his side. "What proof do you have?"

"Michal has been meeting with her nephews on a regular basis," Hushai said, rubbing both hands across his knees. "I've heard the younger ones speak rebellious words when I happened to pass under her window."

"Spying on them, Hushai?" The situation wasn't humorous at all, but the thought of his short, stocky friend playing the spy seemed amusing.

"Only in your best interest, my lord."

"Well, I'll thank you for that. Is the tribe of Benjamin riled up enough to cause a problem?" Would his kingdom ever know a measure of peace?

"I don't think it's serious, my lord. But I do believe Michal will push to see her father's house retain some control in your kingdom. You need to keep on your guard with her," Ahithophel said.

David's fingers sifted the hair across his forehead. Wasn't

he always on guard with Michal? They hadn't had a decent conversation since coming to Jerusalem, since Joab had resumed his place as commander. He barely knew her anymore.

"So I take it you agree, Hushai? Based on what you've heard?"

Hushai nodded. "Yes, my lord. I think they are a fire to be snuffed out before it is too late."

"I'll deal with it then." David leaned back against the cushions. "I have another matter to discuss with you." The desire had niggled at the back of his mind for months. It was time to give it voice.

"We are at your service, my lord," Hushai said.

David clasped both hands beneath his chin, studying the men.

"Our nation has neglected the worship of the God of Israel since the days of Saul." He watched Hushai nod vigorously and Ahithophel's eyes soften. "I want to change this."

"What do you have in mind?" Ahithophel asked, crossing one leg over the other.

"I want to bring the ark to Jerusalem. We could pitch a tent for it, like we did in the days of the judges, and offer sacrifices and worship the way Yahweh intended."

"But where is the ark, my lord?" Ahithophel asked. "We haven't heard of it in years, not since the Philistines sent it back to Beth Shemesh on an oxcart."

"I believe it is in the house of Abinadab in Kirjath Jearim." Hushai leaned forward. "They say the Lord has blessed the man for keeping it."

David's heart soared, the thrill of a new pursuit raising his spirits to great heights of joy. "We will go after it then. We'll gather all the men of Israel and bring the ark to us here with songs of worship."

"I'll see about preparing a new cart for it to ride on," Ahithophel said. "It would never do to use the cart from Philistine days, if it still exists. The ark of the Lord must ride on a newly constructed virgin cart, pulled by young oxen, never given to hard labor. We must give God our best if He is to bless us."

David felt the hairs raise on his arms. "Sound advice, Ahithophel. Get started at once."

༄༄

"You wanted to see me, my lord?" Michal took a tentative step across the polished mud-brick roof to kneel at David's feet. She touched her head to the cold stone and lifted it quickly once she felt his hand on her arm.

"I want to talk with you, Michal." David's fingers traipsed down her arm to her hand and intertwined with hers. "Come to the parapet and look out over Jerusalem."

She allowed him to lead her. Keeping her attraction for David's charismatic personality at bay was a struggle every time she was alone with him. She couldn't allow him to woo her to forgive him or love him.

Love cost too much.

"Do you see the way God has blessed us since we moved here, my love?" He pointed to the surrounding homes and smiled.

Michal let her gaze follow his finger from the bright blue sky to the whitewashed brick buildings sparkling in the blaze of the late afternoon sun. She glanced down at the area homes and spotted a young woman in her courtyard with long, braided, ebony hair bending her lithe body over a small herb mill, whistling like a bird. Michal's eyes darted to David's handsome face. Had he seen the girl?

Sudden jealous thoughts rushed through her. If he brought her here just to show off his accessibility to beautiful women, he was wasting his time.

"I can look down on you from this spot, beloved." David tugged her gaze away from the young woman, apparently oblivious to her. Michal looked over the rim to where he was pointing and spotted the lovely young Maacah and shy Abital with the doelike eyes walking about the courtyard.

"And everyone else in your harem."

He stilled, then turned, leaning his back against the western parapet. "You dislike my privileged view."

She lifted her chin, averting her gaze from his all-too-alluring eyes. "It's nothing special, unless you like looking at women." She glanced at him, but she could not read his thoughts. Turning away from him, she strode into the tent-like pavilion in the center of the roof. Breathing in the scent of spikenard, she was taken aback by the plush comfort of the king's hideaway.

She took a seat on one of the cushioned couches and leaned her elbows against the pillows. The heady scents from the incense burner gave her a feeling of well-being. David stood in the wide opening where the flaps were pulled back to allow a magnificent view of the sky. He leaned one hand against the center tent post, watching her.

"I see this meets with your approval."

Was she that readable? It irked her that he could perceive her thoughts while his own lay behind an impenetrable mask. Michal ran one finger over the embroidered threads on a pillow, then let her gaze skip across the interior of the tent. "Is this the kind of tent you lived in when you traveled in the wilderness?" What would it have been like to have been with him then?

"It's more costly, more comfortable, and roomier." He walked over and sat beside her with only an arm's width between them. "Similar though."

At his nearness, Michal's breath grew shallow. She could feel the warmth of his body sitting so close. Too close. Why did he make her nervous?

She studied the fig leaf pattern on the pillow. "Why did you want to see me, my lord?"

David extended both legs and crossed his ankles. "Two reasons."

She was aware of his scrutinizing gaze but couldn't bring herself to meet his dark, fathomless eyes. If she did, she might drown in their liquid depths. She might let herself feel the strength of him.

She might love him all over again.

She moved the threads on the pillow back and forth beneath her fingers instead.

"Yes, my lord?"

David switched legs, topping the left foot over the right. "First of all, I'd like you to come with me when we go to get the ark to bring it to Jerusalem. You could help lead the rest of the women in worship."

Was he serious? She bit back a laugh. "I can't carry a tune, David." She looked at him then. Surely he knew this.

"You could play a tambourine."

She smiled. "I've never liked to play any musical instrument."

David looked at her, his reaction still unreadable. "I want you there, Michal."

"I'm honored, my lord." Though she didn't see the point.

David lifted his hand to play with a lock of her hair.

She stiffened. "What else did you want, my lord?"

He let his arm drop to the cushion and sighed. After a long pause, he stood and walked to the opposite end of the tent. He turned to face her. "I've heard you've been inciting your nephews and the tribe of Benjamin against me. Is this true, Michal?"

She sucked in a harsh breath. Now this was unexpected. Her fingers stilled on the pillow, and she leveled her gaze first at the floor, then at him.

"No, not against you. But we do believe it is only fitting that some of my family still be recognized as part of the hierarchy of your kingdom, David. After all, my father was Israel's first king, and many people have not forgotten all he did to bring the tribes together and defeat the Philistines. Since all of my siblings are dead, and you refuse to name me your queen since we have no child, I think the least you can do is give my nephews, whom I helped raise, places of leadership in the kingdom. The older ones could be governors or judges in the land or captains in the army. But if you want to avoid trouble with the tribe of Benjamin, you'd best give them something worthwhile."

Michal realized she was glaring at him then, and she hadn't expected her speech to come forth with such venom. But she'd given the matter a lot of thought and had been planning how to approach David for months. Now she had.

"Are you telling me that you have been stirring up an entire tribe in my kingdom, all for the sake of giving five spoiled young men a place of power in the land?" His face darkened, though his voice remained perfectly calm.

"They're no more spoiled than your own sons!" How dare he!

"Are you aware that Merab's sons have been known to speak of rebellion against me, Michal?"

She averted her gaze. She'd suspected but had no proof. "I can't believe they would do that."

"Well, they have. And I'd appreciate it if my wives would keep out of the affairs of state and find useful things to do that didn't involve arousing trouble among the tribes." He walked closer as he spoke and stooped to kneel at her feet. "I'm trying to bring them together to honor the Lord, Michal, not tear them apart."

Michal couldn't pull away from the tender look in his eyes. "I'm sorry." But she wasn't sorry. Not really.

"Just come with me to bring the ark, Michal. Things will improve if you do."

He stood then and pulled her to her feet. Why did he always think his ideas would make everything all right? He was not privy to her thoughts and had no inkling of the hurt places in her soul. And as long as he relegated her to just one of many wives in his harem without making her queen, he never would.

❦34❦

Michal sat astride a white mule at the head of the company of David's wives, watching the sea of men and women tuning a variety of instruments and jabbering with excitement. The noise sounded like the low rumble of thunder before a storm, but one glance at the cloudless blue sky dispelled the possibility. She wasn't sure why she'd come. Until her traitorous heart caught a glimpse of her husband decked out in full regal attire, waiting for the priests to come out of the building and set the ark on the gilded cart.

David had spared no expense in the construction of the cart. Even the oxen wore a glistening harness with gold interlays. She had to admit the royal markings and rich trappings made her heart swell with pride. It was small compensation for David's recurrent indifference, but on a day like today it helped.

Michal pushed the newly embroidered blue veil from blowing across her cheek and lifted her gaze up the hill, where the men were fitting the ark into the place created for it. Moments later a young man hopped into the seat and grabbed the oxen's decorative reins. Another young man stepped in front of the oxen and started down the hill, guiding the man driving the cart. The crowd's noise drifted to silence as the oxen took their first step. The ark lurched to one side, and men and women held their collective breath. Michal released her own long-held sigh of relief as the oxen's steps righted the ark and began a slow descent. It would do no good to see the ark of God tumble into the dust.

At David's wave and joyous smile, the music began in earnest. Michal's heart lifted at the sound of her husband's clear voice rising above the crowd.

She shaded her eyes, watching David follow the cart and lead the people toward the base of the hill to Nachon's threshing floor. She kicked the mule's sides and motioned for the women to follow. Most of the women were on foot, but David allowed his wives the privilege of riding. She wouldn't have come if she'd had to walk the whole way. Head held high, chin tipped up, Michal maneuvered the mule behind David and off to the side. She didn't want to get too close to the ark. Something akin to fear kept her a healthy distance from the ancient golden symbol of her people's faith.

"I will praise You, O Lord, with my whole heart. I will tell of all Your marvelous works. I will be glad and rejoice in You. I will sing praise to Your name, O Most High."

Michal heard David's glad refrain, and her heart surged with a mixture of joy and pain. Why couldn't she praise God like that? What kept her from feeling the radiance reflected not only in David's melodic tones but in the expression on his handsome face?

David paused as the cart slowed, waiting as the oxen carefully made their way down the hill to the more level ground of Nachon's threshing floor. Michal urged her mule to halt, and the rest of the crowd stopped as well. David glanced at her, smiling. Her stomach dipped, and emotions surged to the surface.

"Sing praise to the Lord Most High," David called to the men surrounding him.

"Sing His praise forevermore," they responded in unison.

The young man leading the cart took the final step down from the grassy hill and turned, motioning for the other man holding the oxen's reins to follow. The oxen moved slowly, one tentative step, then another. Michal felt her breath coming in spurts. Hooves lifted, then settled in the dust. The crowd quieted. A moment passed as the people watched, waiting for the cart to steady itself on level ground.

The oxen stumbled, and Michal's heart skipped a beat.

The ark rocked precariously to the side of the cart. Time stilled. The cart lurched again, and the ark tilted, sliding toward the edge.

Oh, don't let it fall.

The young man in the cart dropped the reins and twisted sideways, reaching one hand to block the ark from continuing its downward slide. At that moment, the cart righted itself. But before Michal could breathe a sigh of relief, the young man who had touched the ark fell out of the cart into the dust. Michal watched his wide eyes stare at nothing, his mouth gaping.

"No!" The scream came from somewhere in the crowd.

Michal turned to see David begin a slow trot toward the man.

"Pull him away from the cart," David commanded. Several men bent forward cautiously to obey.

"Is he dead?" She heard David voice the question as though he couldn't believe what his eyes told him.

"He's dead, my lord," Abiathar the priest proclaimed, dragging one hand over his scraggly beard.

Silence, still and foreign in the previously joyous air, settled like heavy fog over the waiting crowd.

"Why?" David's voice sounded commanding.

"Because he touched the ark of God, my lord." Abiathar shook his head, his face a study in misery.

David examined the still form of the young man. "How can the ark of the Lord ever come to me then?" Even from a distance, Michal watched anger and fear mix equally across his dark features. "I can't take it to Jerusalem now." He looked at the priest. "Someone else could die."

An old man, wrinkled and bent with age, leaned heavily on a walking stick as he approached the king. "I don't want it back." The man's voice wavered. "Uzzah was my grandson. God may do worse to my household if I keep the ark again."

"But it has blessed you all these years."

The old man lifted a shaky hand and pointed his finger at David. "Young man, can't you see the boy is dead?"

Michal stiffened. No one should talk to a king like he was a common man. She assessed David's reaction, watching the lines around David's eyes soften and his hand reach to cup the elderly man's shoulder.

"Yes, Abinadab, I can see. Do not worry, we will find another place to take the ark of God."

The old man nodded, then bent over his grandson's body, sobbing. David backed away, and a small group clustered around him. Michal strained to hear but soon gave up when the whispers of men and women drowned out the possibil-

337

ity of making out David's words. At last David emerged and waved his arms for attention.

"I am sending the ark of God to the house of Obed-Edom. He is a Levite living close by. The rest of you, please return to your homes." Tears filled his eyes. "I'm sorry."

He walked away and began the long trek back to Jerusalem. Michal kicked the mule's sides and followed him, the other women falling in behind. No one spoke. Michal doubted anyone could have, given the slumped shoulders and bowed head of their king.

Was the ark worth this? David was acting like a defeated general, one who'd just lost a battle of vital importance. So what if the ark couldn't come to Jerusalem? If God was that sensitive that He would kill someone trying to protect His box, then maybe the people would be better off without it.

Michal lifted her chin and straightened her back, determined to present an air of dignity, even if David wanted to humble himself before the thousands of people trudging the path behind him. Let them fuss and fret over today's unfortunate incident. As far as she was concerned, the ark of God wasn't worth the trouble.

❧

Michal walked up and down the lengthy corridors of David's palace, glancing at varied intervals through the arched porticos to the outer court and wide marble steps leading to the king's audience chamber. She wouldn't call it pacing, though her anxious feet had made the trip enough times to lose count. They'd been gone two days. How long could it possibly take to bring a gold box a half-day's journey to Jerusalem?

Two days earlier Michal had stood in the courtyard where

David had called his mighty men and family members to join him. He had approached her, asking if she was coming with them.

"I can't believe you're going after that thing again, David. Has three months shattered your memory?" She couldn't hold back the words. Couldn't he see the futility in his decision?

David stiffened and looked at her without expression. "We didn't follow the law last time we tried to bring the ark here. This time, if God wills, we will succeed."

Michal's chin lifted, and she glanced heavenward, avoiding his piercing gaze. "Well, I'm not going. I'm not fool enough to think that just because you do things differently there won't be problems." She looked at him then. "If one of your sons had died instead of Uzzah, you wouldn't be rushing off to subject yourself to that again."

Michal averted her eyes, ashamed of the clipped edge in her voice and hating the compassion it drew from him. She didn't want him to humor her. She wanted him to change his mind and forget this foolhardy mission. But when his hand cupped her face and coaxed her to meet his gaze, her resolve began to weaken.

"The Lord has blessed Obed-Edom these three months the ark has been in his home. No harm has come to him and his family, Michal. Besides, the priests have searched the Scriptures for me and discovered why God did not bless our last attempt. The priests were supposed to use the poles made for the ark and carry it on their shoulders. I plan to offer sacrifices as well, to cover the sins of the people." His fingers stroked her cheek. "Are you sure you won't come?"

The memory of his impassioned plea that day only aggravated her now.

Michal stopped her pacing midstride and shaded her eyes with both hands, searching for some sign of the group. The memory of his disappointed sigh at her refusal still rang in her ears. He'd moved on to his other wives, stopping in front of Abigail. Sweet, kind, righteous Abigail. Of course, she'd gladly accepted the role of leading the women in Michal's place.

Michal's fists clenched at the thought of the grateful look on the woman's face. Her eager child had hugged David's legs, and Michal had been surprised David hadn't asked Abigail to lead the women in worship first. She seemed to share the same religious fervor as their husband, so to ask her would have made perfect sense. If not for the problem with the woman's son, Abigail would surely have been David's choice as queen. As it stood, the proud, haughty Maacah had a better chance at that position, if David's affection for Absalom were any indication.

Michal spun around and walked back through the corridors of the nearly empty house. She climbed a flight of stairs to the second story and peered through the window, hoping for a better view. Surely they would come soon.

❦

Abiathar, Zadok, and their fellow Levitical priests lifted the poles of the ark of God, rested them on their shoulders, and carried the ark with measured steps out of the house of Obed-Edom, where it had remained for the past three months. When their feet moved six paces, they stopped. The lowing of a bull and a fattened calf reached David's ears, and he turned his head to watch two more priests grab a protesting bull by the horns and swiftly slit its throat. Blood spurted from the animal and was caught in a basin by a third priest.

The priests cut up the now lifeless bull and placed its parts on a newly constructed altar, sprinkled some of its blood along the sides, and poured the rest of the blood at its base. After the bull was consumed, they brought the fattened calf in front of the altar. Its wide, trusting gaze ended quickly as the priest's blade snuffed out its young life. Smoke rose heavenward from the sacrifice, and David's heart constricted with remorse at the animal's loss, then turned in an instant to his own silent repentance.

They're dead on my account, Lord. Please see the blood spilled on behalf of Your people and accept our sacrifice. We don't deserve Your favor. But we long for it. Forgive us, Lord God. Remember we are but dust.

More bulls and rams were sacrificed, seven of each in all, and with each one, David's soul yearned more for Yahweh. He slipped his royal robe from his shoulders and handed it to a servant. Zadok offered prayers, his arms raised toward the sky. When the last ember from the sacrifices died away, the priests started the long walk to Jerusalem.

David's heart lifted, and he motioned for the singers to begin playing their instruments. The Lord had heard their prayers. He was sure of it. Joy bubbled from deep within him. His feet kept time with the music, his voice raised in song. They would bring the ark to Jerusalem. He would be able to lead the people back to the true worship of Yahweh. Hadn't this been his longing from his youth?

Oh, thank You, Lord God, for hearing our prayers and accepting our sacrifices.

His feet leaped higher, and his arms lifted toward the clouds. He'd never known such unrestricted joy. God was good beyond measure.

The rich timbre of David's voice carried to the palace, where Michal still stood at the second-story window, looking out over Jerusalem. The throng of people following the ark surged toward the ornate tent made of the finest cloth in Israel, their voices now joining David's. Michal's gaze drifted from the ark to her husband leading the multitude.

What was he doing?

She stepped closer and leaned her head out of the window. The noonday sun glinted off a sleeveless white linen vest covering David's tunic. Michal blinked and looked again. Where were his royal symbols—his robe, his jewelry, his crown? Her gaze shifted to the ordinary priests following those selected to carry the ark. David looked like one of them!

Movement caught her eye, and she glanced back at David. Her mouth dropped, but she clamped it shut, gazing in disbelief at the sight below. David was dancing! Like a common man. Dressed like a priest instead of a king.

Praise songs drifted to her, and she focused on the crowd. Peasant women looked on, and even from a distance she saw the admiration, the yearning for her husband. Every woman in Israel was in love with David. And he was acting as their equal. Next thing she knew, he would be adding a horde of common women to his already bulging harem.

Michal hugged her arms to her chest and again stared at David still dancing and raising his arms toward the sky. His devotion was definitely misguided. If he wanted to worship Adonai, fine. But he shouldn't lower himself in the sight of the people. He would lose their respect.

Just like her father had.

A tremor worked through her. She couldn't endure that again. Couldn't live with a king who was driven to madness.

The crowd reached the entrance to the tent, and the priests turned and continued walking. They would be stopping at the front of the tabernacle. There would be sacrifices and feasting and more singing. But Michal had seen enough. She turned from the window and stalked toward the stairs, heart pounding, fists clenched at her sides.

How could he do this to her? He was the king! Kings didn't act like common people. Hadn't he learned that by now?

When she reached the bottom step, Michal took the hall leading back to her apartment, seething. David was acting like a fool. The thought seized her and turned her heart cold. She hated him with a fierceness that took her breath away. Then, without warning, a strange peace settled over her, like an unexpected calm before a storm.

David was a simple shepherd, a usurper of her father's throne. Without her, he had no right to rule Israel. It was time he realized it.

❧❧

David looked out over the dispersing crowd, quiet joy filling all the spaces in his heart. What a day! God's mercy had shined on their efforts, and the ark of the Lord now rested in the tent he had prepared for it. Once again the feeling of awe and humility swept over him, leaving his heart open and bare. But he wasn't afraid anymore. Yahweh had examined his heart, pierced his soul, and cleansed his hidden sins. He felt clean, usable, and the joy of the Lord made his heart sing.

With a parting glance toward the front of the tent where

the ark now rested, David turned and walked to the tent opening. Benaiah stood waiting to escort him.

"Your robe, my lord." Benaiah held David's gold and blue embroidered robe open, and David slipped his arms through the sleeves.

"Thank you, Benaiah." He accepted the crown from Benaiah's outstretched hand and slipped the signet ring back on his finger. "Although I'd almost prefer the humble ephod over this. Brings a man's thoughts in line with how insignificant he really is, you know?"

Benaiah nodded and fell into step beside David as he moved out of the tent and began the walk back to the palace. "Your actions today endeared you to the people, my lord. But I think you were too concerned with Adonai's opinion to notice."

David stopped to look at the guard and smiled. "I'll take whatever blessings God allows, my friend. I couldn't help but feel the need to strip myself of the trappings the people place on me when coming before the Lord. He is Israel's true king."

The marble steps of the palace loomed before them, and the two walked in silence to the halls leading to the royal family's private quarters. When they reached the audience chamber, David spotted Michal walking toward them, head held high, eyes flashing. On instinct he stiffened.

"How the king of Israel distinguished himself today! He uncovered himself today in the eyes of his servants' maids as one of the foolish ones shamelessly uncovers himself!" Michal flung the words at him like sharp barbs, her voice rising with every word.

David stood still under the arch of the covered portico, staring into her hardened dark eyes. The joy of the day vanished under her icy glare, and in an instant David saw into her bitter soul.

She hated him. She stood there acting like his superior, condemning his actions. Why? Because he'd removed the symbols of royalty? How did that make him immodest or shameless? He'd done it for Yahweh, because only Yahweh is king.

But Yahweh did not rule Michal's heart, nor could she understand someone whose life was lived in devotion to Him. The thought sank to the pit of his gut, making him unutterably sad.

She would never understand him. He saw it all too clearly now.

The moment stretched to an eternity until David finally spoke. "It was before the Lord, who chose me instead of your father and his house, to appoint me ruler over the people of the Lord, over Israel." He lowered his voice, but it still carried across the room. "So I will play music before the Lord. And I will be even more undignified than this and will be humble in my own sight." He paused, searching her face for some flicker of remorse, but was greeted only with disdain. "But as for the maidservants of whom you have spoken," he continued, "I will be held in honor by them."

"And I suppose if they look on you with respect, you'll be adding them to our number?"

David almost flinched but caught himself. So that was her problem. She just couldn't accept the fact that he had taken other wives. What did she expect of him? A king took wives to make alliances, to keep war at bay, to strengthen his kingdom. He had swallowed that bitter reality long ago. If she cared about him, she would understand.

But she didn't care. He could see it now in her rigid stance and cold stare. Goliath had looked less menacing.

He met her silent glare with one of his own and straightened his shoulders, taking the kingly posture she expected. "If I choose to add more wives to my family, it is not your concern, Michal. Your part is to support me as a first wife should, in being an example to the others. But seeing as you scorn your role and disdain my choices, I will grant you what your heart seems to desire. You will live in my home, but do not expect to see my face again."

He watched shock register on her beautiful face. But in the next instant, her eyes grew cold once again, her fists balled at her sides.

"Take this woman back to her rooms, Benaiah." David forced his voice to sound casual, hiding his sense of loss. "She is not welcome here." With that, he turned and strode with brisk steps to the roof where he could mourn in peace.

35

Grief. That had to be what he was feeling—as though he had lost Jonathan all over again. He should never have allowed the woman to have such power over him. Didn't he know that? Hadn't he clung to that belief long ago?

He had no one to blame but himself, of course. If he hadn't allowed her innocent beauty to entice him, hadn't succumbed to the longings of youthful love, hadn't thought that the way to the kingdom might be through marrying into Saul's family, he wouldn't be in this mess.

David closed his eyes where he sat among cushions in his rooftop pavilion and buried his face in his hands. It was weakness that made him so miserable. If the truth were known, women held his heart far too easily. And he never should have given so much of it to Michal.

He had loved her once—thought he still did. Until today. But time had changed her. He could still feel the hatred in her glare, see the ice in her eyes.

Could any woman's love last?

Jonathan would never have turned on him like that. But

then Jonathan shared his love for Yahweh. Obviously Michal did not.

Sudden restlessness overtook him. He stood and paced the small room, soon tiring of the confines of the darkened tent. He slipped under the flap and walked along the rim of the parapet.

Was anyone left of the house of Jonathan? He'd vowed he would protect his friend's family, but in all the struggles to advance the kingdom, he'd forgotten. How could he have been so faithless?

His thoughts lashed out at him, berating him. Maybe he couldn't change Michal's heart, but he could do something for Jonathan's offspring, if he could find them. He walked to the stairs where a guard stood.

"My lord the king." The guard bowed in respect.

"Summon my counselors. Have them meet me in my private chambers."

"Yes, my lord." The man turned to do his bidding.

🦋

"Is anyone left of the house of Saul, that I may show him kindness for Jonathan's sake?" David looked around at Ahithophel, Hushai, Joab, Benaiah, and Abishai, trusted soldiers and friends. If anyone could find this information for him, they could.

"You mean besides Merab's sons or the sons of Saul by his concubine, Rizpah?" A scowl worked its way up to Joab's eyes. "Michal has already pushed hard for her nephews' positions in your kingdom, my lord. You've been more than gracious toward her requests by even allowing them to live. Isn't that kindness enough?"

David heard the underlying bitterness in Joab's tone and tented his fingers beneath his bearded chin. Merab's sons were surly, insolent young men, a constant reminder of Saul's slights against him. He had put up with them for Michal's sake.

But didn't Jonathan have an heir?

"Most kings would have killed every member of their rival's families, my lord," Ahithophel said. "Besides, if you pursue this, the people may think you need Saul's goodwill to hold your kingdom together—that you are weak without Saul. And when they find out you've banished Michal, they may think you are grasping to hold their favor. With all due respect, my lord, you are stronger without Saul's family."

David drummed his fingers on the cushion beside him. "I made a vow to Jonathan, Ahithophel. I am bound by honor and by Adonai to keep it."

The older man nodded his acquiescence. "In that case," he said, "I know of a servant of Saul—a man named Ziba. He may be able to answer your question."

David's heart lifted. "Thank you, my friend." He looked toward the standing guard. "Find Ziba and bring him to me."

❧

"Mephibosheth is coming here?" Michal's heart thumped at the painful memory of Jonathan's crippled son. Sometimes, when she lay alone in her bed, Sarah's distraught screams still rang in her ears, and the twisted legs of her nephew materialized before her closed eyes. She should have sought him out and demanded Paltiel allow her to care for him years ago when his mother died. Why had she let Paltiel's aversion to his handicap keep her from compassion? And what would David do with him now?

Fear gripped her, making her blood run cold. She looked warily at Keziah. "When?"

"The servants said the caravan carrying Jonathan's son was seen entering Jerusalem's gates moments ago, my lady. They should be arriving at the palace shortly."

Why would David want Jonathan's son except to harm him? "I have to warn him, Keziah. Before it's too late."

Keziah placed a comforting hand on her arm. "Why do you fear, my lady? You cannot stop the king's decree. Besides, has David harmed your other nephews or Rizpah's sons?"

Michal stared at the woman, her heartbeat slowing a pace. She was right, of course. David had never done anything to hurt her family. Why should she think any differently of him now?

Except that now she had shown him how much she despised him. Her own loathing fueled her fear. He knew she hated him.

And she knew he must hate her in return.

She turned away from Keziah's searching gaze and walked into her bedchamber, flinging herself across the bed. Why had she allowed her feelings to overcome her good sense? Why had she spoken such bitter words?

Now it was too late.

※※

David rested both hands on the gilded arms of his throne, watching the crippled son of Jonathan drag his disfigured feet behind him. It had taken six months to find Saul's servant Ziba and arrange for Mephibosheth to get here. Now Mephibosheth leaned heavily on Ziba's arm across the length of the audience chamber. Pain beat a path to David's heart. The son of Jonathan deserved better.

When the young man reached the throne, he let go of the servant and fell to his face on the tiled floor.

"Mephibosheth?" David's voice filled with compassion.

"Here is your servant!"

David watched the man's shoulders shake. He motioned to a guard to help Mephibosheth to his feet. When their eyes met, David smiled. "Do not fear, Mephibosheth, for I will surely show you kindness for Jonathan your father's sake, and I will restore to you the land of Saul your grandfather, and you will eat bread at my table."

Mephibosheth bowed his head, his voice low. "What is your servant that you should look upon such a dead dog as I?"

David studied Mephibosheth, searching for some resemblance to his old friend. The man was thin and weak limbed, but the somber olive brown eyes were Jonathan's. He smiled, silently thanking the Lord that he could at last fulfill his vow.

"Ziba," David said to the servant, "I have given to your master's son all that belonged to Saul and his house. Therefore you and your sons and your servants will work the land for him, and you will bring in the harvest, that your master's son may have food to eat. But Mephibosheth your master's son will always eat bread at my table." David's gaze shifted to Mephibosheth, warmed by the man's awed smile.

"According to all that my lord the king has commanded his servant, so will your servant do." Ziba knelt, head bowed in respect.

"As for Mephibosheth," David said, smiling, "he will eat at my table like one of the king's sons."

It was the least he could do.

❧36❧

Five Years Later

Michal sat in the center of her private garden, fanning herself from the arid heat and staring at the sparse almond leaves and wilted flowers. Two years after Mephibosheth had come to live near David's home, the famine had set in, and now, three years later, the drought had withered the plants and dried up the soil until the people cried continually at the king's gate for something to be done.

Surely by now David must realize that God was punishing them. Why else would He withhold life-giving rain and allow the heat to zap the moisture from the already dry land? The thought unnerved her. Could she be the cause? Was Adonai punishing the nation because she had despised her husband?

Her gaze drifted across the garden to the life-size teraphim standing guard on either side of the entrance—household gods she had once vowed she would never look at again. She'd changed her mind when she realized David meant what he said and would never come back. Somehow the sight of them reminded her of happier days when David had belonged only to her.

She choked out a brittle laugh. Even the memories mocked her, and she wondered, not for the first time, why she chose to torment herself with them. She bent to pick up a clump of dry earth and flung it at the teraphim. Her mother had once thought of the images as some kind of magic charm against her father's demons. But they'd held no power to help her mother or father then or to help her realize her dreams now. They only managed to fuel her resentment. Ishby would have frowned on the images, and Jonathan would have demanded she destroy them.

She bristled, frustrated at her own confused train of thought. If she hadn't used one as a ruse to help David escape all those years ago, things might have been different.

She brushed the remnants of dirt from her palms and went back to fanning herself. Who was she kidding? If she could do things over again, she would have helped him exactly as she had then. She'd loved him with abandon. And it had been the death of her dreams.

Sighing, Michal stood and walked toward the teraphim, examining the carved wood and intricate gold overlay. David would smash them in a heartbeat if he knew.

You shall have no other gods before Me. Jonathan's words haunted her now. She was acting just like her mother. Perhaps Adonai was angry with her. Could her household gods be the cause of the famine?

The thought made the blood drain from her face, and she thought she might faint. She needed air. But the air was oppressive inside and out, and she was sick to death of the small section of the house in which she was allowed.

Cries from outside the palace walls drifted to her on the still afternoon air. Men and women should be resting on their beds until this heat wave ended. But their voices permeated the cedar beams and marble halls until Michal wanted to tear her hair out.

She whirled about, shoved one of the teraphim on its side, and strode into her bedchamber, longing for relief. Guilt nudged her, but she shushed it away. It wasn't her fault the land was ravaged by famine. How could it be? God wouldn't condemn a whole nation because of one woman.

And why did she even worry about such things? The problem rested with David. Let him find a solution.

🙢🙠

The audience chamber with its marble floors and cedar-lined walls offered little respite from the continuous oppressive heat. David drummed his fingers on one arm of his gilded throne while servants lifted palm branches and papyrus fans to cool the air around him. The prophet Nathan strode across the floor, arms tucked into the sleeves of his brown robe. When he reached the throne, David motioned for him to sit beside him.

"Welcome, my friend. Thank you for coming."

"I could not have done otherwise, my king. You have something you need from me?" Nathan took the seat offered him and rested his hands on his knees. His aqua eyes sparkled, and his lips curved in pleasure. He was a tall man with a straight black beard and hair extending halfway down his back. The lean prophet, a few years David's junior, had taken the Nazarite vow never to cut his hair or drink wine. He had joined David's special council soon after the ark came to Jerusalem.

David studied the simple dress and guileless smile of the

prophet and sighed. Such an uncomplicated, joy-filled life Nathan lived, communing with Yahweh day after day.

"I want you to inquire of the Lord for me, Nathan. I need to know the cause of this famine."

Nathan stroked his beard. "You think the Lord is punishing Israel, my king?"

David sighed heavily. "I wish I knew, Nathan. If He is, I need to know."

The prophet nodded and stood. "I will seek the Lord on your behalf, my lord."

David dipped his head in acknowledgment as Nathan walked from the room.

❧❧

During the evening meal, while David sat with his sons, Mephibosheth among them, Nathan strode into the dining hall. David stood at Nathan's approach.

"What has the Lord said to you?"

Nathan's gaze seized David's, sending chills up his spine. "Thus says the Lord." The clank of silver goblets and the din of voices drifted to silence. All eyes looked to the prophet. Nathan drew in a slow breath and spread his arms wide. "The cause of the famine is due to Saul and his bloody house because he tried to exterminate the Gibeonites."

David's tense muscles relaxed, relieved his own guilt wasn't the cause of such misery among his people. "Did the Lord say what I am to do about this?"

Nathan shook his head. "No, my lord. This is all He said."

David sat back in his seat, his thoughts sifting through the possibilities. He would confer with his counselors and send for the leaders of the Gibeonites. There must be some

way to make amends so the land would be blessed once
again.

❦

The walled gardens directly opposite his bedchamber usually gave David a welcome respite from his hectic court life.
But even here the drought reached, making fig trees fail to
produce and normally shiny flowers droop, their petals falling
like teardrops to the dry earth.

David flexed his fingers and raked one hand through his
thick hair. How could Saul have sought to kill these people?
For as long as David could remember, the Gibeonites, protected by an ancient covenant with their ancestor Joshua,
had been a peace-loving tribe. They didn't try to push their
territory beyond their borders and weren't violent or trouble-
making men. So why on earth would Saul murder them?

David began a slow walk along the smooth stones of the
garden path, hands clasped behind him. Memories of Saul's
bloodthirsty order to kill the priests flashed in his mind's eye.
Though he hadn't been there, David had imagined the gory
details many times in his nightmares. As with the priests,
Saul had also killed the Gibeonites because he cared only
for himself.

He stopped in front of a spreading tamarisk bush and ran
one hand over the prickly branches. They needed water. Bar-
ley harvest was about to begin, and David wondered if his
family's normally lush land in Bethlehem would produce
enough grain to keep them fed. Three years was a long time
to go without a good crop.

Please, Lord, put an end to this famine.

He'd uttered the same prayer a hundred times. Turning

on his heel, he headed back toward his room, glancing at the sundial along the way. The Gibeonites should be arriving in Jerusalem within the hour, if his sources were correct. Maybe then he would finally have some answers.

❦

The trumpet sounded, announcing David's arrival, and the hall grew quiet as the people waited for him to take his throne. Moments after the normal preliminaries, a scribe announced a contingent of foreigners, whose leaders strode forward as a group and bowed low at David's feet.

"May my lord, King David, live forever." An aged man with silver hair and a bent back straightened as best he could and stepped forward, touching the scepter David extended to him.

David assessed the men before him. "What shall I do for you? And with what shall I make atonement, that you may bless the inheritance of the Lord?"

The old man averted his gaze a moment, staring at the mosaic floor, then lifted his head and sighed. "We will have no silver or gold from Saul or from his house, nor shall you kill any man in Israel for us."

David felt a measure of relief rush through him. "Whatever you say, I will do for you."

A collective breath suspended over the room at his announcement. David looked to his sons and advisors. At the sight of Mephibosheth, he paused, reading fear in the man's gaze.

"As for the man who consumed us and plotted against us, that we should be destroyed from remaining in any of the territories of Israel," the man said, commanding the attention of the entire hall, "let seven men of his descendants be delivered to us, and we will hang them before the Lord in Gibeah of Saul, whom the Lord chose."

A trail of gasps moved around the room, and David watched all color drain from Mephibosheth's face. He looked back to the spokesmen as the crowd stilled.

"I will give them." David's voice cut the silence of the court.

"Thank you, my lord," the old man said.

David turned to his scribe and whispered directions, then spoke to Benaiah. "Go, send for Armoni and Mephibosheth, the two sons of Rizpah . . ." He glanced again across the hall at Jonathan's son. "I will spare Mephibosheth, son of Jonathan, and his son, Micha, for Jonathan's sake." David's eyes met Mephibosheth's before turning back to Benaiah. "And send for the five sons of Merab, whom she bore to Adriel the Meholathite. These seven I will give to the Gibeonites, that the Lord may lift the famine from Israel."

⁓⊶

"No! He can't have them. I won't let him!" Michal pushed past Keziah, who had delivered the awful news, and hurried down the corridors, slithering by unsuspecting guards. Her whole body trembled.

Please, God, let it be a lie.

She reached David's audience chamber, determined to force her way in, when one of the guards caught her arms, bringing her to a sudden halt.

"Hold on, mistress. You can't go in there. You do not have permission." His grip tightened as she fought to free herself.

"I have to see the king. He's made a terrible mistake. I must see him!" Michal pounded her fists against the guard's chest until he grabbed her wrists to stop her.

"The king does not wish to see you, Michal." Benaiah spoke from behind her.

Michal turned stricken eyes on the burly warrior, head of David's private guard, the man who had once tried to free her from her father and take her to David—in another place, a lifetime ago. The sight of him now did not hold the same hope it once did. He was wholly devoted to David, and David didn't want anything to do with her. The thought made her heart sink and tears sting.

"Benaiah, you must speak to him for me. They're going to execute my nephews—all five of them. Please, Benaiah, I have to stop him before it's too late." Her broken sobs made her breath come in short gasps. The guard loosened his grip on her. She fell to her knees before Benaiah, hands clasped in front of her. "Please, Benaiah, take me to him."

"I have orders to keep you away."

The quiet words tore at her heart.

"Please!" She was sobbing now, not caring what anyone thought of her. *Malchi, Benni, Rueben, Jacob, Joel.* Her heart cried out their names, remembering each young face despite the fact they were grown men. She hadn't seen them in two years, not since David had banned them from the royal court. Still, they were like sons to her. She couldn't lose them now.

"It's too late, Michal." David's voice broke through her sobs, arresting her breath. "The Gibeonites asked for seven sons of Saul to stop the curse of the famine, to pay for the harm your father brought on them when he tried to exterminate them. Sometimes a few must die for the good of the people."

The compassion in his voice gave her courage to look into his still charmingly handsome face. "Are they . . . are they . . ."

"They're already dead."

She didn't want to cry, to give him the satisfaction. Hadn't he done enough damage?

"Why my nephews, David?" The bitter words came out before she could stop them. "Why choose so many from one family, leaving none to console me? Did you do it to spite me? Am I so odious in your eyes that you had to kill the only men I could call sons?" She rose to her feet, hands clenched at her sides. When she took a step toward him, Benaiah restrained her.

She tried to wrench free. "Let me go!" She turned on him, fury making her beat his thick chest with her fists. "What's the matter? Are you afraid I'll hurt your precious king?"

David's cool voice from behind tamed her flailing arms. "You haven't changed."

Michal twisted her head, her body still held in Benaiah's iron grip, and met David's level gaze.

"Take this woman back to her rooms and post a guard. See that her needs are met." He turned and walked in the opposite direction without a backward glance.

~37~

Michal paced the lengthy chamber, perspiration beading her forehead, her fists clenched. She wanted to scream and wail, but the sounds stuck in her throat. How had her life come to this? She was secluded from all happenings in the palace, the city, and the nation. Except for Keziah, she had no one to talk to on a regular basis, and she would never be held in a man's arms again. The ache of it all made her ill to the core. Seeing David dressed in his finest with a glittering crown on his head, looking down on her with compassion, had made her yearn for him again with a fierceness she thought long dead.

She would have given anything to feel the touch of his fingers against her cheek, to hear his whispered words soothe her grief. And then she had ruined it. Her bitterness had bubbled to the surface before she could stop it, and she'd shown David the side of her she now despised—as much as she had once despised him.

Oh, God, what had she done? How could she ever make it right? Her feet found their way to her bedchamber, and she fell to her knees beside her bed. She didn't really know how to pray. Oh, she had heard David speak words to Adonai many times, but he'd spoken so easily, as though he knew Him. Michal realized with sudden clarity that she did not know the God of Israel. Not the way David did.

She snatched a pillow from the pristine bed and hugged it to her chest, leaning against the wooden frame. Why should she care whether she knew the Lord or not? Adonai had stolen everything—every man she'd ever held dear. Even David. But she could hardly blame God for that loss.

She buried her face in the pillow and rocked back and forth, moaning. Anger nearly choked her as the bitter tears wet the fabric. Why was God so mean to her? Was He punishing her for the way she'd acted, for the lies she'd told?

Was He trying to tell her something?

The thought had never occurred to her before, and with it came a sense of longing. How could David know *Adonai El Elyon*, the Lord Most High God, so well? Was it possible . . . could she know Him too? The thought sent a shiver of fear up her spine.

Did she want to?

What if she came to Him and gave Him everything she had left, and He took the rest? If she'd learned one thing in her life, it was that God could not be trusted. Every time she'd wanted something and begged Him for it, she'd lost it soon after He gave it. Her father's times of peace never lasted. David never stayed home, and after he left her, he never came back, no matter how many prayers she'd uttered.

She gulped a sob and pushed up from the floor, flinging the pillow onto the bed. Sullenly, she wandered into her adjacent gardens and sank onto a wooden bench. Her fingers stroked the clay pot that had once held her favorite rose of Sharon, now dried up from lack of water. Relentless tears smarted again, and she sniffed away the emotion. God had taken the beauty from her only place of refuge.

Why, God? Why are You doing this?

Her thoughts drifted again to her early days with David, the joy they had found in each other's arms. How short-lived it had all been. David was supposed to have been the means to her gaining control of her life and one day ruling at his side. What had happened to it all? She curled both fists and squeezed them, closing her eyes.

Images passed before her thoughts, as though her life were being replayed. Father's rage. David's kiss. Paltiel's arrogance. Her bitter words flung in David's face.

She slowly unclenched her fingers as the pictures played like a terrible dream in her mind. Grief and guilt rose in her chest, filling her with deep remorse. She blinked hard and tried to look heavenward, but her knees grew weak, and heaviness fell like a hot blanket over her soul.

O Adonai!

Her heart twisted in fear and pain. She felt as though a hand pressed down on her, forcing her to her knees.

And suddenly she knew. A window to her soul opened, and Michal squirmed at the sight. What a bitter woman she'd become! She'd been so afraid Father's demons would one day hound her steps that she never realized she'd given herself over to demons of her own.

She lowered her head to her hands, the pressure of guilt squeezing her soul. A sense of humility washed over her, and her spirit felt stripped and bare before the eyes of the One who sees all. How could she even lift her head to speak with Him? He had exposed her shame, and the scars in her cynical soul repulsed her. How could she ever face anyone again, let alone the Lord?

Come to Me with clean hands and a pure heart.

She turned her hands over, examining them. Oh, they were clean on the outside, perfectly perfumed and hennaed too. But she'd used them to seek her own way all of her life.

She lifted her gaze long enough to glance across the garden, where the teraphim sat guarding the opposite gate. She had kept them purposely, knowing David would never approve. Another stain on her hands.

O Adonai, please forgive me.

The weight of her guilt nearly leveled her to the floor, and tears blurred her vision again. She would destroy the idols first thing.

And a pure heart.

Despair slid next to the grief in her soul. How on earth could she ever have a pure heart? Hers was as black as a starless night.

Repent.

The word sang in her thoughts, as though David had strummed his lyre and sung the word in her ear. Repent? Hope filled her. Was it that easy?

Repent, beloved.

Oh, could she? Would Adonai accept her after all she'd done? She moved from her knees and prostrated her body across the smooth stones. Words formed in her thoughts, and she spoke aloud slowly, haltingly, like a baby taking his first steps.

"I have never prayed to You like this, Adonai. I've never come seeking Your forgiveness, never humbled myself before You, never realized my sin. I don't know if You can forgive me for my pride or give me the pure heart You require. But I'm coming to You, and if You will have me, I will submit to You."

Michal's words continued in broken sobs as she named every sin that surfaced—her deceit when she had convinced Father to give Merab to Adriel, her lies when Father had questioned her about David, her angry words poured out at David's feet, and most of all her bitterness. She grew stiff and achy until she finally pushed up to her trembling knees and gazed heavenward.

Was it possible? Her bitterness was gone, melted away like wax seeping into the soil on a hot day. Joy filled her. She was clean! Her heart felt light, and she laughed outright, almost giddy.

"Are you all right, my lady?" Keziah asked, rushing through the door of the house.

Michal could not contain her smile. "Better than I've ever been."

If only she could share her news with David. The thought dampened her spirit, but the joy remained. If God willed, she would see David again to share her newfound faith.

❧❧

"It's been six months, my lord, and Rizpah still stands guard over the bodies of her sons, not allowing the carrion birds to touch their bodies." The messenger had come from the tribe of Benjamin with a contingent of men.

David looked down at the crowd, searching for a friendly face, but saw only troubled glances. His gaze shifted to his counselors, and he motioned for them to approach his throne.

365

Ahithophel spoke first. "Perhaps it's time you gave the bodies a proper burial, my lord. The famine has only partially let up. The Lord may not bless us until the bodies are no longer exposed."

David noted the nods of Hushai and Benaiah. He glanced over at Amnon and Absalom seated to the right of the court. How would he have felt if they had been among the dead? A twinge of guilt nudged him. Perhaps that would explain Michal's outrage when the men were killed. Had he picked her nephews out of his own private revenge? David shook away the disturbing thought. It had not been his idea to execute Saul's family. He'd done it for the good of the people. Still, six months' exposure to the elements was long enough.

"You're right, Ahithophel, it is time to give the men a proper burial. We will exhume the bones of Saul and Jonathan as well and bury them in the cave of Saul's father, Kish."

He excused his counselors and announced his intentions to the men from Benjamin. Maybe then God would bless the land again with abundance.

꿈꿈

A knock at the door, so unusual these days, made Michal's heart skip. She looked up from the pillow she was embroidering with fig leaves and purple lilies and nodded to Keziah, who jumped up to open it. David's guard stood to the side, admitting a messenger bearing the royal insignia. David had a message—for her?

The man stepped into the room, and Michal laid her stitching aside. She watched the messenger bow at her feet.

"My lady," he said, meeting her gaze, "the king has sent word to inform you that there will be a memorial service honoring your father at the end of the week. We will be traveling to the burial cave of King Saul's father, Kish. Do you wish to come?"

Michal's heart leaped, hope filling her. David was going to honor her father? And he was inviting her to come? "Yes. Tell the king . . . tell my lord, King David, that I would be pleased to come."

The guard gave her a curious look. What had the servants been saying about her? Were her words and tone so different that he actually noticed? Would David notice too?

"I will give the king your message, my lady."

O Lord, please let David look on me with favor once again. I don't deserve the pleasure of his company or the status of first wife restored to me after what I've said and done to Your anointed, but please . . . if nothing else, let me share with David what You have done for me.

She watched the messenger close the door behind him, and she picked up her stitching again. What she wouldn't give to move freely through David's house again. Even to interact with his bickering wives was better than this seclusion. And yet, it was nothing more than she deserved. She knew that now. If only God would be merciful . . . Dare she hope? Maybe then she would find a renewed purpose for living.

☙38☙

Michal tugged the woolen cloak over her shoulders and hunkered closer to her mule's neck, trying to block the cool wind from seeping against her skin. The caravan traveling from Jerusalem to Zelah where her grandfather's bones rested was filled with heads of tribes, mighty men, several of David's family, and what looked like the entire tribe of Benjamin. Her father's concubine, Rizpah, was given a place of honor behind the king and to the left of Mephibosheth, who followed the men carrying the bones of Saul, Jonathan, Rizpah's sons, and Michal's five nephews.

The wind picked up as they neared the outskirts of the town, whipping the scarf around Michal's head. She reached one hand to pull the black sheer fabric from her eyes and scanned the crowd. David was separated from her by scores of men. Would she even be able to see the cave when they placed her father's bones within its walls?

Pain tugged at her, and the familiar bile of bitterness rose to choke her. This was her family! She deserved to be leading the crowd, or at least given the honor due Saul's last surviving offspring. Yet David treated her as though she were as dead as the men whose bleached bones they were burying.

She shook her head, forcing her tears into submission. No! She mustn't think like this. Adonai would not be pleased if she spoke out in anger again. She bit her tongue, begging God to keep the bitter words from spilling from her mouth.

Give me a heart of humility, Lord. A heart like David's.

David slipped from his mule, and she watched his men follow his example. They formed small groups around the burial cave, effectively blocking her view. There was no way she could force a path through such a crowd unless she made a terrible ruckus. Not a good way to endear herself to David.

She tugged on the mule's reins, maneuvering as close as she dared. She pulled to the side of the crowd, craning her neck to see. Several muscular soldiers shoved aside the heavy stone, and the men carrying the bones of her family members stepped closer to the opening of the cave.

A trumpet sounded with royal fanfare, and flags whipped in the wind.

David's voice quieted the crowd. "Men of Israel, today we lay to rest with honor the bones of Saul and his beloved son, Jonathan." His voice broke with emotion. "Jonathan, my brother, how wonderful your friendship and how great your devotion." He looked over the crowd, his eyes resting for a moment on hers.

His gaze moved on, and her heart sank. Jonathan's devotion was better than hers. Jonathan would have done all in his power to support David, no matter what.

She listened, eyes riveted on David, as he commended Rizpah for her loyalty to her sons and expressed his sorrow over all their losses. At last, when the words ended and the crowd sang a song of mourning—the song David had written when her father had died—the bones were placed in the tomb, and the tomb was sealed with her father's royal insignia.

Michal allowed the wind to shove the veil over her eyes, grateful that it hid her silent tears. She bowed her head, waiting for the crowd to disperse as men and women mounted horses and donkeys to return to Jerusalem and their surrounding villages. David's entourage took longer to ready themselves, and Michal thanked the Lord for the added time she could mourn in peace. She slipped from her mule's back and stretched her legs, then walked away from the group to the shelter of a cluster of rocks.

Michal's heart ached, but she bowed her head and knelt in the dust anyway, begging God to give her an attitude of thanksgiving. A hand on her shoulder startled her, and she jerked upright.

"It's all right, Michal. It's only me." David's voice sent her blood pumping, and heat poured into her face.

She quickly lowered her head, touching it to the earth. "My lord the king."

She felt his fingers touch her head, and she slowly raised her eyes to meet his gaze. What was he doing here? She wasn't supposed to ever see him again, let alone be close enough to touch the hem of his garment. Could Yahweh have heard her prayers?

"My lord," she whispered. She sat back on her heels, certain he could hear the slamming of her heart against her chest.

He stood gazing down at her, a curious look flitting across his knitted brow. "The daughter of Saul kneeling in the dust is a bit undignified, wouldn't you say?"

His barbed words sliced through her heart. How she must have hurt him.

Oh, Yahweh, forgive me.

She lowered her eyes, not sure she could withstand his scrutiny. "Forgive me, my lord, I was praying. I did not hear you coming, and . . ." His sudden intake of breath sounded like she'd startled him. She glanced at him. "I was trying to show you the respect you deserve." Her gaze dropped to her folded hands, and she held her breath, silently begging him to understand.

He cleared his throat. "You were praying?"

She stole another glance at him and nodded. If she was ever going to explain herself and speak with him, now was the time.

"I've come to know Him, David. Adonai allowed everything to be stripped from me. Everyone I ever loved, I've lost. Even you." She held his interested gaze. "It finally occurred to me that maybe God was trying to tell me something. I wanted to pray to Him, but I didn't really know how. I knew you knew Him, but I didn't. I wanted to ask you"—she averted her eyes—"but I couldn't. So I just started talking to Him, begging for forgiveness."

She looked at David again, and his look stopped her words. His hand extended toward her. She lifted trembling fingers to settle in his palm.

David's strong arm pulled her to stand before him, and she instinctively bowed her head, half afraid of what he would say, thrilled with the touch of his fingers wrapped around hers. Silence spanned the distance between them until she felt him tipping her chin to look at him.

371

"You could have asked me, Michal. You could have asked me long ago."

"I had too much pride then, my lord." She searched his face, trying to read his thoughts. "I'm sorry." She looked away. "For everything."

He released her hand, and the loss made her heart sink, until she felt him trace the outline of her face and then encircle her waist.

"Do you remember the night of Merab's wedding in the garden, when you slipped away alone and we met there?"

Michal met his tender gaze and smiled. "How could I forget? I dreamed of you for months afterward, scheming to get my father to let me marry you."

She watched a reserved smile cross his face. He was holding back from her. She could feel it in his touch and in the way his eyes held hers.

"Was it a mistake, David? Was our marriage all a horrible mistake?" She couldn't stop her lower lip from trembling, and she hated her sudden tears.

His finger covered her lips before he pulled her closer, hugging her against his chest. Her cheek brushed the soft fabric of his royal robe, and she could hear the steady cadence of his heart. "Shhh," he whispered against her ear. "Don't say such things, my love. We cannot second-guess what's past. Nor can we change it."

"But I've failed you, David, and in the process, I've lost something . . . something precious. I never wanted to push you away, and I didn't mean to let bitterness steal my love."

When he didn't speak, Michal's heart beat harder, certain she'd said too much. Did he believe her? Was he weighing every word? Or didn't he care anymore?

"I forgive you, Michal." He spoke so softly she almost missed the words.

She pulled back to look into his eyes, taken aback by the tenderness in his gaze. Had she heard him correctly? Dare she hope?

"You forgive me?"

He stroked her cheek. "Yes."

The trembling started again, and tears broke through, filming her eyes. "Thank you."

He gave her one of his most charming smiles and pulled her against him again. "You're welcome." She felt his grip tighten around her, and she leaned against him, sighing, wishing, hoping he would never let go. But would his forgiveness change anything?

"I'll inform the guard to allow you free access to the palace again," he said as though reading her thoughts. Her heart rose, then sank at his next words. "But I can't promise you much else, Michal." When he pulled back to look at her again, she felt her blood run hot under his scrutinizing gaze.

"You understand that I'm still the king with many wives. And you forfeited your position years ago. I cannot restore you to your former place."

"In other words, I am married to a king but will never be queen." She had accepted the death of this dream long ago. Still, to say it aloud made everything so final.

"The Lord has not desired to bless your father's house, Michal. Today is witness of this." He waved one hand toward her grandfather's burial cave. "He doesn't seem to have blessed our union either."

Must he say such things? True or not, hearing him say it bruised her soul. All she had ever wanted was to be David's wife and queen and bear his son—a son who would be heir to his throne. She had always thought that the uniting of two families anointed by the Most High would bring prosperity to the nation. But nothing had gone right. And she was getting too old to bear children anymore.

"What are you saying, my lord?" She had to know if she would ever see him again. "Are you setting me aside then, for good?"

The pained expression on his face sent a flicker of hope to her heart.

Please, Lord, let him give me a second chance.

"I'm saying I can't give you what you desire."

Her heart nearly stopped, and suddenly the anguish in his eyes made her want to comfort him. "All I desire is your forgiveness, my lord."

"You already have it," he said with an air of impatience. "You know that's not what I mean."

With sudden boldness, she reached one hand to touch the soft waves of his beard. "You mean you cannot give me a son because God has not blessed my father's house. But shouldn't you leave that decision up to God? Must we decide for Him?"

He toyed with a sad smile, and Michal knew she had touched his heart but not his decision. "I'll think about it." He kissed her then, a soft, reserved kiss that promised little.

"Let's go home, Michal," he said, cupping her chin in the palm of his hand.

Michal looked into her husband's handsome face. She hadn't felt his intimate touch in years, and when she had, she'd merely tolerated him. But now, when it was almost too late, she thrilled to walk beside him, and her lips still trembled from his kiss. If only she had sought the Lord early in life when she could have blessed David with a heart bound to him in all ways. Her life might have been so different.

She glanced up as he walked ahead, led her back to her mule, and helped her mount. He kissed her cheek and smiled into her eyes.

"Thank you, my lord."

He nodded and turned away, suddenly surrounded by advisors and friends. Tears filmed again, but she realized these were tears of gratitude, not sorrow. She might never realize the dreams of her youth, but she'd been restored to peace with her husband and, most of all, peace with her God.

Her gaze moved from David, who was busy with kingly duties, to the cloudy blue heavens. The cool wind brushed the black veil from her face, but it no longer chilled her spirit. Yahweh had offered her stubborn soul forgiveness when she least deserved it. And the peace it had wrought in the process would warm her heart through all the years she had left to live in the king's palace.

Acknowledgments

To list all of the people who have encouraged my writing or helped with this project, which has morphed many times over the years, would be impossible. Some I've lost touch with, some have passed on, but some have stayed with me to see this book birthed. To thank them hardly seems like enough, but I hope they will recognize how much gratitude I feel for them—for their encouragement and their prayers.

To those who have remained, I thank you.

My acquisitions editor, Lonnie Hull DuPont, first inspired the story and then gave me a chance to share it sixteen years after the initial idea! Wendy Lawton, the best agent ever, believed in me and this story even though she knew it would be a tough sell. Thanks to all the great people at Revell who have read *Michal* and loved it and made me believe someone besides me would actually want to read it! You've all done so much to make it shine. Special thanks to my editor Jessica Miles, who put up with my many questions and whose suggestions were helpful, encouraging, and right on. Thanks to Twila Bennett for working so hard to market the book—the two-page catalog ad is amazing!

And to Cheryl Van Andel who designed such a gorgeous cover—thank you!

My dear friend and critique partner, Jill Stengl, read and critiqued the manuscript twice. Jill Marie, I thank God for you! To my fellow critique partners and author friends—Tamera Alexander, Meredith Efken, Kathleen Fuller, Maureen Lang, and Diana Urban—thank you for your mega encouragement, your critiques, and your prayers. And a special thank-you to author Deborah Raney, mentor, encourager, and friend.

To my prayer team—Linda LeBlanc, Kathy Kroll, Julie Miller, Joyce Strong, and Dennis and Barbara Smith—for sticking with me year after year. To past prayer team members and friends and family—Scott and Elaine Bills, Kathy Klassen, Susan Conner, Kathleen Rouser, and Judith Peitsch, among others—who have prayed regularly with or without an email update, encouraged my publication pursuit, and fanned my dreams into flame. Thank you!

To my beloved parents, Leonard and Shirley Smith, who were the first to support my writing dream and have always believed in me.

To church friends past and present—thank you so much for your prayers and support!

Finally, to my dear husband, Randy. You are the best husband ever—supportive, encouraging, my strong arm to lean on. Thank you for putting up with twenty years of my writing woes, when there were more lows than highs and more tears than joys. I figured out that you prefer a wife who is sane and writing over one who is crabby and not writing, even if you don't understand how she can put up with the subjective nature of it all. I will love you forever.

And my three sons Jeff, Chris, and Ryan—no one has better

sons! You have taught me as much as I hope I've taught you. Thank you for brainstorming with me; designing my website, business cards, and bookmarks; helping me understand the way guys think; being my moral support; encouraging my dream; and asking my opinion on some of your own writing. You have put up with twenty years of waiting and gave me courage to persevere, letting me cry on your shoulders and rejoicing with me when the dream came true. You all are loved beyond measure.

Above all, I thank God for His precious gift of salvation, for putting the desire in my heart to write David and Michal's story, for giving me an insatiable desire to read and to love His Word, and for allowing this dream to come true.

Note from the Author

Dear Reader,

The idea for a story on the life of King David began in 1989 after I completed and taught a Bible study on David's life. I'd studied the facts, and now I wanted to read a biblical novel that transported me to 1000 BC—that put me *there*. I searched high and low for a novel on David's life and found nothing that satisfied. So I began to write the book I longed to read. I had no idea I was stepping into a twenty-year journey before my dream of seeing the book in print would come to fruition.

In 1991 my first two-volume epic story on David's life was complete. I knew nothing about publishing except what I found in the *Christian Writers' Market Guide*. I sent out twenty-eight queries and garnered interest for the full manuscript with one major publisher, but alas, it was not to be. After exhausting my options, I packed the book into a box, where it remains.

One of those rejection letters came from editor Lonnie Hull DuPont with Harper & Row in San Francisco. Lonnie wrote me a two-page response suggesting I change the focus of my book to Michal rather than David. At the time, books with female leads sold better. To make a long story short,

Harper discontinued their biblical fiction line before I could break in, but the seed for Michal's story had been planted. Ten years later, I finally wrote the book.

In 2001 I started querying again, this time with *Michal, Daughter of the King*. It won fourth place in a writing contest and garnered interest, but no sales. In 2005 literary agent Wendy Lawton fell in love with *Michal* and soon after signed me on as a client. She told me the book would be a tough sell, but she was committed to trying.

In August 2007 Wendy met Lonnie Hull DuPont, who was now with Revell, a division of Baker Publishing Group, at a writers' conference. Lonnie mentioned she was looking for a work of biblical fiction, and that was all the encouragement Wendy needed. She sent Lonnie *Michal*, and within three months Revell bought the series.

Sixteen years earlier, Lonnie had planted the idea for Michal's story, and God brought that story back to her in 2007. While at times I have been impatient, wondering if anything would ever come of this longing to tell David and Michal's tale, God had His plan all along. He brought the book full circle in His timing and in His way.

I hope you have enjoyed Michal's story as much as I have. But my biggest prayer is that this fictional retelling will inspire you to read the real story in 1 and 2 Samuel of the Bible. Biblical fiction was not meant to replace but to increase our love for the real story in Scripture. I have done my best to stay true to Scripture throughout this novel. Any discrepancies or inaccuracies are my own.

Your servant in Him,
Jill Eileen Smith

Jill Eileen Smith has more than twenty years of writing experience, ranging from articles and short stories to reviews and blogs. Her writing has placed or won prizes in several writing contests. In addition to homeschooling her three sons, Smith has taught piano and women's Bible studies. She enjoys baking, traveling, scrapbooking, and the antics of her two lovable cats. She lives with her husband and sons in southeast Michigan.

To learn more about Jill, visit her website, www.jilleileen smith.com. For more about David and Michal, visit www .thewivesofkingdavid.com. Feel free to email Jill at jill@ jilleileensmith.com. She loves to hear from her readers.

Sweeping Tales of Passion and Drama

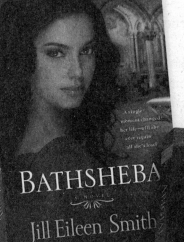

A single moment changed
her life—will she ever
regain all she's lost?

Turmoil marked her life—
what price must she
pay for love?